WRITE LIKE HELL

KAIJU

WRITE LIKE HELL

Sentinel Creatives

www.sentinelcreatives.net
The paperback edition 2020

1

Copyright © Sentinel Creatives 2020
The authors' assert their moral right to
be identified as the authors' of this work

This anthology is entirely a work of fiction.
The names, characters and incidents portrayed in it are
the work of the authors' imagination. Any resemblance
to actual persons, living or dead, events or localities is
entirely coincidental.

All rights reserved. No part of this publication may be
reproduced, stored in a retrieval system, or transmitted,
in any form or by any means, electronic, mechanical,
photocopying, recording or otherwise, without the prior
permission of the publishers.

KAIJU

Also from Sentinel Creatives

The Ritual (by Mitchell Lüthi)
The Zealot (by Mitchell Lüthi)
The Jethro Parables (by Justin Fillmore)
Write Like Hell: Dark Fantasy & Horror Anthology Volume 1
Write Like Hell: Dark Fantasy & Sci-fi Anthology Volume 2

WRITE LIKE HELL

CONTENTS

1. *Foreword*
2. *Big Bloody Ben* – Adam Gray
3. *The Bone Fields* – Mitchell Lüthi
4. *A Boy and his Monster* – Andrea Speed
5. *January Through the Years* – André Uys
6. *Cipactli* – Scott Miller
7. *Honengyo* – C. L. Werner
8. *The Whaler* – Justin Fillmore
9. *One Monstrous Pandemic* – Leon Fourie
10. *Starchild* – Erik Morten & Samantha Bateson
11. *Dominion* – Tyron Dawson
12. *Kaiju Noir* – Matthew Fairweather
13. *Cthulhu vs. Kaiju* – Mitchell Lüthi

KAIJU

Foreword

There's a certain inevitability to any kaiju story. Notwithstanding the rare digression here and there, most unfold with the same irrepressible logic. The domain of routine life, epitomised in bustling metropoles, is suddenly encroached upon by a bafflingly large monster of inscrutable origin and enormous destructive power. Before the disposable citizenry has time to react, the rampage begins. Buildings topple like dominoes, the survivors run for the hills, and a recklessly extravagant military response is crushed in short order—you know, the usual kaiju pageantry. For a brief moment, man comes to know his place in the cosmic food chain—and it's not at the top. It is at this point that the genre embodies the central tenets of cosmic horror and, in its response, promptly bins them.

When these mythical creatures emerge from the depths of the ocean, or from long-dormant volcanoes, it goes without question that the future of humanity's existence is at stake. But instead of reeling in psychosis-inducing terror from the revelation of man's flimsy position, an overweening optimism, baked into the very fabric of the genre, propels the plot onward. Apart from mild apprehension, no significant psychic backlash registers in the minds of the heroes. Rather, in a rare show of global solidarity, a unified front develops, and a crack team of scientists, engineers, and grizzled soldiers of fortune form the vanguard in a hackneyed counter-offensive against the colossus, leading to its demise.

It's tempting to watch such stories from afar, detached and indifferent. After all, mankind always prevails, right? The monster will die, or otherwise return from whence it came, and everything will go back to normal, right? We disentangle ourselves from the interconnected stories of the individuals and look at the narrative as a whole, smiling when humans succeed, despite the cost.

One would think we'd have grown tired of triumphing over adversity by now. A cursory glance at the Marvel Cinematic Universe, or any major blockbuster, reveals not. And it's a testament to how time-worn that storyline is that *Infinity War*—specifically supervillain Thanos—became so popular, so infamous, so upsetting to the average viewer. In the final act, man's every attempt to triumph over evil fails, and Thanos snaps his way to a catastrophic but refreshing break in consensus storytelling.

Kaiju stories rarely indulge plot twists of that sort, preferring to present an indomitable threat and then see it defeated. The monsters central to these stories have every possible advantage, and yet they often lose. There's nothing wrong with this approach to storytelling *per se*, even if it requires a near constant suspension of disbelief in the face of absurdity. But it could be argued that it is that very absurdity that has cemented kaiju's place as a genre unto itself. From its obscure origins as a kind of Japanese post-war expressionism to a universally beloved medium of the modern day, it has always been charmingly ridiculous. It's why *Pacific Rim* pays homage to it the only way it can, by cranking up the apocalyptic zaniness to eleven. There's a ceiling to escalation, however, an inherent limit. The emotional stakes can only be raised so high before there's very little joy to be gained from beating the odds. This effect may go some way to explaining why the sequel was such a monstrous dud. Too much chaos and carnage; too much of a good thing. Fortunately, there are countless other ways one might write a kaiju story, paths that might take more seriously the existential threat such a being poses to humanity.

It's quite possible, if not probable, that an event of such magnitude would be the undoing of humans, a fight we'd lose at the very outset if some super-being were to awaken. And even in the best case scenario, a residue of helplessness and hopelessness would linger long after the monstrosity was vanquished and a sense of 'normalcy' had returned. What's more, it might be thought that the mere existence of such a thing would be enough to shift the nature of our beliefs, for what God could allow such creatures to exist side-by-side with us? It might be enough to make us question our history, and how much we truly know of what is possible and impossible. And lastly, it would doubtless make us pause and think—truly think—about what it means to survive in a world where such beings exist. Would anyone want to continue on in such a place?

Write Like Hell: Kaiju presents a glimpse into such a world. With twelve stories of monstrous beings, this anthology covers huge swathes of genre territory, which is something that delighted us when we first selected the manuscripts that would eventually make it into the book you find before you. Mention a 'kaiju tale' and people often think of titanic figures clashing over cities as mankind watches on, impotent and lost. Well, this collection has that—of course it does! But it has something else, too. A touch of fantasy for the sword & sorcery lovers, a sprinkling of horror for the cult of Lovecraft, and a glimpse at a possible future among the stars.

WRITE LIKE HELL

Big Bloody Ben

Adam Gray

Tip zigzagged between mounds of horse manure—some fresh, some already weeks old—that dotted the streets of southeast London. He was out of breath, and the city air, thick and dark like molasses, did little to satiate his need for oxygen. He hurdled over the lethargic legs of a leper that seemed to blend into the stones beneath him, just as the leper's plea for a shilling blended into the anonymous background noise of the city. Tip turned the corner at Mr Oswald's Store of Exotic Tinctures, whose storefront was decorated with sepia flyers that proclaimed a simple concoction of herbs and fermented rat uterus to cure your genital warts or your money back. Beads of sweat accumulated at the hairline bordering Tip's temples before whizzing off behind him into the darkness and obscurity of night.

Tip was on a mission, and his destination was in sight. Ahead of him lay the nondescript façade of London's least extraordinary police station, where Captain Wilbur Stopforth exercised command.

Captain Stopforth was on night shift, the time when the drunks and crazies unleashed their mischief, seemingly in an attempt to rouse Stopforth from the relative comfort of his hardwood desk and almost-too-narrow chair. The captain was a heavyset man, rotund but not jiggly, like an enlarged turnip with a matching complexion to complete the image. Stopforth was a good detective, a man who did things by the book, if not the most inspired law enforcement official there ever was. Now into his forties, he saw less action than he did a decade ago, but he'd earned his badges—and his paunch. These days, he was more content to ensure his operation was kept tidy.

He was just about to take stock of the department's open dockets, and ensure a balanced case allocation between his detectives, when the dishevelled silhouette of Tip hurtled into his office and planted itself on the chair opposite Stopforth's desk. Tip hunched over, steam rising from his back, in a desperate attempt to compose himself and gain control of his breathing. Tip's fearful excitement was tangible.

"Good heavens, boy! What's the matter with you?" exclaimed Stopforth with a practised blend of condescension and gravitas.

"Ss-s-sir..."

"Out with it, lad. Have you lost your senses?"

"Y-yessir, s-sorry sir," said Tip, his breath beginning to return to him. "It's just that, well, there's been a murder, sir."

"This is London, boy. There's a murder in the city near every weekday, and double on weekends."

"Not like this, sir."

"Say what, boy?"

"There's not been a murder like this before, sir, not what like I've seen, to be sure."

"What's happened?"

"You'd better come see, sir. I don't have the words for it."

"Where?"

"Maypole Street. Quick, sir, before the rain comes."

***

Stopforth would have noticed the hairs dancing erect on the back of his neck. He would have noticed the cold surge running parallel to his spine. He would have noticed the paralysis that took hold of him, and the inertia, and the momentary disappearance of the world. He would have noticed all of these things, were it not for the astonishing spectacle before him. Stopforth couldn't work out what he was looking at, or perhaps his mind simply refused to believe it.

The body was set with shins on the road, knees pointing forwards, torso arched with the solar plexus forming the peak of the parabola, the top of the head dusting the ground to complete the semicircle, face upside down, mouth agape, and eyes opaque, colourless. But it wasn't the positioning of the body that was so strange—so disturbing—it was the texture, the consistency of the body itself. It evinced no sign of life, now or ever. It was a husk, a fossil. A sculpture of white ash. A brittle, alabaster installation. And yet, somehow, impossibly, and until very recently, it used to be Miss Elizabeth Thomas, who sold her company to lonely gentlemen of questionable moral standing. Stopforth gazed at her ghostly form; he had never seen someone exsanguinated before.

"What's happened to her, sir?" Tip asked in a bemused tone.

"If I didn't know better, boy, I'd say she's been drained of her blood."

"How much blood, sir?"

"A lot."

"How, sir?"

"I don't know boy, I don't know."

Stopforth wracked his brain. It didn't make sense, and Stopforth wasn't one who enjoyed things not making sense. He watched on vacantly as a pair of officers struggled to load the human-ish husk of Miss Thomas onto the back of a wagon to be taken to the coroner for autopsy.

***

He stood in the laboratory, observing as Dr Templeton poked and prodded various points of Miss Thomas' moistureless flesh with dissection scissors and a pair of toothed forceps. Stopforth didn't like the cold sterility of labs. They were emotionless, the backdrop for unfeeling men to explore their eerie curiosities. A place where souls were unwelcome and the dead seemed somehow to be at their deadest. Chills darted down Stopforth's spine.

"What's the verdict?" enquired Stopforth in a tone that was jollier than he'd intended.

"It's quite strange," replied Templeton in a tone so sterile it very nearly blended in with the surroundings.

"Yes, strange, but what's actually happened to her?"

"Well, it appears to be an instance of exsanguination, but I've never seen one so perfect before."

"Perfect? I'd hardly call it perfect." Stopforth could not conceal his dismay at the choice of words.

"She's been bled completely dry. But I mean completely. I can tell you, captain, this sort of thing does not occur in nature. Even a man intent on the task would surely fail to draw every drop of blood from the body of another, and that's with the necessary medical training."

"Well, she hasn't done it to herself, I can tell you that much."

"Now isn't that peculiar," muttered Dr Templeton, almost inaudibly.

"What? What is it?" Stopforth's heart began beating more quickly.

"You say there was no weapon recovered at the scene?"

"No, the perimeter was searched, but whoever did this must have taken it with him, either that or hid it impossibly well. My men combed the whole area thoroughly."

"Well, I've found something that might be of interest to you."

Dr Templeton held Miss Thomas' hair aside to reveal the back of her neck. Just below the hairline were three puncture wounds, three points of an isosceles triangle.

"What in God's name is that?" exclaimed Stopforth.

"That appears to be how this unfortunate woman was divested of her blood."

"Some kind of stab wound?"

"Not exactly. These piercings were made with an extremely sharp instrument. Several giant needles, perhaps? No, the holes aren't the right shape. Also the blood had to have been drawn out directly from the body. There was no blood spatter, which would be impossible if the victim was simply stabbed. And to drain her of this much blood using an ordinary medical syringe, one withdrawal at a time, would have taken much too long—days, and even then, it wouldn't be possible to drain all of it... No, this is... something different."

***

The night was quiet. It was hard to believe that, not so far away, something so twisted and violent had occurred, and that whoever was responsible was still out there—a faceless stranger, out of reach like a nightmare forgotten instantly upon awakening.

Stopforth's mind was racing. He stared at the ceiling, but saw nothing. His mind was far away. What had he missed? Who would want to kill Elizabeth Thomas in such a macabre way, and how was he able to do it? Someone must have seen something. Stopforth was no doctor, but he knew draining a human body of all its blood was never going to be a quick process for any man, no matter how strong or knowledgeable he might be. But even if he could, what did he use to do it? No weapon or instrument he'd ever seen or heard of could drain someone of all their blood so totally and with no mess.

"Think, man, think," Stopforth admonished himself. As he waded through the marsh of information and useless facts that crowded his mind, the high-pitched whine of a mosquito oscillated in and out of earshot before reaching its shrill crescendo, followed by an abrupt silence as it landed on a patch of Stopforth's exposed flesh. Suppressing the instinct to flail and swat at where he thought it might be, he lay dead still in the dark, imagining the parasite's needle-like proboscis plunging into him and noiselessly extracting his blood—his life force. A quiet thief, silently stealing life.

The morning glow illuminated the streets in bright grey. "How many mosquitoes would it take to suck the blood right out of someone?" pondered Stopforth. He did not know the answer to that question, a question so outrageous he could never have contemplated having to ask it. But now he found himself seeking out the advice of a man who maybe could.

Stopforth ascended the four short steps that led up to the grand but slightly dilapidated Georgian house. The heavy timber door was furnished with a brass knocker cast in the shape of an unsettlingly large Goliath beetle. Stopforth found it grotesque. He reluctantly placed his hand over the metallic carapace and drew it back before thrusting it back against the door. He repeated the action twice more.

From deep within the house came the sound of papers flapping and the flurrying of limbs.

"Coming, coming, won't be a minute."

Stopforth heard the swipe of a bolt being drawn across the inside of the door, and took a step back. He was greeted by thick spectacles that framed the unfocused, adjusting eyes of a short, balding man with thick white eyebrows and an off-white cravat.

"Yes? Who's that?"

"Dr Whitby, it's Captain Stopforth, Wilbur Stopforth from the London police department. I was hoping you could assist me with some information pertinent to a most curious case."

"I'm afraid I don't know much about any of the goings on around here, you'll find. I tend to stay inside.

KAIJU

No, I wouldn't know anything about any case," said Mr Whitby in a quietly defiant tone.

"Perhaps not, but I'm led to believe that you do know a fair bit about insects?"

"Insects? Not many are enamoured by my field of study. I do not get many invitations for casual conversation on the topic. Come in Mr—What did you say your name was?"

"Stopforth."

"Come in, Mr Stopforth. Would you like some tea?"

***

The ceilings were high and the passageways wide. The house was structurally spacious, but every inch was occupied by some artefact, curiosity, or trinket from various worldly origins. There was a stuffed dodo in the corner of the study, itself adorned with oriental silk and tapestries. Papers printed with diagrams, maps, and sketches were strewn about every visible surface. It was the physical manifestation of a knowledgeable but chaotic mind.

Stopforth sat alongside Dr Whitby at his oversized oak desk decorated with loose papers, books, and glass-topped display boxes containing a vast assortment of butterflies of varying sizes, shapes, and colours, each pinned through the thorax onto the stiff, deckle-edged paper within. Stopforth took a sip of tea, which was adulterated with the leaves from a plant with which Stopforth was unfamiliar. It tasted bitter and earthy. He placed the mug down in front of him and sidled it away as surreptitiously as he could. He did not want to upset his host; he needed his help after all.

Dr Whitby had his eye glued to an elaborate-looking microscope with four tubes, each containing a lens of varying degrees of magnification. The biggest of the four was presently focused a millimetre from the slide directly beneath it. On the slide, beneath an extremely thin, glass square was an even thinner wing that once belonged to a dragonfly. "Just breath-taking," exclaimed Dr Whitby. "Would you care to take a look?"

Stopforth obliged, and found his eye confronted with a network of veins, intricately connected within the ethereal matrix of the transparent surrounding wing. "It's exquisite," said Stopforth, truthfully, but anxious to discuss more pressing matters. "Dr Whitby, could I borrow your attention for a minute? You see, something terrible has happened. Not just terrible, but terribly perplexing, and I would be greatly appreciative if you were able to provide some clarity on the matter. Let's just say it's not the kind of thing we're used to seeing in my profession."

"Well, I'm curious to see how I can be of assistance, although I must reiterate that I can promise nothing," replied Dr Whitby tentatively.

Stopforth recounted the incident.

***

He finished describing the position of the corpse and the sensation he felt as he touched the dry flesh for the first time, as well as the strange marks on the victim's neck that had been discovered on the coroner's dissection table. "What I cannot wrap my head around, Dr Whitby, is how could a man manage to drain every last drop of blood from her, how could he do it so quickly, and how could he do it without leaving so much as a drop of blood at the crime scene? It seems impossible, and yet I saw her there with my own eyes, dry as a desert," stressed Stopforth with due exasperation. "But I did have a thought. The only instance that I can think of whereby blood is drawn from a living being without leaving a drop behind—and correct me if I'm wrong—is when a mosquito sucks the blood of its host. The perpetrator must have used an instrument akin to a mosquito's proboscis, only much bigger in scale. The problem of course being that an instrument of the like has yet to be invented. It simply doesn't exist. So my question is this doctor: does there exist another, much larger mosquito-like creature in the insect world that you know of that is capable of such a feat?"

"No," replied Dr Whitby. "It doesn't exist."

"Are you quite sure, doctor?" asked Stopforth, his voice now dulled with resignation.

"Yes, quite sure. An interesting hypothesis though it might be, if there were an insect capable of such a thing, I can assure you I would know about it. Alas, the idea belongs in the domain of fiction."

"Well, it was worth a try. Thank you anyway, doctor." Stopforth stood, readying to leave.

"Anyway, it wouldn't be a mosquito you were looking for by all accounts. Judging by the description of that wound, you'd be looking for a specimen in the arachnida class."

"As in a spider?" asked Stopforth, somewhat surprised.

"No, as in a tick."

"Are you suggesting a tick could have done this?"

"Don't be foolish," retorted Dr Whitby. "What I'm saying is that whilst we are being fanciful, we might as well be accurate in our fancy. What I mean to say is that your hypothetical perpetrator would not be a giant mosquito, it would be a giant tick."

"But no such a tick exists?"

"No, no such tick exists. I did, however, encounter a local folk legend once on a lepidopterological expedition to Guinea, on the west coast of Africa. The locals spoke of a creature that would snatch onto the feet of children, drain their blood until they died, and then detach itself and disappear. The only way to kill it was with fire. By their accounts, the creature was some subspecies of tick, much like the usual variety, but the size of a human fist. If it were true, it would be by far the biggest species known to man."

"And if it did exist, would it be capable of draining the blood of a fully grown human?" Stopforth asked with renewed exhilaration.

"No," said Dr Whitby. "It would still have to be much, much bigger, and, even more importantly, it would have to exist."

Stopforth and Dr Whitby jumped in unison as a scream penetrated the busy London ambience outside. Nightfall had already descended and the city was dark, but they did not hesitate as they dashed out of the house, down the steps, and onto the street in pursuit of the scream's origin. The scream became increasingly louder until they finally turned into a narrow street, where they were confronted with a harrowing but familiar scene. A woman was collapsed on the floor, wailing, an oil lantern on the cobbles alongside her; she was obviously the one responsible for raising the alarm. Beside her was the white, shrivelled husk of a man. He had been exsanguinated, just like Miss Thomas. Dr Whitby reeled back in horror.

"Who did this?" demanded Stopforth, anxious for answers and charged with adrenaline.

"A thing w-what's like... n-nothing I've ever... l-laid me eyes on," spluttered the woman through sobs and heavy, uneven breaths. She was clearly traumatised.

"Where did it go?"

The woman raised her arm and pointed ahead. Stopforth looked in the direction her finger was pointing, and was able to make out the outline of a huge crater in the middle of the road. Where it led was a mystery. "You wait here and call for help, Dr Whitby," said Stopforth, before turning his attention back to the crying woman. "If I may, Madam," Stopforth said, not waiting for permission before making off with the woman's oil lantern. It was an emergency after all.

***

The stones underfoot were loose and hazardous, and the ankle-height water was foul. The darkness itself seemed to be in a state of decay. The crater led to the underground sewerage network below London, a labyrinth at whose centre Stopforth now found himself. He could not tell how long he'd been trudging through tunnels saturated with human waste, and he could not recall having ever smelled anything so putrid. The timid amber glow of the oil lantern provided the only light in London's murky underbelly.

Above the sloshing rhythm of his own footsteps, Stopforth heard a new sound: a faint gurgling. Following the source of the noise, he quickened his pace. After a short while, he arrived in a chamber where various tunnels appeared to connect. He was listening for the strange sound when he stumbled over something in the shallow, grey water, nearly falling flat and submerging himself in the process. Looking down, he could make out the silhouette of a body. As his eyes adjusted, further details came into focus. The white, shrivelled skin, bloodless but no longer dehydrated; the body had become inflated with sewerage water. Beneath the paper-thin skin, the life force that had once flowed through this unfortunate soul's veins had been replaced with liquid human excrement—an unholy transfusion. As Stopforth bent over to get sick, he noticed that there was not just one body in the water, there were hundreds—London's watery catacombs. He started running in panic; any direction would do.

But Stopforth was quickly cut short. Before him, not more than thirty paces away, rising out of the gloom was the most hideous abomination out of Hell's loathsome menagerie. A huge, bulbous abdomen, grey and pulsating, the size of an elephant. Eight red, crustaceous limbs protruded from the oblong frame, each segmented and tapered into sharp points upon which it carried its mass. A disproportionately small head crowned the narrowest point of the creature's body, couched between tweezer-like pedipalps and a serrated hypostome. Stopforth stared into the beady black eyes of the giant tick. Then he ran.

Stopforth could hear the thrashing of water as the creature gave chase. It was alarmingly quick for something so big. Stopforth could feel the mushy compacting of waterlogged bodies beneath his feet. He did not have time to care too much. He darted down sewer tunnels, one after another, turning down intersecting passageways as often as possible in a bid to lose his ravenous pursuer. But the tick was relentless.

No matter which way he turned, the beast was at his shoulder, hunting him without mercy.

And then all remaining hope drained from Stopforth's heart. Ahead of him, the tunnel was cordoned off by an iron grate, allowing only for the passage of water. Stopforth shoulder-charged it, but to no avail; the grate held firm. He turned to face his would-be executioner. The tick was only a few paces from him now, but it had slowed to a walking pace. As it approached—now almost within touching distance—Stopforth raised the oil lantern. He wanted to properly see the creature before he perished. But something strange happened. As he raised the lantern, the creature reeled back in what Stopforth recognised to be fear. Could it be that this beast was scared of fire? He swung the lantern round in front of him, casting fiery shadows on the tunnel walls, and the tick retreated further. Stopforth charged. The hideous parasite took off back down the tunnel.

It was difficult keeping up with the creature; it was quick and unperturbed by the darkness. But Stopforth was motivated to ensure that this nightmarish manifestation from the underworld did not escape to continue its long-undetected massacre. The chase continued through an endless maze of interconnecting tunnels and avenues, forcing Stopforth into sudden turns and sidesteps. Just as Stopforth felt as though he might not be able to keep up any longer, a dead end emerged ahead—the end was literally in sight. Right before the tick seemed destined to careen into the stone wall ahead, though, it began to ascend into a vertical tunnel above. But, for a moment, it slowed, and without thinking too much about it, Stopforth leapt, grabbing onto a back leg and wrapping his left arm around it. The lantern remained tightly clutched in his right fist.

***

The Palace of Westminster stood serenely in the moonlight, as motionless as an oil painting of itself. There was no wind, and the permeating drizzle that plagued London had dissipated momentarily. The River Thames below was calm; the water dribbled by, oblivious to the frenetic lives of men and happenings beyond its banks. Most of the city was asleep by now, and only a handful of people were on the streets to witness as a gigantic grey mass exploded upwards through the road from the sewers beneath. Those with keener vision would, in addition, have noticed the dwarfed figure of Captain Wilbur Stopforth clinging to what looked by all accounts to be a giant red leg. Debris scattered outward from the huge subterranean projectile, and a plume of dust and lime mortar billowed up in its wake.

The mass landed with a doughy thud before scuttling off furiously in the direction of Big Ben. By then, Stopforth wasn't sure whether holding onto the tick was the wisest course of action, but he was committed to the probably ill-conceived strategy and locked his arm even tighter around the leg. As they barrelled over an abandoned cartwheel lying in the street, the glass outer case of the lantern caught a broken spoke and shattered. Stopforth applied the now exposed flame to the indented, milky hide of the tick, staining it black with soot. The creature's entire frame began to convulse, and then its bulky movements quickened, like a horse shifting from a canter to a gallop in response to the spurs of its rider digging into its hindquarters. It cannoned forwards on a collision course towards the granite column of Big Ben, the steadfast overseer of the city, the great timekeeper.

Soon, Big Ben was towering high above them; they had reached its base. "What now?" thought Stopforth. "Where are you headed?"

As if to answer his question, the tick propped itself up against the exterior of the Clock Tower and began to climb, navigating the grooves and inlays as it scaled the south face. If Stopforth had ever intended to dismount, he had clearly missed his chance, as the ground had receded too far to survive the jump. He would not be disembarking any time soon.

The streets ebbed further away as the tick continued its upward journey. Stopforth could not hold on forever; he needed a plan. The tick had just made it up to the fourth lateral division of the tower, and would shortly reach the belfry above. It scurried over the face of the clock using the immense minute-hand as scaffolding. Clasping the bottom of the oil lamp tightly at the base, Stopforth carefully removed the burner from the oil chamber, which remained intact, making sure that the wick continued to burn. Holding onto the tick's leg by wrapping his own legs around it, he poured the kerosene over the parasite's rear hide. Then he bided his time as they passed the Roman numeral twelve of the clock face; he did not have long before the wick burned out. As soon as the tick reached the belfry, Stopforth struck the wick against the area where he had emptied the kerosene. It ignited on contact and Stopforth sprung from the great leg, landing on the outside ledge of the belfry. The tick continued its ascent, a plume of smoke trailing behind it. As the flames grew and became hotter, a hissing sound emanated from within the body of the creature; the blood inside was beginning to boil.

Stopforth peered out from the relative safety of the belfry threshold in order to track the creature's progress. It traversed the topmost iron roofing plates with ease. All that lay before it was the cast-iron spire rising out to form the needle-like summit of the tower. The tick commenced the final stage of its ascent. Its legs clung around the spire, heaving its enormous mass towards the tip in a fruitless bid to outrun the trailing blaze. Its strength was failing fast, and its movement had become lethargic and less deliberate. After an agonising effort, it reached the pinnacle, balancing precariously atop the lance-like point. Smoke billowed from the creature's rear, causing the clock tower to resemble the chimney of a crematorium. The tick held itself in the skyline for one tranquil moment, one final glimpse at the world below. And then without warning, the tick collapsed, the spire impaling its bloated abdomen.

A flood of crimson cascaded from the sky, showering London in a thick blanket of second-hand blood. The smell was ungodly. None of the four clock faces were visible beneath the sea of red, but it was midnight, and Big Ben began to chime the hour.

"Bloody hell," said Stopforth.

KAIJU

The Bone Fields

Mitchell Lüthi

LONGSHIPS

Thoril braced against the cold wind and gripped her oar tight as the storm buffeted the longship *Varúlfr*. Beneath them, all around them, the ocean was a broiling black cauldron, heaving its might against their own. It had not yet found them wanting.

Inge hunched up beside her and grinned madly as the sea crashed over the side of the longboat. Her shaven head was lathered with sweat and rain, and the tattoos that covered her skin shone as though freshly inked.

"Njǫrd is in one of his moods again," she called over the wind.

Thoril spat out salt water and wiped her lips. "He is always angry this time of year. Halvor was foolish to make us stay for so long."

She stared along the aisles, past the ragged band of figures that made up the rest of the company. Halvor stood at *Varúlfr*'s helm, unbowed by the frantic gale that hammered the ship. His long hair was soaked through, matted against his head and neck. His eyes remained fixed on the horizon, in search of their sister ship, *Kveldúlfr,* who had disappeared into the storm.

"Halvor's raids are always the most rewarding," said Inge. "That is why he chose to stay, and that is why we chose to come. This old god's anger is a small price for what we have taken."

Thoril nodded. It had been a bountiful raid, and Halvor's company had made enough for them all to secure land and power upon their return home. They had stuck to the coast at first, like any other raiding party, and taken what they could from the farms they found there. But Halvor was ambitious, and they'd soon found themselves sneaking into larger settlements and then sacking them. It had been slaughter, but one well worth the wait. She glanced over her shoulder, towards the covered stern of the boat. She'd even managed to secure a slave on this expedition—her first. He sat huddled up beside two others, shivering into his soaking rags.

"Fritjof better not have gotten himself lost." Inge squinted her eyes against the rain. "Or sailed *Kveldúlfr* to the ocean floor, then we'll never see half our spoils. Afterlife or no, I'll hunt him down and wring his thin neck until his eyes pop out."

Inge had another reason for wanting to see *Kveldúlfr* again. Her lover, Akes, sailed with Fritjof. The warrior had spurned her advances at first, but Inge was not easily dissuaded. The first night on Bretland soil had seen them share a bedroll, and they'd spent every night together since.

"Not even Fritjof would dare sink his ship when he carries Halvor's cargo. You will see, once the storm relents, then you will see that stupid boy's face again."

Inge slapped her on the back and grinned. "I'm more interested in what's between his legs."

KAIJU

Thoril rolled her eyes and sank her oar into the water. The pull of the waves was getting stronger and she struggled to find a rhythm. Others in the company, Herleid and Ovil—but others, too—had already given up. They sat wrapped in great furs beside sheltered braziers, taking what little warmth they could.

"Halvor will tell us to stow away the oars soon," said Inge, her smile fading. "Then we will need to hold fast until the storm passes, or join Fritjof at the bottom of the sea."

Thoril shrugged. Halvor was too shrewd a sailor to let a mere storm defeat him, but when one's time came, even the trickster himself would be hard put to evade his fate. She turned to the sea and watched as it rampaged and turned beneath grey clouds. For too long she had been away from the open waters, and her mood had dampened with each day they had moved inland. Now that she was back—cold as she was, wet as she was—she felt her spirits soar.

Her eyes narrowed as a wave rose up beside *Varúlfr*. It drew the ship towards it, until they were tilted horizontally against it and a gauzy mist of water splashed over them. Halvor rode the wave expertly, bringing the longship over it before it could crest and plummet them all to their doom. As the wave diminished beneath them, Thoril thought she saw a flash of silver below the surface, the scales of an enormous shape riding alongside them. But when she blinked again, it was gone.

"Land!"

She shook free the vision and looked up as the call rang out again.

"What land is here?" Inge rose from her seat beside her, stepping up onto it in an effort to see over the heads of the rest of the company.

"There is nothing," Ulfgar said from the seat opposite them. He ran a hand over his stubbly head and shrugged. "Not for many days, still. There must be a mistake."

"There is… something." Inge leaned on Thoril's shoulder for support and rose on her toes for a better look. "I see a thin line, barely a smudge, but it has the look of land about it."

"To your oars!" Halvor's voice boomed above the storm. He strode between the aisle, pulling the crew back down to their seats. "We make for the shore, and a break from the storm!"

Inge plopped back down beside her and laid her hands on the oar. Together, they pulled deep against the chopping waters for the smudge on the horizon.

***

The howling wind relented as they navigated their way into a sheltered cove, where the ocean was strangely dead and still. The land around them was unfamiliar and Thoril felt herself tense as she stared up at the grey crags above. *Where had they come from?* She had never seen this place before, and the maps did not speak of it. Unless the storm had blown them further off course than she realised.

Halvor had them moor *Varúlfr* along the coast, and then set a team to repair what little damage the storm had done. Thoril took up her sword and shield, and walked along the beach with Inge while the rest set up camp. She could see Halvor's pathfinders moving up ahead of them, slipping in and out of the trees that hemmed in the shoreline.

"Maybe they will find us another farmstead?" Inge thumped her sword against her shield and smiled. "Or perhaps a little lord and his castle, too far from anyone to call for help. That would be enough to settle my debt with Dag, no?"

Thoril stayed quiet. Her own debts had been covered weeks ago, and she did not have it in mind to raid again.

Inge stared at her from out of the corner of her eye and then bumped into her with her shield. "You are never smiling, even when things are good. 'Troubled Thoril', that is what they should call you in the songs."

"Only because that hole in your face never closes," she replied, returning the shove.

Inge laughed loud and skipped about her, kicking up clumps of sand.

Troubled Thoril!
Aesirs' daughter did not smile
Troubled Thoril!
Cold as Jötunn, with rage like Freyja

Thoril dropped her sword and shield, and covered her ears. "You sing like a dog, Inge. If the gods could hear you now, they'd cut out your tongue."

"Good enough for the beer halls, but not for Troubled Thoril, eh?" Inge made to push her again, but Thoril raised a hand.

"It's Bjarki," said Inge, following her gaze.

Halvor's chief pathfinder was bounding over the beach towards them, his sword and shield strapped to his back.

"What have you found?" Thoril called as he loped past.

Bjarki slowed, breathing heavily. "*Kveldúlfr*. We've found her, she's up ahead."

"See, I told you," said Thoril, turning to the other shield-maiden. "Fritjof is too much of a coward to lose his ship. He will be sitting fat on Halvor's loot, like Hreidmar and his dwarves."

Inge knitted her brow, her eyes still tracking the pathfinder as he jogged over the sand. "And of the crew, are they all there?"

Bjarki shrugged as he picked up his pace, heading towards the camp. "There is no one."

***

Halvor's company—over twenty warriors, all told—stood at the top of a dune, and stared down at *Varúlfr*'s sister ship. Fritjof had moored her on the beach, away from the draw of the tide. Her oars had been stowed away and sails furled, but there was no sign of life anywhere aboard.

Bjarki and his trackers stood by Halvor, engaged in whispered conversation, while the rest of the party edged down towards the ship.

"Do you think an ambush?" Inge's question lacked any conviction, but Thoril shook her head anyway. She couldn't see any of the signs of a fight from the dune; no bodies littered the sand, and there wasn't a drop of blood to be found around *Kveldúlfr*.

"They must have moved inland." She waved her shield towards the dense forest beside them, and then squinted into the gloom herself. A coarse thicket covered the land between the beach and the rock face that loomed above. The trees were tightly packed, leaving hardly enough space for a man and his shield to pass through, and malformed roots snaked their way across the forest floor. Fool that he was, it was unlike Fritjof to leave his ship unguarded, and for what? A walk through parts unknown?

A shout from aboard the boat saw Thoril's eyes snap back to *Kveldúlfr*. Ubba and Katja, two of Halvor's senior blooded-warriors, had clambered up the rungs of the ship and were waving everyone closer. The pair of them were covering their faces, and Ubba retched up something watery before climbing back down.

"I do not like this," said Inge as she grabbed Thoril by the shoulder. The two navigated the steep incline together, slipping and sliding as they made their way onto even ground.

They were among the first to reach the bottom of the rise, and they pushed their way towards Halvor and his trackers, who had moved down ahead.

Ulfgar gave them a curt nod and shifted up to let them through. He was normally the first to crack a smile, but his face was grim. "Might have been better we remained away from this bay." He gritted his teeth and turned to look at the sea. Beyond the shelter of the cove, the storm still raged, and the wind still howled. But beneath the crags of this new island, everything was peaceful. "I am reminded of the tales of *Náströnd* in this place, of the cursed and the damned."

That hall is woven
of serpents' spines
There Níðhǫggr sucked
corpses of the dead
and the wolf tore men

31

on Dead Body Shore

Thoril shivered. "You are always one to set a mood."

"It is not me." The old warrior thumbed his hand, and then rolled his neck, before meeting her eyes. "Old Ove has felt it, too. We were not meant to come here."

Inge guffawed. "Ove always *feels* something, but sometimes it's just the madness inside his own head."

"Mock him if you like, but he has seen more than you can know, more than you can understand."

Inge shrugged at that, and they walked in silence for a moment, behind Halvor and the pathfinders. Ulfgar took such things seriously, more so than most. To argue with him was like pushing a bull through mud with its horns pointed at you. He bore his faith on his skin, and his shaven scalp was adorned with symbols of protection—Othala runes, the Fe, and tributes to Heimdall himself.

Inge was about to snap back with a delayed retort when she gagged. "That smell."

Thoril made a face and covered her nose with her forearm. "Like rotten fish." Her eyes started to water at the stench that assaulted her senses, but she walked forward gamely, even as others choked and swore behind her.

The rest of the party gathered at the base of the longship, and waited as Bjarki and Ulfgar clambered up the rungs and stared over the side.

"They've left their shields." Thoril glanced up at the rack, which remained untouched.

"That's Akes'," said Inge, pointing her sword towards a red and white shield above them. "They must have needed to move quickly."

KAIJU

Thoril nodded, but she felt the first hint of uneasiness grip her as she watched Bjarki and Ulfgar turn to face the gathered party.

"It is a serpent's brood," Bjarki stated solemnly. He made the sign of the Fe and spat at the boat. "This is Jörmungandr's lot, and we are not welcome in this place."

Ulfgar dropped down onto the sand, and then helped the older warrior down.

"It is an ill omen," he said, once Bjarki was on the beach beside him. A crowd of confused faces stared back at him, until Halvor strode forward and nimbly clambered up the side of the boat.

"Eels," he said simply as he stared down at the hold. "The storm must have seen them dumped in Fritjof's boat, nothing more."

Ulfagr mumbled something from below, but Halvor silenced him with a wave of his hand. "There is nothing of the Midgard serpent here. Do you think we would have found this ship if the World-Snake had come upon it?"

Ulfgar shrugged, and thumbed his palm nervously. "I simply say what I see."

The jarl shook his head, and then stared at the party for a moment, sweeping his gaze across the dunes. "Fritjof is a fool," he said. "We all know this."

Some of the men chuckled at his words, but most were quiet. Ulfgar had put them on edge.

"He has left his ship unguarded and charged off to see what treasures he can find for himself. He means to leave us with his ship, like a nursemaid." Halvor jumped down from the boat and dusted his hands off. "But we are not his nursemaids, are we?"

Thoril found herself muttering her dissatisfaction with the idea along with the rest of the party.

"We will move inland and find the fool, then he can make a bed from the eels he left in his boat!" A grin split Halvor's face as the mood lifted, and raucous laughter was joined by his warriors.

"Come, now," said Halvor once the laughter had receded. "Fritjof can't have made it far." He nodded to his pathfinders, who moved off quickly into the forest. "There is still a little light before nightfall."

As the company moved towards the tree line, Inge pushed past Thoril and headed towards the boat.

"What are you doing?" Thoril sighed and followed after her friend. "You heard Halvor, we don't have much light left."

"I want to see." Inge dropped her gear into the sand and turned to Thoril. "Are you not curious to see what Jörmungandr has left us?" She didn't wait for an answer before pulling herself up the side of the boat.

Thoril sighed again and dropped her own gear to climb onto *Kveldúlfr*.

The wood had started to rot, and the smell of decaying flesh intensified as she pulled herself up.

Inge exhaled as she reached the top and stared down into the hold. "Gods, Bjarki was right."

"What is it, Inge?" Thoril asked, hearing her tone. She didn't wait for a reply before peering down herself.

The entire floor of *Kveldúlfr* was covered in a writhing, seething mass of serpentine bodies. Their silver forms shifted in the half-light, wrapping themselves around one another in a slippery embrace. Thoril nearly gagged at the sight of them, and turned away as the smell threatened to overpower her.

"There are so many." Inge curled her lips in disgust and watched as the creatures rolled across the floor of the boat. "Fritjof and his company will have much to clean once this lot rots in the sun."

"They will have no help from me," said Thoril. She took one last look at the flowing mass of bodies, and then clambered back down the rungs. "Come! Inge! Or we will be left behind."

WRITE LIKE HELL

THE LIVING AND THE DEAD

Of Halvor's company, four were left to guard over *Varúlfr*, and another two to wait by Frtijof's ship in case of his return. The rest set out into the dark forest, with torches lit against the coming of night.

"I have not seen nor heard any sign of beast or bird in this place." Ulfgar swatted away a gnat with his torch. "Only these bastards."

"Your blood is too pure," said Inge. "But I have the cure." She swigged from her flask and handed it to Thoril. "They will not eat you if your blood is poison."

Thoril shrugged and took a sip, almost spluttering as the bitter liquid went down her throat. "What is this?" she asked, wiping her mouth with a hand, then looking at the flask sceptically.

"Baht gave it to me as a gift before we left. It was all he had left from his journey East."

"No wonder his mind is so addled." Thoril sniffed at the container and made a face. "I would rather be eaten, I think."

"Suit yourself," said Inge, taking back the spirits. "But don't cry to me when your skin is raw from scratching."

Ulfgar snorted. "Inge the generous."

"It is *Inge the Bloodied*, now that I have fought the Christians and stolen their silver." She adjusted the shield on her arm and stared up into the canopy.

They had walked for many miles beneath the outstretched limbs of ancient trees, and there had been no sign of Fritjof or his company. Not long after leaving the shore, Bjarki had found a single path that cut its way through the forest. It was the only way past the near impenetrable undergrowth, and Halvor led them on it towards the great crags they'd seen from the boats.

"There are no stars." Inge frowned up at the branches, and then shook her head. "They hide from this place."

"They're hidden behind clouds," said Thoril. She'd felt uneasy since finding *Kveldúlfr* and its slippery cargo, and didn't need Inge's superstitions compounding that. "There was a storm, remember?"

"Or it is that this place is outside of our own." Ulfgar glanced around him, holding his torch close to the trees. Their boughs and roots were scarred with age, and the leaves seemed to shrink away so close to the open flame. "Beneath the roots of the World Tree, there exists a place of terrible suffering, it is Hel's kingdom."

Thoril rolled her eyes. "But we have not died, Ulfgar. Ove is getting into your head with his stories. Unless you think we sunk to the bottom of the sea in that storm?"

The warrior shrugged. "Who's to say that we didn't?"

"Our flesh!" Thoril pulled down her sleeve and pointed to her bare skin. "Our sweat and thirst! Do you think the dead suffer these things?"

Ulfgar flinched at the tone of her voice and raised a hand in supplication. "It is only a thought, I do not mean to anger you, *storm-maiden*."

"It is not you, Ulfgar." Thoril took a deep breath and rolled her knuckles against her shield. "I am sorry. It is this place, the quietness is getting to me."

"It gets under my skin, too," said Ulfgar. "When these bastards aren't busy eating me." He swung his torch at a cloud of insects, and then beckoned to the other shield-maiden. "I'll try some of your poison now, I think."

Inge grinned and handed him the flask. "It gets better after the first sip, promise."

Ulfgar raised a sceptical brow and took a hesitant sip. His face paled and his brow creased as the liquor passed his lips. "This is what Baht calls a drink?" He spat on the forest floor and groaned. "No wonder he always stinks of cat piss."

Inge grinned and took back the flask. "It has kept me warm through many a cold night, and it's better than being eaten alive."

"That it is," said Ulfgar pressing on ahead. He waved an arm towards the thinning trees as a pale moon emerged from behind the diminishing canopy. "It looks like this dark forest has finally come to an end. Now we will see what wolfish murderers and serpent spines haunt this island."

***

The forest opened up into a wide valley nestled between steep, windswept hills. A thin strip of silver hinted at the existence of a river not far ahead. Its snaking path ran the length of the valley, and then disappeared beyond the grey walls of the mountain range in the distance.

Halvor ordered the company forward, beyond the shelter of the forest, towards the river. The warriors were relieved to find themselves with empty skies above their heads once more, and moved with purpose.

As they moved out from the undergrowth, Thoril couldn't help but notice the lack of stars. Even without the cover of clouds, the sky was like a black sheet, with only the wan light of the moon guiding their way.

"We will camp by the river." Halvor led the company himself, setting a gruelling pace that soon saw them all wet with sweat and breathing heavily. He waved his axe at his chief scout and motioned to the grey peaks.

"Bjarki and Sigurd will move into the mountains while we rest." He turned to his warriors, walking backward as he took them all in. "Do not sip too heavily on your mead this night. I think we will all need to be sharp come the morning."

His warriors grumbled to themselves, but accepted his warning without rebuke. Most were too tired for thoughts of drink, and the idea of a proper night's sleep was enough to keep them motivated.

Inge had gone off to see if she could not join Bjarki and his scouts, and Thoril found herself walking between Ove and Ulfgar. The moon had not yet reached its zenith, and its pale light made everything look a shade of grey.

"There is no sign of that fool or his company," said Ulfgar. "No tracks, no fires, nothing of our friends. Halvor leads us on a merry chase." He spat at the ground and shook his head. "This place is empty."

Ove snorted from beneath his hood. "It is not empty, Ulfgar. You are just blind to what occupies this land." He waved a hand at the mountains before them and smiled. "We walk where few have walked before, in the place between the living and the dead."

It was Thoril's turn to snort now. "Old Ove, you have seen so much, and yet your stories are always the same. The living and the dead, the beasts of *Náströnd*, the serpent that eats the world. Why have we seen none of these things? Every year you cry your tale, and every year we ship back home, alive and richer than before!"

"I only repeat what I have seen, girl." Ove made the sign of the Fe with a gnarled hand, and then turned to look at her. His skin was weathered by years of salt and sun, but his blue eyes were as piercing as ever.

He stared at her for a moment, and then smiled. "You have seen something, too, I think."

Thoril shrugged, but in her mind's eye she recalled that flicker of silver beneath the waves, that formless shape slipping through the sea.

"It is no blessing to have hold of the sight," Ove continued. "To see one's future played out before one's very eyes has damned many a man to insanity. But you must be better than that."

"What is it that you saw?" asked Ulfgar.

"It was nothing." She shook her head, readjusting her shield on her arm. "Ove is mad, you know that as well as I."

"I have seen it, too, girl," Ove barked. "It is the world's end that slithers behind your eyes!" He retched out a hacking cough and laughed. "Do not be afraid. Soon they will all see!"

Thoril snarled at the old warrior and picked up her pace, leaving the pair of them behind. It was only when she was at the head of the company, and Ove's choking laughter had faded away, that she felt her mind settle.

He is mad, she thought to herself. *Him and Bjarki both.* Still, there was something in the way he had looked at her that made her think otherwise. The old man had seen more years than any of them, and his words, though often veiled by myth, were rarely false.

She sighed to herself and tightened her grip on her shield. Either way, she would meet her fate head on.

The first night on the island was cold, and Halvor ordered massive fires to fend off the chill. He cared not that someone might see them. After all, who would dare attack Halvor and his company of bloodied? The warriors drew lots for sentry duty, and those that could, tried to slip in a few hours sleep before dawn.

Thoril and the other shield-maiden had laid their kit out beside one of the bonfires, and sipped from Inge's bitter liquor while Ove told stories of the night, and of the first fires.

"When Loki, Odin, and Haenir crossed the vast mountains, they came across a herd of oxen!" The old warrior took a bite from his dried meat and crinkled his nose. "Fresh meat, not like what we've been nibbling on, eh, Ulfgard?"

Ulfgard blinked into wakefulness at the sound of his name and stared across the fire at the old warrior. "What now?" he said.

"Come, come," Inge rolled across the grass and extended her flask towards him. "Don't be boring, Ulfgar. Sit with us."

He shook his shaven head and pulled his blanket tighter about his chest. "I have the next watch. It would look poor for me if Halvor caught me drunk. You heard what he said."

She stuck out her tongue and took a steady draught from the bottle. "You will be sad when there is none left."

He shrugged and closed his eyes. "As long as I get my sleep, I do not care."

"What about you, Ove?" Inge turned to the veteran. "Something to fend off the cold and make your heart kick like a newborn's?"

"I already see things that are not there," said Ove, chewing on his meat. "I rather not tempt fate with your fire water."

"More for me and Thoril, then," she said as the others laughed. She took another sip from her flask and squinted into the darkness surrounding the camp.

The mountains were mere silhouettes in the distance, looming over the sides of the valley like the bastions of some great castle. The river they'd seen from afar was, in fact, two concurrent streams racing beside one another towards the sea. They'd bathed in its water, and even fished, but there was no life to be found in it, and the warriors had made do with dried meats once more.

For a moment, she thought she spotted a movement on the ridge above their camp—a single figure stepping into the moonlight. She squinted up at the hill, trying to bring it into focus, but whatever it was she'd seen had gone.

"You alright, girl?" Ove cocked his head, a strange look on his face.

"It's nothing," said Inge, shaking her head, and then bringing her eyes back down to the fire. "It is only shadows."

"Is it nothing, or is it shadows?" Ove showed his teeth before winking at Inge. "They are not the same."

The shield-maiden rolled her eyes and leaned back on her bedroll. She was tired of Ove and his riddles. "It was both and neither," she said, turning her back to him and the fire. He could figure that one out for himself. She closed her eyes and let the warmth of the fire, and the soft hum of her friends chatter, lull her to sleep.

In the morning, Ulfgar was gone.

KAIJU

***

Bjarki shook his head as he walked over to Thoril and the others. "There is no sign of him. Sigurd saw him take the watch, but after that, he did not return."

"Where did he stand sentry?" Thoril had been the first to wake, and to find his bedroll empty.

"Not far from here," Bjarki said. He pointed to the base of the ridge, on the other side of the river. "He took over from Eyva and left camp well after midnight. His watch was to end a few hours before dawn, but no one has seen him."

"He can't have gotten far," said Inge, staring at the ridge.

"But why would he have left us in the first place?" Thoril licked her lips and followed Inge's gaze. The drink had given her a splitting headache, and she was finding it hard to concentrate. "It makes no sense," she concluded.

"I am inclined to agree," came a deep voice from behind her.

Halvor stood next to Bjarki and nodded to them each in turn. His mane of hair was wet from the river, and his beard had grown out. Flecks of white and grey dotted the scruff, making him appear even more distinguished.

"It is not like Ulfgar to disappear like this." Thin lines creased his forehead as he frowned. "I suspect he has been taken by whoever has been tracking us this last day."

Thoril and Inge's immediate questions were ignored, and Halvor silenced them with a wave of his hand. "Bjarki spotted them when we landed. A small band, maybe three or four in total. They have been shadowing us since we moved inland, but I had not expected them to act so boldly. Not against our numbers."

Inge shivered, remembering the silhouette she'd seen on the ridge. "Who are they?"

"I cannot be sure. Locals, perhaps. Or other folk like us who've been washed up by the storm. The pathfinders have been instructed to catch one of them, if possible. Then we will see."

"And what of Ulfgar?" Thoril's eyes narrowed as she watched her jarl. She already suspected the answer.

"There is nothing that can be done. We don't know the land, and Bjarki says the surrounds turn into more gulleys and ravines than he can count—too many places to disappear. We will find what has happened to him when we catch one of his captors."

Thoril nodded. She knew Halvor did not allow for dissent. What was done was done, and she'd just have to hope Bjarki and his trackers were as good as they thought they were.

"None of this to the others." Halvor met her eyes, and then stared down Inge and Ove. "I would not have fears of shadow-men spread through the company. They will learn of this when the time is right."

"We will keep your secret, Ironnson." Ove smiled. "But do not think to catch these spectres, or to harm them. They cannot be hurt. They walk between the worlds. This I know, Ulgfar knows it, too."

"We will see, old man," said Halvor, already turning to leave. "There is little that walks in this world that does not fear the sharp end of my axe."

They walked for half a day before someone spotted smoke rising behind them, and Halvor called them to a halt. He signalled to Sigurd and those scouts not out searching for Ulfgar and his mysterious captors. They quickly moved up the ridge to get an eye on where the smoke was coming from.

"Could be Fritjof and his lot," said Inge. She dropped her kit on the ground and placed a foot on one of the larger rocks around them. The valley had started to narrow as they closed in on the crags, and rocky debris littered the floor around them.

"Could be, could be." Ove sucked on his teeth and tracked the scouts up the hill. "Could be a funeral pyre."

"Best not to wonder on such things until we can be sure." Thoril shielded her eyes from the sun with a hand and stared at the rising plumes of black smoke.

"There is another," she said, pointing a little ways away from the first cloud. "It is smaller, but it is the same."

Inge clambered atop the rock and leaned against Thoril as she tried to get a better look. "She's right, there is more smoke from somewhere further back."

"We will find out just now," said Ove, gesturing to the ridge. Halvor's scouts were racing down the incline, trying their best to remain sure-footed as they hurtled down towards them.

"It's the boats!"

The cry went up like wildfire, and Thoril felt a familiar feeling of uncertainty crowd out her other thoughts. *We are trapped here*, she thought as she joined the milling mass of norsemen crowding around Halvor.

"It is true," said the jarl plainly. "Our ships have been set afire. Both *Varúlfr* and Fritjof's ship, though it does not look like the fire on *Kveldúlfr* has taken so well. She may still be salvageable."

"What are we to do?" A voice called from the amassed warriors.

Thoril could see the company was close to panic. Tired men and women, stranded far from home on an island they'd never seen before... It would not take much to push them over the edge. To his credit, Halvor did not seem perturbed by the situation. He rolled his shoulders and turned to Sigurd. The two engaged in quiet conversation, both of them glancing up at the clouds of smoke in the distance, before Halvor raised a hand to silence the company.

"We have no choice but to return to the ships and to see what we can salvage from the fires." He nodded to Sigurd, who moved to gather the remaining pathfinders. "We will wait for Bjarki's return, and then we shall make with haste for the coast."

"And of Fritjof?"

It was Inge's voice that Thoril heard. She turned to see the other shield-maiden standing beside two of Halvor's largest warriors, Theodaric and Henrik. "What happens to Fritjof and his company, and what of Ulfgar? Are we to leave them here, to this island and its people?"

Halvor gave her a look of warning, and then rolled the handle of his axe with his wrists. "There is nothing that can be done. We must look to our own preservation now."

His words were met with agreement by the gathered company, but Inge was not yet done.

"If it were you, we would stay until we found you, or we were all dead."

Halvor smiled, revealing a row of straight, white teeth. "But it is not me, shield-maiden. And I say we go."

Before Inge could continue her protest, Halvor whistled and waved at the remaining pathfinders. "You have until nightfall, and then we are gone."

Inge gritted her teeth, but looked up at Thoril's approach. "Just like that."

"Maybe Bjarki will find something, perhaps of Ulfgar or Fritjof, or both?"

Inge shook her head and wiped at her eyes. She was tired and she was hungover, and she wanted to see her friends again. "It might already be too late. There is something wrong about this place. There is no life here, not even a bird, just these pests that want to drain us of our blood." She swiped at the air, as if to make her point. "Halvor must know it, if we leave now we may seal their fates."

Thoril nodded, but there was nothing more she could say. Halvor had spoken, and his word was law.

***

Night had long since fallen when the first of Bjarki's scouts returned. Tired eyed and wary limbed, they slowly streamed in. They spoke of a great ravine, guarded by the walls of ancient pillars. Of figures cut from stone and strange sounds in the trees. They spoke of an uneasiness that settled upon them, and a feeling of being watched, of being stalked, hunted. But of Fritjof and Ulfgar, there was no sign.

"We wait on Bjarki," Halvor told the company. "When he returns, we will make for the coast, for our ships."

They waited until the night grew cold, when even fire barely kept the chill from their bones. The camp sat in a state of frozen anticipation, with each warrior ready to move at a moment's notice. But that notice never came. Halvor grew restless and took to pacing around the perimeter, harassing his sentries and forcing them to take deeper forays into the night, to search for the pathfinder. It wasn't long before Thoril and Inge were sent out with a party, into the black of night with only their torches to guide them.

"We will find nothing like this," said Inge. "Stomping around in the night like fools, hoping to fall upon Bjarki by luck."

Thoril lifted the torch above her head and watched the flickering shadows around them. They had been walking for hours now, with still no sign of the pathfinder. What hope she'd had of finding him had diminished, and she just wanted to return to the camp and to the warmth of the fires. She sighed as she stared up at the hills that loomed above them. The peaks were hidden by the night, and what little light the moon shone down on them failed to illuminate the darkest corners of the valley.

"What else would you have us do?" Thoril lowered her torch. "You heard Halvor, we must look to ourselves now. If we don't find Bjarki, we have to leave without him."

Inge shook her head. "Halvor will not leave his precious pathfinder behind."

"Then we must do as he says, and search every crevice of this valley before dawn."

The other shield-maiden rubbed a hand over her scalp. She had not shaved it in weeks, and stubble now covered the tattoos that spiralled across her head.

"Ove has taken it well," she said. "Ulfgar is like a son to him."

Thoril took a swig from her flask and wiped her mouth. "He said he *knew* what was coming. Him and Ulfgar both."

"How could they know?"

"You know what they are like." Thoril turned to her friend and waved at the sky. "The gods tell them stories, or plant ideas in their heads… At least, that is what Ove wants us to think. It is either true, or he is mad. Sometimes I think it is both."

They walked in silence for a moment, keeping within hailing distance of the rest of the party. Arvid and Dagfinn were barely a dozen yards from them, while Uskar and Tommen ranged ahead, their torches appearing like mini stars in the distance.

But, of course, there were no stars here. Thoril hadn't seen one since they'd arrived. She looked up at the sky, careful to keep her footing on the uneven rocks that surrounded the gully.

"It is like Ove says." Inge came to a standstill beside her. "This island is of another place."

They were still standing together, staring at the emptiness above them, when Uskar's horn rung out in the darkness. It blew once, then twice, and then there was silence.

"He's found something," said Thoril as she skipped down from the rocks. More torches were moving through the valley now, heading towards where Uskar's horn had sounded from.

"If it's Ulfgar, I'll box his nose in for leading us on this merry chase." Inge's face shone with hope, and she jogged ahead of Thoril towards the gathering torches. "Then we will see if Ove saw that coming, too," she called over her shoulder.

Thoril smiled at the thought and picked up her pace.

WRITE LIKE HELL

THE DESTROYING FLAME

There were no smiling faces to greet them when they reached Uskar. A band of norsemen stood around three indistinct bodies, bound and gagged with rope.

"It is the Christians," said Tommen at their approach. His eyes were wide, and a sheen of sweat covered his upper lip. The other warriors looked similarly spooked, and fidgeted with their blades as they waited.

"How is this possible?" Thoril stared down at her own slave, who'd been left back on their longship when the company moved inland.

The man's greasy black hair hung over eyes that flickered back and forth across the gathered warriors. His beard was covered in spittle where the gag was loose, and welts had already formed upon his hands.

"It is a trick," said Sigurd, stepping towards the slaves. "Fritjof is playing with us, it is one of his games."

His words were met with silence, and Thoril found herself thumbing her own sword nervously. How had they gotten ahead of them? Who had left them out here to be found?

She knelt down beside her slave and gripped his jaw with a hand. The man bit harder into his gag, and his eyes darted inside his skull, averting her gaze.

"What happened to you?" she asked, tilting his head towards her own. Even if he could understand her, she doubted he would have responded. Something had scared him, and the other slaves, too.

She rose from the floor and nodded to Sigurd. "Let's get them back to camp, see if Ove can make sense of what's happened here. He's spent more time with the Christians than any of us."

Sigurd pulled the nearest slave to his feet and prodded him forward. The wiry blond man gargled from behind his gag, but stumbled forward without resisting.

"Where are their guards?" said Sigurd as he pushed the last captive to his feet. He yanked the man by the collar and drew him close. "Where are the others?" Spit sprayed from his mouth, and his face reddened. The Christian tried to make himself small, cowering away from the massive norseman, but his grip was too tight.

Thoril placed a hand on the warrior's shoulder and shook her head. "It is no use, Sigurd. They cannot speak our tongue. All they know is our rage and the sharpness of our blades."

"You are right," he said, releasing the man. "They are a weak people, made weaker by their god who dies." He kicked at the slave lazily with his foot, and then strode forward, in the direction of camp.

"Ove will know what to do." Inge helped Thoril guide her slave forward. The man was surprisingly strong beneath his rags, and Thoril felt the bulge of muscle on his arms as she directed him back towards the camp. It was his eyes that held her, though. They rolled madly in his head, and did not stop, not even when they'd reached the safety of the encampment.

"It is useless," said Ove, scratching his head. "I cannot make sense of anything they say." The slaves had had their gags removed, though their hands were still securely bound, and were sitting in the centre of the camp. Ove circled them slowly, nodding and shaking his head as he asked them question after question in their native tongue. The responses were hurried and garbled, though the Bretlander tongue always sounded that way to Thoril.

"Ask them how they found themselves inland," Halvor's voice boomed above the confused chattering of the Christians. "Was it Fritjof? Is this some game he is playing with us?"

Ove translated the words and then waited as the leanest of the three replied. After a moment, the veteran turned to Halvor and shrugged.

"He says they came through the earth."

"What foolishness is this?" Halvor stopped his pacing and turned to the captives. His axe rested in the crook of his arm, and his eyes shone red in the firelight. "Do they mock me, Ove?"

The old man raised a brow and met the jarl's stare. "I think, given their position, they would not dare, Ironsson."

Halvor glanced at the slaves, his eyes narrowed into slits, then he spat at the fire. "Find out what happened here, Ove. And no more of these stories, I will have the truth."

"I will do what I can, but I am not familiar with all of their language. There are words that do not make sense to me."

"See that it is done." Halvor spared one last look at the captives, and then stormed off into the night.

Once the jarl was gone, Thoril sat down beside Ove and watched as the slaves chattered amongst themselves. Much of their panic seemed to have receded, but they still flinched when she arrived.

"They are scared." Ove scratched his nose with a thumb and looked to Thoril. "They were asleep on the ship, and woke up to screaming—probably Eluf and his men."

"What, then?"

"I am not sure. The language they speak is strange, littered with metaphor… So, I cannot tell quite what is true and what is an allusion to fact. Why they were spared I cannot tell, but it has something to do with the blood of their three-faced god—it is not pure, or it is too pure, I do not know."

"What of Eluf and the other's guarding *Varúlfr*?"

"Nothing. Only their screams."

Thoril frowned at the old warrior. He was right, it sounded like nothing more than the mutterings of madmen. Hardly enough to satisfy Halvor or the others.

"Did you not see this," she asked. "In your dreams?"

"There was nothing of the Christians, nor of the burning ships." Ove turned his hands over, mapping the scars on his knuckles with a finger. "This place blinds me to our fate. I only see fragments, but it is not enough. It is worse with the Christians. What I do see is blurred, as if from a great distance."

Thoril leaned back, resting on her hands. "What are we to do? No Fritjof, no Ulfgar, and now no Bjarki."

"Halvor will want us to stay. He owes Bjarki a debt of blood, and will not leave this place without him. Even if it means he risks us all."

That night they caught their first glimpse of the strange people who had been tracking them. Sigurd saw them first, standing upon the ridge above them. But then more were spotted, until the hills seemed filled by their presence. Dozens of figures moved silently across the forsaken landscape, torches raised to the starless sky. Halvor ordered the company to battle-readiness, but the observers seemed uninterested in an open fight.

"I do not see a blade among them," said Sigurd as he strode between the massed ranks of norsemen. "Catch one alive if they come at us."

But the onlookers seemed content to simply watch from a distance. They moved away if any of Halvor's party got too close, only to reappear further along a moment later. The warriors grew frustrated, and some of them lobbed stones at the figures, to little effect.

"They are testing us." Thoril moved up beside Inge and Ove, taking her place in the shield wall. "Probing for a weakness, or trying to bait us into chasing after them."

"It might work," said Inge. She nodded to a band of younger warriors at the foot of the hills. The men were slowly hyping themselves up, and only the appearance of some of the company's veterans stopped them from racing headlong at the watchers.

Ove lowered his shield and rubbed his eyes with an arm. "They are young and foolish, but we were all like that once. Halvor will see them in line." His words were soon followed by the hoarse bark of the jarl, and the offending warriors quickly fell back into place.

"You see," said Ove, staring back up the walls of the valley. "Not even youthful vigour ignores the will of the jarl." He squinted into the darkness and blinked before turning to Thoril and Inge. "I fear we will need his strength before long, both of his mind and his axe."

The three stood together until the early hours, watching the watchers. It was only when the sun rose, and the figures retreated into the many caverns and ravines that splintered off from the valley, that the band finally found rest.

That morning, they found Fritjof and the crew of *Kveldúlfr*.

KAIJU

***

Their bodies, over thirty of them, had been nailed to stakes and hung rotting beneath the sun. The forest of corpses was found by one of Bjarki's pathfinders, upon the ridge nearest the grey walls of the ravine. Halvor had led the party up the hill as soon as he'd heard the news.

Swarms of gnats clung to the dead in such numbers that it was impossible to make out the features of the deceased. By the smell, it was clear that they had been here for some time. Longer, perhaps, than was possible.

"We must burn them," Halvor declared. "This is no way for a viking to enter Valhalla." He pointed towards the thin line of trees that ringed the hill. "A mighty pyre for the fallen, to usher their spirits on to the next life. Then we will deal with those who dared take up swords against our brothers."

The norsemen took to the task with vigor, while others set to removing the crew of their sister ship from the wooden stakes. It was a gruesome task, and Thoril found herself retching as she cut the bonds holding an elderly warrior to the post. Removing the nails from his wrists proved to be more horrid, and she was forced to step away from the corpse for a moment.

"They will thank you for it," said Ove, walking towards her. "Once they find rest in the great halls of our fathers."

Thoril nodded and wiped her brow. Braziers had been lit alongside the dead, and the smoke fended off the worst of the insects, but the heat wasn't helping with the smell.

"If we had not come upon them, the dead might have returned." Ove drew a blade from the folds of his sleeves and approached the stake. "To leave a body like this, with the head towards the heavens, is to encourage the becoming of draugr. You can see here"—he tapped the swollen leg of the corpse with the knife—"even now, the corruption has begun. These bodies will soon welcome unlife, and then we will have to kill our brothers and sisters, even if it is no longer truly them." He shook his head sadly and began the grisly task of removing the nails from the warriors hands and feet.

Thoril watched quietly, and then helped Ove take the body down and place it on the floor, beside the others. Behind them, the pyre had grown, and now covered much of the surface of the hill.

"They will see this fire from Tronde." Ove smiled sadly and patted her shoulder. "And when we return home, we shall feast to the memory of those we lost here."

Thoril wiped her hands on her breeches and stared down the line of posts. "Any sign of Bjarki or Ulfgar amongst the dead?"

"Inge searches now for them, but she will not find them here, I think."

She looked quizzically at the old warrior, but Ove simply shrugged. "This is not the fate reserved for Ulfgar. As for Bjarki, I suspect he would not let his body be caught like this, not by whoever haunts these hills."

"You think he is still out there?"

"It is what the jarl believes, and if anyone can hide himself away in a place like this, it's Bjarki."

"Then why not return to us, if he is still alive and free?"

Ove sighed. "I do not have all the answers, girl. And in this place, I can see as much as you. It is just a feeling, that is all. Perhaps Inge will come upon their bodies both, and then we can mourn their passing with the rest of them. But until then, I sense there is more to come for both Bjarki and Ulfgar."

"Halvor will want us to continue on, won't he?" Thoril said the words softly, so that only Ove could hear.

"He will not let this go unpunished, and he will not leave Bjarki to suffer this same fate." Ove raised a hand and gestured to the bodies still bound to the poles. "There must be a bloodening now, and vengeance for our fallen. Halvor will bring violence to those who have done this."

Thoril nodded, and watched as another body was removed from its stake. "Good," she said, gripping the hilt of her sword. "Vengeance it shall be."

They watched from the hills as the pyre was lit, and great plumes of smoke blew across the valley, aiding the dead in their journey beyond. It was Inge that first recited the words of Hialmar's Song. She had found Akes' body with the rest of them, and the words rung out cold from her mouth.

Flies from the South
The famished Raven
Fly with him
The fallow Eagle
On the flesh of the fallen
I shall feed them no more
On my body both
Will batten now

The sad notes of a tagelharpa joined her voice, and then the soft, rhythmic beat of a drum, too. Thoril watched as the flames roared across the hastily built pyre, and felt her heart go hard at the thought of her fallen raid-mates. To survive the swords of the Bretons and Njord's angry seas, only to be slaughtered on a strange island, far from home. She scowled. Ove's predictions be damned, she would see her kin avenged, and she would see Tronde again.

When the last note of Hialmar's Song faded, the company put the funeral pyre behind them and set off towards the mountain pass. Sigurd made sure there was always a sword and shield between Halvor and the empty hills, but the jarl ignored his mothering and moved speedily to the front of the band.

The remaining pathfinders fanned out, occupying both the high and low ground surrounding the norsemen. They would not be caught out by those who had butchered Fritjof and his crew.

It was sometime after noon that one of the scouts returned, in a state of nervous excitement. He was quickly taken aside by Halvor, who questioned him intensely, before being sent back out into the hills.

"Something is afoot." Inge shifted her shield over her shoulder and watched as the pathfinder disappeared up a rocky outcrop.

Halvor signalled to a band of veterans, and soon had them following in the scout's footsteps. The warriors were less light of step, and smaller rocks and stones rolled down the side of the hill, causing a groan from the disgruntled warriors closest.

When the scout returned, with his escort of veterans in tow, he was carrying a small object in his hands. Thoril tried to get a proper look at it, but whatever it was lay hidden beneath a bundle of rags.

"Let's see what he's found," said Inge, pushing her way to the front of the company. Thoril and Ove followed, ignoring the cursed complaints of the other norsemen as they navigated through the press.

Halvor was standing with Sigurd and Tommen, staring down into the bundle, a strange look on his face. The scout was talking rapidly into his ear, but it was clear that Halvor wasn't listening. He placed a hand into the rags and retrieved the object, lifting it above his head for all to see.

"This is what we face in this Gods' forsaken place." He spat at the ground and rotated his hand so all the gathered warriors could get a proper look. "Truly, it is a being cursed."

The jarl's fingers were wrapped around the pale white surface of a skull. Though distinctly human, the shape was warped, and the cranium jutted out unevenly. The forehead was sloped and smooth, and elongated in a manner that seemed almost serpentine. Thoril felt her stomach churn as she gazed into its empty sockets.

Behind her, she heard the Christians praying frantically to their dying God, before they were forced into silence by their captors.

"Behold the beast." Halvor turned the skull in his hands and stared into its ever-smiling face, before letting it fall from his grasp. "And what awaits it." He stomped a foot down hard, smashing the skull to pieces, and then rolled his shoulders. "Only the godless could do this to themselves. Only the godless could force their skulls to such a shape, to mimic the unfit and deformed…" He sneered in disgust, then pointed at what remained of the white bones. "We will see the same thing repeated, a thousand times, if needed." With that, he turned his back on the company and strode towards the crags.

The warriors followed him without hesitation, and two dozen norsemen jogged up the last hill before the opening of the ravine. But when they reached the summit, even Halvor was forced to take pause. A low muttering spread amongst the ranks as more of the company came into view of the grey walls of the mountain pass.

"This I did not see," said Ove as he stared at the opening. "How did I not see this?"

Before them, on either side of the mouth of the ravine, the rock walls had been cut and chiselled. Two great carvings looked down upon them. Hewn from the surface of the rock itself, the shapes formed were almost as tall as the crag itself. The artist evidently had some skill, and the representations were almost lifelike.

Thoril felt her skin crawl as she gazed upon the first of the two carvings. On the left of the passage, a great snake stretched out across the length of the wall. Its coils were wrapped around a depiction of the mountain itself, while its angular head stared down on the entrance to the passage, its massive fangs exposed. The carver had somehow managed to create the impression of colour without its use, and Thoril could almost see the silver scales of the beast beneath the sea once more.

In contrast, the other engraving seemed more primitive. Rather than the smooth corners of the serpent's depiction, the angles used were all sharp and rough, at times obscuring parts of the carving entirely. Despite that, Thoril could still make out most of the piece. It depicted a man sitting on his haunches, with his legs crossed. His one hand was raised, with two fingers extended to the heavens, while the other was pointed downward, towards the ground beneath his feet. As Thoril got closer, she could just make out the poorly hewn shapes of more serpentine bodies wrapped around his own.

"Eels," said Ove as they approached. He was right. What she'd mistaken for snakes were, in fact, dozens of eels covering his skin like armour.

"This is an old faith." Ove made the mark of the Fe with his one hand, and pulled his axe from his belt with the other.

"You have encountered these images before?" Thoril frowned at the veteran, and then stared back up at the carvings as they walked beside them.

"This one, yes." Ove pointed to the man and his armour of eels. "But this." He screwed up his eyes and stared at the snake. "I have not seen something like this before, not even on my journeys to the land in the West."

"Who is the man?" The shield-maiden stepped onto the sand that made up the floor of the ravine and helped Ove down from the rocky ledge beside her.

"He is a figure from pre-history. Neruk, Elil, Nergal, The Destroying Flame, he has gone by many names, and has had many worshippers. His time has passed though, with the coming of the Christians, and the worshippers of Allah."

"The Destroying Flame." Thoril clenched her jaw and took one last look at the carving of Neruk. His eyes seemed to follow her, and she felt she was being watched even when it was finally gone from sight.

A shout from behind her stopped her in her tracks, and the whole company turned to see what had caused the commotion.

Henrik and Eyva were trying to pull the Christians into the ravine, but they had dug their heels in and wouldn't go any further.

Thoril saw her own slave pulling at Henrik, sheer panic in his eyes, while the others had fallen to their knees and were begging their captors not to force them to continue.

"On your feet!" Henrik shouted. He smashed a meaty palm into her slave's face and dragged him through the sand. The others grabbed onto the viking's legs, slowing him to a halt, and giving her own slave enough time to get back to his feet.

"They will kill them," said Ove, but Thoril was already moving towards the huddle of bodies.

"Enough," she called as Henrik kicked his knee into the lanky Christian's face. The man sputtered blood and grabbed his nose as a moan erupted from his throat. She lifted her sword threateningly when Henrik caught her eyes. "He is mine." She pointed her blade towards her slave and nodded. "I will not have you kill him because he has slowed you down."

He shrugged. "They will not go any further."

"I will take him," she said, lowering her sword. "If he does not come, then I will punish him as I see fit, with blade or fist, but it will be *my* blade or fist."

Henrik shrugged again, but let go of her slave and took a step back. "Be it on you," he said, finally.

Thoril nodded and grabbed the slave by his collar. Understanding seemed to have dawned on him and he did not resist, knowing that his life was truly at risk. She prodded him forward with her shield and walked him back towards Ove.

"What's gotten into them?" Inge joined her as she guided her slave. She stank like spirits and smoke.

"I don't know," she replied. "They are scared easily, these Christians."

"Or they know something we do not." Inge cackled, and swigged deeply from her flask. Thoril couldn't see where she'd placed her sword or shield, but she wasn't in the mood for a fight.

Her slave seemed to have calmed, and the other prisoners had followed after him, preferring to face their fears than face a beating from an angry norseman. She watched him carefully as they walked through the opening to the ravine, and saw that he was talking softly to himself, reciting what seemed to be the same words over and over. He was at prayer, she realised. She glanced at the other Christians and saw that they were doing the same thing. She didn't know why, but it made a shiver run down her spine.

WRITE LIKE HELL

HELVEGEN

The ravine opened up until there was enough space for the company to walk side by side, without touching the walls. Halvor stayed at the front, and sent roving bands of warriors forward, sometimes joining them himself. His voice became a near constant feature as noon turned to late afternoon. He shouted reassurances and words of praise, of vengeance and anger. It was only when dusk fell, and his voice grew hoarse, that silence fell over the warriors.

"That skull," said Thoril as Halvor called them to a halt for the day. "How did it come to be shaped in such a way?"

Ove clicked his teeth, and dropped his shield and bedroll to the ground. "It is through binding that such deformities occur. I have seen it once before, though not to such an extent. As an infant, the skull is bound with rope and cloth. The pressure forces the head to grow in such a way, or the child dies. One or the other."

"Why would anyone do such a thing?" Inge slumped down on the ground beside Thoril and made a face. "To risk death, only to be rewarded with deformity. It is madness."

Ove stretched his back out and yawned. "It is beyond me. It was a long time ago that I last saw it, and the man I had seen was already dead, so he could not answer my questions."

Inge chuckled and rolled onto her side to stare at Thoril. "The Christians seemed troubled by it. Go on, ask yours what he fears."

Thoril turned her head to her slave and watched as he chewed on the dry meats she'd provided. The man's eyes met her own for a second, before he lowered his head and focused on his meagre dinner.

"Ask him, Ove." Thoril rubbed her hands together and nodded to the old warrior. "Maybe it will help us figure out where we find ourselves."

"It is not so easy." Ove frowned. "These Bretlanders speak in dialects I am not familiar with."

"Try." Thoril took a bite from her own supper and chewed it slowly, gesturing to Ove as she swallowed.

Ove sighed and walked towards her slave, who ignored him until he felt a boot prod him gently in the side. The veteran knelt down on his haunches and started speaking in the Bretlander tongue, using his hands to articulate and emphasise points when communication seemed to break down. After a while, once the first fires had been built, Ove rose from his knees and wandered back over to them.

"And?"

Ove eased onto his haunches and palmed his hands. "Neruk, the old god carved into the mountain... The Christians think he is someone else."

Inge rolled her eyes. "Who do they say he is? Another god who dies?"

"Addir-Melek," said Ove. "The blasphemer. I had not heard of him until now, but they believe he is a servant of the devil, and that this is the way to hell."

"Servants of the devil, ancient gods, and the path to Náströnd itself." Inge lay on her back. "What are we to believe, Ove?"

"Perhaps they are the same thing," said Thoril.

"Not you, too." Inge kicked dirt towards her and laughed. "You are always the one telling Ove and Ulfgar off for their stories, Troubled Thoril! Now you believe them?"

"I do not say that they are real, just that they represent the same thing." She crossed her legs and put her hands between them. The night air was bringing with it a chill, and smaller fires would soon be lit all around the camp.

Inge rolled onto her stomach and stared out into night. They had stopped where the ravine grew widest, and the towering walls were less imposing. Inge traced the movement of their scouts, following their torches as they moved alongside the edge of the ravine. Great shadows hung to the sides of the incline, and it was only when one of the torches grew closer to one that she saw it was not a shadow but a gaping hole in the side of the rock. There were dozens of them, scattered all about the valley. She squinted against the darkness and watched as one of the torches disappeared down a tunnel, only to reappear moments later at another tunnel further along.

"This place is a never-ending maze," she said, turning back to her friends. "I will be glad to see it behind us, if we ever make it off this island."

Thoril nodded, but Ove remained quiet, deep in thought. He remained like that even when the smaller fires were lit, even when Inge and Thoril were wrapped up in their bedrolls, fast asleep.

***

"Wake up, Thoril! Get up!"

Thoril awoke with a jerk, and instinctively went for her sword. Her eyes adjusted to the darkness, and she saw Inge sitting over her, her eyes wide and a nervous look on her face.

"What is it?" She wiped the sleep from her own eyes and rested on her elbows. Ove was nowhere to be seen, but the rest of the camp was being woken up by sentries and those who couldn't sleep.

"Listen," said Inge, holding a finger to her lips.

She listened. It was soft at first, barely a sound on the edge of hearing, but as she focused it grew louder, until it was all she could hear. A low moan, punctuated by silence, carried itself across the camp, repeating itself over and over.

"What is that?" She moved into a sitting position and stared into the night.

"At first I thought it was the wind echoing through those tunnels, but then it got clearer." Inge shifted until she was kneeling beside her, and touched her arm with a hand. "Thoril, it is a person. Someone in great pain, calling out."

"Where is Ove?" Thoril dragged herself up from the ground, her tiredness forgotten.

"He is with Halvor. He thinks it might be Ulfgar, but who is to say." Inge joined her standing, and the two started walking towards the camp's perimeter.

The rest of the company was wide awake by the time Halvor had planned on a course of action. His scouts had moved out the moment the voice on the wind made itself heard, and had identified one of the tunnels as the source. Sigurd and a band had already moved into the tunnel, and the rest of the company would follow.

"It is Bjarki or Ulfgar, or both." The jarl stood by the fire in the centre of the camp and stared into the gathered faces. "It does not matter. It is one of us, and we will not let his cries go unanswered."

The gathered norsemen were in full battle-gear, their shields held at the ready. Many of them had applied ochres and paints to their faces, and only their eyes shone out beneath blood-red visages.

"Sigurd leads the vanguard. His veterans will mark a trail for us to follow. Then we will have our vengeance, and these vile beings will know that Halvor and his Bloodied have fallen upon them!" He raised his axe and let out a guttural howl, thumping his shield as the rest of the band joined him.

Thoril found herself howling with the rest of the party, and the weight of days fell from her shoulders. Finally, they would confront the enemy face-to-face. Finally, they would bring steel to flesh, and release the frustration that had followed them since landing on the island. She would follow Halvor into the tunnels, and she would bloody her blade once more.

She accepted the torch offered to her as she walked past the fire, in Halvor's wake, and moved into a jog beside Inge and Ove. The other shield-maiden had a look of glee on her face. No doubt she was running through the same emotions she was. But Ove only smiled sadly when she glanced at him. He was too caught up in his stories, in his games of fate, and the will of the gods. The will of the gods was with them, and with their hero Halvor! How else could they perform such feats of strength and courage against the Bretlanders? How else could they survive the storms thrown at them. Even the Christians, with their miracles, could not compete with the chosen Bloodied of Halvor.

The entire company moved towards the tunnels, and Thoril even saw the slaves being pushed along in the direction of the entrance. They would all bear witness to the wetting of her sword.

She gripped her shield closer to her chest as the warriors were forced to press together. The tunnel entrance was narrower than it looked, and she smelt burnt hair as the norsemen bunched up.

KAIJU

The air grew hot, and sweat quickly soaked her undershirt. Beneath her feet, the rock was smooth, and she could feel a slight incline. They were heading underground.

The tunnel grew wider the deeper they went, and soon there was enough space for the band to move unhindered by one another. Halvor waved the norsemen forward and took stock of his surrounds.

The walls around them were smooth, as though the result of a current or stream. Small passages ran along the side of the main tunnel, but none of them were foolish enough to explore lest they lose the main party.

Sigurd had been true to his word. Red paint stained the walls, marking out his path ever downward.

The sound of suffering continued as they mapped out the tunnels, growing louder as they explored its depths. It wasn't long before Thoril wanted to cover her ears, or to scream loudly, anything to block out the noise. She could see the others were growing uncomfortable with it, too, but with Halvor in the lead, they plodded on regardless.

By the time the tunnel ended, becoming one great cavernous chamber, the groaning voice was all anyone could hear. Thoril ground her teeth as they emerged from the passageway and lifted her torch up to fully see the hall. The light flickered as a cold current blew through the gallery, and she turned to see about a dozen other tunnels lined up beside the one they'd just come from. They'd have openings all across the island, she had no doubt about it.

She spotted another of Sigurd's red spots of paint, marking out their route so that they did not get lost, and then turned to take in the chamber.

The light of their torches barely illuminated the walls closest to them, let alone the hall itself, and Thoril found herself staring into pitch black on all sides.

"Where is Sigurd?" Inge had to shout above the reverberating groan that seemed to come from every passageway at once.

"He must be here!" Her own voice sounded thin and soft, but her friend nodded anyway. Rather than shout again, Thoril pointed towards Jarl Halvor, and they both started to walk towards him.

Before they reached him, Inge raised a hand and turned to Thoril. She pointed to an ear and frowned. Almost as quickly as it had begun, the groaning voice on the wind had gone quiet.

"Is that a good thing?" Inge bit her lower lip and watched to see how the jarl would respond.

Halvor raised a hand, bringing the company to a halt, and tilted his head. He stood like that for a moment, listening to the darkness. It was only then that Thoril saw a flicker of movement amongst the shadows made by their torches.

She squinted and lifted her own torch higher to dispel the void that surrounded them. Her breath caught in her mouth as another figure moved within the shadows, and then another.

Just beyond the orange glow, shapes had begun to emerge, dozens of them, until the whole cavern seemed filled with darting forms, moving in and out of the light. Thoril could make out faces now, as the inhabitants of the cave grew more brazen. Wrapped in cloth and bound by rope, the leering visages that greeted her were misshapen and deformed, like the skull they'd uncovered in the valley. To see such disfigurement brought to life made her stomach churn, and she felt herself shrink back behind her shield.

"They carry no weapons," said Inge from beside her. Thoril looked, and watched as one of the figures stepped into the light, before disappearing once again. Inge was right. The man was unarmed and unarmoured. Aside from the rags he wore, and the head bindings, he carried nothing.

"We will make short work of this." The shield-maiden grinned beneath her own torch and strode forward more confidently than before.

Despite the appearance of the watchers, they made little attempt to attack or slow the war party. They kept to the edges of the light and tracked them as they moved deeper and deeper into the cavern. Thoril noticed more tunnels on the walls, and some even on the floor beneath them. She was sure there were more above their heads, but the ceiling was shrouded in a darkness not even the light of their fires could push back. More of the deformed figures appeared from these passages, but they kept their distance, content to watch Halvor and his Bloodied move through the cavern.

Thoril felt her foot step in something wet and stared down at a small pool of water, then dragged her boot out and tried to kick it dry. Ove was knelt down beside another of the puddles, his brow furrowed.

"It is salt water," he said, when Thoril turned to him.

"But we are days from the sea."

"Maybe, but these tunnels… We do not know how deep they go, or what lies beneath the island. They may be flooded by the sea when it storms."

Thoril shrugged. She cared little about the comings and goings of the tide, or for flooding tunnels, provided she was not there when next it happened.

WRITE LIKE HELL

The puddles of water grew more numerous and larger. She was sure she saw movement within some of the black pools—silver shapes writhing within their depths, but when she looked closer, there was nothing.

Inge was the first to notice a change in the ground beneath their feet. She let out a groan and pointed her torch at the floor. Thoril felt her hackles raise as something broke under her boots. The others were noticing it, too, and even Halvor spat in disgust.

The floor was littered with hundreds of bones, and one could hardly make out the ground beneath them. It was like staring at some macabre shoreline. Thoril saw more of the warped skulls, elongated and serpentine in shape, but there were others, too. The skeletons of all manner of beasts blanketed the chamber, and cracked beneath their feet as they moved over them.

The watchers maintained their distance, but seemed less rushed to get out of the norsemen's way, and Halvor nearly caught one with the side of his axe. Others darted back into the tunnels whenever the band made to attack them, but it was clear they were readying for a fight.

When they had walked for some time over the bone carpet, Halvor called the party to a halt.

"Listen," he said as his warriors sipped from their flasks and wiped the sweat from their brows. Deep inside the cavernous chamber, Thoril could hear the sound of a drum ringing out. It beat a slow rhythm, but the sound was unmistakable. Another sound joined that of the percussion, a low hum that seemed to echo through the tunnels.

"Where did they go?" Uskar turned to the gathered warriors and waved a hand at the empty tunnels. He was right: the watchers had disappeared, leaving only the vikings in the chamber.

The drumbeat upped its tempo, and Thoril felt the hair on the back of her neck rise as a fell voice joined it. It droned out words she could not understand, but the meaning was clear: Death. The End.

Other voices joined it, singing out from a great distance, but closing in with every chanted note.

"Shield wall!" Halvor called, dropping his own flask and lifting his axe. His warriors rushed to obey, and wood clashed against wood as the vikings joined in a defensive formation.

The shadows around them started to move, but this time, the figures were not content to hide away. They raced towards the band, charging across the bone floor, even as their feet were cut to shreds by the jagged remains.

The voice in the chamber reached a sickening crescendo, and suddenly hundreds of torches were lit all around them, finally illuminating the chamber entirely. Thoril nearly baulked at the sight. The bone floor stretched out as far as she could see, and there was no visible end to the cavern itself. She'd been right about the tunnels above their heads: the ceiling was covered by them, as was large swathes of the floor.

What caused her to flinch, however, was the sheer number of figures that were bearing down on them. There were *hundreds*. Some were hunched over, their deformities afflicting more than just their skulls, while others seemed small and ungainly on their feet. It didn't matter. Unarmed or not, she didn't know if they could be beaten.

Halvor beat his axe against his shield in a steady tempo, over the sound of the drum in the depths. He glanced at his warriors and grinned. This was what

Halvor was made for: overcoming the odds and proving the gods favoured him.

Thoril felt her nerves calm, even as the cave dwellers bore down on them. She dropped her torch, no longer needing it, and drew her sword.

"Brace!" Halvor leaned into his shield, as did the rest of the company.

When the horde of deformed monstrosities met the shield wall, it was with a blood-curdling scream, followed by the crump of bones breaking and flesh being torn. Thoril threw her weight behind her shield and stabbed out between a narrow gap formed between her and Inge's shield. She was rewarded with a garbled cry, and the pressure against her arm was relieved, before another body flung itself at her.

She repeated the process again and again, until her arm grew tired, but still she carried on. Blood covered the floor, running in a steady stream across the bones, and still they carried on. Jarl Hover shouted out orders, pushing the press ever forward as they butchered their way through Flintjof's murderers.

The savage people that inhabited the cave were unrelenting, despite their losses, despite their lack of weapons. They used their numbers against the norse, and Thoril saw more than one of her brothers pulled down by their sheer weight, before the shield wall closed around the gap again.

When she felt she could not lift her sword again, and the sweat in her eyes was blurring her vision, the attack finally faltered. The steady beat of the drum in the distance finally fell silent, and the only sound was the bark of Halvor and the screams of those who fell beneath their blades.

"Finish!" Halvor cried, breaking from the shield wall. He swung his axe in a vicious arc, dispatching two foes in as many seconds, then catching another with the back of his boot. He smashed his shield down into the mutants skull until it stopped moving.

"With the jarl!" a voice cried, and the shield wall broke, releasing twenty angry norsemen upon the thinning ranks of the cave dwellers.

Thoril charged out with Inge, leaving Ove to deal with the wounded abhorrents strewn across the battleground.

Tired as she was, she felt her strength renewed at the thought of avenging her fallen raid-mates, and of bringing this cult of death to an end. Her sword slashed at exposed necks and chests, arms and legs, until all she saw was blood. It was only when the last of the death worshippers had disappeared down the tunnels, and the beating drum had faded for good, that she heard the soft, sibilant whisper.

She glanced around her, and saw that others had noticed it, too. Most of the warriors were standing still now, listening to the wind, and Thoril was gladdened to see so many of their number left. She flinched as the hissing sound grew louder and turned back to the tunnels that surrounded the chamber.

Theodoric was walking towards the nearest opening, his head cocked to the side as he sought out the source, while the rest of the company slowly edged back towards Halvor.

"Any ideas?" Thoril asked of Ove as they rejoined the shield wall.

"You have already seen it. You know what lurks beneath the tide." Ove closed his eyes and shrugged. "Now we must meet it."

Thoril crinkled her brow and held back a snarl at the old man's words. "It is—"

Her words were cut off by a cry of alarm, and then a high-pitched scream. She turned towards the tunnels in time to see a flicker of silver, and the smooth scales of a gigantic form as it moved past the nearest opening. A giant tail appeared for a moment, and then it was gone, leaving an opening as empty as it was a moment before.

Thoril felt her heart pounding in her chest, and her legs started to shake beneath her. Theodoric was running back towards them, a look of primal fear on his usually stoic features.

"It is Jörmungandr!" he cried, smashing past the now reformed shield-wall. "The Midgard Serpent is here."

Halvor shook his head, but gripped his axe tight in his hand. "Stand fast," he cried, but his voice wavered and his face was pale. "We are Odin's kin, and we do not run."

From the tunnels all around them, another wave of figures appeared. They started to sing in that strange tongue of theirs, and Thoril could hear the drum pick up its beat in the distance again. Her whole body was shaking now, as fear gripped her heart. She thought it would stop entirely, but a hand clutched her shoulder gently, and she turned to find Ove smiling at her.

"We must not fear this," he said, nodding to the tunnels. The hiss was growing louder, and it seemed to come from all the passages at once. "Soon, we will either feast in the halls of our fathers, or we will kill this thing and become like gods ourselves."

She took a deep breath and nodded, somehow conjuring up a smile for Ove. The old warrior patted her on the shoulder again, and then joined the shield wall beside her.

When the great serpent finally appeared, it was from one of the holes above the gathered norsemen. The beast pushed through debris, sprinkling them all with stone and dust, before it thrust its head out into the open. Thoril nearly cried out, but kept her fears in check as the giant snake slithered out into the cavern. The creature was impossibly large, its head the length and breadth of a longship, while its body seemed without end. Row upon row of fangs emerged from behind black gums, and massive red orbs stared out from its arrowhead-like face. Two muscular appendages hung from the beast's sides, and ended in sharp claws the size of a man. The silver scales that covered it were a mess of scars, and massive cuts long since healed. What creature could do such a thing to such a beast, Thoril wondered as it lowered itself to the ground.

All around them, the snake-worshippers were emerging, chanting and cheering as the serpent moved closer to the norsemen. Some were foolish enough to get too close to the snake, and were crushed beneath its coils. Others moved to flank the serpent, and encircled the vikings so that there was no clear route of escape. Though, by the look on Halvor's face, escape was not on his mind.

The norseman rolled his shoulders and tested the sharpness of his blade against his forearm.

"You see this," he said, turning to face his warriors. He raised his arm and nodded to the thin stream of blood running along it. "This blood is the blood of norse, of Odin's son. It is the blood of Freyja and of Vali. It is the blood of Balder. This blood is the same blood that will course through Thor when Ragnarok comes, and Fenris and Jörmungandr light fire to the world. It is like poison to the beast." He looked over his shoulder at the approaching serpent and the gathering cultists. "Now help me kill it."

His warriors moved in behind him, still in shock at the sight of the serpent, but emboldened by his words. Halvor seemed to grow before them, his size and strength swelling to match his words.

For a moment, it seemed that they could perform this impossible task. That they could slay this beast with axe and sword, with spear and shield. Indeed, when Halvor moved into a loping run, his axe raised and a war cry on his lips, it seemed an inevitability.

Thoril chased after him, her own sword raised, howling and cursing with the rest of the band as they closed on the serpent. The creature hesitated, unused to being attacked, unused to anything but fear. It gave Halvor the time he needed to make the last few meters. He leapt into the hair, pushing aside the cultists who scrambled into his way, and embedded his axe in the serpent's side. The beast lashed out, but Halvor had already rolled out of the way and retrieved a short blade from his belt.

Then the rest of them were on it. Thoril stabbed deep into the creature's quivering flesh, yanking her sword back and vomiting as the stench of rotten fish erupted from the wound. She wiped her mouth and fell back before the thing could slam its tail down on where she'd just been. Others thrust their blades into the creature's flank, while the rest took to clearing up the horde of deformed that were still biting at their heels. She caught sight of Halvor crawling up the snake's flank, using his stabbing blade like a climbing tool, and then he was gone, hidden behind the beasts lashing body.

KAIJU

Inge crashed in beside her and cut down with her blade, piercing through flesh and bone. She grinned madly at Thoril, and then rolled out of the way, before the serpent could react. The norsemen were clinical in their approach, and dozens of the snake worshippers were killed, even as the serpent itself was cut to a bloody mess. Still, the beast's skin was thick, and its scales deflected much of the damage done.

Uskar was the first to fall. He lingered too long, trying to retrieve his spear from the snake's chest. The beast didn't even use its fangs to kill him, it simply smashed its head down against the ground he was standing on, leaving nothing but a red paste behind. The next to fall was Theodoric. Encouraged by the jarl's actions, he tried to clamber up the side of the snake in order to get close to its head. His hand slipped against the smooth scales and he tumbled to the ground, only to be crushed beneath the serpent's coils.

For a while, they fought like heroes, battling back both serpent and cultist. Blood ran like rivers from the creatures flanks, and great welts had formed all along its chest. The warriors learnt to move and duck out of the way whenever it slammed its body against the ground, and roll out of range of its massive coils. Thoril fought harder than she'd ever fought before, and was rewarded time and time again as blood spewed out from the creature's wounds. Even the serpent's worshippers began to doubt the strength of their god, and a great cry went up each time one of the viking's impaled the beast.

But the creature was old, and it had fought many battles. When it finally caught sight of Halvor climbing between its scales, the serpent struck with blinding speed. The jarl let out a cry as the creature caught him between its jaws, and a massive fang penetrated his

79

chest. Thoril nearly dropped her sword and fled, but anger coursed through her at the last second and she found herself slashing out at the beast violently.

To his credit, when Halvor died, it was with a sword in his hands and a howl on his lips. Even as the serpent tore the life from him, he sunk his knife deep into the creatures gums, causing it to thrash madly, before it flung the lifeless corpse across the bone fields.

Halvor's Bloodied fought on for a while longer, but with each moment that passed, another of their number fell. Norsemen were consumed whole by the creature's gaping maw, crushed beneath its coils, or swarmed by the cultists. Tommen, then Eyva, Henrik, and then Ove and Inge—all of them were butchered.

Thoril screamed in rage as the serpent killed them, until a hand pulled her away from the fight and she was running. Fleeing from the end of the world, back the way she'd come.

***

She didn't know where the torch had come from, but she held it out before her as she ran. The sounds of battle had long since faded, and all she could hear were her feet sloshing through puddles and cracking old bones. Those who had fled with her were dead. Caught by ambush after ambush of the serpent worshippers, only Thoril remained. She had to survive—only she could tell the saga of Halvor and his band of Bloodied. She paused at the entrance to one of the tunnels and saw that a red mark had been painted on the wall. *Sigurd*, she thought as she moved towards the entrance. She frowned and looked at the floor. She didn't remember there being bones at the entrance to the tunnel. Her torch still raised, she walked over to the next tunnel and saw that the same mark had been painted on its walls, and on the next, and the next. Thoril shivered as the torch began to flicker. She didn't have long before it went out. Gritting her teeth to hold back the fear that threatened to overwhelm her, she moved on. If she could just find the right tunnel, she had a chance.

In the depths of the cavern, a drum began to beat.

WRITE LIKE HELL

A Boy and His Monster

Andrea Speed

Toshi wondered why third dates were such a big deal. He knew why they were for him—he probably hadn't had one since college. He'd pretty much written off any romantic attachments. After all, the truth of his existence was so weird, he wasn't sure he had room for a relationship. But then he met Mason—in line for doughnuts, of all places. He was cute and charming—and hey, he liked the same fancy-ass doughnuts he did. He was relatively fit, with deep brown eyes and perfectly messy black hair that seemed more rushed than sloppy. He was funny, and maybe a little caffeine-juiced, but Toshi decided to give him his number all the same.

Their first date wasn't technically a proper date—they just met for coffee, and to make sure the other person wasn't a complete lunatic. It went better than Toshi had anticipated, and found they liked many of the same bad movies and good television shows. He was also a reader, which shouldn't have impressed Toshi, but it did. He knew lots of guys who were perfectly smart and otherwise appealing, but hadn't picked up a book since college. He might have lost most of his childhood podge, but Toshi had always been deeply nerdy at heart. Discussing books with him was almost foreplay, although he was careful not to tell Mason that. He didn't want to scare him off.

Their second date was the first proper date. They attended a food truck festival, and Mason, clearly a foodie, introduced him to all of those places. He knew who had the best breakfast sandwich, the best dim sum, the best tacos. Toshi was kind of amazed to be around someone who knew that sort of thing, and his passion for food was infectious.

When he got home later that night, Toshi was as giddy as a teenager with their first crush. He liked Mason, and he was pretty sure Mason liked him, too. Maybe this could be a thing. Except… His eternal roadblock. Okay, that was melodramatic. Toshi was not in fact eternal. Jerry probably was, but no one knew for sure. Still, there was a problem.

For the third date, Toshi realised he had to do something different. His college boyfriend, Eric, had broken up with him because he knew Toshi was hiding something from him. Eric was convinced it was a side-piece, but the truth was so bizarre, Toshi couldn't tell him. Now he was in the terrible position of trying to keep his secret even better than before, or risk it all and show Mason the truth and see where the chips fell. He wasn't sure that was the best option, but a relationship that started with a lie was doomed to fail. Yes, it was weird, and there was a very good chance Mason would run screaming into the night, never to be seen again, but that was a risk he was willing to take. Truth had to be the way forward.

Toshi tried to plan the third date down to the second, but soon recognised it for the fool's errand it was. He couldn't make it any better by sticking to a rigorous schedule. He just had to let it happen and deal with the aftermath.

For date three, Toshi took Mason out to a Thai restaurant he knew about. It didn't look like much, especially as it was located in a failing strip mall location, but the food was great, as was the atmosphere inside. Outside, not so much, but you can't have everything. Afterwards, he invited Mason back to his place, and he accepted.

Although it was a long drive out, Mason seemed impressed when he saw it. Toshi lived in a sprawling, ranch-style house on a ten-acre piece of land that gave him all the privacy in the world. His nearest neighbour was three miles away.

Mason let out a low whistle. "I didn't know you were loaded."

"I'm not. It's kind of hard to explain."

"Was this your aunt and uncle's place?"

Mason already knew his parents had died when he was young, and that he'd been raised by his aunt and uncle. Toshi hadn't wanted to tell him that part so soon, but it kind of slipped out on the second date, and he had some explaining to do. He'd skipped over the most troublesome detail, but that was what this was all about.

"No, but this is where we lived once we moved to the States," Toshi said.

Mason nodded. "It's wild. I thought all the property up here was government owned."

"It is, more or less."

Mason looked at him with furrowed brows. "You bought it from the government?"

"Kind of. Come on, I'll show you."

Mason was beginning to get suspicious, and Toshi didn't blame him. The long, winding driveway ended at a free-standing garage. Toshi's car was the only one parked inside its spotless interior, but it held enough for several more. Toshi kept nothing in there, and neither did the support people. Everything was held in the warehouse.

Instead of heading for the house, he started round the back, and assumed Mason would follow him. He did, although when Toshi caught his eye, he raised an eyebrow in curiosity. *He doesn't think I'm a crazed killer, does he?* Toshi had no idea why his mind went there. Perhaps he'd seen too many horror movies. He didn't think Mason's mind had jumped to the worst-case scenario, but he didn't know for sure. You don't really know anyone—you simply hope you do. Walking around the house was no easy feat. The large, two-storey home Toshi alone occupied featured a grandiose library and two 'guest rooms', neither of which had ever seen a guest. Every so often, he'd dust and remove cobwebs in there, which made him feel a bit like Mrs Haversham, precisely the kind of reference you'd expect from someone with a personal library.

They passed a small herb garden on their way, before cresting a small incline. Mason gasped upon seeing the gracious spread of land Toshi called the 'backyard', not least its most obvious feature: a mile-long airport hangar, painted white to reflect the heat back into the sky. "Don't tell me you have your own private airport…" said Mason. He was only half-joking.

"No, that's simply the roof."

"The roof?"

They walked in silence until he reached the outside of the hangar, or 'warehouse', as it was officially called.

WRITE LIKE HELL

Toshi put his hand on the smart lock. It scanned his fingerprints and palm, and the hangar door popped open with a pneumatic sigh. Mason stared at the high-tech lock with trepidation, perhaps thinking that Toshi was leading him into his large, elaborate murder shack. Toshi didn't blame him, but that was mild in comparison to what was about to happen.

Lights flicked on automatically as they entered. Several crates of supplies were piled up against the sidewalls, and a very unassuming industrial elevator appeared near the back. They used to stack the crates to hide it, but after the incident with the trespassers, it seemed pointless. Upon seeing it, Mason did a slight double-take. "Why is there an elevator in here?"

"As I said, this is only the roof. Things get more interesting downstairs. And no, this isn't my murder shack."

Mason laughed nervously. "I wasn't thinking that," he said like someone who'd genuinely considered it.

"I like you, Mason, which is why I have to be perfectly honest with you. If you want to bow out now, I don't blame you. But let me show you this before you make up your mind, okay?"

Mason seemed even more alarmed now, but he nodded. At least that confirmed he kind of liked him, too.

Toshi stepped into the elevator and waited for Mason to join him. As he stepped inside, Toshi hit a button and they started sinking downwards. "So, do you remember that thing that happened in Japan in '03?"

Mason thought about it a moment. "Oh, you mean that nuclear meltdown that was covered by that ridiculous story? Yeah."

"Funny thing, that. The 'nuclear meltdown'? That was the cover story. The ridiculous story was the true one, but the authorities figured no one would believe it. They were correct."

Mason stared at him in disbelief as the elevator came to a smooth stop. "What? Wasn't the story some bullshit about a giant monster?"

Toshi nodded, leading the way out. He brought Mason into a low-lit, cavernous room that smelled faintly of salt water. The water feature was in one of the connected rooms, but the scent pervaded the complex. It had the same ratio of saline as ocean water, minus the pollution, and featured some aquatic life. If not for the living coral, some species of fish, and a ton of seaweed, it would otherwise have been a giant swimming pool. Jerry hadn't liked the empty, lifeless water at all.

"Correct," Toshi said. "A gigantic lizard wreaked havoc on the outskirts of Tokyo, and at a U.S. military base. Stupid, right? It's why the nuclear story was so much easier to believe." There were a couple of megaphones lined up against the near wall like they were grandma's knick-knack shelf. Toshi picked one at random, held it up, and spoke. "C'mon, Jerry!" he said, before putting it back into its assigned slot. "Of course, there was a minor nuclear reactor incident, but it didn't melt down. As I told you, my aunt and uncle were childless, and didn't really want any kids, so I was having a difficult time settling in. And one day, on the pier, I saw the most extraordinary thing."

The ground started shaking in bursts. Relatively faint to start with, but growing louder by the second. Mason grabbed the wall. "Is this an earthquake?"

"No, it's my friend." The shadows at the far end of the room shifted, and Mason screamed.

WRITE LIKE HELL

The shaking was Jerry galloping towards him like a happy puppy. A 100-ton, 300-foot-tall puppy with dark green, serrated scales, glowing red eyes, and a mouth about half the size of a blue whale, full of jagged ivory teeth. Toshi pushed a button on the wall. A slot opened with a metallic grinding noise, and a marshmallow the size of a hay bale plopped onto the floor. Jerry came to a stop. A pinkish-grey tongue the size of a stretch limo darted out from between its lips, picking up the marshmallow with surprising grace. The marshmallow was a mere nugget to Jerry, but as much as she wanted sugar, she could only have so much of it per day. A hyper Jerry was no more favorable than an unhappy Jerry.

Jerry lowered her head and Toshi petted the only smooth part of her, the top of her muzzle. She made a sound like a beater car in desperate need of a muffler, a loud, rumbling purr you could feel in your chest. Up close, it was clear her mouth had more room than many parking garages, but Toshi wasn't scared of her. He was the only one who wasn't. "You don't have to be scared, Mason. She won't harm you, not while I'm here. And if she sees you're my friend, she'll leave you alone."

Mason was sitting on the floor with his back to the wall, his eyes bulging in a state of permanent shock. His mouth was opening and closing, but no sound came out.

Toshi nodded, still petting Jerry. "I know. It's weird, right? Monsters exist. Not only that, I live with one, because the Japanese and American governments think it's best."

Finally, Mason spoke. "What?"

"As I said, I was on a pier, and I saw this monster appear out of the ocean. Everybody was running away and screaming, but... I don't know. I was a kid, and I was lonely and miserable, and maybe I had a death wish and didn't realise it. But when Jerry started towards the dock, I just held out my cotton candy. She sniffed at it and ate it, and didn't eat me. According to the scientists, who really scratched their heads over this, Jerry bonded to me and only to me. She let me climb on her head and ride her as she stomped around the countryside. At times, I thought I might fall, but she never let me. She looks after me like I'm her kid. The military really poured it on when she attacked, and tried their best to kill her. They used every missile and bomb in the toy box and they couldn't make a lasting dent in her. But when I asked her to stop, she did. They don't know what she is, where she came from, or how to stop her. All they knew was I could. So, in the end, I helped them capture her. The U.S. military retrofitted this place to hold her, and moved me and my family here. This used to be some sort of underground nuclear bunker, but they made it a two-mile long monster habitat just for her."

Toshi knew from experience that she'd let him pet her for hours. Toshi paused a moment to stroke Jerry's scaly muzzle, taking care to ensure he didn't rub her the wrong way, lest the ridges slice up his hand like the teeth of a chainsaw. He smiled as the beast purred at his touch. She'd happily allow him to pet her like this for hours.

"I think, in the beginning, they were just holding her here until they could figure out how to kill her. But she turned out to be a gold mine. For one, her droppings are a kind of super-fertiliser. Seeds that would ordinarily take weeks to germinate can grow in a matter of days. The skin she sheds turned out to be tougher and more bullet-resistant than Kevlar, and the molecular composition of her talon sheaths have baffled scientists, who've since attempted to replicate it. She even has the capacity for rapid regeneration, which they're also researching, in hopes that humans might someday benefit from it. And now that she's a source of advancement and profit, they wouldn't dream of killing her. Capitalism triumphs over safety concerns every time. Not that I'm saying I'd be happier if they were working on killing her, 'cause hell no. Jerry's probably the best friend I've ever had. That may sound pathetic, but it's true all the same."

He didn't mean to downplay anything that had happened. Jerry went on a rampage, people died, and so much property damage was done it was almost incalculable. It was a terrible thing, and Toshi felt bad about it every day. But he was a stupid, lonely kid who inexplicably made friends with a monster. At the time, it was easy for him to let the actual damage just slip by. And as far as he was concerned, it was mostly self-defence, since the military had attacked Jerry first. But with the benefit of hindsight, he knew there was little else they could've done. Jerry was massive, unknown, indestructible, and more than happy to swallow trucks and tanks whole. Jerry was a threat, whether or not he realised it at the time.

Neither had he realised he could stop her until he did. Up until that point, he'd never had any control in his life. He was an orphan living with people he barely knew, who treated him like a space alien. Much like Jerry, Toshi had always felt like a monster. Maybe that was the thing that scientists kept missing. They were on the same wavelength, connected on some unquantifiable level. Of course, if he'd told them that, they'd have thrown him in a padded cell and thrown away the key. Or worse, have him sent to the military psychiatrist he'd seen in Japan, whose reductive questions had driven Toshi nigh insane. He'd been tempted to shovel some of Jerry's droppings on his car. A super-fertiliser it may have been, but it also smelled, and could strip paint. It was far worse than keying it.

Even with Toshi's hand simply resting on her muzzle, Jerry continued to purr. Sometimes he slept in the warehouse because it was comforting to her, and he didn't want her to get lonely. Toshi honestly had no idea why a monster bonded with him. It may well have been the cotton candy, but it was soon made clear that she'd only permit Toshi to feed her, as anyone else who tried got eaten. It was to Toshi alone that she responded. He wondered at times whether their mutual loneliness had bound them together.

The scientists had studied Toshi almost as much as they'd studied Jerry, desperate for answers. Their best conjecture was that Jerry had recognised the boy as a juvenile of her own species, and decided not to kill him. But that presumed on her part a measure of sapience it wasn't clear she possessed. Although, whenever he read books aloud to her, he could swear she understood at least some of what he was saying. She seemed to enjoy horror novels best. On occasion, he'd project movies on the walls of the enclosure for the two of them to watch. She seemed to enjoy cartoons and travelogues most. This, too, the scientists had wanted to study, but they had yet to discover a definitive reason for the admittedly strange behaviour. Toshi was just as baffled. It wasn't like she'd watch anything if he wasn't there. If he was out for a long time, she'd get bored and hostile. Despite all the safety measures, if Jerry wanted out of her makeshift habitat, she could get out. Perhaps she'd only remained for Toshi. He wondered at times what would happen if, inevitably, he became ill or died. None of the scientists ever answered that question, but the answer seemed obvious to Toshi. Her rampage would begin again, only there'd be a different city to destroy. If that happened, Toshi wondered if she'd find some other kid to bond with. He dearly hoped so, else she'd be unstoppable. Even after studying her, they were no closer to figuring out how to slow her down, let alone kill her.

Toshi scratched the side of Jerry's jaw. Her skin felt a little like tree bark crossed with stone. Rough, but not unpleasant to the touch. From the feel of her scales, it wasn't difficult to see how her thick hide might repel bullets. Toshi was amazed she was able to feel his fingers at all. Perhaps she couldn't and was simply humouring him. Again, that suggested sapience, and he couldn't be certain of how smart she was. No one had managed to discover a way to communicate with her besides him. Toshi fell silent, and at least a minute passed before Mason asked in a hushed whisper, "They don't know what she is?"

"No. For a time, they thought she was a dinosaur who'd been trapped in arctic ice and had awoken with its thaw, but she doesn't fit the known physiology of any known or even speculated terrestrial dinosaur. A more recent theory suggests she's of non-terrestrial origin, and that she hitched a ride on a meteor or something."

It seemed to take a minute for Mason to understand what he was saying. "So, they think she's an alien?"

"I know, right? Ridiculous. But that might explain why she's so unknown to anyone attempting to type her species… and why she has nuclear breath."

"Nuclear breath?"

"Yes. When she wants to, she can breathe fire, much like a dragon, but far worse. The fire she breathes is so hot, it rapidly super-heats the air, and the resulting combustion is instantaneous. And she's fireproof, so it doesn't bother her. She can also live underwater for months if she has to. Her powers of adaptation are so advanced and versatile, the scientists soon gave up studying it. She can adapt to anything, and under any conditions—vacuum, pressure, lava, radiation, ice, you name it. One day, the sun will expand and burn the Earth to a cinder and she'll be the only thing left."

She was a monster whose size put her at odds with the rest of the planet and its inhabitants, but she wasn't evil. Evil bespeaks intent and a desire to destroy, and that simply wasn't her. People started shooting at her, and she retaliated. She only took out the military base after they shot missiles at her. She acted in self-defence. People reacted to her with violence because of her size and strangeness. Humans don't take kindly to being shoved off the top of the food chain, but hey, life's a bitch.

Mason finally stood up. He hadn't prized himself off the wall, but it was progress all the same. "She really is bonded to you, isn't she? Is that what they mean by 'imprinting' on something?"

"Maybe. As I said, they stopped studying me a long time ago. I was a dead end." The scientists had tried to discover if there was something unique about him, such as whether he had ESP, but no, he was little more than a chubby, Japanese, and entirely unremarkable, boy. Jerry was likely the same for her species—a regular, similarly chubby, 300-foot monster—but there was no baseline for her development. Maybe she was special among her kind. They'd never know unless they found another creature just like her, and they weren't all too certain they wanted to find out. It may have demystified the creature, but Earth could barely accommodate one Jerry, let alone two. That would be a catastrophe.

"But you must be special. I mean, she likes you, right? That makes you unique," said Mason, clearly trying his best to apply reason to the situation. Whatever helped him accept the reality of what he was seeing, Toshi guessed, even if the two of them couldn't be neatly categorised.

"I guess so. But only she knows why, and she's not telling," said Toshi. Jerry continued purring, and looked at him through half-lidded red eyes. Her running registered seismically, as little earthquakes, which is why it behooved him to be so far from neighbours and on government land. The locals still picked it up, and he'd seen the online conspiracies about it. One suggested fracking, another ventured it was an ongoing underground development, but no one came close to guessing at the true source. Then again, 'giant monster' sounded bananas. You'd even be laughed off the darkest corners of Reddit for suggesting such a thing.

"Should you be telling me this? I mean, the government doesn't want this to get out, right?" asked Mason, a note of concern in his voice.

"Actually, they don't really care. I was free to tell anyone I wished, because as soon as I said the words 'giant monster', no one would believe me. As for monitoring my comings and goings, they don't care about that, either. It's not like I can take her out for a walk." What would he do, try and sell her to a foreign country?

Mason took a steadying breath and moved a step closer. Only the one, but again, it was a start. He was still shaking a little, but was mostly calm. "Am I the first person you've brought down to see her?"

"Yes. Although, before we got the new security features installed, a couple of trespassers managed to get around the defences on the perimeter and broke in. We only know about this because their tennis shoes were found in Jerry's stool. The lock is really to protect people from their own curiosity."

About a week later, they'd heard a couple of 'guerrilla press' from a far-right extremist site had been declared missing in the area, so it was easy to put two and two together. They wanted to see what the government was up to, broke into the property, and Jerry found them first. If she came across someone she didn't know, or hadn't been introduced to through Toshi, she'd eat that person. It wasn't personal; Toshi was the only mammal she didn't view as food. He bet, if those guys were looking for the aliens that the government was supposedly hiding, they didn't expect it to be so big, or so carnivorous. Not that he could ask. At least it would have been over fast. Jerry didn't play with her food, mainly because it was too small to be worth the bother.

"Oh, wow. Yeah, I can see that." said Mason, taking a cautious step in Toshi's direction. "Not that I want to, but you're the only one who can touch her, right?"

"Yeah. Other people can if I'm around to calm her, but that's about it."

"Wow. And here I thought your big secret was a kink or something. I never imagined it was a giant alien monster."

"No one ever does, which is why she's such a surprisingly easy secret to keep." All humans know on some level that certain things are too ridiculous to entertain as reality, and city-destroying monsters tops that list. Toshi suddenly clicked and raised an eyebrow at Mason. "A kink? What, did you think I had some airplane hangar-based fetish?"

He smirked, but it was more of a queasy grimace. Mason was handling it well, but it was still a lot. "I had no idea. I once met this guy who... You know what? This is the wrong time and place for that story."

"Oh, come on. You can't say that and not tell me."

"I'll tell you when I don't feel faint, but it ends with me deleting Tinder from my phone."

Toshi was dying of curiosity. What kind of fetish could the man have had, he wondered. There were probably people who had monster fetishes, too—which, *ick*. But he supposed he couldn't talk, having emotionally bonded to a giant space dinosaur. That probably meant he couldn't judge anyone for anything ever again.

He finished scratching Jerry's muzzle and gave her a little boop on the nose, which she seemed to like. There was a thud and a tremble in the reinforced floor as her tail flopped about. She didn't wag it like a dog, but Toshi had learned to pick up signals from how she moved it. Much like cats, her tail often told a story, if you knew how to read it. That was her happy flop, suggesting she was content and pleased to be with him. Toshi had tried to create a chart for the support staff and the scientists so they could better interpret her moods, but as it turned out, her tail signs were harder for others to interpret correctly. It wasn't rocket science, but they didn't get the nuances that Toshi did. Maybe those weird military people who tested him for psychic powers back in Tokyo had been right. Maybe he did have some sort of low-level psychic connection with her. Just because they couldn't measure it with their instruments didn't mean it couldn't exist. Except that made him sound as crazy as some of those Reddit people, who insisted the Tokyo incident was actually the start of an alien invasion, and most people around the world had been replaced by alien doppelgangers, waiting for the signal to wipe out the remaining humans. Which actually sounded pretty cool. **Reality was rarely that dramatic, even if that did sound appealing.**

Toshi caught Mason's eyes and found his fear had drained away to nothing. "So, are you saying this isn't the worst date you've ever been on?"

Mason smiled. "I don't know. I'm going to have to think about that. It's pretty close. My therapist may have to decide."

"Which reminds me, if you ever tell anyone about this…"

He chuckled faintly. "I'm a crazy person. Yeah, I get that. I mean, I may have pissed myself, but thanks for trusting me this much."

"There's spare sweatpants upstairs. We keep a crate up there of multiple sizes, for obvious reasons. We haven't had a new soldier here in a while, but when they first see her… it's a messy day at headquarters, I can tell you that much." And then there were those who ran screaming from the place, leaving the military, and perhaps their sanity, behind—but the less said about that the better. Jerry had no control over how people reacted to her; it was a shame she didn't.

Mason laughed, and Toshi felt some tension releasing. If he could laugh about this, then they were okay. They could move beyond this, and that was good. Maybe he could have something resembling a normal life. Him, his boyfriend, and his 300-foot monster. Not a normal family unit, by any means, but still better than some.

KAIJU

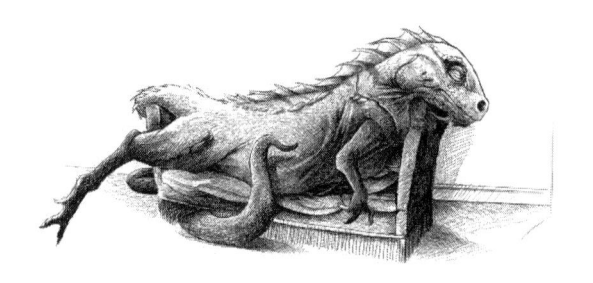

January Through the Years

André Uys

January, 1946

Kent's oft-lamented dreary weather painted the landscape in a bleak greyscale, yet bestowed an enchanting sense of depth to Brittany's surroundings. Scotland's moors might be renowned across the world for the eerie ambience that inspired the literary greats, but she'd always felt that the Dengemarsh had a greater sense of vibrancy, of life, to it. Anyone who hadn't grown up in New Romney would mistake this landscape for lush pastureland, but a local would enthusiastically tell you that "the soil remembered" when this was all part of the River Rother, and that the marsh was never far away.

Brittany remembered *oba-chan*, as her grandmother had insisted she be called, taking her for walks along Dengemarsh Sewer—a terrible name for a river, but a spellbinding stroll. Her quiet, dignified voice would enthral Brittany, and send her youthful spirits soaring as her grandmother regaled her with tales of her native country and its close ties to her adopted one. Brittany closed her eyes as she remembered one such occasion.

"You are a child of two island kingdoms. Two tiny, isolated dots of land, somehow able to hold sway over vast dominions. The world's water besieged them both, and so they mastered the water in turn; mastery that was never far from subservience. These two nations share the temperament granted by the water, but they also share the water itself.

"This river takes its name from the Denge Marsh, from which it springs. The Denge Marsh, in turn, takes its water from the English Channel, fed by the Atlantic Ocean. The Atlantic Ocean tempestuously greets its sibling, the Indian Ocean, down at the tip of Africa. The Indian runs the Indonesian gauntlet to finally give of itself to the Pacific Ocean; after an interminable journey, a single drop of water arrives on the shores of Japan."

Brittany came to and realised that she had wandered a bit far off the beaten track while lost in her reminiscences. She was on her way home from the bank, having already taken a considerable detour to stroll along the marshlands masquerading as farms. She had needed a touch of childhood to take her mind off the harsh realities of her adult life, but now it was back to the practicalities of that life—the life of a war widow.

Geoffrey's pension from the army was barely sufficient to cover her grocery bill for the month, let alone maintain the picturesque but costly manse her grandfather had built out in the woods. Perhaps it was time to take in a few boarders, she thought.

She felt a wash of icy pain pour through her chest at the thought. That house meant family. Growing up, she and *oba-chan* had driven her parents mad in that house. When Father died, she and her grandmother had provided her mother support and love during her grief. Later, her mother had consoled her in turn when age had finally caught up to the most vital person in Brittany's small world. She had met and married Geoffrey before her mother's passing would have left her alone in the house, and she had been given just enough time to dream of restoring it to its status of 'family home' when the Second World War had hit. She might have dreaded the solitude in that house, but filling it with strangers was far worse.

There were other ways to make a living. She had volunteered as a nurse during the war. Rather than moping about and hoping to live off her husband's death money, she thought it time to make use of the skills learnt during that hellish time.

Her decision made and her resolve restored, Brittany lifted her gaze to the horizon and quickened her step. Her maudlin amble was at an end and it was time to find her bearings.

She marched on through the unfamiliar terrain until she gradually became aware of a softening of the soil underfoot. She had crossed the Dengemarsh already, so she must be closing in on one of the streamlets that led off it. In the distance, she thought she could make out a faint shadow that might betoken the woods that surrounded her property.

Her determined tread faltered as she heard a curious crooning sound. It was utterly alien to her, especially considering the native fauna, but there was a distinct note of distress. Any hesitation that she might have had evaporated as another piteous wail assailed her. She crashed through the undergrowth, orienting herself according to the occasional cry of need. Finally, she came upon a tuft of rushes obscuring a shallow puddle.

Inside the puddle was something Brittany had never before seen. It was some form of reptile, she surmised, judging by its scaly hide, but bulkier than the lizards with which she was familiar. Its head, on the other hand, evoked something almost equine. Her analytical examination came to an abrupt halt as she beheld its eyes. In place of the anticipated vertical slit common amongst reptiles, a circular pupil regarded her. The look in those almost-human eyes was pure misery.

Without a second thought, she picked the creature up and cradled it to her chest. As she tried to comfort it, she staggered under its unexpected weight. She took in its full size and realised that the puddle could not have been as shallow as she had assumed. It was *big*. Roughly the length of a cat, it weighed twice as much due to its solid frame. Its stubby legs were slightly shorter than those of a cat, but, on all fours, its back would probably stand at approximately the same height.

She had never seen nor heard of a reptile that size in England, unless one indulged in mythology, but she knew that the deserts of the world had some gigantic specimens—called 'something' monsters, and quite understandably so. But there was nothing monstrous about this creature. Its size simply seemed natural, befitting its frame and appearance, although she had no idea why an adult of its species would be in such distress. It behaved almost as an infant in want of its mother.

"That's it—you're coming home with me," she found herself saying out loud, before she knew the decision had even been made. As she shifted the little creature into a more comfortable position and set off for the five-minute walk to her home, she idly thought that it might not be quite so lonely after all.

WRITE LIKE HELL

January, 1947

Brittany couldn't wait to get home and soak her feet after a long shift at the hospital in Rye. She knew, though, that she still had a long walk ahead of her from the bus stop to her home. These days, she was earning enough that she could have afforded not to walk home, but a year of frugality was hard to shake. Besides, she had a bottomless abyss waiting for her at home, and there was no telling how much Gila would soon be eating…

Work at the hospital paid well, and she was quietly proud to no longer be in need of her husband's pension. Mrs Rateliffe from Lloyd's had called her a few weeks before to ask why she hadn't been collecting her cheques. Brittany wasn't sure how to express her feelings on the matter—that taking that money every month was akin to looting her husband's corpse. She knew that wasn't a commonly held notion. Instead, she told the old secretary that she had remarried and no longer needed the income. *Strange how that satisfied the poor dear, but my independence would have scandalised every bone in her body!*

Regardless, she had no intention of working at the hospital all her life. She was 31 years old at the time, and she wasn't going to spend her twilight years making ends meet while emptying bedpans. A question in the back of her mind added to her concern, but remained unacknowledged: how much longer could she keep up with Gila's appetite?

She was busy working on an idea of sorts. If doctors made house calls, why couldn't nurses? She had taken a look around her in New Romney and realised that those the war had left behind were mostly the women, the elderly, and the youth. The young ones all flocked to the bigger towns and cities, the women married again and moved away, and the elderly were left behind to care for themselves. She knew this, because they would share a bus with her when they needed to go to the hospital in Rye.

Most of those visits were for things a nurse could do. A check-up on this, a shot of that, filling a prescription—she would, of course, leave diagnoses and prescriptions to the doctors, but why couldn't she take some blood in the comfort of the patient's home? Why couldn't she pick up the prescriptions for a number of people and drop them off as she made her weekly round? Nothing stopped her performing the basic physicals—the ones she had been doing every day for a year—in a location more convenient for her patients.

Fleshing out the details of her bold new idea kept her going through the drudgery, the aching feet, and the few dark nights when all she could do was lie in bed and sob at the thought of the life she had lost when Churchill had made that fateful declaration.

***

As Brittany opened the front door, she felt a wry smile tugging at the corner of her mouth. Dog owners could expect an enthusiastic greeting upon their homecoming, and cat owners settled for a brief brush against the legs, if only in a mute appeal for food. She, on the other hand, merited a lazy opening of one eye from Gila, the lid drooping down over his oval pupil again in short order, as he lay curled up on a sofa.

It seemed her initial impression of the reptile was incorrect. He must in fact have been close to full maturity, but he had since grown rather quickly. Gila was now the size of a large dog—about a metre from head to scaly tail, and coming up to half a metre in height—and must have weighed twice as much as your typical German Shepherd.

She would have dearly loved to head straight for a bath, but she knew how hungry he always was. How she knew that, she didn't have the faintest notion, as he never really showed it. She headed to the freezer and took out some frozen fish.

She had tried red meat at first, but he wouldn't touch it. He showed some interest in chicken, but walked away after a few bites. On that first night, she had been in a fine state, convinced that her newest friend would die of starvation by morning. It was only after she thought back to where she found him, in what could only be considered a quasi-marine habitat, that she had an idea. She rooted around in the rubbish, finding the remains of the fish she'd had for dinner the previous night. Before she had even approached him, he stood up on his four stubby legs for the first time since she had picked him up. Though his features were not terribly expressive, there was nevertheless a palpable eagerness emanating from him.

She tossed almost Gila's own weight in fish in front of him and backed away. She felt slightly uncomfortable watching him eat. There was something too clinical in the way he dissected the food with deft swipes of his razor-sharp claws, contrasted with the subsequent savagery of rending the meat with his disquietingly powerful jaws.

She drew herself a steaming bath and ignored the sounds coming from the family room. She started when she realised that she had begun to call it that again—the 'family room'. After her mother had passed, even once Geoffrey had moved in, it had always just been 'the lounge'. She shook her head and chuckled quietly to herself. *Clearly, I see myself and Gila as a family!*

Settling into the steaming water, she let slip a subdued moan of pleasure. She could feel her muscles relaxing to the point where they approached the same consistency as the bathwater around her. She imagined her entire body disintegrating and becoming one with the water, and she floated in a perfectly serene state for an eternity. *Geoffrey will be angry with me for letting the water grow cold—*

She snapped back to the present moment and cursed herself roundly for falling into the same old trap. Rule one of widowhood: never let your guard down.

After her bath, wrapped only in her grandmother's old robe, she sat down next to Gila on the couch, settled her head on his dependable solidity, and stroked the little nubs that had begun protruding from his scaly back.

WRITE LIKE HELL

January, 1948

Mr Burns stared at her through the Hanging Gardens of Babylon he called his eyebrows. He might be a lecherous octogenarian, but his weighty gaze still held an immense authority.

"I am terribly grateful to you for coming out to our homes and saving us that horrid trip, but I'm concerned for your wellbeing, young lady," he croaked. "I see how you scurry to and fro in this town, seeing to all our needs, but there isn't one of us that tips the years under 60. Where are you supposed to meet a likely young gentleman?"

This was a recurring theme among her patients. They were all too eager to avail themselves of her services, but the thought of a single woman making it on her own still rankled. She knew, however, that Mr Burns was one of the few who was genuinely concerned, so she bit back the smiling retort that came so easily these days and gave the question due consideration.

"Mr Burns, I'm afraid that's simply not on the cards any longer," she smiled, with what she hoped would be seen as wry amiability. "I suppose the easy way out of this conversation would be to protest that I'm 'over the hill' and that no biddable bachelor would be interested in an old widow like me, but, truthfully"—she shrugged—"I feel like I'm just hitting my stride. I feel strong, confident, and in control. So, it isn't that."

She paused briefly as she gathered her thoughts. "My nursing practice takes up all of my time. When I started this, I envisioned seeing about five patients a day—at most. My primary concern was whether I would have enough patients to make ends meet. Now, I'm beginning to despair of ever having a moment free! I leave home before dawn and only walk through my front door again once the sun has set, and I still worry that I'm not getting to you all often enough. That is a reason for my ongoing solitude, but it isn't *the* reason."

She drew a deep breath. "My Geoffrey was my entire world." Saying his name aloud still sent ice down her spine. "When he marched his way into my life, I gave up every last shred of self—I existed for him alone." She forced a self-deprecating chuckle. "It doesn't sound particularly healthy, I know, but it was an all-consuming love. In the first place, one simply cannot move on from that inferno of emotion to the softly glowing embers of a comfortable and affectionate marriage of convenience. In the second place, were I to find another Geoffrey, I don't think I would want the inferno again! One cannot give all of oneself twice."

Mr Burns regarded her levelly for a while. Finally, he gave out an exaggerated harrumph, the exclusive province of the British elderly, and spoke. "You're far from over the hill—in fact, were I a decade younger, I'd tell you exactly what I think of your hill."

Brittany burst out laughing. She recognised his lewd comment for what it was: an olive branch, a knife to cut the weight of the moment. "If you were a decade younger," she said as she swatted his shoulder and made to leave, "I might have wanted to know!"

As she strolled down High Street to her next appointment, she had a quiet chuckle as she thought back to Mr Burns winking at her on her way out the door, the Amazon jungle briefly dimming the glint of mischief in his eye.

***

WRITE LIKE HELL

As the sun valiantly hurled its last rays over the horizon before its battle with the evening was lost, Brittany noticed something wrong with the vague silhouette of her front door. She approached cautiously until the unusual detail resolved itself. There was no front door. It was lying about a metre away, where it had been deposited after being ripped off its hinges. She felt a surge of panic familiar to anyone who had lived alone, far from others, for any length of time. She quashed the thought and forced herself to think rationally.

If this had been the work of human intruders, the door jamb itself would have been broken, or hanging off one hinge, at most. No, the state of the door and the distance it had been hurled bespoke a bestial strength. While it was an outside possibility that some form of bear had found its way over from Europe, the more plausible scenario was that her very own little beastie was responsible. Her panic was gradually replaced with sharp concern.

She hurried inside to find Gila innocently dozing on his favourite sofa—a sofa he now draped himself over, rather than curled up in. She stopped in place and finally came to terms with his immense size. He was now easily the size of a horse, at least in height and length. No horse had ever possessed such sheer *mass*.

It was time to acknowledge that Gila was still growing. Her first impressions upon finding him, that his cries of distress were infantile, were indeed correct. If she was lucky, he was nearing full maturity now. She refused to consider that he was only an adolescent. *What am I going to do with him if he gets bigger?*

It wasn't only a matter of space in the house. She was making a considerable amount of money now, but her seafood bill was approaching titanic proportions. As she approached him, she noticed scattered bones across the floor of the family room. The bones were definitely not from her stock of fish in the freezer. She had been buying deboned stock, worried that he might choke on the bones. Apparently, that was no longer a concern. *Neither is my grocery bill.* Clearly Gila had been out hunting for himself, hence the ruined door.

She made a mental note to leave the back door open for him in future—once her front door was fixed, at least. For now, all she wanted was to curl up next to him and take solace in his reassuring bulk. She wormed her way into the available space, taking care to avoid the spines that ran in a line down his back and tail. As she began to drift off, she had the distinct impression that his forelegs were becoming skinnier, and his hind legs more squat and powerful.

WRITE LIKE HELL

January, 1949

Brittany poured herself a stiff drink. It had been building for a while now—a vague sense of unease, a momentary chill that had nothing to do with the weather, restless sleep filled with dreams of amorphous, saurian terrors. A gradual, tidal encroachment of deeply buried anxieties upon the shores of her conscious mind. And on that day, the inevitable crash of the wave.

Her day had been going well. She had just concluded a handshake agreement with the mayor of nearby Lydd, and would be allowed to extend her network of home nurses to the elderly of that town, who faced the same problems she had identified in New Romney two years ago.

When she eventually conceded that she needed help, she was amazed to discover how many widows who, like her, were looking for ways to assert their independence. Most of them had worked as nurses during the war as well. Soon, she was able to rent a small office on High Street and tend to the administration of her 'Angel Network', as she privately thought of her girls. She still made one or two house calls a day, but she feared that would soon come to an end. Travelling in between New Romney and Lydd would take up a lot of time, and the paperwork was only increasing.

She had decided to celebrate her upcoming expansion by taking the rest of the day off. She was even whistling as she took a stroll along the Dengemarsh Sewer as a scenic detour on her way home, which must have been why she didn't hear a thing before the river erupted in spectacular fashion right in front of her.

As she froze in the grip of fright, the water settled and a monster was revealed. Screaming would have been a blessed respite, but her throat had constricted to the point where breathing seemed a faraway dream. This dread apparition was towering over her, ready to rend her limb from limb, extending a hostile... Fish?

As her frenzied heartbeat slowed down, her throat opened up for a snatched breath and the blurring at the edges of her vision subsided. She recognised the unmistakable outline of Gila. However, this was a Gila transformed by one crucial detail: he was standing on his hind legs.

She knew he had continued to grow, but it was just so easy to dismiss when she saw him every day. Seeing him standing, albeit slightly hunched over, put his size in an entirely new light. He dwarfed her 1.58m height, of course, but he was taller than even her Geoffrey had been. Not only that, but he was easily three metres in length from tail to snout and carried an immensity of muscle that defied description. He reminded her somewhat of a few pictures she had seen of creatures called 'dinosaurs', but those were frail, spindly things compared to her Gila.

Her hand trembled as she took the fish from him. She noted how dexterous that forelimb had become. It was clearly no longer ideal for holding his immense weight. There was something disturbing about it; only humans and primates should have such manual capabilities, she thought.

***

She put down her empty glass and shook her head. She pondered whether the beast she had been so afraid of was really her Gila—her only family for the longest time, her constant companion. No. She would not let her highly strung emotions take him from her.

She would, however, bow to the demands of reality. Gila was simply too big to live in the house with her. In the morning, she would head out into the woods and create a comfortable, spacious den for her beastie. She would ensure that he knew she was not kicking him out—simply 'expanding their home'.

Tonight, though, she would pour herself another drink. Simply to banish the silly flight of fancy. The ridiculous notion that she caught a flash of hostility when she took that fish.

KAIJU

January, 1950

Brittany strode into the eerily silent woods. There were no bird calls, no brief rustling in the bushes, and no near-silent susurrations. She wondered why that was. Gila may have been an apex predator, but he only fed on marine life. Why would birds and small mammals fear him? Why would snakes, so prolific in this area, stay away from something that must be a close cousin?

She followed the broken branches and the gashes in the tree bark. Those gashes were more than three metres high now. Eventually, she came upon Gila feeding. Where on earth had he found a *seal?* She supposed that they weren't too far from the ocean, but she wasn't aware of any seals that big along their stretch of coast.

She thought of how powerfully he had launched himself from the river a year ago. Water was clearly his natural habitat. How far afield could he roam if given the wide ocean as a hunting ground?

She didn't want to watch him feed, so she focused on the rest of his anatomy. His ridge of small spines had developed into a double row of large, razor-sharp plates. She theorised that these were used in underwater navigation. As his body had grown, his head, at first elongated, had become more proportional, and the gradual widening of his jaws had eliminated any resemblance to a horse he might once have had. In terms of size, the sheer scale was difficult to comprehend. He was easily two times her height, and half that again in length. He probably weighed more than 10 tons.

At first, she had come to see him every day. Whether she had been imagining his anxiety or not, it gradually lessened. She began to allow work to distract her, and fairly soon she was visiting once a week. This had been her first visit in a month. There was some element missing in their interactions. There was never any physical contact; every time she neared him, a flutter of fear danced in her breast. As for him, he had never once sought her out physically, not even when he was an infant. She simply didn't feel comforted by him anymore, either because she no longer needed that comfort—now that she was a well-respected businesswoman—or because her fears kept her from being vulnerable around him, the way she used to be. That didn't mean she didn't love him. She had grown wise enough to realise that he had served as a surrogate child when her maternal instincts needed it most. Regardless, he *was* her child, and she his mother. Her discomfort and fear might keep her away at times, but she would always come back, she thought.

KAIJU

January, 1955

New Romney had been Brittany's home for her entire life, but she was a victim of her own success. The Angel Network had reached every corner of Kent, and she had built up enough capital to fund a push into other regions. Unfortunately, its expansion into new territories would also require a new administrative hub. She couldn't launch a campaign to take over England from the sleepy town of New Romney, after all.

The little house she had found in London was a far cry from the rambling spaciousness of her country manse, but she didn't need much space. Besides, she would never sell her home. Whenever the open air of the country called, she would return to wash off the city. There would always be one thing drawing her back.

She approached that one thing. She hadn't visited Gila often in the past five years, but she had always come back. Before, she had barely noticed his rapid growth, since it had been happening right before her eyes. Due to her infrequent visits, she was able to fully appreciate his size.

His head brushed the tops of the highest trees. She estimated his height at six metres, and his length at close to 10 metres. There was no way of measuring, but she felt sure that he weighed between twenty and thirty tons. The fact that he had not yet been spotted by others was a testament to his stealth, of a level no creature that large had any right to. She had known from the start that he was unusual, but she was coming to understand that he was unique. Nothing like him had ever been encountered by humanity. Earth's ecosystem simply didn't have a place for something that ate other creatures and had such an advantage in terms of speed and power.

If there had been more of Gila's kind, humans would never have evolved from the primates.

No, she was convinced Gila was from another world. Brittany couldn't be bothered with the mechanics and implications of that sweeping truth. It was enough that she had been given a companion when she had needed one most.

She climbed up a tree. How her girls would laugh if they saw their primly elegant boss scrambling from branch to branch, she thought. She reached the top of the tree, high enough to look Gila in the eye. Whatever had made his eyes seem so human had disappeared. His pupil was not quite the reptilian slit, but it was certainly no longer round, nor even oval. The void in that fiery yellow iris was a thick, flat bar with a slight bulge in the middle.

"Gila, I'm leaving for a while. My business has taken off and I'm needed in London if I'm to continue growing. I'm sure rapid and continued growth is something you can understand… I will be back to see you. I might not be able to come as often anymore, but I will always come back. This is goodbye, but it is a little goodbye, not The Big Goodbye. I love you dearly, little beast."

If Brittany had spoken to a pet dog like that, she would have felt a fool. Staring into that eye, though, one couldn't deny that there was a powerful and sophisticated intelligence at work. She got the distinct impression that Gila understood every word and nuance—possibly her stab at humour, too. However, if she were expecting sorrow, or even passing regret, she would be disappointed. All she felt from him was cold indifference.

KAIJU

January, 1966

Brittany looked up from her work for a moment to ask her secretary for a cup of tea. She buzzed the intercom, but didn't receive any response. Irritated, she made to get up to give Kelly a piece of her mind, when she caught a glimpse out her office window. *Gracious, it's dark outside!* Now that she thought about it, she vaguely remembered Kelly popping her head in to say goodbye. How long ago had that been? It must have been a few hours.

She got up and stretched a back that was beginning to ache more and more with every passing year. She stared out the window, down at the fiery swathe that made up London's night lights and sighed. *So, this is what it feels like to have 'made it'.* All she felt was tired.

How naive her thoughts of a 'campaign to take over England' had been. True, she'd done it, but it had been a decade of hard-fought battles. While she had stayed in Kent, she could be dismissed as an up-jumped country girl playing at men's business, but the moment she stepped into London, she unleashed a storm of epic proportions. No man was willing to tolerate competition on a national level from a woman. They all insisted that she was far too soft, and should go back to running a household. Ironically, it was those selfsame qualities that gave her an advantage over the men.

Whenever a problem arose, there would be two ways of addressing it. The men would invariably apply brute force thinking, whereas Brittany would find the solution that would benefit her clients and staff the most. The men would win every fight, only to find that their clients had quietly gone over to The Angel Network while they had been swinging their battle axes.

WRITE LIKE HELL

Of course, their insinuation that she was only fit to run a household also worked in her favour; her administrative prowess made her organisation far more efficient than theirs.

It had been a long, drawn-out war, and it was far from over, but she was no longer the underdog. The Angel Network was the single largest home health-care provider in Great Britain.

She decided to have that cup of tea before she headed on home. While it was brewing, she switched on the news. Her attention immediately zeroed in on the footage they were playing in the background while the news anchor spoke.

"After years of reports from local fishermen of something 'monstrous' lurking in The Channel were dismissed, the government was quick to take notice when one of its submarines encountered a large, unidentified return on their radar screens. After receiving no response to its urgent hails, the HMS Dreadnought fired upon the source of their signals. The return disappeared, but, mere minutes later, all communication with the submarine crew was lost," crackled the anchor's voice. "The footage you are seeing in the background is of the creature presumed to have destroyed the HMS Dreadnought. It seems to be on a direct path to London, and the authorities are scrambling to evacuate the city. Meanwhile, the military has fired almost every weapon in its arsenal at this monster, with little to no effect. In fact, it seems our efforts have only served to enrage it further." The anchor looked shaken as he continued. "Our experts tell us that it is a heretofore undiscovered species of amphibian. Best estimates put the monster at eighteen metres in height and close to one-hundred tons. The devastation this creature has left in its wake is—"

Brittany mechanically switched off the television. She hadn't returned to New Romney once in 10 years. It seemed, in his hour of distress, Gila was coming to find her.

January, 1981

15 years later, Brittany thought back to that night as she walked into the water.

The media had speculated that the "monster" seemed to be searching for something in London, opening up buildings as if they were cans and peeking in before moving on to the next one. This was eventually dismissed in favour of the more popular theory: it simply revelled in destruction. Brittany knew the truth, though.

She did not have the courage then to go comfort her neglected child.

When Gila gave up, he simply turned around and headed back to the water. The nation's mighty defenders, with their ships and their guns and their scanners, simply lost him. There had been scattered sightings of him over the years, so she knew he had kept growing. The last confirmed report had him as a shadow just beneath the surface of the Japan Sea—a shadow well over one hundred metres long.

Brittany shivered as the icy water reached her neck. Her doctor had given her two months to live. Well, she had achieved everything she wanted to in her life. There was just one final wrong to be put right. Her body went numb from the cold as she struck out for the open water.

The last thing she saw before the paradoxical warmth lulled her to sleep was a colossal alien eye, and she was gratified to note that there wasn't an ounce of indifference in it.

KAIJU

Cipactli

Scott Miller

Among the Reeds

Tepin wriggled his toes into the soft clay at the water's edge. Palms swayed lazily overhead in the warm breeze and sunlight speckled his skinny arms. The air was filled with the hum and buzz of insect noise. Black clouds of tiny bugs hovered above the river like flocking birds, and water-striders traced vanishing patterns upon its surface. Something rustled in the ground cover, and he turned his head in time to notice a family of small reptiles scurry out from the forest floor in search of their next meal. Tepin rested his chin on knobbly knees and heaved a contented sigh. Alone, at last.

A skink clawed its way up his legs, coming to a rest on his knees, and he laughed. "That tickles!"

Its eyes swivelled with curiosity, and its pale blue tongue darted out, tasting the air. Tepin mirrored the little creature, sticking out his own, and smiled. He adored lizards, and they seemed quite fond of him, too. The wind carried with it the distant sound of laughter from further upstream, and what sounded like his own name, but he thought little of it. He was much too mesmerised by his find, and desired a closer look.

Tepin proffered a cupped hand to the skink. "Come on, cuetzpalli, don't be shy." After a moment's hesitation, it clambered aboard. "There you go," he cooed. Its eyes were hard and fiery, and its scales shimmered and shifted colour in the noon sun. He took great care handling the lizard, and even greater care admiring it, soaking up every detail he could.

"Tepin!"

Tepin shrieked, first in alarm, then in searing pain. He flapped his hand about in a panic. From the tips of his fingers dangled the skink, its razor-sharp teeth embedded in his soft flesh.

The chimes and bones around Tēya's neck rattled as she threw her head back in laughter.

"Help!" cried Tepin, staring up at her haughty face.

"As you wish, lizard boy," she said with a smile, clutching her belly. Tēya knelt down beside him and wrapped her hand around the skink's belly. She gave it a gentle tug, but it squirmed at her touch and bit down harder.

Tepin yelped in agony. "What are you doing? Get it off already!"

"This should do it, little one," she said, licking her lips in concentration. She pinched the skink at the base of its neck and prized it off. It writhed in her grip, hissing through a mouthful of blood. She regarded it with disgust, hissed back at it, and tossed it over her shoulder.

She sat down and fished a hand into one of the brown leather pouches secured at her waist, before popping something into her mouth. "I wish I knew what you saw in those things," she said, chewing and shaking her head.

"I don't know… I like them, and they—"

"Hand," she demanded, spitting a greenish-brown mush into her palm.

"…They like me. They're my friends. Ow!"

"Friends wouldn't bite each other, Tepin," she said, dabbing the wound with the paste.

He narrowed his eyes at her. "They might… If they get scared."

She nodded her head thoughtfully. "They might. But even so, you're not a lizard, little one."

"Am, too!" cried Tepin, bearing his teeth and clawing the air with invisible talons.

Tēya laughed. "Hold still, please." She gestured to the river's edge, where several skinks were tanning themselves on rocks, just beyond a skirt of yellowing reeds. "See? Lizards spend time with their own kind. This is true of all the beasts of the forest."

Tepin was silent for a moment and stared at the ground. "Then, what am I?" he asked, his small voice cracking.

She lifted his chin with a fingertip, feathering his tear-stained cheeks with her thumb. "You're a proud son of the Jaguar, Tepin," she said, her mouth curving into a broad smile. "And the children of the Jaguar never get scared." She gave his wound one final inspection. "There! All better."

The little boy wiggled his finger and looked up at her with a half-smile.

"Come," she said cheerily, holding out her hand. "Let's go visit your brothers and sisters."

He gave a slight nod and grabbed hold. Together, they began walking upstream, in the direction of the distant laughter.

Tepin and Tēya walked hand-in-hand beside the river for a time. It was by no means a long journey—at least, it wasn't intended to be. But it became increasingly clear to Tēya that her young companion was quite unlike other children. Most younglings would've kicked up a fuss, but not Tepin. He was fascinated—by everything. She could scarcely take two steps before feeling the familiar tug at her wrist, and their trek was once more at a standstill. A litany of attractions littered their path, each one more captivating than the last. A dome-shaped mound of clay overrun with ruby-red ants. A large bird whose long, tapering beak contained all the colours of the rainbow. The drunken dance of a bumblebee as it doddered between brightly-coloured flowers. The severed tail of a lizard he insisted on keeping, even as it thrashed in his grip. She'd humoured him as best she could, hiding her irritation behind weak smiles, but as Tepin began stuffing the tail into his pouch, she could feel her patience dry up.

"Really, Tepin... You're keeping that?"

He tightened the drawstring of the pouch and gave it a little pat when he was done. "Only to give it back to him," he stated at last.

Tēya palmed away the sweat from her brow and sighed. The sun was at its highest point now. "Tepin, they often lose their tails, but they grow back eventually. There's no need—"

The little boy's mouth became a hard line, and he crossed his arms in defiance.

Tēya glared at him. "What?"

"If I found something you lost, I would give it back to you."

Tēya rolled her eyes. She should've known better than to argue with children, let alone this particular child. "You're so strange, little one," she said, conceding.

"It shouldn't be strange to be kind."

Tēya almost chuckled at the simple wisdom of the boy. "Who told you that? It was one of the elders, wasn't it... When they've had too much jagube, they get a little"—she twirled a finger at her temple and stuck out her tongue. "You know?"

"No, no one told me."

"Are you su—"

The wind laughed once more, louder this time.

"We're nearly there," Tēya surmised. "Let's go," she said, grabbing his hand.

WRITE LIKE HELL

Beneath the Mire

Tepin and Tēya followed the distant voices until they'd lost sight of the river. The sun's strength was beginning to fail, staining the sky a deep shade of blue as it fell. A gentle breeze, far cooler than before, brought relief to their inflamed skin. But it brought something else with it, too—something that stopped the little boy in his tracks. "What is that, sister?" he asked in between sniffs.

The smell was strange yet familiar. It reminded him of something he'd once discovered on one of his adventures—a small rodent with its feet clasped together, baking in the heat. He was used to seeing them on sticks, roasting on an open flame until they shone pink and tender. This odour was much stronger, and he blinked back tears as they strode further into the stench.

Tēya rolled her eyes and pushed ahead. "Come on," she said, waving him forward. She'd grown tired of his questions, and saw no reason to stop.

When Tepin caught up to Tēya, she was standing atop a small, sandy hill. "We're here," she announced.

Tepin joined her and found himself staring down into a chalky clearing in the forest the shape of a half-moon.

Tēya laid a hand on her small companion's shoulder. "Looks like fun, doesn't it?"

A dozen or so children were at play below, with no adult to stop them—laughing and yelling as they ran about the place, kicking up dust in their wake.

Tepin grunted a response, his attention elsewhere. The scene was nothing unusual, but Tepin still felt odd at the sight. The patch-turned-playground itself had caught his attention. The endless sprawl of the forest came suddenly to a halt here, as if it dared not venture further. Instead, it grew around the circular patch of dry, cracked earth. It was a wasteland in the centre of a verdant jungle, like an oasis' perfect opposite. The clearing was hemmed in on one side by what he took to be the river, but it looked different to his eyes. The surface was covered in vast islands of spongy moss and tufted shrubs, and what water he could spy beneath was thick and murky.

Tēya sensed his unease. "Do you not want to play with the others, little one? You'll have fun, I promise."

He met her gaze for a moment, before looking back. "Did something scare the forest, sister?"

"Tepin, we should really head down now. I promised their parents I'd keep an eye on them, and we've taken long enough to get here."

"Sister, please," he insisted, pointing.

Tēya relented, crouching down beside him and squinting into the distance.

"It looks like something ate a piece of the forest, and now it's scared to grow back." Tepin made a snapping mouth of his hand. "See?"

Tēya was unconvinced. It looked much the same as it always had. In truth, she'd never known a time when it hadn't looked this way, and the thought of questioning it had never occurred to her. Neither had it occurred to the wizened elders of her tribe, for whom it seemed every blade of grass held some infinitely grander story. Tēya shook her head, and was about to dismiss the question when she saw in it an opportunity and changed tack. She stroked her chin in mock-thought and allowed her eyes to dart back and forth as if giving it serious consideration, before turning to face him. "You know,

WRITE LIKE HELL

Tepin" she began. "I've actually never noticed that before... You might just be on to something."

"Really?" Awe had transformed the boy's face.

Tēya nodded and stared off into the distance, trying her best to remain engaged. "But what could have done this? It must've been very large."

"That's what I also thought!" Tepin said proudly.

"Tell you what, little one," she said sidling up to him. "Let's go ask the others. Maybe they'll know something we don't. How about that?"

"Okay!" Tepin couldn't contain his excitement, and began hopping from one foot to the other.

They shuffled down the sandy hill together, the grains, still warm from the midday sun, stinging their feet. Once they'd reached the bottom, Tepin sped off towards the noisy pack of children. Tēya didn't bother calling after him, deciding to spare her throat—and her aching feet—the trouble. She'd fulfilled her duty, as far she saw it, and Tepin wasn't the only child in her care. He could be someone else's problem for the time being, she thought, and strolled towards the edge of the forest. There, a group of young girls were taking refuge from the heat.

***

Yāōtl was taller than the others—stronger, too—but not by much. His head was shaved, save for a ragged strip that ran down the centre, and bands of fluttering feathers hugged his glistening forearms. Stone plugs weighed down his lobes, flopping about his neck as he ran.

He scooped up the ball in one fluid motion and sped off, leaving his playmates choking on dust. His temples throbbed to the beat of his heart, and droplets of sweat clung to his brow. The boundary line was in sight—just a few metres more. Out of the corner of his eye he spied a figure gaining on him, and another appeared just ahead to block him off. He clutched the sun-dried fruit firm to his gut and willed his legs into a sprint, weaving from side to side as he pushed ever onward. After a moment, he snuck a look behind and smiled. The figure had slowed and was shrinking from view. He whipped his head back to find a pair of burly arms fixing to tackle him to the ground. With cat-like grace, he shifted his weight to one foot and dashed out of reach, but not before driving his elbow into his opponent's face. The boy staggered from the blow. His eyes rolled back in his head and his body folded like a banana leaf, crashing to the ground. The others rushed over to his body, hurling abuse as they went. Yāōtl sped on, imagining they cheered for him. He cleared the line with a tumble and lay on his back until his breathing found a steady rhythm once more. He rose as the others beckoned him over, and whipped his weary legs into a trot.

The boys, some no older than ten, greeted him with a scowl when he arrived. They gestured angrily to their friend on the floor, who'd begun to stir.

Yāōtl walked over to him, clutching his side. "Better luck next time," he said, holding out his hand.

Hual waved it away and staggered to his feet. "Get off." His one eye was sealed shut, and he spoke as if through an extra set of teeth.

"Are you alright? You took a nasty fall there."

Hual snorted and massaged his jaw. "Spare me, Yāōtl. You know what you did."

Yāōtl looked dumbfounded. "Win, you mean? Come now, Hual, don't be a sore loser. I won fair and square, let's not kid ourselves."

"No, you didn't—you never do. Playing fair simply isn't in your nature, neither is honesty."

Yāōtl looked him up and down, a look of pity on his face. "And winning clearly isn't in yours."

Hual spat out a gobbet of blood onto the dirt. "At least I play by the rules, Yāōtl. You do your best to break them. It's a wonder anyone plays with you, and I'm a fool for expecting anything less."

"It's my game, isn't it? The rules are mine to break if I choose. Perhaps you'd have better luck picking flowers with the girls—there's a game you can't lose."

Hual rolled his shoulders and took a wobbly step forward. Before taking another, a friend laid a hand on his arm.

"Come on, Hual. It's not worth it, you know that," he said, trying to turn him away.

"You should listen to your friend while you've still got your wits," said Yāōtl, tapping his temple with a finger.

Hual shrugged off the hand and stomped towards Yāōtl, stopping inches from his face, their eyeballs practically touching. Hual lurched his neck forward in a feint. Yāōtl shut his eyes out of instinct, nearly tripping over himself as he reeled.

Hual's lips, sealed with dried blood and spit, were wrenched open in hearty laughter. Others joined in, and Hual began to walk away. Yāōtl's face flushed with embarrassment, and then rage. His eyes flickered back and forth, searching for someone to offload on.

"Excuse me? Does this belong to you?"

A small boy, with an equally small voice, stood in front of Yāōtl, holding above his head a large, dried guanabana.

***

Tēya batted aside an overhanging palm leaf as she passed under the canopy. She couldn't help but smile as the shadows enrobed her, soothing the sting in her skin. She greeted the girls warmly, one by one. "Xōcoh, Necā, Tapa."

The girls were sprawled out on the forest floor, napping, overcome with drowsiness from the heat.

Tēya placed her hands on her hips and scowled. "Has the sun drained you of all manners?"

Tapa turned in her sleep, while the others sat up and rubbed their eyes.

Tēya tutted and dropped something in Xōcoh's lap, a bulging leather pouch with crude stitching. "Here," she said, lying down beside them. "Fresh water from the river south—not that you deserve it."

Without a word, Xōcoh brought the pouch to her lips and squeezed out a thin stream into her parched mouth.

"Water?" slurred Tapa, stirring.

Necā, now fully awake, snatched the pouch from an unsuspecting Xōcoh. "Elders first," she cried as she took off into the jungle. Xōcoh, the youngest of the trio, began sobbing. Necā took two steps before being tackled to the ground.

"And I'm the eldest." cried Tapa. Necā withdrew her arms and legs like a frightened tortoise, shielding the sack. Tapa beat out a rhythm on her back with her bare fists when she refused. "Give it here!"

Tēya groaned and cocked an eye at the miscreants. "That's enough!" she bellowed.

The young girls were stunned. A shower of leaves fell as birds scattered in the treetops. In the distance, the boys craned their necks in confusion. Even Xōcoh's tears dried up for a moment.

"There's more than enough for all of you, and if you insist on behaving like boys and not sisters, I will drink it all myself," she spat.

Necā regarded Tapa's hand warily before taking it and dusting herself off. The girls bowed their heads in shame and mumbled out apologies as they passed the pouch around. They drank their fair share from the battered container and handed it back to Tēya, before settling on the ground once more. They sat in silence for a time and stared out across the breadth of the clearing, watching the boys prance across the barren field as their game resumed. The girls were afraid to make eye contact, let alone pass the time with idle chit chat.

Tēya wiped her mouth and tossed the empty pouch aside. "Why aren't you playing with the others?" she asked, breaking the silence.

Tapa smiled weakly and stabbed the ground with a stick. "It's too hot."

Tēya snorted. "That's never stopped you girls before. What's going on?"

"It's Yāōtl. We never play when he's around."

"The high priest's son?"

Necā grunted. "He's a cheat," she said, finding her voice again.

Tēya frowned. "What do you mean?"

"He doesn't play by the rules," said Tapa.

"No, never. He changes them when he's losing," added Necā. "And if anyone challenges him, he gets angry and hurts them."

Tēya squinted into the distance. A great number of children were at play, their tiny bodies glinting in the sunlight as they darted about. "Are you sure? It seems like harmless fun to me, and besides, all your friends are out there. Why don't you join?"

The girls looked at each other. "We're not allowed—none of the girls are." Xōcoh started whimpering again. Tapa reached out a hand to comfort the young one, before continuing. "The boys, especially the younger ones, don't have a choice," said Tapa. "If they say no, he hurts them anyway."

Tēya could feel her anger mounting with every passing second. Yāōtl was much like his father Cuāuhtl, high priest and beloved adviser to the emperor, but lacked his better qualities—wisdom, courage, and leadership. By fate or chance, his worst traits had trickled down to his insufferable son—trickery, selfishness, boundless vanity. She rose to her feet without realising it and readied to leave, her face swollen with rage. "Stay here," she commanded. They didn't dare move an inch.

As Tēya left the forest behind, she felt the desire to look back, and peered over her shoulder. She finally understood what Tepin meant, in his own way. The forest did look scared, tormented by some invisible horror, ready to uproot itself and flee with newly-sprouted legs. Tēya dropped to her knees and examined the ground. Its uneven surface hinted at trailing roots, and the trees themselves seemed to grow at an odd angle, away from the area. Was the patch getting larger, or was the forest retreating into itself? Surely neither, she told herself. Just Tepin's imagination getting the better of him—it wouldn't be the first time. *Tepin!* The realisation finally hit her. She was so desperate to get rid of the boy, to check in on the others, that she'd all but forgotten about him. She cursed out loud and broke into a sprint.

Tepin peered into the bottomless murk and slapped a hand to his mouth. The stench was unbearable, and the sight ghastly to behold. This was no river but a bog, a watery tomb where all living things ensnared in it would surely die. Black ooze dripped from branches, their gnarled forms like outstretched hands, begging to be wrenched free. Dozens of fish bobbed on its roiling surface, their eyes staring back unblinking, covered in flies. Large bubbles burst with a loud pop at the surface, releasing plumes of yellow smoke. It wasn't long before Tepin's vision blurred with tears, forcing him to look away.

"Are you sure?" Tepin asked, coughing into his hand. "It doesn't seem safe."

"Of course it is, boy. We play this game often. It's one of our favourites."

Tepin looked past him, into the faces of the other children. They couldn't bring themselves to look him in the eye, and whispered amongst themselves. He pointed at them. "The others don't seem to want to play. They look scared."

Yāōtl stared down at them and waved Tepin closer. "I think they're just jealous," he said, his hand cupped to his mouth.

"Jealous? Of what?"

Yāōtl drew a finger to his lips. "Quiet..." He dropped to his knees so that they were the same height.

"Not everyone gets to play, you see. Only the older boys are allowed, and I decide who. It's a *special* game."

The boy grew silent for a moment, mulling it over. The other children barely took notice of him, and had never thought to include him in their fun. Yet here was an older boy, nearly an adult, that not only wanted to play with him, but had promised to satisfy his curiosity if he did. If he were to turn him down, he might never know the truth. In his mind, it was decided.

"And if I play with you… you'll tell me what happened to the forest?" Tepin asked.

"That was our arrangement, wasn't it? I always keep my promises, boy, you can ask the others." Yāōtl turned and glowered at them, and they started nodding furiously. "See? Do we have a deal?" he asked, rising to his feet.

Tepin raised a brow at him. "Swear it."

"Really?" he chuckled. "You're an odd one."

Tepin folded his arms.

"Alright, fine." Yāōtl's expression turned serious and he placed a hand over his heart. "I swear it."

"Okay, I'm in."

***

It wasn't long before Tēya crossed paths with Hual. She found him seated on the ground, a short ways from the other children. Quite unlike him, she thought, the boy rarely kept to himself. She noticed his posture—his head knocked to his chest, and his hands clasped around it, gripping it steady. He swayed back and forth like a mother rocking her newborn to sleep.

Tēya crouched down beside him and placed a hand on his shoulder. "Hual?"

He flinched at her touch and scrambled backwards on his hands and feet.

"Hual! It's alright, it's me, Tēya."

He paused, and she watched the panic drain from his bloodshot eyes as they fell upon her. That's when she noticed his torso caked with dried blood, the gash at his cheek that refused to close, and the socket sealed in black. She carefully took his head in her hands. "What happened to you? Who did this?"

Hual began to tell of how he came to be injured, but no sooner did the question leave her lips had an answer proposed itself. An answer she knew, but feared, to be true. She roused him to his feet and slung her arm about his shoulders. She turned her pouches out in search of something to ease his pain, but found nothing. She decided it best to return to the village, where he could be properly treated. With any luck, they'd make it back before the sun's power was spent and the cool blanket of night shrouded everything in shadow. She was plagued with doubt about the trip ahead, and wrestled with the thought of leaving Tepin to his own devices.

They came to a stop at the edge of the clearing, and Tēya looked back. "Hual, you didn't see a small boy there, did you?"

A twist of teeth and tongue crept up his shaded features. "You'll have to be more specific than that, I'm afraid."

Tēya thought a moment. It was little use. However she phrased the question, Hual or anyone else wouldn't know of whom she spoke. Tepin spent every waking moment with lizards, not boys his age, and even his parents had given up worrying after him. He had no friends to speak of, save her. In all likelihood, after discovering his kin possessed neither scales nor feathers, he probably wearied of them and went off in search of a lazy stream to marvel at.

"Never mind," she said, finally, and the two pressed on through the soft vegetation. She'd have to come back for him, and trek through the pitch-black jungle alone.

***

The game was simple: make it to one end and back—and don't fall in. Simple enough, and yet just as dangerous. Tepin looked on as Yāōtl demonstrated. Rocky outcrops dotted the surface of the bog, spanning ever outward in a long line. Some were smooth and broad, some half-submerged in rancid water, or else covered in slippery lichen. All of them were smaller and further apart than the last, until only a distant spike of crumbling stone remained of the final obstacle. For once, a game whose rules even Yāōtl couldn't break, unless he wished to cheat death itself.

The agile teen made quick work of the circuit, leaping from rock to rock with a confidence that grew with every hurdle—as did his showmanship. He made as if about to topple over and slide at times, or fall short of his target by a hair, always inches away from plunging into the water. But he recovered every time. The crowd watched on as if bewitched, gasping in unison with every stumble, cheering every time he pulled through. It was more than a simple demonstration—it was a performance. In a game where breaking the rules meant certain death, Yāōtl had managed to cheat all the same—only it was his audience he cheated, whose emotions he toyed with for his own entertainment. Tepin would've been impressed were he not battling confusion. He sat with his back to the ridge and fished the lizard tail from his pocket, turning it over and over in his hands as he thought. He couldn't figure out what was so special about the game. Straightforward and difficult, but not special in any way. Tepin was having second thoughts. The noise, the crowds, the unbearable smell—it was all beginning to wear on him. He'd always puzzled everything out himself, so why should this be any different? Before he could dwell any further on the matter, a hand slapped him on the shoulder.

"Got it?"

Tepin blinked away his thoughts. Yāōtl towered above him, grinning from ear to ear.

"I think I'll be going now," he said, rising to his feet.

"I guess you'll never know why the forest is scared, then."

Tepin sighed and returned the skink's tail to his pouch with the utmost care, patting it twice. "That's alright. Well done on winning," he said, and turned to walk away.

But for once, winning simply wasn't enough for Yāōtl. He tore the pouch from Tepin's waist, and the young boy's loincloth fell around his ankles. The crowd erupted around him in a chorus of laughter, battering his senses.

Yāōtl added his cackle to the rest of them. "What's the matter, lizard boy?"

Tepin gulped down the lump forming in his throat and drew his lower lip between his teeth in a snarl. He leapt at Yāōtl, pushing off hard against his bent knee. He thrust his one hand to the sky, just grazing the pouch with his fingers. His other he balled into a tiny fist and struck out, connecting with the prominent lump in Yāōtl's throat. They fell hard, landing on top of one another. Yāōtl gasped for breath, while Tepin used his whole body to wrestle the pouch from the older boy's vice-like grip. The teen shoved him off with a kick to the chest, and for a moment, they were both prone on the floor, struggling to breathe. Yāōtl got to his feet first and set off at a sprint towards the ridge, the little boy close behind. Atop the muddy incline, Yāōtl cocked his arm back and threw.

"No!" Tepin screamed, but it was too late.

He watched in horror as the pouch sailed through the air, landing on the surface of the bog with a plop. Tepin raced to the ridge and leapt to the first rock in an attempt to pluck it from the surface. He hoisted himself over the edge and made a panicked grab at the bag, but it was just beyond his grasp. Tepin screamed out in anguish as it was swallowed up by the forbidding waters of the wretched, stinking bog, never to be retrieved again.

"Oh, what a pity."

Tepin raised his tear-soaked cheeks to find Yāōtl standing on the embankment, a triumphant grin on his face, his voice as thick with mockery as the bog-water that sloshed around them.

"That wasn't a very nice game now, was it? And to think, this could all have been avoided if you'd simply kept your promise. There's a lesson to be learnt here, and I intend to teach you."

Tepin looked pleadingly into his eyes.

"On your feet, *now*."

***

Tepin arched his back in a long stretch. "Again?"
"Again," said Yāōtl.

The little boy breathed out a sigh and gazed up at the darkening sky. The first stars had emerged from hiding, like tiny jewels embroidered in pale purple silk. "Look, I think I've learnt my lesson, and I really should be getting home. Nantli's making tam—"

"Again, damn it!"

Yāōtl's game wasn't going as planned. For hours now, the boy had cleared every hurdle with an ease that made his face prickle. Worse still, he seemed almost to be enjoying himself, quite having forgotten about the pouch of prized goods he'd torn from him earlier. He watched on alone, cursing bitterly beneath his breath. The other children had fled in favour of a warm meal in the comfort of their homes, and he spared a curse for them, too. The evening's chill had wormed its way into his skin, and his stomach growled its emptiness. It was starting to feel like *he* was being punished, not Tepin. This couldn't go on.

"Stop, stop, stop. You're doing it all wrong," he said, waving his hands in frustration. "Horribly wrong."

"What? I am? Why didn't you say so earlier?"

"Consider it a kindness you didn't deserve. Now comes the real test."

Tepin raised a brow at him. "I thought it was a special game, not a test."

"Good, so there's nothing wrong with your ears after all, yet you can't follow simple instructions." Yāōtl began hopping one-legged, steadying himself with see-sawing arms.

Tepin scratched his head. "I don't understand."

Yāōtl snorted. "Of course not, you're hopeless. Like this, watch." He crouched low on one leg and kicked off. He tilted hard to one side as he landed and had to brace himself with a palm.

"Like this?" Tepin followed suit, his landing a little more self-assured. "I think I've got it," he said, flashing a smile.

Yāotl glowered at him. "Oh yeah?" Without warning, he sprang into the air and vaulted over two slabs in quick succession. "Beat that," he blurted out between ragged breaths.

Never a game, and no longer a test, it was a race— one Yāotl had no intention of losing. But no sooner had Yāotl regained his breath than Tepin whistled past his dumbstruck face. He spat into the water and tore after him.

Tepin gripped the short spine of stone with his toes and pivoted about to look back. A thin layer of mist had blanketed the surface of the bog, and it shone a pale grey in the moonlight. A voice rang out and he nearly lost his footing.

"Lizard boy!"

Tepin narrowed his eyes to find Yāotl cutting a path through the sheet of cloud towards him, leaping from stone to stone with both feet. He shook his head at the sight. *Cheater.* His eyes darted from darkness to darkness in search of an escape, but the only path available now lay behind the older boy.

"End of the line," Yāotl taunted.

The grey waters below began to writhe, and Tepin felt warmth creep up his face. The perch he sat atop listed to one side with a sudden groan. He leapt off as it disappeared beneath the mire, and landed inches from Yāotl.

The older boy walked forward, his nostrils flaring with rage. "I've been thinking," he began with a lick of his lips. "What happens to little lizard boys when they hit water?"

Tepin gulped and felt the hair on his arms stand on end as he drew closer.

"Do they sink?" Yāōtl took another step forward and wrapped a tattooed hand around Tepin's throat. "Or float? Let's find ou—"

Yāōtl shrieked as a jet of hot, foul-smelling smoke burst from the surface of the bog, hitting him squarely in the face.

Tepin pushed him aside, ducked beneath his flailing limbs, and began wriggling through his open legs. A moan escaped Tepin's lips as the older boy seized him and wailed on his back with his bare fists, but he managed to squeeze himself through. Without looking, he leapt to the nearest rock.

"Get back here, you little worm!" Yāōtl staggered after him in the pitch dark, his eyes sealed shut.

Unwilling to waste his only opportunity, Tepin made haste across the waters, ignoring every sound but the throb of his heart at his temples. He'd clambered up the embankment and rolled down to the other side when a shrill scream rent the air.

"Tepin, help!"

Tepin looked back to find Yāōtl clinging to the sunken rock face, his body half-submerged in muck, screaming his name between mouthfuls of rancid bog-water. A deep thrumming, like the swell and crack of pitch-black rain clouds, drowned out his name. Tepin gazed up to find not a single cloud in the sky. "I'm done playing games, Yāōtl," Tepin called out. "Give it up, already."

"This isn't a game, I promise!"

"I'm going home," said Tepin, turning to leave.

"This isn't a ga—" The boy's head was jerked underwater for a moment, only to pop up a second later with a wet, sucking noise.

"Yāōtl?"

"Tepin, please! There's something in here, help me! Tep—"

"Yāōtl!"

The little boy's jaw hung open at what he saw next. The roiling waters had taken form, rising up and out in a tall column of churning sludge. Once it reached its full height, it curled and crashed down on Yāōtl, dragging his body down with it. Tepin backed away slowly, a strangled cry at his throat, and ran for the forested ridge.

WRITE LIKE HELL

Beyond the Palms

For the first time in his young life, Tepin was lost—hopelessly so. Where children his age whiled away their days in the sun with friends, every minute he could spare he'd spent alone in the forest. He'd come to know it intimately. There wasn't a lazy stream he hadn't played in, a tree he'd left unclimbed, or a plant whose name he couldn't recite from memory. It was his second home, if not his true one. When he was sad, the shroud of leaves cradled him; when he felt like running, it gave him winding paths to rove; and when he felt like flying, it lifted him up towards the canopy, to where the leaves fluttered wildly against the breeze. He'd spent so much time there, his nantli used to jest that she wasn't his mother at all.

"The forest raised you. All I did was bring you into the world, my child… But even I'm not so sure of that. You may have ripened on the branch and dropped to the floor when it was time I'd found you."

Her voice brought a smile to his face. He opened his eyes, half expecting to see her sitting at the foot of his bed, her eyes flickering in the firelight and a mug of steaming cacao in her lap. But the image faded and his vision swam with inky blackness. The forest had grown dark and unforthcoming, and Tepin no longer recognised his home. It was foreign to his every sense. The trees stood closer together then, inches apart as if huddling for warmth. He strained his ears for familiar sounds but heard nothing. The soft burble of water, the gentle creak of swaying branches, the birds that roosted noisily in the treetops—it had all vanished, replaced by an oppressive stillness that turned his blood cold. A musty smell perfumed the woods, drawing the air tighter around him, and he found it difficult to breath. *Fear*—that's what it was, and the forest reeked of it. He nestled himself in a tree's hollow and rocked back and forth on hugged knees, wishing himself elsewhere.

His thoughts drifted to home, to warm walls of curved stone, and the snap and hiss of flames licking dry wood. Of his parents, his *tetahnantli*. His nantli kneeling in the kitchen, her hair damp at her temples as she toiled. The rush of steam as she heaved the lid of a clay pot aside to reveal a dozen or so plump parcels lying dormant inside. She'd scoop the still-warm tamales in her broad arms and carry them to the table, where she'd find his tahtli snoring in the corner, his lips stained milky-white with sour octli. A wooden spoon would fly across the room, barely missing his head.

"Tahtli!" she'd say in that voice that spelt trouble, her hands firmly at her hips.

Tepin chuckled. *She's mad now, pata. You'd better get up.* Without warning, the scene began to shrink from view, until it was but a dim speck in a sea of blackness.

"Tepin!"

Yāōtl's face flashed before his eyes, his pale skin loosely draped across his skull. His mouth hung open in a frozen scream, even as he spoke, and tears welled up in his pleading eyes. "You did this!" he rasped as Tepin turned away, and reached out. "Look at me!" Tepin felt the icy touch of swollen digits wrap around his throat.

"Tepin, look at me."

He knew that voice. It took a moment for his eyes to adjust to the presence of light, but sure enough, it was her. "Tēya!"

Tēya set the torch to one side and swaddled him in her arms. "We've been searching high and low for you! Your parents have been worried sick."

"I'm sorry," he blurted out between choked sobs.

She stroked the back of her hand against his cheek. "No, I'm sorry, Tepin. I shouldn't have left you. I'll explain later, okay?" Before Tepin could respond, she'd turned away and called back the way she'd come. "Found him!"

Specks of flame danced like fireflies between the trees, drawing nearer. Moments later, three bulky figures stood before them. Tepin thought them beasts at first, birds of a sort that had learned to walk like humans. They were covered from head to toe in feathers, and their heads were enclosed in great golden helms shaped like the beaks of giant eagles. They brandished long, tapering spears and broad shields, each one engraved with leering faces and intricate geometric patterns.

"Damn, just the small one," said one of them. "It will do little to ease the worry in Cuāuhtl's heart to see this one returned." He turned and gestured to the other warriors. "Come, we cannot linger here."

"Wait," said Tepin. "What—who are you?"

One of the trio planted his spear in the ground and stepped forward, tucking his helmet into the crook of his arm. "We are eagle warriors, boy, the winged fury and sharpened talons of the emperor."

"Eagle warriors? Are we being attacked? What's going on?"

The elite soldier chuckled. "Hush, boy. The shaman's son has gone missing. He fears something has happened to him, and we scour the earth at his breath, his word."

"You haven't seen Yāōtl, have you, Tepin?" asked Tēya. She watched as the question drained the blood from his face, and a distant look took root in his eyes. "It's okay," she cooed, drawing him closer to her bosom and rubbing his back.

The eagle warrior shifted uneasily. "Some darkness has touched him, the same that haunts this place. I can feel it," he said, gazing up in the dim light. "I fear for Yāōtl."

"Wherever he is, he's probably making someone's life a misery," she spat, turning to the eagle warrior.

"You'll get your pretty tongue cut out with talk like that. He's one of us, girl, and even if he wasn't, I have my orders." With that, he plucked his spear from the ground and slipped his bulky helm over his head.

Tēya nodded solemnly. "No, you're right."

The eagle warriors bade them farewell, and she watched as their torches went out one by one as they fled into the forest to continue their search. She picked up her own and draped a blanket over Tepin's shoulders. "Come, let's get you home."

***

"I'm done," said Tepin, pushing his plate to one side.

"You've hardly touched your food, pilli."

"I'm not hungry, pata," he said, even as his stomach groaned.

Tahtli licked his chops, overturning the plate onto his own with childish glee. "More for me."

Nantli slapped his hand away. "Pig! We're keeping some for later. This is where drinking all the time gets you—a layabout by day, and a ravenous fool by night."

"If you weren't so hard on me, I wouldn't have to drink so much," he said with a wry smile, and ducked as a wooden spoon grazed his bald head.

"How I married the village idiot, I'll never know." She rested her chin on her palm and sighed. "If my *nonan* were still around, I'd never hear the end of it."

Tepin's mouth couldn't keep from quirking up.

His father slapped a hand over his mouth in surprise and pointed. "Did you see that?" he said, nudging his wife with an elbow. "He smiled! What a relief. I was starting to think an impostor had joined us for dinner."

Tepin laughed—they all did.

"Now if only we could do something about this," he said, gesturing to the plate piled high with untouched food. All mirth drained from tahtli's face, and his tone turned grave. "Why won't you eat, son?"

Tepin shrugged and lowered his head.

His father leaned back, resting his steepled fingers on his paunch. "Tepin, what happened out there?"

But the boy said nothing, and stared off into nothingness.

His mother shook her head and rose from her seat. "There he goes again... Head in the clouds," she said, gathering up crockery in her arms. "Tepin, answer your father, please. We have a right to know why you're home so late."

"It's okay, Malintzin," said the boy's father, holding up a hand. "Tepin, please. You can tell us."

"Behind the forest, at the clearing. That's where I was."

"By the bog?"

Tepin nodded, shifting uneasily on his seat.

His father stiffened in his chair and leaned forward. "Tepin... I told you not to go there. We both did."

"I know, pata," said the boy, his eyes still downcast.
"Did something happen at the bog?"
Tepin nodded.
"Did you see something?"
"I'm not sure what I saw."
"Was the high priest's son involved?"

Tepin slowly raised his head and nodded once more, and tears streamed down his cheeks. "It's all my fault," he sobbed. "I left him there."

At that, his father curled round to Tepin's side and placed a hand on his shoulder. "No, it's not. Come with me and I'll explain" he said, steering him to his bed.

Tepin wriggled into the soft folds of his blanket, and his mother shortly appeared in the doorway to hand him a steaming mug of bitter cocoa. Once he was settled, his father took a deep breath and began to speak.

"Many, many lifetimes ago, long before you were born, the sun disappeared beyond the mountains and never rose again, covering the world in shadow. After a time, the snake god decided to reignite the sun, but found he couldn't do it on his own. He needed help, and so slithered across the starry night in search of a torchbearer, until eventually he found one. He put his faith in one of his siblings, the goddess we call the woman in the jade skirt. She accepted, and brought light to the world once more. When the sun rose that day, our ancestors, simple farmers, woke to the sound of rain. Thinking little of it, they set out to tend their tall fields of maize, as they always did. As they worked, black clouds gathered, blocking out the sun and covering the world in darkness. Great flashes of light, like a hundred tiny suns, rolled across the sky, and the earth was covered in water. Soon enough, the farmers' fields were waterlogged, their food spoilt, and their homes swept away with raging rivers that flowed into an endless sea."

"You're scaring him," said his nantli.

His tahtli stopped, noticing that his son had disappeared from sight. "Should I go on, little one?"

A tiny voice spoke from deep within the shivering blanket and a pair of wary eyes peeked out to regard him. "Yes, please," said Tepin.

"Are you sure?" he asked.

"Please. I want to know."

Tahtli reached out a hand to pat what he took to be Tepin's head. "Alright. Now, where was I... Ah, yes. Without food or shelter, our ancestors were left with little choice but to adapt—and fast. Quick learners they were, for soon they weaved for themselves small boats from floating palm leaves. But a man cannot survive without food—well, perhaps only in your case," he said with a wink, before continuing. "Soon, small nets and gut were cobbled together from the same plant. The fish they caught at first were small, no bigger than rats— barely enough to feed a man, and certainly not an entire village. Soon enough, their hunger drove them beneath the waves, where the fish were half the size of a man. Our ancestors rejoiced. At last, no one would go without food or shelter..."

His father paused to clear his throat and move the coals around. "And for a time, this was enough..."

A groan issued from within the warm bundle, but his father pressed on.

"Eat, fish, sleep—months passed this way, until every day resembled the one before it and the future looked certain. With too much time on their hands, the villagers became restless. More than that, they began to tire of life, and mourned the world that once was. The hills and valleys, the winding paths and nesting birds—they wept for it all, and thought the gods had abandoned them. Until, one day, the fishermen thought up a way to pass the time.

"They challenged each other to plunge deeper and deeper into the ocean, to gather as many fish as they could. Eventually, the waters were barren of life, and the fishermen, having spent so long in the water, had started to resemble fish themselves. Gills appeared at their throats, their fingers fanned out like fins, and they soon forgot their former lives—and their partners on the surface.

"Their wives, as hungry as they were impatient, decided they'd waited long enough and dove in after them. They combed the waters for hours, but found little, save for a few measly fish. They'd first deal with their hunger before resuming their search, they decided. They hauled their catch onto their floating homes and began gutting the fish one by one, unaware that they were killing their husbands. They were consumed with guilt when they'd realised their mistake, and threw themselves overboard as a sacrifice to the woman in the jade skirt. The goddess took pity on them and tried to save them, but something got to them first—her minion, *Cipactli*, a creature so large even the oceans could barely contain it. The creature hadn't eaten in weeks, and devoured them with relish, disobeying its master. As punishment, the water goddess pursed her lips and blew the oceans away in a single breath. When the wind died down, all that remained were the rivers, lakes, and streams we see today."

"Still filling his head with nonsense, are we?" Tepin's nantli stood in the doorway. "It's getting late, my love. Let the boy sleep, will you."

"In a minute. We're nearly finished."

She stooped to kiss them both on the cheek before leaving.

"And what about Cipactli, pata?" asked Tepin in a whisper.

"Ah, well. That's where it gets interesting. Once the storm had passed, she found the mighty Cipactli. He was flopping around on his belly like a sardine, begging for mercy as he choked. There wasn't an ocean big enough for him, then, and so she decided to shrink him down. When he was small enough for her liking, she picked him up and tossed him into the smelliest, filthiest swamp she could find. There he was to remain, to live out the rest of the age and every age to come, until his debt was paid." His father drained the last of the bitter drink and rolled his stiffened neck once or twice.

"Thanks for the story, pata."

"Story? It's no story, Tepin. You must keep your distance from that place."

"So, Cipactli lives in the bog?"

"I can't be sure, son, but this isn't the first time something like this happened. Just promise me you won't go back."

"I won't."

His father breathed a sigh. "Good, good. Do you have any questions?"

"No, pata."

He chuckled and rose from the bed. "Well, that's a first." He leaned over Tepin and planted a kiss on the warm bundle. "Goodnight, son."

"Goodnight."

But Tepin couldn't sleep that night, couldn't shut out the noise in his head long enough for rest to take hold. He wanted to believe his father, that what happened to Yāōtl hadn't been his fault, and that some ancient creature had devoured him, just as he'd done the villagers—that there was nothing he could've done to save him. With all his heart, he wanted to believe that. Until the morning light shone pale through his window, he tossed and turned. Finally, he threw off the covers and got dressed. He had to see it for himself, he decided, and slipped out the door.

WRITE LIKE HELL

Above the Sky

Tepin hadn't thought anyone would've been awake at this hour, but the village was swarming with guards. These weren't the soldiers he'd grown accustomed to seeing, either, not the usual rank-and-file troops. Their bodies were covered in plumage, their heads swallowed up by metal beaks. He'd come across them in the forest with Tēya just the night before. Eagle warriors, the emperor's personal guard. While many soldiers aspired to join their ranks, even the most fearsome peasant would be rejected. Only those of noble birth could become eagle warriors. Tepin understood then what the captain had meant when he mentioned that Yāōtl "was one of them". He wasn't referring to just anyone. If it wasn't for Tēya, they may well have continued their search without sparing him a second thought. For them, the son of a retired farmer—and a perpetually drunk one, at that—simply wasn't worth their time.

The faint rustle of leaves caught a soldier's attention, and he rammed the end of his spear into the quivering thicket Tepin had vanished into. But even the most adept tracker would've met their match in the young boy, who moved unseen through the dense foliage.

He soon found himself hurtling across the clearing and staring down into the bog. There was something different about it. The waterline had receded, and rocks he'd leapt across not a day ago were gone, along with the nose-wrinkling scent of decay. Even the water looked a shade clearer to his eyes, possibly good enough to drink.

Something caught his eye. He hopped down to take a look, his feet sinking into the muddy bank. He plucked it from the water and held it up, paying little attention to the shadow stretching across the water's surface. Tepin's eyes widened. "Cipactli?" he said out loud. A voice responded and Tepin froze.

"Looking for something? Or, should I say, someone…"

Tepin turned to find the eagle warrior captain staring down at him. He was slapping a length of braided rope against his palm and smiled knowingly.

***

Tepin awoke to find himself staring into the hollow sockets of a grimacing skull, floating before him in darkness.

"Explain yourself, boy—and well," it said, snapping its brittle jaws together in time with the words. When no response came, the skull leaned to one side as if studying him. "Come, now, don't be shy," it said. Golden-ringed fingers curled around it, beating out an impatient rhythm against bone.

"I—"

"Speak up!" the skull cried, dashing itself against the stone floor. A dozen sconces flickered into life and a gaunt face leered out at him.

Tepin's head sunk to the floor in a low bow.

The high priest sat back down on a creaking, high-backed throne of polished bone and braced a hand to his teetering headpiece. He wore a towering crown of gold, resplendent with in-laid jewels and striking patterns. It was so heavy that it listed to one side, fixing his face in a permanent scowl. His arms disappeared into the deep sleeves of his blood-red robes, and a staff, carved into the form of a coiling snake, lay upon his lap. He tugged at the golden collar around his neck, out of which fanned a multitude of feathers, and cleared his throat. "I'll ask you one more time. Where is my son?"

"I don't know," said the boy, raising his trembling head.

Cuāuhtl staggered to his feet and hobbled over, leaning with both hands on the hissing serpent head. "No?" The high priest nodded to someone behind Tepin and a whip spiralled out from the shadows, tearing into the boy's back. "How about now?"

Tepin winced but shook his head. "N-no."

"How strange." The high priest's hands disappeared into the yawning folds of his robe for a moment. "Then how exactly did you find this?" In his spindly fingers he twirled Yāōtl's feathered armband.

Tepin said nothing.

"No? Did that do nothing to jog your memory?"

"Please let me go. I don't know where your son is."

"Captain?" the high priest called out.

"Your grace?" the captain responded.

"It seems there's been an error. You've caught the wrong boy. They all look alike these days, don't they… Help him out of his binds and take him back to his parents."

"At once," said the captain, and the chamber fell quiet for a moment. He started to snicker, as did the high priest, and soon enough, uproarious laughter was echoing off the stone walls of the dimly lit room.

The high priest nodded to the shadows once more, a sardonic smile playing about his lips as the whip tore another rut into Tepin's back.

"You've wasted enough of my time, boy," he said above Tepin's screams of pain, and snapped his fingers. "Guards—"

Before Tepin could be dragged away, he blurted out a single word. "Cipactli!"

The high priest wrenched his face closer. "What did you say?"

"Cipactli! He took Yāōtl! I couldn't—"

"Enough!" the high priest bellowed, slapping him hard across the face. "I thought I told you not to waste my time," he said, massaging his hand. "The world-monster didn't live past the fourth age, foolish boy. It is from his flesh that the world—and not the one inside your tiny head—was remade. No, my son was not taken by such a creature. It is impossible."

"But my pata said—"

"Ah, so that's who it was. That's who filled your head with drivel. You could no longer content yourself with whispering your secrets to the plants; the guilt had become too much. You ran to him and confessed. He heard you out, but knew not what to do, so he soothed the ache in your heart with lies."

Tepin struggled against his restraints. "It's not my fault!"

"It's all so clear now—so painfully clear."

The high priest tore off his robes and cast aside his walking stick, bearing his wiry body in the torchlight. There was scarcely an inch of his body that wasn't covered with scars, each one as deep and determined as the last.

"What are you doing?" asked Tepin.

One of the guards knelt before him, proffering a knife of black obsidian.

Cuāuhtl held a finger to his lips, before testing the point of the blade with his thumb. "Preparing."

Preparing for what?

Slow and steady, the high priest ran the blade across the length of his chest. His eyes rolled back in equal parts pain and ecstasy. Blood flowed freely from the gash, forming a crimson puddle at his feet. All the while, a deep thrumming issued from his throat, a chant in a language far more ancient than Tepin could understand. The knife clattered to the floor and the high priest's eyes flickered open. As if he'd plucked the thought from Tepin's mind, he answered.

"A sacrifice."

Below the Waves

"Move!"

Tepin had lingered a second too long, and winced as an elbow caught him between the shoulder blades, knocking the air from his lungs. It felt like he'd been climbing all his life, and was no closer to reaching the top of the temple.

"I haven't got all day, boy," the captain said, "unlike you."

When he felt his legs might give way beneath him, he staggered over the final step and collapsed on the floor. Not a moment later, he was jerked to his feet by a guard, and an arm was slung about his torso. Tepin was about to thank him for saving him the trouble when he recalled why he was there in the first place. This was where he was going to die, and he knew precisely how. In his short life, he'd seen it play out hundreds of times.

When the moment came, the villagers would flock in their hundreds to watch, shepherded by a shrill sound that could chill marrow. One by one, the convicts would be laid out on the rounded stone dias, and one by one, their still-beating hearts would be torn from their chests. To complete the ritual, their heads would be cleaved from their necks and tossed down the temple steps, into the baying crowd below. The cycle would repeat until blood flowed like water and the smell of iron clung to your skin. There was no point in arguing, begging, or pleading. The high priest's decision was final. Once condemned, no one was spared.

But despite it all, Tepin had managed to find something worth appreciating about the moment. Minutes from crossing over the threshold, he stared out in wonderment at the panorama of his home. From atop the temple, he could see everything. The village below was impossibly small, its inhabitants like ants as they went about their daily tasks. The forest looked endless, its leaves shimmering in the blazing sun with a vibrancy he'd never seen before. Beyond the lush greenery were the rolling hills and grassy trails he'd walked countless times before. He drew his gaze further and further out, until only the soft shadows of the mountains were visible on the horizon, towering above the clouds. Behind him lay the ocean, a perfect mirror of the azure sky. He savoured the salty air and strained his ear for the faintest sound of crashing waves.

His reverie was shattered when two figures mounted the final step, their hands clasped. The high priest followed close behind. If not for the guard propping him up, Tepin would've crumpled to the floor from shock. "Nana! Pata!" he screamed.

"Tepin!" they cried out, hobbling towards him with outstretched arms.

"Get back!" A guard wedged himself between Tepin and his parents, and held a whip above his head. "Don't make this harder than it has to be."

Rage coursed through Tepin at the sight of his shackled parents. Now more beast than boy, he strained against his binds and writhed like a serpent in his captor's grip. There was little the guard could do but carry him to the other side of the platform. But Tepin wasn't about to go quietly, and lashed out with what little energy he had left. He buried his elbow in the guard's throat, crushing his windpipe. Tepin clattered to the floor, looking up in time to see his captor disappear over the edge. He screamed as he rolled down the endless steps, until his head split open with an audible crack and his body disappeared into the gathering crowd of villagers.

"Bind him!" commanded the high priest.

Tepin felt a bicep curl around his neck as two guards tied his feet and hands together.

"You'll be begging for death before I'm done with you," Cuāuhtl whispered into his ear as he was lifted up.

He didn't have the strength to resist anymore, and spared one final look at his parents' horrified faces while the guards set about lashing him to the dias. Tears came to his eyes, and he mouthed an apology to them. The high priest brushed off his hands and straightened his tunic, before walking to the edge of the platform to address his audience. It had begun.

The words with which Tepin had grown so familiar sounded strange in that moment. They were distant and muffled, little more than a murmur. He couldn't hear his parents' panicked cries, nor taste the salt on the breeze, and the rope that irritated his hands was quite forgotten. As if a valve had been tightened within his mind, all sensation slowed to a ponderous drip, and then stopped entirely. Tepin had retreated into himself, until all he was left with was a visual of his body, floating through an infinite void. It was there that he left a simple message.

KAIJU

You helped me once before. Please, help me again.

Tepin gasped awake and the world of sensation rushed in, overwhelming him. His eyes seared with pain, his lungs burned as if he'd just taken his first breath, and his limp extremities prickled.

A blurry Cuāuhtl hovered above him and tapped him on the cheek. "I want you awake for this," he whispered, raising the obsidian dagger high above his head, aiming for the boy's heart.

But the stroke never fell. A sound like rolling thunder rang out, and the high priest gazed up in alarm and confusion at the cloudless sky. Seconds later, a scream erupted from him and he vanished. Something had struck the temple, tearing clean through the masonry, taking the high priest with it and covering the boy's body in pink mist. Moments later, several more thunderclaps boomed in the distance, and the villagers began to scream and scatter. Tepin's parents rushed forward to where he lay and cut his bonds with Cuāuhtl's knife. They helped him to his feet and started to descend the steep steps, but turned back.

"Wait! I have to see what's going on." Tepin couldn't help himself, and peered over the wall. He knew that sound. It was Cipactli—it had to be, he thought. It wasn't.

From the forested ridge at the southern end of the village charged hundreds of soldiers with a tremendous cry. They were clad in shining steel plate draped with crimson cloth, and carried long poles topped with two blades. The one was narrow and pointy, and the other broad and curved like the black teeth of the macuahuitl.

Tepin watched as eagle warriors descended on the scene, beating their shields and screaming battle cries of their own. The forces were about to clash when, at the last second, the eagle warriors halted their charge. Something had spooked them, and they soon broke formation. They were already fleeing by the time Tepin glimpsed what made them scatter.

Yet more soldiers had emerged from the woods, but they weren't your usual rank-and-file infantry. They sat atop muscular, four-legged beasts as tall as two men or more, and wielded both sword and spear. They looked nothing like men at all, their entire bodies encased in gleaming armour as they pressed forward. Tepin watched with morbid curiosity as they chased the fleeing eagle warriors down, either running them through, or else impaling them at the end of their spears. Whoever survived the onslaught was brutally dispatched by row upon row of simple, sword-wielding soldiers.

Tepin had just managed to tear himself away from the grisly scene when the ground shook beneath him with the sound of another thunderclap, raining down pebble-sized fragments of stone around him. He looked around for his parents, but they were already making their way down the steps. He called to them above the tumult, but they disappeared into the throng of anxious villagers.

The soldiers were beginning to stream past the steep walls of the temple, penetrating deeper and deeper into the village. Tepin watched as the eagle warriors struggled to contain them. Ordinary civilians didn't stand a chance, it taking little more than a single swing of the sword to fell them. The eagle warriors didn't fare much better. In the forest, where cover was plentiful, they may have stood a chance, but not out in the open.

After a few skirmishes, the lightly-armoured infantry were easy enough to pick off, but just as they'd managed to even the odds, some new threat would pose itself. Tepin watched in horror as a thirty-strong group of eagle warriors led by the captain of the royal guard piled into the throng of infantry, only for a separate enemy detachment to emerge at their flank. They held long, thin tubes and were busy filling them with something. They didn't look like any weapons he'd ever seen—hardly weapons at all. When they were done, they balanced the slender instruments on forked hooks in the ground and hugged them tight.

Tepin raised his head to get a better look, but a series of deafening cracks forced him back down. When he peered over again, smoke was billowing from the narrowest point of the tubes and two thirds of the captain's force lay prone on the ground, clutching gaping wounds in their sides. No matter their number, they all met the same end—hacked to pieces by an array of weaponry they'd never seen nor understood.

The enemy soldiers had flooded the village at that point, and began to corral unarmed civilians, both the young and old, at the end of spears and swords. Some fought back with their bare fists, some with rocks and crude weapons of their own. They ultimately fared no better than the soldiers, and succumbed to the endless tide of silver and crimson.

It was hopeless. Tepin sunk to his knees on the steps of the temple, bereft. A small group of spear-men had spotted him and were mounting the steps. For a moment, he felt it didn't matter—none of it did anymore. If he resisted, he'd perish. If not, he'd be captured and live as a slave. He decided then and there that he'd rather die. He gathered up what loose debris he could throw and bounded back up the steps, all the way to the upper terrace, to make his final stand.

Tepin unleashed volley after volley of stones at the approaching spear-men. Most of them landed wide of their target, or were batted away by their heavy shields, but others struck true. Every so often, they'd hit their helmets with a satisfying clink, sending them tumbling down the steps. It may have only prolonged the inevitable, but it brought a smile to his face all the same. Soon enough, he'd run out of things to throw, and scoured the platform for a weapon of any kind. His eyes lit up as he spotted the high priest's dagger. He clutched it to his chest and scrambled into the corner as the spear-men bore down on him, mounting the last few steps to the upper platform. They approached him with their shields raised and their spears down-turned. He seemed more caged animal than boy then, hurling every abuse he could at them while waving the knife about with murderous intent. One soldier stepped forward and removed his helmet, his spear and shield clattering to the floor. His companions looked at him as if he'd lost his mind, but slowly backed off. They began speaking to each other in a tongue Tepin didn't recognise.

"What are you doing, Roderigo? Are you insane?"

"Silencio, Juarez. Can't you see he's but a child?"

"Child or no, he means us harm," said the other.

"And we don't, Diego?" snapped Roderigo. "No, we're taking this one alive."

With that, Roderigo held up his hand in a gesture of peace. "No tricks, see?" he said, slowly extending it. "Give me the knife."

Tepin drew back into his corner and stabbed out at the proffered hand.

"Coño!" Roderigo pulled back with a yelp and closed his mouth on the wound. The other two wheezed with laughter. "Shut up and hold him steady."

Diego and Juarez took up their shields in both hands and moved to hem him in.

"No!" Tepin screamed through manic swipes, until his knife was firmly wedged in Diego's shield, missing the Spaniard's eyeball by a hair.

They tossed their shields aside, freeing up their hands, and grappled him to the floor. "Got him, capitán!" But no response came.

"Probably bled out from that flesh-wound," sneered Juarez.

Diego looked back to find Roderigo frozen in place and staring off into the distance, a puddle of urine slowly collecting at his feet.

"Capitán?"

Nothing Capitán Roderigo could've said would've done the sight justice.

Hearing the screech and crack of timber, Tepin scrambled to his feet to peer through a crack in the masonry.

A creature of unspeakable size was clearing a path through the woods before them, flattening trees like cattails as it stomped towards the village. Towering high above the canopy, the soldiers had to take a step back and crane their necks to take in its full immensity. It parted the tree-line like a green curtain, revealing itself in all its horror. If the terrible beast bore a resemblance to any living creature, it looked most like a crocodile, one that had just emerged from centuries of sleep in a swamp—but even that falls short of capturing its hideous appearance. From tapering snout to thrashing tail, it was covered in thick, interlocking scales that shone dark green beneath the filth. Sharp, bony protrusions ran down the length of its back in diamond-shaped rows, and Tepin was immediately reminded of the rocky platforms he'd leapt between for Yāōtl's amusement. Its hulking, dreadful form was supported by short, muscular legs, each one ending in a webbed foot from which curled sharp talons.

It paused for a moment and scraped a clawed hand across its pale, ribbed belly, removing tufts of moss and sprawling lichen. It swayed its massive, mud-encrusted head back and forth, peppering buildings and villagers both with mud and ooze. It opened its eyes, the nictitating film drawing back, and putrid yellow orbs leered out. The monster wrenched open its gaping maw to reveal row upon row of conical teeth, and its pale blue tongue darted out to lick the air. Jets of foul smoke erupted from crater-like nostrils at the tip of its long snout, and the membranous sack of skin beneath its jaws began to quiver and inflate as it drew breath. A loud, baleful cry erupted from its breast, sending a tremor through the temple, shaking loose stone and bursting eardrums. A warm stench, like rotten fish, followed as it lumbered forward to the terrified screams of villagers and soldiers alike.

A horn sounded behind Tepin, and he watched as a hail of iron balls screamed through the air, hitting the creature in the belly. The shots rebounded off his hide, only serving to irritate the beast. It dragged a bulky claw through lines of dazed infantry. Most of them died on impact, or were tossed into the sky, landing a great distance away. The three soldiers spared a glance back at Tepin, before racing down the steps to join the others in retreating.

As the soldiers fled in panic, the beast-men rode ahead in tight formation, their swords raised, spurring their frightened mounts into a gallop toward the colossus. Puffs of smoke filled the air as the tube-soldiers offloaded into the beast. They hacked and slashed at its haunches, but with every swipe their swords blunted and chipped, until their blades were ground down to the hilt. The monster seemed not to notice the men at its feet, until one of them plunged their sword deep into the soft flesh between its scales. A howl rent the air and the creature brought down a webbed foot upon the company, turning both beast and man to paste. The remaining soldiers were flung from their rearing mounts and fled with the rest of their kin to the shoreline. Dragging its ponderous tail behind it, the creature bounded after them.

Cowed by the beast's sheer presence, the villagers had fled past their homes and into the trampled forest, but began to emerge as its whipping tail disappeared from view. Tepin raced down the steps as it passed the creaking temple, joining the villagers in chasing after it as it disappeared beyond the steep hills to the beach.

The soldiers were fleeing for their lives, many of them falling over themselves to reach the shoreline. Hundreds of ships were at anchor on the crystal-clear waters. The soldiers had piled into tens of smaller boats and were paddling frenziedly to reach them. He couldn't see the beast anywhere, but he did notice an oily black pool of scum and slime rise to the surface. An inky shadow broke off from the dark stain, and the ships began to buffet as waves rose and broke with its approach. The smaller boats began to topple over and sink as a column of salty water shot into the sky, before crashing down on the remaining vessels. The beast raised its emerald-green bulk above the tides and seized one of the larger ships in its hefty claws. The ship's wooden hull screamed in protest as the creature tugged on either end, before snapping it clean in two. It lifted both halves high above its gaping maw and shook the ruptured craft, until men began to fall into it. One by one, every boat and every soldier met the same grisly end. By the afternoon, nothing remained of the fleet but floating wreckage and drowning men. With the threat vanquished, the beast looked back at the villagers brave enough to follow and observe the destruction.

"Tepin?" said a voice, squeezing the boy's hand.

"Yes?"

"Is that Cipactli?" asked his father with a frown.

"I'm not sure, pata."

"What did you do?"

"Nothing much. I just asked for help," he said, and his parents smiled back at him.

KAIJU

Honengyo

C. L. Werner

The village lay strewn across the shoreline, a vast swathe of rubble and debris. Broken timbers stabbed up at the sky like accusing fingers. The cracked pillars of a toppled torii lay in the dirt like shattered bones. A little shrine sagged against the side of the hill as though pushed over by a tremendous hand.

Gazing down on the scene from the hilltop, Shintaro Oba was awed by the destruction on display. The samurai was no stranger to such scenes. He'd been there when the forces of the Shogun razed the castle of his clan and left it burning in the moonlight. But that devastation had been wrought by an entire army. This had been done by a single creature. At least, so his companion claimed.

Kawajiri Ujio stroked the neck of his horse, trying to ease the animal's agitation. A smoky, reptilian odour hung in the air, a scent that was noxious to both rider and steed. "Lord Torogawa wanted you to see this for yourself before I take you to him." He pointed down at the smashed village, indicating a spot just beyond the fallen torii gate. "One of the monster's tracks. The others have been washed away by the tide."

Oba could see the outline of an impression, but it was vague at this distance. "I want a closer look," he said. He kicked the ribs of his horse and urged it down the path that circled down to the destroyed village. His steed resisted, only reluctantly obeying his command. The horses bred by the Hoshin clan were known for their boldness, yet that musky reptilian stench had them as frightened as rabbits. Even Kawajiri, a far more accomplished rider than Oba, was having troubles keeping his mount under control.

Finally, the two samurai reached the spot. Oba's expression was grave when he studied the impression. There was no denying it looked like a track, but the vastness of its size was incredible. Their horses might lie side by side in that track and still have room to spare. The size of a creature that could leave such a footprint was beyond anything Oba had seen before, and he'd seen many monstrosities since he'd started hunting demons across the provinces of Mu-Thulan.

In shape, the track was wide with a broad heel. There were three long, clawed toes at the fore and an impression that might indicate a fourth. The depth to which it was sunk into the earth told of a tremendous weight. Oba saw the crushed fragments of a stone Jizo statue at the bottom of the track, pulverised by the creature that trod upon it.

"I confess, at first I thought this couldn't be what you claimed it was," Oba told Kawajiri. "I thought it must be enemies of your clan trying to ruin Nokoshima and using an old legend to hide their actions." He shook his head as he gazed across the shattered village. "Now I'm ready to believe what you've told me."

"Lord Torogawa expected you'd need convincing," Kawajiri said. "In Nokoshima Province, all of us have heard the legends, but few more than half-believed in them." He swept his hand across the destruction around them. "Three villages have been annihilated. Now we believe. Now we know Honengyo is real."

***

Once before, Oba had been admitted into the presence of Lord Torogawa. On that occasion, he'd been drawn into the struggle between the Hoshin clan and a pirate gang that was preying upon their ships. He'd helped end that menace, defeating the sorcerer leading the pirates and his shark-demons. But he was an enemy of Shogun Yoshinaga, while the Hoshin clan were loyal vassals. With such a state existing, Lord Torogawa had been unable to provide any official recognition of the samurai's service. It had been strain enough on the clan's honour to allow Oba to leave without turning him over to the Shogun's agents.

Now, despite the obligations of feudal loyalty, Lord Torogawa sought Oba's help. He'd sent riders looking for him throughout the neighbouring provinces until, at last, Kawajiri was able to beg his help and bring him to Nokoshima. It was a testament to the daimyo's desperation and need that he should risk the ire of the Shogun by asking help from an outlaw.

Oba sat on the floor of the reception room, facing towards the raised platform on which Lord Torogawa and Chamberlain Hidetoro Kayama reposed. Behind them, picked out upon a silk banner, was the mon of Clan Hoshin. The suggestion in the design, of a great beast rising from the sea, now took on a much more sinister meaning.

Kawajiri and two other Hoshin samurai sat to Oba's side, their swords laid out on the floor beside them. Opposite the samurai, on Oba's other side, was an old man in the yellow robes and black sash of a priest. His head was shorn down to monkish baldness, but a long moustache drooped from his upper lip. The priest kept his head bowed, but Oba could feel his eyes studying him with almost intense scrutiny.

"You do our clan honour by accepting our summons," Hidetoro greeted Oba. "Please understand that we wouldn't have presumed upon you if things were otherwise than they are now."

Oba nodded to the chamberlain. As an enemy of the Shogun, it would be unseemly for Lord Torogawa to speak to him directly, so the daimyo's intentions had to be conveyed through the medium of Hidetoro.

"Across a conflict of loyalties, debts of honour must be acknowledged," Oba stated.

"Yes, you helped us before," Hidetoro replied. "Though your Clan Sekigehara were supporters of the Emperor, you defended our province from an Imperial sorcerer." He looked back at the daimyo before continuing. "Though we are loyal to the Shogun, we couldn't return good for ill. It would have been a stain upon our clan to do so."

"And now you ask me to come back," Oba said. "To help you again."

"We could think of no one else," the chamberlain sighed. "Your sword, the Demon-Killer, has prevailed against many foes…"

Oba held up his left hand while his right dropped to the bone-hilted uchigatana lying beside him. "Against demons, Koumakiri has powers that bypass their infernal protections. But against monsters that don't come from the realm of Kimon, it is only a sword." His eyes narrowed as he looked directly at Lord Torogawa. "Is this Honengyo a demon, or is it some other manner of being?"

Lord Torogawa gestured to the priest. The old man shifted forwards so that he sat between the raised platform and Oba. "Honengyo is as old as the mountains and the sea. He was here before the first Yamajin arrived to build their huts. He was here when the Koropokguru still dominated the land, before the first kings drove them into the wilderness." The priest pulled at his moustache. "There are some who believe he is a god, to be venerated and honoured. Others hold that he is a monster to be feared and despised.

"For many hundreds of years the priests of Mount Odo have paid tribute to Honengyo as the guardian of Nokoshima. Once a year, when summer fades into autumn, a sacred cow is tied to a raft and set adrift for Honengyo. When he accepts our tribute, he drives fish from the deep ocean into our waters and the province prospers."

"But this time, something has gone wrong," Oba surmised. "Now, instead of improving your fishing, Honengyo is destroying your villages."

"Three villages have so far been razed by the monster," Hidetoro stated. He made a chopping motion of his hand against his palm. "One after another. All in a row. After the first, we evacuated the people from their homes. The next village that lies in his path has also been evacuated, but beyond that is the town of Hokkashiri. To lose the town would devastate the province. We'd be unable to maintain the prosperity the Shogun expects. Our clan would be uprooted and sent to a lesser province. Perhaps even disbanded."

Lord Torogawa threw back the sleeves of his kimono. "I will not let that happen," he said. "It is my prayer that your experience hunting and destroying demons can overcome Honengyo, whether he is a god or a monster. If the task is beyond you, then know that I have marshalled my forces at Kuroyama, the village that Hidetoro spoke of. Whatever my samurai may accomplish by force of arms, we will strive to achieve at Kuroyama."

"Each time, Honengyo has allowed twelve days to pass before his next attack," Hidetoro explained. "That means there are four days left before we can expect him at Kuroyama."

Oba nodded and turned back to the priest. "These sacrifices you made to Honengyo I feel must be the key to this crisis. The last was made before the first attack?"

"Immediately before," the priest confirmed. "Four monks took the offering down to the shore at Imori. What happened there, we don't know. The monks have been missing ever since. It has been agreed they must have been Honengyo's first victims."

Oba pondered the priest's words. "Without evidence, it could be reckless to agree on anything," he said. "I would see this place at Imori."

"What do you think to learn?" Hidetoro asked.

"A clue to why a monster that has only brought prosperity to your people before now brings destruction," Oba said. He laid his hand across his swords. "Something happened to change things. As you've seen before, ruthless men won't balk at inflicting the worst misery to achieve their ends. It may be that your enemies are at work again."

"Another of the Emperor's sorcerers?" Hidetoro shook his head, aghast at the suggestion.

"It may be another onmyoji," Oba said, recalling the pirate-wizard. "If so, I will seek him out. Whoever's behind this, whatever they've done, I will put an end to this." He cemented his vow by lifting up Koumakiri. He drew the blade a few inches from the sheath, then slammed it back again. The metallic sound echoed through the room.

"Your commitment pleases me, Shintaro Oba," Lord Torogawa said, again defying convention by acknowledging the outlaw. "You do honour to your ancestors." He lifted his hand, displaying four fingers. Slowly he lowered one of them. "One day is spent already. In three more, Honengyo will attack. I will meet him at Kuroyama with my army. I doubt our chances for victory, but we will not run from this fight." He shook his hand before him. "Three days, that is all you have to prevent the battle."

***

The destruction of Imori was every bit as complete as what Oba had seen at the other village. There was only a slight difference. Here there had been no evacuation, and the ruins were infested by crows drawn by the stench of the bodies entombed in the rubble.

"Only a few escaped the attack to tell what happened," Kawajiri told Oba as they walked down what had been Imori's main road. The Hoshin samurai paused and bowed respectfully at the toppled mess of the house they were passing. "They said that Honengyo rose from the sea during the night. His roar split the darkness and the earth trembled from his steps. Many in the village were awakened by the turmoil, but they were frozen in shock as the monster strode through the surf.

The survivors were those who had sense enough to run the moment they heard the roar. Too late did the other villagers recover their senses. Some tried to hide in their homes, others sought to flee into the hills. All of them were crushed beneath Honengyo's feet."

Oba nodded. He could see the image of clawed toes stamped into the crushed buildings, silent testament to the colossal beast that brought them to ruin. "Where on the beach did the monks make their offering to Honengyo?" he asked his guide.

"This way." Kawajiri directed him towards a weathered outcropping of rock. There was a faint suggestion of carving about it, as though it had been crudely sculpted ages ago, then worn down by the elements into its current shape. Oba thought of the savage Koropokguru. Before humans had driven them into the forests, the dwarfs had been fisherfolk who dwelled beside the sea. Perhaps this had been one of their shrines. Something revered by the dwarfs. Maybe it was connected to Honengyo. It was possible that the tradition of making offerings to the monster wasn't the invention of Mount Odo's priests.

Oba inspected the area around the rock, his eyes roving across the tide pools and clumps of seaweed thrown up by the surf.

"We checked the beach for miles," Kawajiri said. "In both directions. We could find no trace of the monks."

Something in one of the tide pools caught Oba's eye. A flash of colour moving beneath the water. He darted forwards and caught the thing in his hands. He pulled it up from the pool and studied it in the open air. "When you searched, there might have been nothing to find,"

Oba said. He held the creature he'd caught out to the other samurai. "Now there is."

The thing in Oba's hands was a crab, no different than the crustaceans common to any beach. It was the scrap of yellow cloth caught about its legs that made it remarkable. There was no mistaking it as coming from a monk's robe.

"Then, they were here," Kawajiri nodded.

"I think they still are." Oba turned the crab around so that its flailing claws couldn't nip at his arms. "They've been here for some time. Long enough to draw scavengers." He tossed the crab back into its pool.

"The tide would have washed up any bodies by now," Kawajiri objected.

Oba began removing his armour. "Not if someone didn't want them to be found. I'm convinced that they're still here." He set his arm guards down in the sand and began undoing his cuirass. "If they are, I'll find them. It would be useful to know how they died. It might tell us who killed them... and why."

Oba stripped down to the cotton fundoshi that girded his loins. He handed Kawajiri his uchigatana but kept the smaller wakizashi. "Keep a watch for me," Oba said. "I can hold my breath for three minutes. If you don't see me come up for air, then you'll know I won't be coming up at all."

"May the Dominance grant you luck," Kawajiri told him, invoking the name of the supreme god.

Oba turned and marched out into the waves. He used the side of the rock to steady himself as he trudged through the water. Once it was deep enough, he kicked away and began to swim. He ducked his head under the surface, straining his eyes to peer at the bottom. He dove and swam, navigating the marine growths that sent feathery tendrils up from the bottom. Several times he resurfaced to suck breath back into his burning lungs. Then he dove down once more to continue his search.

The sun was beginning to fade from the sky and Oba knew he couldn't continue the hunt much longer without light. He mustered his reserves for one last dive and plunged once more towards the bottom. This time, his vision was rewarded with a glimpse of bright yellow among the weeds. He swam towards the suggestion of colour, drawing aside the clumps of vegetation.

A grisly sight was waiting for him. Four monks stood suspended in the water, their tattered robes billowing around their pale bodies. Their flesh was ripped and torn, ravaged by the sea creatures that continued to pick at their remains. But to Oba's eyes there were other injuries, ones that struck him as too deep and regular to be the work of marine vermin. Certainly, it had been no fish that had tied their feet together and fasted the ropes to large stones. This was murder.

Oba could feel his lungs crying out to him for air, but he was determined to make a closer study while the light was with him. This was the end of the third day. If he waited, he would need to linger in Imori until morning. Twelve hours wasted that he couldn't afford to spare.

Defying the demands of his body, Oba swam around the corpses. His eyes locked upon a dark shape that protruded from one of the monks, almost hidden by his tattered robes. The samurai reached for it before he recognized what it was. Jerking his hand back in alarm, he recovered from his close call. Taking the frayed robe, he used it to grip the object and work it free from the cold flesh.

He could feel his body screaming at him for air. Spots danced before his eyes and a dreadful pounding rumbled in his ears. Still, Oba wouldn't give up. He used his short sword to slash way the section of robe he'd wrapped about the object. Only when he had a secure grip on it did he kick his way up to the surface. He gasped for air as he breeched the water. Then he shouted to Kawajiri on the beach. "I found them!" he cried. "And I found something else!"

Once Oba was back on shore, he showed Kawajiri the weapon he'd removed from the dead monk. It was a steel star, its edges sharp as that of a sword. Even after being submerged for weeks, there was still a greenish residue on its points. Oba warned the other samurai to be careful. "It's coated in poison resin," he said.

Kawajiri looked at the object with increased loathing. "A shuriken. Then the monks were murdered by ninja."

"Every ninja clan uses a shuriken of a shape distinct unto itself so that they might boast of their prowess." Oba shook his head. "Of course, with ninja, the only dishonour they know is to fail in the task they've undertaken, so they aren't above trying to implicate another clan for their crimes when it suits their purpose. The pains they took to hide the monks makes me think this shuriken was left by accident. The ninja didn't want their involvement to be known."

"Do you know which clan that shuriken belongs to?" Kawajiri asked.

Oba stared at the murderous implement. "I've seen this before. This kind of shuriken is used by the Kokuryu." He looked away from the weapon and his voice grew solemn. "The Kokuryu ninja clan serve the

Shogun. If they're here, then it means Yoshinaga sent them here."

***

The fishing village of Kuroyama had been transformed into an armed camp. The bell in the watchtower clamoured as the inhabitants were driven from their homes by armoured samurai. A long line of refugees with bundles slung across their backs hastened up towards the hills. Behind them, groups of soldiers took over their huts to employ as barracks. Pavilions and tents sprouted along the beach as more soldiers built their bivouacs.

"I didn't realize Clan Hoshin could muster such a force," Oba commented as he gazed down upon the army.

Kawajiri's expression was dour. "Many of these are samurai and ashigaru from allied clans," he said. "Others are ronin paid from our treasuries." He pointed to the half-dozen catapults lined up along the top of the cliff, then gestured to the enormous ballistae arrayed at the edge of the village. "Craftsman were hired from five provinces to build those weapons." He turned and indicated three huge ships lying at anchor in Kuroyama's waters. "The Shogun allows each clan only a single atakebune." For a moment, a smile flickered on his face. "Though we'd yet to sell or scuttle the pirate ship your sword won for us in summer. The third warship was loaned to Lord Torogawa by Lord Tsugimoto of Shinanno."

"Your clan has spent much gold and many favours preparing for this fight," Oba stated.

"Every weapon at our disposal has been called upon." Kawajiri clapped Oba on the shoulder. "We've even asked the famed Shintaro Oba and his Demon-Killer to help us."

Oba frowned at the accolade. "I can only strive to be worthy of your trust." His eyes roved across the gathered army. It was the largest fighting force he'd seen since the destruction of Clan Sekigahara. To think any beast could stand against this many warriors was incredible, yet he'd seen the footprints left by Honengyo and the devastation the monster could wreak.

A strange spire of rock projecting from the bay attracted Oba's attention. There was something familiar about it. As the waves rolled back and exposed a little more of it, he saw why. Though farther out in the water and more eroded, it had the same suggestion of ancient carving about it. He drew Kawajiri's attention to the rock. "It looks like the outcropping at Imori," he said.

"You think it's a koropokguru idol?" Kawajiri asked.

"When our ancestors took this land from the dwarfs, what could be more natural than to build their settlements in the same places?" Oba scratched his chin as he continued the thought. "The shore must have been farther out then and the rock stood clear of the water. There may have been other idols present at the other villages Honengyo destroyed, ones that were completely submerged."

Kawajiri followed the speculation. "You think these idols have something to do with Honengyo? That in some way the Kokuryu are using them to draw out the monster?"

"We know the monks went to the rocks at Imori to render tribute to Honengyo," Oba said. "If they could manage such a thing for the good of Nokoshima, perhaps others could use it to work evil."

"Then, we have to stop Honengyo here," Kawajiri growled. "Because there's a stone very much like this in Hokkashiri. The 'lucky dragon' the sailors call it. It sits right in the heart of the bay."

Oba felt the weight upon his shoulders increase. If there was any doubt that Honengyo would avoid the town, now he had none. Whatever the ninja had done, he was certain it would be repeated at Hokkashiri. "Our hope now is that the Kokuryu have to perform the same rite to lure Honengyo from the sea at each village."

"That would mean they're already here," Kawajiri said. His eyes hardened as he looked down on the mass of warriors. "With so many ronin and samurai from other clans, it will be hard to unmask who is a ninja."

"They might be disguised as a common ashigaru, or even a camp follower," Oba cautioned. "Nor could you neglect to look among the warriors of your own clan." He raised his hand to stifle the outraged protest Kawajiri was going to make. "Ninja are masters of deception. One of their spies might lurk unseen for years, loyal and faithful in all respects, until that moment when his true loyalties are called upon by his clan. Never underestimate their cunning. It is a mistake few men are fortunate enough to make twice."

"How will we find them if we don't know where to start?" Kawajiri asked. "We can speak with Chamberlain Hidetoro, get his help trying to find the Kokuryu, but what if they remain hidden?"

"We've one advantage," Oba said. "They don't know we suspect their involvement. If we can't find them, then we can still keep vigil over the idol.

Tomorrow night, if the pattern holds, they must commit the ritual that brings Honengyo out of the sea."

The two samurai descended from the heights and made their way through the armed camp. At every side they passed warriors inspecting their armour and tending their weapons. Ashigaru gunners practised with their tanegashima matchlocks, peppering their cliffside targets with bullets. Sohei warrior-monks from Mount Odo chanted prayers over their broad-bladed nagintas. Companies of ronin sharpened their swords and strung their bows, eager to prove themselves in the coming battle and perhaps earn for themselves a position in Clan Hoshin.

"Any one of them might be a ninja," Kawajiri whispered. "How can we hope to spot them?"

They were walking away from the bivouacs of the warriors and into the clustered tents of the camp followers. The smell of food cooking was everywhere, but there was an undercurrent of perfume wafting from the pavilions of geishas. Professional sword-sharpeners had ready work for themselves as they honed the edges of the katanas awaiting their attention. Armourers mended the neglected gear of mercenaries, pounding out dents and patching tears.

Oba's attention was drawn to the tent of a fortune teller. An old woman with a crooked back beckoned to those walking past, encouraging them to attend the divinations of her mother. This was an even more ancient crone with a bulbous nose swaddled in a heavy cloak. She was poised behind a bamboo table. The ill-favoured prophetess read the future by drawing joss sticks from a clay jar. Her hands proved thick and hairy when she did so, calloused from hard work.

"That one," Oba nudged Kawajiri. "She has a man's hands."

"Not much there to be a ninja," Kawajiri told him. He pointed at the rug on which the prophetess sat. Oba saw at once what he was referencing. The crone's body was truncated, her dimensions reduced by some horrible accident. From the knee down, her legs were missing.

Oba had to concede that the Kokuryu might employ a cripple as a spy, but not as an active agent in a scheme such as they were now engaged in. Yet, as he walked away, he couldn't help glancing back. For just a moment he thought the younger hag was watching him. He knew it was irrational, but he couldn't shake the impression that he'd seen her before.

"There's something wrong with those two just the same," Oba said. Then he sighed. "If I was sure what it was, I'd act. But if I'm wrong, all I'd accomplish is to warn the Kokuryu that we know they're here."

"We'll speak with Chamberlain Hidetoro," Kawajiri assured him. "He'll help ferret out these ninja. Wherever they're hiding."

Oba couldn't share the younger samurai's confidence. He'd come against ninja of different clans before, but none had been so ruthless and cold-blooded as those of the Kokuryu. "One day to catch them. If Hidetoro's men can't do that, it'll fall to us to stop them."

"We can set a hundred samurai to keep watch on the rock," Kawajiri suggested. "Make it impossible for them to carry out this ritual."

"No," Oba said. "We can't do that. Right now, we have an idea of their plans. If we make the ninja suspicious, they'll change those plans. Then we won't know where or when they'll strike." His hand closed around the bone-hilt of Koumakiri. "Just the two of us. If Hidetoro can't find the Kokuryu first, then we'll have to lie in wait for them and hope our presence goes unnoticed."

Oba stared out to sea. He pictured the monster that even now was lying off shore, waiting for the call that would bring it rampaging into Kuroyama. "If we can't stop them, Lord Torogawa's army must face Honengyo."

***

Night hung over Kuroyama. The camp was eerily silent now when compared to the previous evening. Gone was the murmur of carousing warriors guzzling sake to bolster their boasts. The music of flute and samisen were silent, the songs of geishas absent. Many of the tradesmen and specialists had decamped over the course of the day, retreating inland in advance of the coming battle. Everyone knew that time had run out. Before morning, Honengyo would appear and try to destroy the village.

Oba had a clear view of the rock spire from where he lay hidden. An overturned fishing smack was his shelter, its side propped up so that he could see across the beach. Kawajiri was similarly concealed only a few yards away. There were dozens of the boats lined about the shore. The others had been soaked in oil, intended to be used to create a wall of fire when the monster arrived. Oba hoped that the ones they hid beneath would be camouflaged by the others.

Hidetoro had sent dozens of samurai and retainers to prowl the camp, trying to sniff out the ninja. Their efforts had only unmasked a few thieves. The Kokuryu remained free. The chamberlain harboured the horrible thought that the martial build-up at Kuroyama might have made the conspirators bypass the village and move ahead to Hokkashiri. This hideous prospect was one he didn't dare suggest to Lord Torogawa. At this late date, there wouldn't be time to move the army, even if they were sure.

Oba was convinced the Kokuryu were here. If their intention was to ruin Clan Hoshin, then crushing this army would be an even greater coup than destroying Hokkashiri. Whatever clan assumed control over the province would benefit from having the town intact. The villages would be easy to rebuild, Hokkashiri much less so. No, Honengyo would be set loose here. Oba was sure of it.

Many hours passed before the samurai gained confirmation. The moon was retreating into the west when Oba saw motion on the beach. The strange figure he saw seemed unreal. At first, he thought it must be a child, such was its stature, but the proportions were off. No child had such broad shoulders and stocky build. It took a moment to realize that what he was looking at wasn't human at all, but one of the koropokguru.

The dwarf moved stealthily, but seemed clumsy beside the figures that moved alongside him. If Oba's notice hadn't been drawn to the koropokguru, he doubted he'd have seen the black-clad shapes that stalked towards the water. They, at least, were human in their dimensions, though the realization offered no comfort. Oba knew they could only be Kokuryu ninja.

Carefully, Oba squeezed himself under the edge of the fishing smack. The sound of sand shifting under his weight made him freeze. He kept his eyes on the advancing ninja, watching for the least sign that they were aware of him. Every moment, he expected one of the assassins to spot him as he crawled out from his shelter. He wanted to pass warning to Kawajiri in case the young samurai had failed to spot their enemies, but there was no way to do so without betraying their location. All he could do was wait and hope his luck held.

Oba emerged from beneath the boat and crept around behind it as the Kokuryu continued to approach. He saw now that one of the ninja was carrying a small raft. Another carried a black goat, the animal's mouth and legs securely bound with leather thongs. Between them was the koropokguru, his misshapen body swathed in the same black raiment as the ninja, except for the masking folds of the fukumen across his face. Oba saw in the ugly countenance the visage of the 'crippled crone' telling fortunes, her seeming infirmity explained by the dwarfish physiognomy. Prowling behind the others were two guards, one armed with a sword, the other with a sickle and chain.

Unable to coordinate with Kawajiri, Oba evaluated which of the enemies presented the most immediate threat. Arrayed in a loose kimono, he knew he'd be without the security of armour to defend against the vicious blades of his foes. He decided upon the ninja with the kusarigama, knowing that if the killer could befoul his sword with the chain, it would leave him easy prey to attack by the other assassins. He closed his right hand around Koumakiri, easing the uchigatana from its sheath. His left clutched at the sand. Tense seconds passed while the samurai waited for his enemies to draw closer.

The leading ninja and the dwarf passed the concealed samurai without noticing him. More wary than his companions, the swordsman caught sight of Oba. He hissed in alarm and lunged for the samurai. Oba dodged aside as the deadly ninjato slashed at him, its keen edge pitted with spots of rust to ensure even a slight cut would poison the blood. He didn't pause to engage the killer. His left hand swept forwards, casting a fistful of sand into the ninja's eyes.

Oba didn't confront the blinded enemy, but bound past him to rush the ninja with the kusarigama. He caught his enemy before he could react. Koumakiri struck the assassin's shoulder, crunching down through his black jacket. The cleaving blade bit deep into the chain armour beneath the cloth and ripped into the man's body. The ninja made a feeble cast of the kusarigama, but his throw missed Oba. Wrenching his blade free, the samurai left his enemy writhing in the sand and turned to meet his other foe.

The swordsman started towards Oba, then darted aside, the eyes above his mask glaring at Kawajiri as he erupted from beneath his shelter and charged towards the assassin. "Stop the others," he called to Oba. "I'll handle this one."

Oba felt guilty leaving Kawajiri. He knew the samurai was brave and skilled with the sword, but those attributes counted for little against enemies as treacherous as ninja. At the same time, he knew he had to stop the Kokuryu from carrying out their plot.

The other ninja and the dwarf were wading out into the surf. The assassin with the goat laid the animal on the raft. When the killer turned to stare at the pursuing samurai, he was surprised to find that she was a woman. A familiar voice snapped a command to the ninja who'd been carrying the raft. "Stop Oba! Kill him!"

Yasune Meiko! Oba knew now that she'd been disguised as the daughter of the fortune-telling crone. He'd last crossed paths with the vicious spy on Cripple Mountain, when the Kokuryu were extracting gold for the Shogun's treasury. Now he once again found himself confronted by the ruthless ninja.

The killer dispatched by Meiko drew his sword and rushed towards Oba while his comrades pushed the raft ahead of them into the waves. Oba could just make out the blackened blade of the ninjato as the assassin advanced. He held its blunted tip beneath the water. When he drew closer, he tried a variation of the ploy the samurai had used with a fistful of sand. Whipping the ninjato up suddenly, he sent a spray of saltwater into Oba's face.

The samurai was expecting such a trick, and turned the instant the killer started to move. He spun around just in time to block the attack that followed. Steel rang as Koumakiri met the assassin's blade. The ninja pressed his assault, straining against Oba's strength, trying to force his way past the samurai's guard.

Oba felt the ninja try to trip him while they struggled, but the water retarded his efforts. Suddenly, his enemy changed tactics, jumping back and ending the resistance against Koumakiri. Oba stumbled forwards. As he did, the ninja drew down his mask and spat a mouthful of ink at the samurai. This time, he wasn't able to dodge the blinding attack, and he cried out as the spittle stung his eyes.

For an instant, Oba should have been helpless, but he denied the ninja the moment his low trick had gained him. Even as he cried out in pain, the samurai threw himself forwards, plunging under the water. He sloshed his body from side to side, letting the ink wash away as he swam beneath the surface. His vision was cleared when he drove himself upwards.

The ninja was waiting for him. The assassin sprang at him, bringing his sword slashing downwards in a double-handed stroke. Alarm flashed in the enemy's eyes when he saw his mistake. Before, Oba had gripped Koumakiri in both hands. Now he held the uchigatana in only one. While underwater, he'd drawn the shorter wakizashi. It was this blade that he now plunged into the assassin's side, ripping it free with a vicious twist. The ninja sank into the waves, his face contorted in an expression of shock.

Oba turned from his vanquished foe and started back towards the raft. Meiko and the koropokguru had progressed far in the time it had taken him to overcome the rearguard. They were out near the idol now, both of them clinging to the sides of the raft as they treaded the water. Oba sheathed his swords and started swimming towards them. It was against the possibility of having to swim that he'd left his armour behind. Now he strove to gain the most from that decision.

Meiko saw the samurai striking out through the waves. She reached onto the raft and ripped away the thing binding the goat's mouth. The animal began to bleat in fright, protesting its rough treatment. "The potion," she snarled at the dwarf. The koropokguru drew a clay jar from beneath its jacket and tendered it to the ninja. She forced its contents down the goat's throat. Her companion grew agitated the more she poured.

"No!" the dwarf protested. "Too much! Too much!" His hairy hands tried to pull the jar away. Meiko didn't hesitate. She pulled back and slashed the koropokguru's throat with the edge of a shuriken. He reeled back with a bubbling cough before sinking into the deep.

KAIJU

Meiko emptied the jar and flung the vessel away. She pushed the raft out towards the open sea. She watched it as the waves carried it off. "You're too late, Oba," she declared, turning back to the samurai. "I've used more of the potion than before! Honengyo will smell it and come for his offering faster than he ever has!" Her voice dropped to a vicious laugh. "Then the poison in the koropokguru's brew will enrage the monster. He'll make straight for Lord Torogawa's army and destroy it utterly!"

The ninja swam around to the idol. She climbed up onto it, steadying herself on the slimy perch. Oba saw the bloodied shuriken clenched in her hand. "Try to reach the raft, samurai," she taunted him. "Just try!"

"You'll die, too, when the monster comes," Oba shouted at Meiko.

"There's no shame in dying for the Kokuryu as long as my mission is a success," she retorted. The shuriken flew from her hand. Oba dove under the water as the missile came towards him. The sudden attack had given him no time to prepare, no chance to charge his lungs with air, but he knew he couldn't risk surfacing while Meiko was watching for him.

Once again, Oba forced himself to ignore the demands of his burning lungs. He swam below the surface, striking out for the sunken idol. With every stroke, his body weakened, the agony in his lungs increased. But he knew that every push brought him nearer to his goal and the confrontation that was his only hope of survival.

Oba reached the far side of the rock spire. More intense than the agony of holding what little breath he had was the necessity to restrain himself, now that he could breathe again. Instead of sucking down a great gulp, he restricted himself to slight inhalations that would go unheard by the enemy crouched only a few feet above him.

Meiko continued to look for him where he'd been. She had another shuriken at the ready, poised to throw it the moment he showed himself. Warily, Oba reached up to the rock. He waited until a rolling wave drew himself higher—and then he struck!

The samurai's hand locked about the ninja's ankle. Exerting his full strength, he dragged her from her perch and sent her plunging into the water. Oba drew his wakizashi, ready to face his enemy the moment she showed herself. He paddled at the waves, ready for the least sign that might betray the ninja.

A tingling at the back of his neck made Oba swing around just in time to avoid the throwing star that sailed past his nose. Meiko had copied his own tactic, staying underwater and swimming to the other side of the idol. While he'd been searching for her, she'd regained her original position.

"There's no escape for you," Meiko spat as she drew another shuriken from her sleeve. "This is the last time you'll interfere with the Kokuryu!"

Oba saw death in the woman's hand, but before she could send the poisoned blade hurtling towards him, the sea outside the bay exploded in violence. From the depths arose a sight to stun even a ninja.

***

Honengyo! From the footprints and destruction wrought by the monster, Oba had formed a rough impression of the beast. Now that he saw it, however, he found his imaginings were sorely lacking. This could only be one of the primordial behemoths vanquished by the gods at the beginning of the world. Locked away in the deep places until the Time of Wrath should set them free again.

Oba realized he was gazing upon something beyond any demon or monster, but one of the dreaded kaiju.

The creature was gargantuan, perhaps two hundred feet tall if the water he rose from was as deep as Oba estimated. Honengyo's shape was bipedal, two enormous legs supporting his bulky body. A pair of powerful arms swung from sloping shoulders, their clawed fingers pawing at the air. A long tail, as thick around as the Ten-Thousand Year Chrysanthemum in the Emperor's garden, thrashed the water behind the colossus, churning the waves into foam. The whole of the behemoth was covered in thick grey scales like an immense lizard, gradually fading to white on its chest and belly. The head was reptilian, pulled forwards in a fanged muzzle, two yellow eyes set deep into its heavy skull.

Oba could see the raft with the goat tied to it caught in Honengyo's fangs. The monster made a lurching twist of its neck, throwing the raft forwards and then snatching it from the air. He didn't bother to chew the tiny morsel, but gulped it down whole.

Almost at once, the change could be seen in the mammoth reptile. The yellow eyes blazed with fury. Honengyo threw his head back and bellowed, the shrieking ululation ripping across the sky. The long tail slammed into the water, sending a great wave rolling towards the shore.

That wave smashed over the rocky spire. Meiko was thrown over the side, plunging into the water beside Oba. For the moment, the samurai couldn't spare any attention for the ninja. It was enough trying to maintain his own grip on the idol while the waves spilled over it. Then he felt her arm curl around his throat from behind. Viciously, she drove his head against the rock, trying to smash his skull.

Another great wave rushed over the idol as Honengyo trudged towards the shore. Oba's fingers dug at the rock, grasping at the holes left by centuries of erosion. He clung to the ancient idol, well aware that to lose his grip would see him washed out to sea and towards a watery grave.

Meiko's grip tightened, threatening to choke him. Feeling his consciousness fading, Oba twisted his head and bit down on the black-clad arm. He tasted the ninja's blood in his mouth, bubbling over his teeth. The sudden attack was enough to break her hold. As her grip loosened, another surge crashed over the rock. Meiko was swept away from the idol. Oba's last sight of her was a dark shape being washed off into the distance.

Oba knew he'd suffer the same fate if he remained where he was. Rallying his strength, fighting back both exhaustion and injury, he pulled himself up onto the spire of rock. His hands found holds in the pitted surface, securing his place as more waves crashed against the sunken idol. Each successive surge was weaker than the one before. The reason was obvious enough. Honengyo was moving away. Lumbering towards the shore.

From the rock, Oba could only watch as the kaiju approached Lord Torogawa's army. The first who stood in the behemoth's path were the warships. Each atakebune raised anchor and rowed itself into position. On the decks, scores of bowmen took aim, their arrows soaked in pitch. Faintly, Oba could hear the shouted command. "Loose!"

Flaming arrows sailed across the water, a burning volley that clattered against Honengyo's scales. The monster paused in his advance, lowering his head to peer down at the warships. A second volley peppered his face and chest, the blazing arrows extinguishing themselves with a fiery hiss as they fell into the water. The kaiju drew back and emitted a thunderous roar at his antagonists.

A third desperate volley was loosed against Honengyo, but with as little result as the others. The kaiju rushed at the nearest atakebune. His clawed hand slammed down against the deck, crushing archers and shattering timbers. The other hand came around and snapped the mainmast, leaving it to crash into the sea. Frantic bowmen continued to shoot at the monster while sailors abandoned their vessel and dove into the turbulent sea.

Honengyo roared once more and pressed down on the stricken ship. The atakebune was plunged under the surface. As water rushed into the holds, it lost its buoyancy and hurtled to the bottom, sucking down with it those who'd remained aboard.

The other warships tried to turn away and escape the fate of their comrade. The manoeuvre drew the kaiju's attention. Roaring, Honengyo seized one of the fleeing vessels. Even as men dove into the sea, the monster pulled at the atakebune. The sound of groaning timbers rang out as the tortured ship tried to resist the tremendous pressure being exerted upon it. At last, the behemoth's primal strength prevailed. The superstructure cracked apart as Honengyo ripped the warship in half. The segments bobbed in the waves as they drifted away from each other.

The last atakebune took on sail, trying to retreat from the bay. Honengyo's long tail rose from the sea and slammed into the warship. The impact pulverized every man on the deck and snapped the masts as though they were twigs. Stricken a mortal blow, most of its soldiers and crew dead, the mangled atakebune floated listlessly in the spot where it had been struck.

Honengyo turned from the demolished warships and continued to plod his way towards the village. Samurai, some distance up the beach, raised their bows and loosed. Their burning arrows weren't intended for the kaiju but for the oil-soaked boats arrayed along the shoreline. Oba thought of Kawajiri when they ignited and wondered if his friend had been able to get away, if he'd won his fight with the ninja. Certainly, it was a grim image to think of his body lying there being consigned to the snarling flames.

The kaiju paused when the beach before him erupted into a wall of fire. His eyes glared furiously at the barrier. A snarl of anger rumbled from his throat. Honengyo lashed his tail in the waves, throwing up debris from the bottom.

Any hope that the fire would hold the beast back vanished when Honengyo charged up from the surf. He plunged through the flames, their burning kiss unable to penetrate his scaly hide. The monster kicked burning boats into the village as he smashed through them, scattering the ronin hidden among the buildings.

Samurai officers called for a different kind of fire as they directed ranks of ashigaru gunmen to shoot the hulking reptile. Hundreds of matchlocks crackled as they peppered Honengyo with bullets. The behemoth was startled by the stinging barrage. The guns fared better than the bows, leaving shallow divots in the thick hide. But it wasn't enough to turn back the beast. Honengyo rounded on the ashigaru and charged their position. Soldiers were trampled under the kaiju's feet, obliterated in the blink of an eye.

Before the massacre could be complete, the catapults on the heights took action. Their arms sprang forwards and hurled massive boulders down upon Honengyo. The first stone startled the monster, slamming into the ground a few yards away and spraying him with sand. The second was more true in its aim, striking the monster in the side. The impact knocked him down. A third boulder smacked into the kaiju as he tried to rise. The behemoth slumped back against the earth, stunned by the impact.

Oba could hear the fierce war cries as a troop of cavalry galloped towards the stricken monster. Back-banners bearing the mon of Clan Hoshin snapped in the wind as a hundred samurai charged Honengyo. Each warrior held a long spear with a vicious barbed head, a design called a 'dragon cutter', and used by the conquerors of Po against the giant lizards that infested the islands. The riders kicked their horses, forcing the animals past the repugnance the kaiju's scent provoked in them. Closing upon Honengyo, they stabbed at the beast. Many spears broke against the thick scales, but others pierced the monster's hide, drawing blood from the flesh beneath.

The attack roused Honengyo from his stupor. His wrathful roar panicked the horses, breaking the tenuous discipline their riders had maintained. Samurai were thrown onto the sand as their steeds bucked and bolted in every direction. Some warriors clung to the necks of their mounts, desperately trying to stay in the saddle.

Honengyo snatched at the fleeing horses, grabbing up several in his claws. He rose to his feet, his side festooned with dozens of spears. The kaiju glared at the catapults as their operators hurried to rearm the weapons. With another bellow of anger, he threw the captives caught in his claws at the siege weapons. Screaming horses and wailing men slammed against two of the catapults. The brutal impact smashed their frames and collapsed them. Crewmen cried out as dislodged boulders and broken timbers crashed down on them. The survivors fled from the position, running off into the hills.

A triumphant growl rumbled through Honengyo's fang-filled maw. The huge reptile lumbered onwards, stomping on the reeling samurai in his path. His eyes narrowed with suspicion when he saw the ballistae ahead of him.

Oba held his breath, anticipating this phase of the conflict. The gigantic crossbows were the last weapon in Lord Torogawa's arsenal. If the dragon cutter spears had been able to pierce Honengyo's hide, then there was every reason to expect those of the ballistae to perform even better. The question that troubled him was whether it would be enough.

The kaiju paused a moment, seeming to consider the same question. Honengyo raked one of his claws down his side, tearing loose the spears embedded in his flesh. Another shrieking roar shook Kuroyama as the reptilian colossus stormed towards the men who dared to oppose him.

Oba could see Lord Torogawa standing before the ballistae. In the daimyo's hand was his war fan. He used this to signal the crews, snapping it closed as they launched their attack. Twenty feet long, the huge arrows were sent hurtling across the beach, their steel heads gleaming in the moonlight.

Honengyo snarled in pain as one of the giant arrows pierced his leg. A second struck his belly, the white scales turning black as the reptile's blood seeped out from its wound. The beast bent down as he reacted to the attack, and the third shot slammed into his chest. Even out on the rock, Oba could hear the meaty impact of each hit. Honengyo's pained howls echoed into the night. The kaiju slumped down onto his knees, his body shuddering from agony pulsing through it.

Cheers rose from the ballistae crews and those warriors who'd yet to flee the battlefield. Lord Torogawa appeared sombre, watching the stricken beast. He unfolded his fan, signalling for the weapons to be reloaded. Stirred from their exhilaration, the soldiers hurried to crank the windlasses and rearm the ballistae.

Honengyo roared at his enemies and staggered back to his feet. Blood streamed from his wounds, but now the kaiju appeared oblivious to either hurt or pain. He charged towards the ballistae, his claws raised as though eager to rend the tormenting machines between them.

A group of Lord Torogawa's retainers hurried the daimyo away. The crews of the ballistae held their ground. One managed to crank off a shot as Honengyo rushed them. At such range, the arrow ripped clean through the reptile's leg. The kaiju staggered, but his rage was undiminished. He crouched before the ballistae and shattered them beneath his clawing hands. He threw handfuls of debris at fleeing soldiers, smashing their bodies as they tried to escape.

Honengyo stood amid the carnage, his long tail swatting the tents and pavilions lining the beach. His eyes focused upon Kuroyama. He threw back his head and screeched wrathfully. Then, limping on his injured leg, the monster attacked the village. Houses that had withstood typhoon and earthquake crumbled under his assault. Warriors sheltering in the structures were massacred as the kaiju expended his rage. Pounding feet flattened entire buildings, obliterating the men inside them. Scaly hands ripped into huts and threw the rubble across the countryside. The monster's tail battered entire streets, whipping through them like an avalanche.

When Honengyo turned from Kuroyama, only death remained there. The kaiju stared at the destruction as though pleased by what he'd done. His clawed hands reached to the ballista arrow in his belly and wrenched it free, casting it aside as though no more than a nuisance. As the monster lumbered back into the sea, he pulled out the other arrows and dropped them in the surf.

Oba's last view of Honengyo was when the kaiju reached the deep water outside the bay. The reptile drew back and voiced one final, triumphant roar before submerging. Returning back to the depths from which he'd been called.

***

It was some hours before Oba felt strong enough to manage the swim back to shore. With every stroke, he neared the horrible devastation wrought by Honengyo on Lord Torogawa's army. Parts of the beach were black with crows as the scavengers picked at the carcasses of men and horses. Here and there, he could see people moving through the havoc, searching for the wounded or trying to find the bodies of the noble dead.

He made landfall very near where he'd first fought the Kokuryu the night before. The sands were black with soot from the boats, but of the ships themselves there remained only charred outlines. Oba wondered again about how Kawajiri had fared in all that had happened.

While his thoughts were on his friend, the samurai was surprised to see his armour tied in a bundle and lying on the beach. Oba walked towards it, perplexed by how it had gotten there and who had left it.

That mystery ended when Kawajiri emerged from behind a pile of debris. The samurai's kimono was bloodied and he had a gash across his scalp, but from the way he moved, Oba judged that his friend had suffered less injury than himself during the night.

"You beat the ninja, then," Oba congratulated Kawajiri.

"I killed him," Kawajiri corrected him. There was gravity in his voice, grimness on his features. "We only killed them. Their mission was a success."

"We learned what they were doing. Lord Torogawa can take precautions to keep it from happening again." Oba pointed out to the sunken idol. "Tear those things down. Then they won't know where to go to call Honengyo again."

Kawajiri shook his head. "It doesn't matter." He waved his hand at the destruction scattered along the shore. "They accomplished what they set out to do. The pride of Clan Hoshin has been humbled. Lord Torogawa will atone for what has happened here."

Oba bowed his head. He knew what atonement meant. For such a failure, the daimyo would perform seppuku as the only way to regain his honour.

"Clan Hoshin has been humbled," Kawajiri said, bitterness in his voice. "Lord Torogawa will die." He clenched his fists. "And Chamberlain Hidetoro will be the new daimyo."

Oba blinked in disbelief. "Hidetoro? How do you know this?"

"Because that was what the Kokuryu were sent to accomplish," Kawajiri said. "When Lord Torogawa allowed you to leave Nokoshima, Chamberlain Hidetoro informed the Shogun. Yoshinaga considered it to be an act of disloyalty and so arranged all of this to punish both Clan Hoshin and Lord Torogawa." Kawajiri's hand closed about the grip of his sword. "As for how I know this, Hidetoro told me after Honengyo returned to the sea." Slowly, he drew his katana from its sheath. "I was to wait here, to see if you had survived. If so, he ordered me to kill you."

Oba studied his friend, evaluating the samurai's condition and comparing it to his own. Whatever gap there was between their relative skills was more than balanced by his own fatigue. More, Kawajiri wasn't a loathsome ninja. Oba couldn't countenance employing trickery against him. Their contest would have to be an honest fight.

"I regret it had to be this way," Oba said as he drew Koumakiri. He held the sword before him. "I ask only that, if you win, you cast my sword into the sea. Take my head to Hidetoro as a prize, but not my sword."

Kawajiri was silent a moment, his eyes staring at the ground. "I can promise you nothing," he said. "Fight well if you would preserve the legacy of your clan."

With a shout, the young samurai sprang at Oba. The katana flashed downwards in a vicious sweep.

Oba side-stepped the attack and retaliated in kind. The heavy uchigatana crunched into Kawajiri's ribs. He sagged against the biting steel, his katana falling into the sand.

"You let me strike you," Oba gasped. He'd seen Kawajri fight before. He knew his friend knew better than to leave himself exposed in such a manner. He rushed to the wounded samurai and lowered him to the ground.

"It is better... to die... than to owe... one's loyalty... to a traitor," Kawajiri coughed as blood bubbled into his mouth. He grasped Oba's arm. "Thank... you... for saving me... from such... dishonour." The samurai continued to look up at him, but there was no vitality left in his eyes.

Oba stood over his dead friend. When Clan Hoshin's retainers found the body, they'd believe Kawajiri had died trying to fulfil his duty. They'd never know he'd died to preserve his honour.

Sheathing Koumakiri, Oba turned and faced the sea. "If you ever rise again from the depths, Honengyo, you'll find a daimyo in Nokoshima worthy of your wrath."

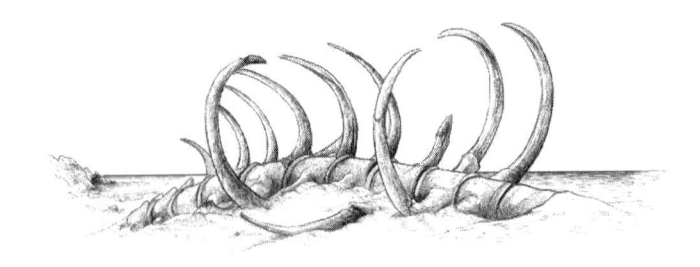

The Whaler

Justin Fillmore

"The *Agnor Rose* was a poorly-built schooner from the island called Britannia, many seas up from here." The frail old man pointed his finger to the night sky. "The craft was owned by Samuel Enderby & Sons, and leased to the South Sea Company, which the rulers of Britannia created for the purposes of killing //'áú. But you need not worry about those names."

The old man's lean, muscular body was flickering in the firelight. He dug his toes into the warm sand. "The bones you see along this coast tell you all you need to know about Britannia's brutality. And if you go back down to the Kuiseb mouth, where we come from, and follow the river inland, you will find the people bones left behind by other companies of Britannia."

He spat and muttered a curse to himself. The wind carried the whispered words towards the sea. He stood gingerly, revealing his traditional buckskin loincloth and crooked frame. Old age prevented him from standing totally erect. He held a staff in one hand, fashioned from one of the many whale bones that rested in the sand around him. He looked around and motioned with his staff. A small necklace decorated with seal teeth clattered around his neck. "They call this coast of skeletons the Gates of Hell, because the cruel Atlantic Sea and the barren Namib Desert are stitched together by the bones of the dead." An uncomfortable silence fell on the little bodies of the children huddled around the fire. "Well, if this is where they enter hell, let us welcome them with open arms." He grinned at the petrified young faces looking up at him.

"Grandfather…" A girl with bushy hair waved her hand.

"Yes, my love."

"What is a 'schooner'?"

"Ah, right you are, little one. Forgive me. Old men get side-tracked from time to time. And usually they are left confused by their own wonderings." He tapped his fingers on his coarse grey hair. He slid them down to his chin and patted his dry lips. "Back to my story." The children around the fire relaxed their bodies, some reclining, and some choosing to lie on their backs.

"A schooner is a type of sea ship, you see. They are long crafts made out of the big trees you find far from here. These trees can grow to become the size of the leviathan." The old man stretched his arms far apart as he spoke. "They kill these trees, too, and fashion long planks that are burnt, bent, and nailed into place. It looks like this."

The old man cupped his hands together and floated them above the fire. His hands formed the shape of a hull. "Planks cover the top, here." He grabbed the little girl's hand and placed it flat over the top of his hands. "Two tall dead trees are planted on the flat surface, here and here." He pressed his index finger into the little girl's hand, once aft to the stern, and once forward the bow. "The men hang big cloths from these two trees.

The cloths catch the wind and use him to send the ship forward." He blew a long, steady breath and sent his cupped hands snaking forward. The children were mesmerised.

"Now, a schooner is the smallest of the whalers, you understand. You might see her as big as the buck. But there are other ships that make her look small, like she was standing next to a giraffe. Because she is the smallest of the whalers, she is fast, and she is cheap to supply and crew. But she can only carry two whaleboats. The whaleboats are made like her, but smaller, with no trees planted on top. They are like her two children that she carries in each arm. But when she puts them down into the water, they are deadly. It is them that do the killing."

"Excuse me, Grandfather." Another child, this time a young boy, interrupted. He sat up from the sand, leaving a small, prone dent behind him. "I want to hear about our !Hõá. Our man. You said the story was about him, not ships."

The old man chuckled. "You little geckos are too clever for me. Always one step ahead." He took his seat on the old tree stump that connected the circle of children around the fire pit and placed his staff down in the sand beside him, getting comfortable. "Our !Hõá was part of the crew aboard the *Agnor Rose*. He was but one small part of the ant's nest on the ship. And just like the ant's nest, there is always activity. No one can afford to rest too long, otherwise the ship will either sink, or the men will return to shore with empty pockets— equally terrible fates." He shifted his bony buttocks on the stump.

"The *Agnor Rose* had one master. Captain John Hanlon. He was a good man, but at the end of the day, he was ruled by money. It's funny to think of it, a man ruled by something he imagines to be real." A smile appeared on the old man's face. "There was a second in command, the ship's first mate, Mr Grosvenor. Not only did he have authority on deck, but he would take the small whaleboats out on the water, and there he would transform into the most efficient killer since the scorpion. He would use the harpoon, a cold-hard spindle, and wield it like the scorpion's tail. It became one with his arm as he thrust it into the back of the //'áú." The old man had picked up his staff again, this time motioning it like a harpoon towards the child closest to him. The child flinched and the rest of them grimaced.

"Evil," said the flinching child.

"Yes, my love. But it is not the act of killing that is evil—it is the method and the treatment of the victim. That is true evil. You and I might kill the buck, but we kill him quickly, taking his pain away. He does not suffer. We thank him for his life and we eat what we can. We thank his family, and we use his skin to keep ours warm. And when one of us dies, we give thanks, and we offer the body to the soil. It nourishes the earth and makes it fertile for the buck to feed. This is harmony. This is respect."

The old man clicked his tongue. "You see, I am wandering off on my own path again." The children laughed. "Back to our man."

"Like us, our man travelled from the Kuiseb mouth, up the Skeleton Coast, but he did not stop here." He prodded his finger into the sand. "He was young and strong, so he walked on and on, into the tribes far north. These tribes speak many different languages, and they have skin even darker than our own. It was among these tribes that our man learnt to speak the language of Britannia. This allowed him to use his skills aboard the evil ships that kill, maim, and waste the //'áú.

A skinny girl with black plaited hair interrupted this time. "But Grandfather, why would our man join the evil killing ships?"

The old man shook his head. "Too, too, too clever. You children think a lot. It is good to question like this." He motioned to the skinny girl. Will you please hand me that satchel over there?" She did as he asked and handed him a leather carrier with ends that could be tied around the waist. "Go sit down again, my child. I must continue my tale." He reached into the satchel and drew out two items of clothing. He stood awkwardly and drew leather pants up over his legs, remaining topless. "Pants, fashioned from the black rhino himself. Thick enough to repel an arrow, and light enough to be worn thus." He waved his hands alongside his clothed legs. He bent down and drew the second item on, over his neck. "A jacket, with the exterior fashioned from the same rhino. The best part is the interior pelt, taken from the lion and stitched together. This gives you a jacket that is impenetrable, and as warm as your mother's bosom." The old man danced about, modelling his new look. The children cackled with laughter and rolled around in the sand, clutching their stomachs and smacking their legs.

"Alright, alright. Settle down. Do you geckos want to hear about our !Hõá or not?"

"We do, grandfather."

"Please, grandfather, don't stop. We'll listen."

"Please."

The children quietened down and assumed their previous positions.

"Only because you begged me. I don't take kindly to being mocked." He sat on the tree stump again and stoked the coals. He added a few more logs and waited for them to crackle. The fire sent sparks and flames into the evening air. The stars above seemed brighter now.

"Our man's name is Xa-a-tin, but the men of Britannia called him Xa. And to continue Xa's story, I must become him. I am no longer your grandfather—I am Xa." The old man pulled his jacket closed and narrowed his eyes, trying to mimic a much younger man. He cleared his throat.

***

Xa had been walking throughout the night. He was determined to reach the city before the next lot of whalers left port. His calf muscles burned from overuse, and sweat droplets covered his forehead. The droplets gleamed in the moonlight.

Xa was carrying very few possessions. His coin purse held enough for one drink, and he was out of food. His traditional bow hung over his right shoulder. His bone-tipped arrows were concealed in a cylindrical leather pouch that hung on his back, held in position with two thin straps, one over each shoulder. He wore nothing but his loin cloth. His last two possessions were a pair of pants and matching jacket, fashioned from treated animal hides. Xa's feet ached. They had become as leathery as his loin cloth, and they were the same colour as the dirt road.

The port at Namibe was held by the Portuguese. But they had a treaty in place that allowed for ships from Britain to trade produce, livestock, and slaves. Whalers of the South Sea Company used it as a station to resupply along the coast of Africa, especially on voyages that went further south to the Antarctic.

Xa passed through the poorer communities of the city, south of the harbour. Crude shanties, and huts made from wood and mud, were scattered about. Some of the locals grew maize and potatoes for subsistence. The wealthier among them kept livestock as well. Xa could hear the sound of his own breathing as he walked through the ramshackle villages. His feet scuffled in the dirt, crunching the gravel as he went. The sound became rhythmic and comforting.

As he neared the port, the buildings grew in stature and prestige. He marvelled at the architecture and sheer man-power required to accomplish such grandeur. It impressed him every time he entered the city. This must have been his ninth or tenth time in Namibe. He couldn't quite recall. Xa walked with his eyes fixed upward at the brick marvels. He did not enjoy the stench of the city. Man and beast lived too close for comfort, sharing in each other's waste. He headed straight for the port, where the smells were more oceanic. The filth was not much better, however. He needed to join a whaling crew that was headed south at sunrise.

The night-shift harbourmaster greeted him as he came alongside the docked ships.

"Xa-a-tin, back for another season, you old sea dog?"

Xa nodded. "You know me, Felix. I work as I have need."

"Is that a joke, Xa?" The African with big white teeth smacked his own leg. "You haven't stopped working! Every time that I see you take a whaler south, I go to sleep. Then when I wake up, you are back here. 'Like a man possessed,' as my mother says."

"Your mother is the best. I would know."

"Hey, you piece of dog shit. Watch it!" The African pointed his finger sternly. Xa stared back at him. The two erupted into laughter, and Xa walked off. Someone shouted from the ship nearby, rebuking the noise. Some ships had lights flickering on deck. Some weren't lit at all. They swayed gently, mirroring the weather conditions. Xa took a seat on the boardwalk. The nearby jetties sprawled like wooden fingers into the water at equal intervals. Xa made himself comfortable, sitting with his legs crossed. He came to accept hunger as a natural part of life, despite his protesting stomach. He would eat after he procured a job.

The sun rose a few hours later. Xa had nodded off here and there, but the blinding light warmed his body and forced his eyelids open. He got to his feet with a struggle. His muscles were stiff from last night's walking. Hunger clawed at his insides again. He moved towards the nearest ship. The first white man that he approached greeted him with insults and told him to get lost. The second man happened to be Mr Grosvenor.

Eaves Grosvenor was three heads taller than Xa. He had broad shoulders, and his trousers were tight around his chiselled legs. He wore a tricorne at all times. The crew reasoned that it was because he was an ex-navy man. Some claimed that it was because he was simple and thought his position warranted it. Regardless, his face was sunburnt beneath the hat. His previously white shirt hung loose on his torso, yet the sleeves were rolled tightly at the elbows. A blurry ship's anchor was tattooed on his left forearm, and a harpoon was tattooed on his right.

The arm with the harpoon held Xa firmly by the shoulder now, half-dragging him up the gangplank that joined the ship to the jetty. Xa felt like he could be crushed by this man like a soft !Nara melon. The British called them butternuts. Xa never understood the term.

"Cappin'! Cappin'! Go' a man here what wants a job." Mr Grosvenor held his left hand at the side of his mouth to project his voice. A regal-looking man appeared on the upper deck and walked down the stairs.

"*Who*, Mr Grosvenor. You have a man *who* would like a job."

The first mate screwed up his face as he tried to soak in the finer details of the English language. "Yeah, like I said Cappin'. Go' a man here who wants him a job."

The captain sighed. "The King can't say I didn't try with you lot." He looked around with his hands held together behind his back.

"You have an appointment with the King, sir?"

"No, Eaves, I don't. It's a turn of phrase. Never you mind."

The helmsman peered over the edge of the banister on the upper deck. He wanted a look at the job-seeker, and the conversation drew him in. The captain extended his hand to Xa. Mr Grosvenor, who was still clutching Xa, finally let go. Xa rotated his shoulder a few times and shook the captain's hand. He had learnt this custom long ago.

"Captain John Hanlon, at your service." The regal man tipped his hat. His ponytail hung between his shoulder blades. He wore a smart blue coat with gold buttons, black pants, and leather boots. The gold lining on his pants, coat, and hat matched. It glowed in the morning light, outlining his slender body. "What can you do, old boy?"

"Greetings. I am Xa-a-tin. Most call me Xa. Well, captain, I do everything, except the killing." Xa nodded with certainty.

Mr Grosvenor found that funny. "Don't worry boy, I'll be doing the killing around here."

"What do you mean, Xa?" The captain wanted clarity.

"I can cook, clean, dress wounds, and I am familiar with all manner of flensing, cutting-in, and boiling down." The captain could see that it was not Xa's first time on a whaler. He noticed Xa pointing to the bricked tryworks and the fifteen-foot cutting spades. "I was taught to use the try pots a few trips ago. I can keep the fires going, and cut the blubber into 'bible leaves,' too. This is where I am best, with the cutting spade. My people use spears like it." Xa performed the movements as he spoke. "Put it in, between the eye and fin, and cut." He thrust his arms forward. "I can also swim with the sharks to mount the body with the hook." Xa bent his fingers like a hook. "Draw him up"—he pulled on imaginary chains—"and take the blanket-pieces. Just like peeling a melon with a stone."

Captain Hanlon and Mr Grosvenor were suitably impressed.

"I work hard." Xa nodded again. "And if I don't, you have my permission to throw me overboard." The three men laughed together.

"Give me a moment, Mr Xa. I must convene with my number two." The captain placed a delicate hand on Mr Grosvenor's shoulder and took him aside. Xa could hear their muffled voices, but he couldn't make out the words.

"What say you, Eaves?"

"I like the son-of-a-bitch already, Cappin'. Christ, his eyes lit up like stars when he described the work. And the blighter has a joke in him, too. What more do you want in crew member?" He looked at Xa over his shoulder. "We can use all the help we can get."

"Yes, I like him, too. Experienced. And you're right about the eyes—uncanny. What's more, these African chaps do fine work for little recompense. The Company can't have any complaints. Right, that's that." Captain Hanlon pat the larger man on his chest as he walked over to Xa. "Welcome aboard, sailor." The captain saluted Xa. "As I'm sure you're aware, 'we work like horses and live like pigs.'" He turned to his first mate.

"Mr Grosvenor?"

"Cappin'?"

"Have the surgeon look him over. We can't have him bring any disease aboard. Once he's given the 'all-clear,' take Mr Xa to the cook and get him a warm meal and a stiff drink."

"Right you ar' sir."

"And Eaves…"

"Yes, Cappin'?"

"For Christ's sake, get the man some deck shoes."

Captain Hanlon ascended the wooden staircase to the bridge.

***

The *Agnor Rose* set sail for the Cape of Good Hope. She would hunt southern right and humpback along the way. The journey from The Port of Namibe to the Port of Cape Town would only take a competent crew five days, given favourable conditions. Captain Hanlon set that number at a conservative ten days, assuming there would be the usual impediments along the way. He knew the Skeleton Coast was treacherous, but it was also prime whaling territory. He gave his crew another ten days for hunting on top of that. They would be just shy of three weeks at sea.

The crow's nest had only spotted one pod of Humpback in five days, and they had lost it all too quickly. Contrary to popular belief, whale hunting was slow and tedious. The tedium was interspersed with a brief but thrilling chase, and if you were lucky, a kill. Days of hard labour followed that, and then it was back to boredom.

On the sixth day, the crow's nest spotted a pod of twelve southern right whales. That meant feeding was good for the leviathans. The *Agnor Rose* chased them as best she could, with Captain Hanlon barking orders at the helmsman on the bridge. His orders were separated by intervals where he would lift his spyglass to his right eye, holding it with both hands. When he did this, he muttered calculations to himself. That was followed by the next order, and so on, until he felt ready.

Captain Hanlon lowered his spyglass for the last time and walked forward to the banister of the upper deck. The first mate was on the deck below. "Mr Grosvenor, lower the boats!"

"Aye Cappin'." The first mate repeated the order with gusto to the second mate. "Mr Turnbull, lower the boats!"

"Aye, Mr Grosvenor. You heard him, chaps. Get it done."

Mr Grosvenor, Mr Turnbull, and four others boarded the whaleboat that was lowered from the davit, port side. The boat was pointed at both ends and painted a bright red. This made it easier for the mother ship to spot. Mr Turnbull took his position on the narrow piece of wood at the stern. As the boatheader, he held the steering oar and commanded the boat. Mr Grosvenor took his position at the bow oar. He was the chief harpooneer. The other four men rowed the comically long oars. Mr Turnbull set them off in the direction of the pod. "Fast and steady, chaps. Let's get us a beasty."

Several hours later, the crow's nest spotted the two whaleboats in the distance. Mr Turnbull had his boat headed in the direction of the *Agnor Rose*. And they had a southern right in tow. The oarsmen were tired and their hands throbbed. Mr Grosvenor looked doubly fatigued. He sat at the front of the boat, legs dangling over the edge. His hands clasped a barbless blade that rested over his knees like a Spanish guitar. It was bloody from the kill. A lit cigar dangled from the corner of his mouth, and his tricorne was at a downward angle on his head. His clothes were soaked through with blood and salt water. His muscular body was still.

The second whaleboat that had launched with Mr Turnbull's played a supporting role. They were rowing slightly behind the other boat. Their 900-foot hemp line was also fastened to the hole in the whale's tail where the fluke spade had gouged out the flesh. The two whaleboats dragged the leviathan tail first. Sea birds were circling in the sky above, which meant that sharks would be circling in the ocean below.

Xa watched the boats as they dragged the corpse to starboard, coming from the stern of the *Agnor Rose*. The beast's head was at the stern when it was fastened to the mother ship. A hole was dug through its head and a wooden beam was sent through the fleshy tunnel. Chains were secured to the beam and cutting-in commenced. Xa was given the inglorious task of entering the bloody, shark-infested water in order to mount the whale and fix the hook to the incision made by the boatswain, Mr Cockburn. Mr Cockburn took charge of the blubber removal and barrelling process.

Once Xa's task was complete, he braved the ocean again and climbed the rigging onto the deck. He helped Mr Cockburn make a few more accurate incisions as the hook was drawn up into the rigging. Blanket-pieces were severed from the carcass and cut into 'bible leaves' for the trying-out process.

Xa assisted with the lighting of the fires beneath the two iron try pots. The blubber was then boiled in the pots, and the subsequent oil stored in barrels. The stench of burning fat was inescapable. The smoke clung to hair, clothing, and the very air itself. The oil seemed to soak through every corner of the ship. The crew lived and breathed oil, day and night. When cutting-in had all but sapped the lifeblood from every member of the crew, the whale was decapitated by the captain and relieved of its baleen. The final task was the scouring of the deck, tools, and sailors.

Xa seemed to have boundless strength. He cleaned as though it was his only purpose in life. His shipmates commented on his stamina and they, too, witnessed the unnatural brightness in his eyes. The captain congratulated him for his efforts.

***

Three days passed with little action. Regardless, there was a mammoth amount of work required to keep a schooner sailing towards the horizon. But the tasks were repetitive and far from glamorous. Xa was treated well by the crew of the *Agnor Rose* after his showing with the southern right. The menial tasks were given to more unskilled men. That was when Xa lost favour with the only other African man employed by Captain John Hanlon.

Bakari of Congo spent the bulk of his days at sea below deck. He was treated as an unskilled labourer, and his tasks fit that station. He despised Xa for being elevated—but there was more to his disdain.

"Cooky, you see this man, Xa." Bakari's tar-black skin was glistening with sweat as he mopped the crew's mess. His arms were as thick as tree trunks. He wore a loose-fitting shirt with a tiny brocade waistcoat that pinned it into place on his chest. His oversized pants were held up with a piece of hemp rope, fastened at his belly. The legs of the pants were always rolled up to his knees to prevent them from getting wet, and his leather sandals had seen better days.

The cook grunted a sound that meant 'yes.'

"Cooky, he has bad eyes." Bakari paused and leaned on his mop. He removed a small handkerchief from the inner pocket of his elegant waistcoat and wiped his bald head. "My grandmutha', she is a healer back home. She taught me about the dark magic. You can know it by the eyes." Bakari extended his pinky and fore finger on his right hand, aiming them at his eyes, and then at the cook's.

The cook rolled his eyes and wiped his hands on his apron.

"Cooky, you white men don' believe it to be. But I tell you, Africa is ruled by the shaman." Bakari folded the handkerchief delicately, placing it back into the inner pocket of his waistcoat. He dipped the mop into the piggin and sloshed it around. Bakari slapped the soapy mop onto the floor of the crew's mess and kicked the piggin forward, resuming his work.

The cook shook his head.

"You can shake your head, Cooky. Shake. That won't help you when *Cassimbo* comes."

The cook was intrigued. He lowered his knife from chopping onions and wiped his eyes with the back of his forearm. "And what is 'Cassimbo' supposed to be? A spooky ghost?"

Bakari looked back over his shoulder at the cook. "No, Cooky. 'Cassimbo' is the smoke that comes over the sea. It covers everything. You can't escape it. It traps ships along the coast and sends them into the Gates of Hell."

The cook had heard the locals at the Port of Namibe talking about this. Captain Hanlon had assured the crew that it was a natural phenomenon entirely. The upsurge of the cold Benguela current along the Skeleton Coast, also known as the Gates of Hell, gave rise to a thick ocean fog that seemed to last for months at sea. This was because the warm wind of the Namib Desert blew from land to sea. The desert coast was harsh and unforgiving, and saw next to no rain annually. Nobody dared live there, and nobody dared wash up there, either. Death would greet both unfortunate parties.

The cook picked up his knife and pointed it at Bakari. "You people need religion, mate. It'll save you from all this foolish nonsense." The cook lifted the gold crucifix that hung around his neck and kissed it. "God is more reliable than make-believe tales."

Bakari threw his head back and laughed hysterically at that.

***

On deck, Captain Hanlon and Mr Grosvenor had assembled the crew amidships, including the lonely soul stationed in the crow's nest. The sky was greying overhead, and the wind was making its presence known. The fore-and-aft rigged sails whipped and snapped. Deafening whistles rushed around the booms that were used for spreading and manoeuvring the sails.

"Men, a storm is upon us." Captain Hanlon surveyed the sky with his hands clasped behind his back. His hat was tucked under his left arm, and his ponytail lashed him on the back as the wind blew it. "Mr Turnbull, secure the rigging."

"Aye, captain."

"Mr Cockburn, secure the tools and keep my tryworks dry, for God's sake. I still aim to hunt leviathans hereafter."

"Aye, sir."

"Deckhands, batten down the hatches. This one's going to be a bit of a bastard. But the trick is to keep my *Agnor Rose* moving." He stroked the mast like petting a lover. "We will avoid the coast at all costs. Skip to it, you beautiful blighters!" A touch of authority, a dash of control and an underhanded insult—that's how a good captain maintained morale in a difficult situation, and Captain Hanlon was pleased with his efforts.

"Mr Grosvenor, with me on the bridge. The helmsman might need your steady hands to assist with the wheel."

"Aye, Cappin'."

Back below deck, Bakari had finished scouring the mess. The cook sent him to the hold to secure the provisions. "Men need to eat, and men need to drink at sea," he told Bakari. "Bugger the storm. Our bellies will keep us alive." He patted his own.

Bakari braced himself between the doorposts of the hold as the ship began to sway. He imagined the size of the swell and shuddered. Nets hung from the ceiling with provisions stored therein. Bakari tugged on them to make sure that they would remain fastened. One came loose, spilling biscuits onto the deck. Bakari swore in his native tongue. He lowered himself onto his haunches so that he would be able to sway with the ship as he returned the biscuits to their packaging. Once he had the net secured, he ducked under it and moved to check on the water casks at the back of the hold. As he stood upright, he got the fright of his life. He pinned his back against the sidewall, palms spread flat against the wood. He shook uncontrollably and let out a whisper. "Ancestors, save me."

There, in the shadows of the hold, sat Xa-a-tin. His legs were crossed and he wore only his loincloth. A circle of coarse salt surrounded him. In his lap rested a traditional, wooden smoking pipe. It was about a foot long, carved from a solid log. One end was crooked and bored out. It appeared to be stuffed with some sort of herb. The embers glowed and smoke rose from it, scenting the air.

A line had been drawn from Xa's salt circle. It ran into a smaller salt circle in front of his. Within the smaller circle was a single lit candle and a child-like charcoal drawing of a strange animal. It had the head of a snake, the body of a fish, and the feet of a lizard. Bakari looked from Xa to the drawing, and back to Xa again. Xa's arms rested on his knees and his eyes shone like stars. It looked as though his eyeballs had been replaced with pure light. He seemed to stare right through Bakari's trembling body. What disturbed Bakari most of all were the eyes of the charcoal drawing. The creature's eyes were burning holes into the deck. They shone magnificently, just like Xa's.

Xa heard Bakari's cries in the distance, as though they came from underwater. His eyes dimmed as his awareness re-entered the hold. He tilted his head as he looked at Bakari. Xa's face was deadpan. "Brother, I have not come for you. Say no word of this to the crew and you will live."

Bakari's mind whirled. He was being offered a deal by the devil. He knew that. Save himself, or save the crew. He could not do both. "Ancestors, receive me." He turned and dashed out of the hold. He leapt up the stairs, three at a time, towards the main deck. He was shouting as loud as he could, but the wind muted his cries.

***

The fog had engulfed the *Agnor Rose* completely. Captain Hanlon stood on the bridge. He had traded his spyglass for his compass. The ship was pitching and heaving now. She was taking on more water than she could handle. Mr Grosvenor held the ship's wheel tightly as the wind tore at his clothes. His tricorne was lost at sea. The helmsman was hanging onto the wheel as well. The two men fought with all their strength to keep the ship headed as the captain ordered.

"For Christ's sake, Eaves, keep my bloody ship pointed towards the waves." Captain Hanlon had one arm behind his back and the other pointed towards the oncoming swell. His hat was tucked into his jacket. "If you allow us to be turned in the reach, we will roll. I guarantee you that."

"Aye, Cappin'. Trying my goddamn best."

Captain Hanlon leaned closer to Mr Grosvenor so that he would not need to shout. He spoke into his first mate's ear. "I haven't seen your man, Xa, running around like us cursed dogs."

"Oh, so now he's my man, is he?"

"Touché, Eaves. Touché."

"You what, Cappin'?"

"Never bloody mi—

The captain was interrupted by Bakari, who emerged from the lower deck waving his arms and shouting like a lunatic. Bakari was yelling with all of his might, "Cassimbo! Cassimbo!" He drew Captain Hanlon's attention, and more importantly, Mr Grosvenor's as well. The first mate's grip loosened long enough for the wheel to bite. Mr Grosvenor's arms were jolted off of the wheel and he staggered backwards. The wheel spun freely, knocking the helmsman to the deck. The ship turned to starboard, positioning herself parallel to the oncoming swell. The captain turned to see Hell's Gates opening.

The first wave broke onto the deck of the *Agnor Rose*. Bakari was the only person not tied down. His body was broken as the water hauled it across the wooden structures. What was left of his corpse was claimed by the creatures of the deep. The rest of the deckhands, and the three sailors on the bridge, were washed off of their feet. Their mouths filled with salt water and their lungs convulsed in agony. The ship's masts were almost horizontal now as she battled to restore her balance.

Captain Hanlon regained composure as the *Agnor Rose* levelled out again. He had just enough time to signal the end of the fight to Mr Grosvenor, who was on all fours. The first mate crawled to the wheel. A vertical wooden lever protruded from the deck beside it. The first mate kicked it with both feet. The davits swung with force overhead. The release of tension snapped the ropes on the starboard side. The whaleboat that had been secured to it was freed at the bow, but the stern was tangled in the rigging. The boat dipped its nose into the water, with its rear jammed in the air. It hung like withered fruit from a tree, rendering it useless. The second whaleboat slapped the water like an open hand and bobbed next to the mother ship. A third lifeboat, much smaller than the whaleboats, hit the water abaft. It heaved and filled with water faster than a pitcher in a well. Captain Hanlon staggered towards Mr Grosvenor and helped him to his feet. He shook the man's hand. "Eaves, it's been a pleasure, as always."

"No, Cappin'. Don't."

"Eaves, no more out of you, that's an order. Now get off of my bloody ship, and take the others with you. Head for the coast."

"Aye Cappin'." Mr Grosvenor's heart sank in his chest.

Captain Hanlon cupped both of his hands around his mouth and gave his final order. "Abandon ship!"

The echoes rang out in the fog as the remaining men relayed the order. Mr Grosvenor and the helmsman untied themselves from the metal rings in the deck. They jumped overboard and made for the whaleboat. Others followed suit. Some grabbed what would float and took their chances in the water, and some were sent to their eternal rest before they could escape.

KAIJU

The second wave towered higher than the first. It sucked the ship towards itself as it grew. Captain Hanlon held onto the wheel tightly with both hands and closed his eyes. The gigantic squall rolled the *Agnor Rose* and sent the ship to the bottom of the Atlantic. Captain John Hanlon accompanied her all the way down.

***

The surf was chaotic. The foam looked whiter beneath the dark clouds. It was blown back towards the sea as it capped the waves. They broke at all angles as they made landfall along the coast. The consistent swell slamming into the shore created a deafening rumble, interspersed with the fizz of water washing the sand on the beach.

The sea water flowed around Xa's brown ankles, forming craters as it receded back into the Atlantic. He revelled in the tickling of the sand beneath his feet. This was his natural home. His skin was dry, his hair unchanged, and his eyes shone like stars in the night. Xa-a-tin was an unmoved statue. The large dunes of the Namib formed an insurmountable wall behind him. Whale skeletons jutted from the sand up and down the beach. Xa rested one hand on his staff, which he had lodged into the sand beside him. His other hand was held aloft, welcoming the remaining sailors to the graveyard that they had created.

The *Agnor Rose* had been closer to the coast than her captain had calculated. The Cassimbo fog and raging swell had seen to that. Flotsam appeared first. Wooden shards and rigging were scattered in the shallows, some being deposited onto the beach.

Drowned corpses were emerging from the fog, like the living dead clawing their way out of their watery graves. Some floated face down, while some looked as though they were crawling on the sand—an illusion created by the waves carrying them forward.

The only remaining whaleboat moved through the fog, amidst the dead and debris. The bow of the boat cut through the foam, urged on by Mr Grosvenor, who was the acting boatheader. He held onto the steering oar with both hands. Four men had taken to the task of rowing, and the rest of the surviving crew were huddled together like shivering rats.

"Heave, men, heave!" Mr Grosvenor had not given up yet. He removed his right hand from the steering oar and formed a peak with it above his brow. Relief settled within him. "Land ho!"

The crew turned to see their salvation. Their spirits buoyed within them. The four men rowed with renewed vigour. The breakers helped the whaleboat along. She rode them into shore with increased speed. The soaked crew felt the hull crunch into the sand beneath them. They scrambled to their feet and disembarked over both sides of the boat. Mr Grosvenor exited last, dragging the fatigued to safety, until he, too, was on his knees. The remaining crew numbered twelve souls. Mr Grosvenor, their new master, made it thirteen.

The men crawled up the beach on all fours, like tired animals. Mr Grosvenor spotted Xa first. The twelve behind him formed a crude half-moon as they knelt in the sand. Mr Grosvenor knelt in front of them, at Xa's feet. He rocked back with knees bent, placing his hands on top of his burning thighs. He cocked his head in order to look into Xa's eyes. Xa seemed to have grown in stature, and his eyes glowed like two suns.

"Who are you, really?" Mr Grosvenor's face searched Xa's body for an answer. "And how did you get to safety?"

Xa lowered his gaze from the horizon. His eyes were whirlpools of fire within their sockets. Mr Grosvenor stared into the flaming abyss.

"Behold, you stand on Hell's doorstep. I am the gatekeeper. You will enter at will, or you will be dragged in, kicking and screaming." Xa pointed to the dunes that stood behind him.

The sailors didn't like that. "What's he on about, sir?"

"He's cracked, sir." Another chimed in.

"Let's move off the beach. Find help," one of them pleaded with the others.

Mr Grosvenor watched Xa resolutely. He would not be condescended by an African—and in front of the men who looked to him for direction, no less. "Who do you bloody think you are? How dare you give me orders?"

"I am *kxá//'áú*—the Sand Fish."

"He's lost it, sir. His goddamn eyes are demonic." The sailors weren't having any of it. "Sir, let's get out of here. We can head up the coast, or down."

One of them was getting angry now. "Let's finish this nut off and find help." The sailor rolled up his sleeves, fixing for a fight.

"I agree, sir." The man next to him clenched his fists.

Mr Grosvenor was unmoved. He looked directly into Xa's eyes as he explained their situation.

"There is no help here. We find ourselves shipwrecked on the Skeleton Coast. That means we now kneel on soft desert sand. To the south you will find gravel plains. And to the north you will run up against rocky outcrops. Heading back to the boat is pointless. There is no way we can launch through the persistent surf. Besides, the only way to launch along this coastline is to find marshlands and make your way out to sea through that. But we aren't hauling that boat hundreds of miles in our condition."

"So we go inland, sir." The sailor with his sleeves rolled would not relent.

"If you're lucky enough to scale these dunes, you'll die of thirst on the salt plains." Mr Grosvenor knew that their situation was dire. "We are trapped here. And he knows this." He pointed at Xa, who was unmoved, too.

"The path to hell is this way. Follow me." Xa turned to face the dunes. He beckoned the sailors with his staff.

"Never," Mr Grosvenor replied.

"Very well."

Xa held his staff aloft. He spoke ancient words, unintelligible to the sailors. The dunes shook before their eyes. The earth trembled as though struck by a quake. Xa lowered his staff quickly, holding it parallel to the ground. The dunes sank into the ground, as though they had been hollow all this time. They revealed a sand plain that stretched far inland, like a desert sea. Xa spoke the ancient tongue again. The sailors got to their feet, with Mr Grosvenor standing in front of them. He rushed towards Xa, arms raised.

The ground split at Xa's feet, forming a crevice that opened into the distance. Mr Grosvenor skidded to a halt in the sand as an enormous creature emerged from the crevice. It scuttled out of the earth like a centipede. The brown scales on its back chittered as it moved. It was the size of several ships lined up end to end. The head of the thing was triangular and viper-like. The sailors froze in fear and disbelief.

KAIJU

Xa knelt before the beast now. It unhinged its jaw and opened its mouth to reveal snake-like fangs the size of a whale, and a forked tongue the size of the *Agnor Rose* herself. The beast barked like Cerberus itself, "Rak-rak-rak-rak." A fin-like appendage rose from its back. Webbing joined the fin to its reptilian tail. Thousands of bristled setae moved in wave-like motions along its belly on the underside. It barked again, "Rak-rak-rak." Its jaws snapped shut. The creature's cetacean eyes were on the side of its head. They too were whirlpools of fire, just like Xa's.

Though the thing appeared to be earth-coloured, its scales and four relatively short legs seemed to change colour according to the environment. Its back, fin, and tale mirrored the colour of the storm clouds above. Its head and undercarriage were a sandy yellow. Mr Grosvenor estimated the girth of the beast to be equivalent to four whaleboats laid end to end. One could certainly sail all four beneath it with room to spare, so high it stood from the ground.

"Run for your lives, you devils. Run!" Mr Grosvenor gave the rallying cry, but did not turn from Xa. "I will see the end of you, Xa-a-tin."

Xa was still kneeling before the beast. He swayed from side to side, in unison with the creature's head, which did the same. "Then it is decided. Kxá//'áú will have you first, Mr Grosvenor."

Mr Grosvenor had heard enough. He launched himself at the kneeling bushman. The beast's tail whipped around in a flash. The scales had receded to reveal a cruel needle at its end. The needle pierced the first mate's torso mid-air. It raised his convulsing body aloft as his innards drained onto Xa kneeling below. The sailors scattered in different directions, like terrified insects. Xa thanked the Sand Fish for anointing him.

Xa stood and turned to look at the sailors running as fast as they could. He called out to them. "Kxá//'áú will have her revenge!" He looked to the sea. "You have taken the Sea Fish and sent them to their graves." He gestured to the whale bones along the beach. "But they are kindred of the Sand Fish. She will do to you what you have done to her brothers and sisters. There is no escape."

The creature moved with frightening speed. It appeared to swim on the surface of the sand with a sidewinding motion. It blocked the path of three men who were heading north on the beach. They staggered backwards as they fought to clear the sand from their eyes. They were close enough to hear the Sand Fish breathing. Its scales pulsated as it inhaled, and its nostrils flared as it exhaled. One of the men turned to run. The beast bit him in two, swallowing his top half. His legs stood stationary in the sand for a few seconds, and then slumped to the ground. The sand turned into a red paste around them.

The two remaining men pleaded for mercy. The beast flicked its forked tongue at them. The tongue was carpeted in small trichome-like hairs. The hairs were expelled from the tongue, and they inserted venom into the men's faces, like a hundred hypodermic needles acting at once. The concentrated hemotoxic fluid caused immediate organ failure.

Two sailors who witnessed the onslaught made for the ocean. The beast moved through the shallows with ease. It pierced one man repeatedly with its needle-tipped tail—first through the legs, disabling him, and then the rest of his body. The water turned crimson. The second man stood still with his hands covering his face. The beast swallowed him whole.

Another sailor had returned to the bushman. Xa's upper body was dripping with Mr Grosvenor's blood and entrails. Two more men tried to pull the sailor back, each holding onto one of his arms as he tried to reason with Xa. "Call it off, for Christ's sake. Call it off. What have we done to deserve this? We have families back home."

Xa's eyes shone through his bloodied face. "Your children will be fatherless—just as you have left the calves of the sea." The beast returned to Xa. It drove one of its fangs down, penetrating the top of the pleading sailor's skull, skewering him as he stood. His body split down the middle. His friends held equal parts of him. The Sand Fish barked again. It clobbered the remaining two sailors left and right with its enormous head. Their bones shattered as they flew into the sand.

The last four sailors were sprinting southward on the beach. The beast bounded into the shallows and retracted its four pillar-like legs, lowering itself onto the seafloor. It swam along the coast with its setae moving like fins in the water. It caught up to the sailors quickly, swimming parallel to them. It moved past the first three in order to cut the leading man off. The man turned inland, trying to get away, but the beast was too fast. It swung its tail, sending him hurtling through the air in the direction of his crewmates. One stopped to assist him. The beast crushed both men with one of its front legs, having extended all four for land use.

Two sailors of the thirteen were left. One stopped in his tracks. He was overweight and panting from all of the running. He wore white chef's overalls, and a golden crucifix hung around his neck. He made the sign of the cross and removed a single-shot pistol from his trousers. He held the barrel up to the side of his head and fired a lead pellet through his skull. His rotund body collapsed into the sand. The beast took the final sailor alive, holding him in her mouth. She made her way back to Xa and disappeared into the crevice.

Xa knelt and thanked her in the ancient tongue. The earth closed and the crevice was no more. The dunes reformed as the landscape returned to its original form. The massacred bodies were the only evidence of the Sand Fish's exploits. The sailors had mistreated the earth and her kin, but the score had been settled.

***

"Grandfather." The little girl with bushy black hair sat up from her place in the sand. "I don't believe this story of yours." She shook her head. "I like our man, Xa. But it is not true."

The old man chuckled as he stretched his limbs. "And what is so difficult to believe, my love?"

The girl tilted her head and looked up to the sky. "Beasts like that don't exist. There is no such thing as a Sand Fish." The other children shushed her. They didn't want her to spoil their fun.

"Ah," said the old man. "Kxá//'áú—the Sand Fish. You don't think she is real."

"No. Besides, my mother says that monsters don't exist." She had her hands on her hips now.

"Your mother is clearly wrong. She made you, didn't she?" The children burst into laughter. The fire was all but glowing coals now. It was getting late. "Never mind, little one. You have a long life ahead of you." He patted her on the head. "You can decide what to believe for yourself." He turned to the rest of them. Some were yawning, others stretching. "I am clever enough to know that you children are getting tired. Best you get to sleep, before all of your mothers come looking for me. He took his leather jacket and pants off and folded them neatly. He placed them back into his satchel. His loincloth was all that remained on his body.

"But, grandfather, we don't want to sleep. Can't you tell us another story?" A young boy spoke for the group.

The old man pointed to the huts in the near distance. "Your parents are waiting for you there. You go ask them to tell you a bed-time story while you drift off to sleep. Those are the best kind, anyway."

The children protested, but got to their feet. They dusted the sand from their skin and stretched some more to delay the inevitable. As they were turning to head to the huts, the ground shook beneath their feet. The earth rumbled and the coals in the fire pit glowed brighter. The old man was sitting cross-legged. He held a long pipe from which he was drawing deep breaths. His eyes shone like suns and he looked younger in the moonlight.

"Goodnight, children." He put the pipe down and waved to them. "I must sleep now, too. I have a long walk ahead of me in the morning."

WRITE LIKE HELL

One Monstrous Pandemic

Leon Fourie

The dimly lit lounge P.K. entered did not feel very inviting, but that was a feeling he had regarding most upmarket estates. He pondered if architects who worked on such high-profile construction gigs were specifically taught to implement generic design methods that would keep guests from getting too comfortable in certain rooms. Wealthy folk rarely entertained guests with any other intention than putting their status on display, and the luxurious decor assured him that that particularly home was no different.

His host, a middle-aged woman whose trendy, silver-hued hairdo resembled a perfectly manicured wig, directed him to a leather chair opposite the post-modern coffee table with a flashy finger nail. Once he was comfy, she tucked her long dress tight beneath her and sank into her chair, her features fading into the shadows cast by her hair. "Now, Mr Kruger, would you please explain why you've been pestering me for over a month? You've left more messages than those blasted telemarketers." Her words scolded him questioningly, her posture imposing, demanding answers.

"Please, call me P.K.," he said nervously, his fingers fidgeting with the sleeve of the formal shirt that scratched at his wrists, reminding him why he never wore it. "To better explain myself, I'll have to first give you some context. I apologise, but there is no straight answer, no brief explanation. Would you lend me your ear awhile, Ms Madison?"

"Since we're all detained in our homes due to this lockdown, I don't have much to do, fortunately for you. The fact that you'd flout the law bothers me, but I'll give you the benefit of the doubt… for now." A subtle warning. If he didn't watch his step, she'd have him forcibly removed.

"I admit, I was surprised when you returned my call, especially with the current situation. I thought now, even as the media preaches caution, you would be less inclined to grant me access to your home. I'm grateful, for this is of the utmost importance, but I am curious as to why you'd take such a risk for a stranger." A man of his age knew all too well the value of being polite.

"It doesn't really matter now, does it?" she snapped at him. "Please start explaining yourself before I make you leave."

A lightning strike lit up the room through the windows. His fingers dug into the armrests for a moment, before settling back in, his panic fading with the sudden flash. It took a moment for him to start talking.

He reintroduced himself, clarifying that 'P.K.' was short for Petrus Kruger, not the abbreviation for a violent assault with the flat of one's hand, a little joke he'd hoped would ease the tense atmosphere—which it failed rather miserably to achieve.

The well-spoken man was an investigator of, and expert in, all matters supernatural, fictional, mythical, and monstrous. He had a keen interest in the occult in particular, as that was his first brush with literature and the doorway to the world he came to inhabit. In his words, it started when he was a teenager living in then-Verwoerdburg, back in the seventies. The local library was one of the few neutral establishments that had evaded suppression by the church, where its efforts to enforce conformity and strip one of imagination ran aground. It also served as his antisocial childhood hideout growing up. He practically lived in between the shelves labelled 'fiction/fantasy', and would on occasion delve into mystery and crime novels, which felt like logical extensions of those genres.

His house was a conventional—that is to say, devout—home. As such, he had to stow his many treasured books beneath his mattress like contraband, and would spend many late nights reading them by candlelight. One such book was responsible for his first encounter with a creature he would only learn to call a 'kaiju' much later in life.

He had taken from the library a dusty old book containing many short stories relating to the occult, magic, and the like. Every new story made him wish he could escape his drab, ordinary life and take part in adventures far grander than reality. In the last few pages he found handwritten notes in a foreign tongue, below the title "Calling the Beast".

In an act that was tantamount to tempting fate, he snuck out one evening and walked into the nearby bushveld. There he recited the faded words in the dead of night. When it appeared as if nothing had happened, he returned home, disheartened. It wasn't the first time he'd attempted something like that. All the other methods were based on stories shared by friends, family, and ghost tales passed down by the older generations, and were similar in execution to folklore legend Bloody Mary.

"I was actually quite upset that I allowed myself to believe in such nonsense at that moment. It didn't last long—the thought, I mean—before something happened. The events that followed held such great significance that they steered the course of my entire life," he said, barely concealing his excitement while recalling the events of that night.

Before he got in bed, a sudden storm appeared, clouds filling a sky that was crystal-clear mere moments earlier. He remembered staring out the window at the rain and occasional lightning when movement in the drops drew his attention. A heavy shadow was cast against the curtains of floodwater, towering over the field where he'd read the passages out loud not long before. A roar that sounded like rolling thunder sent chills down his spine. When his eyes recovered from a blinding lightning strike, the shadow in the rain had vanished.

P.K. fell quiet for a moment, deep in thought.

"I hope you plan to do better than some ghost story," she said, derailing his metaphorical train, or just derailing his thoughts.

"Apologies, I sometimes wonder what my life would've looked like if not for that evening… I assure you there's more."

As the night continues, P.K. reveals how his interests with everything outside the ordinary took an obsessive turn and his family grew suspicious. They searched his room in his absence and confiscated every last book they found. They considered his behaviour outlandish, and blamed it on the devil's influence, for which he was made to attend weekly supportive prayer sessions. When he reached the age of sixteen, when men could volunteer for the military, his parents forced him to join, thinking it would make a respectable man out of him.

"It nearly worked, too. If everything had stayed absolutely the same, in the terribly bland and hopeless way that military life habitually does, I would've been stripped of any and all interest in the supernatural. I was doubting myself then, ready to write off the events of my past as the tricks of a teenage mind, a fanciful product of the reading material I'd consumed in excess. Then I happened upon a division of the army that, strictly speaking, never existed."

The event that would ultimately seal his fate, binding his life forever to the pursuit of fact beyond the appearance of fiction in reality, happened in his final month of conscription. When a freak storm flooded the base, he was tasked with informing a ranking officer of changes to their deployment schedule. The Angola Border war required more forces than they had available, and as such, the ranking officer he sought attempted in secret to contact creatures from the arcane to serve as cannon fodder. The scene it left behind, that young P.K. had stumbled upon moments after it had flopped, was the moment that determined his path.

His father passed away the year after he returned from service, and his mother a month later. As the only child of a wealthy real-estate tycoon, he was left with a sizable fortune. This fortune would fund all his future exploits.

KAIJU

He recounted his steps from the moment he left South Africa for Cairo. He'd hoped the land of the ancients held more answers. He learned that most epics, myths, and legends were rooted in tales told by a travelling storyteller from the East, believed to have originated from Japan. After several years of search and research, he left Egypt. Once P.K. landed in Japan, he learned of the beasts known as 'kaiju'.

"See, I honed my abilities as an investigator, making additional money in my travels as an inspector of all things strange. People are deeply superstitious the world over, regardless of the region, and I hoped there was some truth to the beliefs they held. How wonderful would the world be if even half of those 'fantasies' were true? Every myth contains a hint of truth. I found a well inhabited by a disembodied voice while in Giza. It took me months to figure out a safe means of descending into its depths, where I discovered a bottle without a lid, floating in the water. From it came the voice that scared locals out of their minds. When I smashed it, not knowing if it would set free some unspeakable evil or what, the voice disappeared."

He told his tale with such excitement that he jumped to his feet and started pacing around the room. "I spent well over a year thereafter researching all there was to learn about djinn, hoping to understand what I'd found. The reason I travelled, though, was to learn as much as I could of the creature that I may have summoned all those years ago. Whenever a storm appeared—and not just a small cloud break, but complete with thunder, lightning, and torrential rain—when one of those appeared, the creature appeared, as if to remind me of its presence. I believe that I only see it then, but the creature is always close by. It always appears as a shadow cast against the rain, barely visible but undeniably there, if that makes sense." He turned to his host, who'd gone quiet, to confirm that she was still present. "I think I may have even caused the pandemic that now endangers the globe, which brings me to the events of last year," he said, sitting back down with a deep sigh.

"I finally found information relating my experiences, and many others, to the existence of kaiju. Genies, C'thulhu, minotaurs—you name it, it comes back to the kaiju. The phrase 'Adam and Eve' actually refers to the first men and women of the human race, and not to a single perfect couple moulded in the hands of an omnipotent being. They struck a deal, so to speak, contracting the first kaiju ever in exchange for more knowledge. Whoever was in power at the time didn't like that one bit, and kicked them out of their idyllic homeland that we came to call 'The Garden of Eden'. I theorised that they were exiled to our plane of existence then, and that kaiju were as much gods as Zeus and Odin, but our race was the property of another deity that didn't know how to play nice with others," he concluded like a detective that had made his final, shocking deduction.

In regions rocked by some great calamity, ghost stories had a tendency to follow. The effects of the catastrophe would be greater if there was still some element of mystery attached to it. It was hardly surprising, then, that the dense jungles of Vietnam were home to many a ghost story. The local fishermen spoke of seeing lost soldiers emerging at night while out on the water, as well as the creatures responsible for their demise.

At the end of 2018, a change and newfound consistency in their stories reached P.K. The stories spoke of a colossal creature that would appear in the thick mist and abduct those who ventured into the jungle. It was known to wander into towns on occasion, too. It was hard to say if this was simply due to the increased usage of social media globally and access to it that these stories were only now making their rounds, or if there was a recent change in that forest. As far as he was concerned, it called to him, and that was all he needed to know.

"I spent little over eight months among the locals, living in a rented flat on the outskirts of town. After several failed attempts at listening in on conversations in public social places, I resorted to hiring one of the locals to act as a tour guide. He was familiar with, and even enjoyed, many of the stories, and even taught me a little of the lingua franca. But mostly, he was quite adept at eavesdropping, which was exactly what I needed him to do. Coincidentally, we crossed paths when he attempted to pickpocket me after hearing how I'd agreed to rent the flat without negotiating on price," he added.

There were several features of the stories they all held in common. The beast was only present when thick fog came rolling in. Its appearance wasn't restricted to night-time, but it was more likely to come out of hiding then. One such evening, when the power went out due to a blown transformer, its growls rattled the very earth beneath the city, scaring everyone still awake into quiet hiding. The streets were never as abandoned as that night.

Rain came pouring down, revealing at the end of the street another familiar apparition. It marched out of the city limits and toward the forest. As it entered the fog, its shape became clearer. Any fiction writer would've been tempted to call it a werewolf were it only ten times smaller. P.K. had been following the creature at the time, but seeing it solidify in the fog brought a real sense of danger. He was no longer being stalked by a disembodied smudge in the rain, but rather, a threatening monster. He returned home, biding his time until he could go exploring the forest.

"I never really had any intentions with these creatures. The mystery and intrigue that surrounded them inspired me to seek answers. I wanted to know how many of the myths and legends came from real places in our history."

When he had as much information as he believed could be gained from the Vietnamese village, he rented a Jeep and set off into the dense jungle. A rugged vehicle was the only way one might traverse the rock-strewn terrain. He followed the faint paths for as long possible, and took note of anything that might bring him closer to finding the creature.

A subtle mist with a thick miasma filled the air as he crossed into a more treacherous part of the wilds. His stomach turned as he attempted to breathe the putrid air. He was convinced that either something had died in the area, leaving the lingering smell of rot, or that he'd found his first clue in search of the forest fiend. Not long after, the vehicle got stuck in loose mud that could've passed for quicksand, forcing him to continue on foot.

He nervously ventured forth, uncertain of what predators could be skulking beneath the brush that covered the forest floor. He used hanging vines and low-grown branches as safety rails while he stepped on and over the looser rocks, fallen branches, and moss-covered roots that were less likely to swallow his shoes than the marshland mud below. The canopy blocked out so much light that each step took more guesswork than hand-eye coordination, and he hoped he wouldn't mistake a snake for a vine.

"The smell coming from the creature acted as its 'area of influence', if you will. The research I did during the intervening years made it clear that most altercations and calamities during recent history had been influenced by the presence of kaiju. Those who'd tried writing about them at the time were branded conspiracy theorists due to how absurd their views seemed. Wars, plagues, financial crises, these events were due to the varying size and shape of the kaiju, whose influence had begun to extend further. That's the theory, at least, and what I found proved it."

Woodland creatures were highly unlikely to act violently. Even as someone who feared their potential danger, P.K. knew they were no risk under normal circumstances. The presence of the monster seemed to have driven several creatures into a frenzy. Swarms of bats swirled around in anger, while others seemed stricken with sickness, as birds and squirrels hardly moved at the sight of the human intruder. Every living creature was under attack in one way or another.

A bat, dropping mid-flight to the ground, drew his attention. He moved in to inspect it, only to discover it had died upon impact and a strange, black smoke was rising from its jaws.

As he looked up from the tiny corpse, he found himself looking at crude gravestones made out of boulders that were carved upon. He made his way over for a closer look and found several helmets and old-fashioned firearms at the base. It was fairly easy to deduce that these were the burial grounds for soldiers that had died here during the war, or even shortly after. The carvings on the back of the stones seemed familiar, closely resembling the summoning spell he himself had performed all those years ago. The other symbols he had seen in books on how to bind the occult entities into servitude—or, in this case, guard duty.

"I was in awe of the power of the structure, as it represented a last-ditch effort to defeat one's enemies and defend the fallen. I hoped, mistakenly, that I could release the land of its curse if I were to deface the stones. In hindsight, I should've left well enough alone…" His words were laden with guilt.

"Technically, I should have known better. I've had this creature—this shadow—appear at every turn, never once doing anything else than caution me. Maybe it did do more that I was unaware, but before I decided to convince others of its existence, it was a harmless phantom, albeit a frightening one. When I finally managed to reveal it to a group of like-minded members of a secret society in Japan, they all committed suicide, driven mad by the revelation. You let it be—that's how one chooses the greater good, but meddling was in my nature. I kept hoping it would pay off."

A flash from the window sent him crashing against the backrest of the puffed-up chair with a frightened expression all over his face. His heart settled after some time, then he apologised. He inched over the edge of his chair and cautiously continued.

"I carried with me a small excavation kit, a miniature garden shovel, and some brushes for the odd event in which I discovered something worth investigating. I used the little shovel and loads of force to remove what I could from the stones. I was so

KAIJU

preoccupied with the task at hand that I lost all sense of awareness of the environment around me. The fog had started to creep in, and that made the hostile region all the more dangerous," he recalled.

The roar of the beast startled him. He started running, only to trip and tumble to the muddy ground. His eyes searched what little of the landscape he could make out for movement as he rose to his feet. Overheard, a shadow moved, letting in a ray of light in the otherwise dingy patch of jungle. The creature had been present all along, watching him from the treetops. Bats streamed past, converging on the behemoth wrapped in thick fog.

He followed the creature until it disappeared into the waters off the coast of Hanoi. It settled just below the surface, close to the mouth of a large stone cavern, where the bats blended in with the local colony. When it was fully submerged, the fog that clung to its massive form disappeared, as did the creature.

The week following my sighting, a group of people brought their equipment with which they hunted, captured, and fished for food and resources to sell. They mostly kept their activities to the bushier sections, close to the coast where last he saw the creature. By the time he noticed they were capturing bats as well, the first few shipments had already been hauled off to the town, where'd they be shipped off to whomever was interested in fresh, exotic produce.

He attempted to warn them, those who relied upon the area's natural abundance to provide for their families, about the danger that lurked in the water. He even tried to scare them off using local legends. Unfortunately, they couldn't afford to care about the risks, and ignored his warnings. They wouldn't listen to him, and he was running out of time. Instead, he tried to interfere with their trade by alerting a health inspector to their unhygienic practices. He might, then, have enough time to drive away the bats, so he thought.

He attempted to follow the delivery drivers as they left for the city to distribute their goods, hoping to find out which retailer he would have to spook in order to stop these mutated munchies from causing mayhem. He had little way of proving that they were unfit for human consumption, but at the very least, he suspected they'd be poisonous, possibly fatal.

Heavy rain caught the convoy while they were driving through a quieter region. As P.K. slowed down and attempted to drive cautiously while not losing sight of them, a flash of lightning reintroduced a familiar sight. He swerved hard to avoid it as it appeared in the rain, blocking off the road. He came to a standstill just off the main motorway. He clutched his steering wheel as he struggled to gain control of his breath. By the time the storm had cleared, he'd lost them, and could do little more than attempt to stop the next shipment from causing more harm.

He sat in the car next to the road, waiting for the next truck with the supplier logos to pass. It dawned on him then that the wolf-like creature was sabotaging his attempts at interfering, clearly aware of his intentions. The thought scared him, as it meant that the beast would not only be able to find him wherever he went, but likely knew where he was going and why, even before he himself had decided. His thoughts were interrupted when the second row of trucks came flying by, and he renewed his pursuit.

"This was how I came to be in China. More specifically, I was in Wuhan when it became 'Ground

Zero'. By the time I got there, the first shipment had already been packaged and supplied to several establishments and vendors in the area. The speed and efficiency with which that happened said more than I wanted to know about their hygiene standards. I wouldn't be able to dissuade them from using any other shipments that came in. My hands were tied."

He returned to the caves, occasionally leaving the area to do more research into finding a way to either drive the beast further into the ocean, or the bats from the cave on the coast. By the end of that year, local authorities started sending foreigners home due to a rapidly spreading pandemic. The night before he left, he swore he heard maniacal laughter echo in his mind, almost mocking his futile attempts. He boarded the plane with a crushing sense of defeat, hoping to return once he could figure out how to deal with the unorthodox problem.

"It was during my flight back that I realised I was unable to do a single thing unless I dealt with the other enemy that would sabotage my attempts at every turn. It became more aggressive as I got closer to uncovering the mysteries surrounding its kind, and it would loom over me like a curse unless I figured out how to escape it." He looked at his host as he finished his sentence. She had been sitting almost breathlessly on her chair for a little longer than was comfortable.

As he rose up from his chair to confirm that all was still well, she stopped him with a simple, "Please continue." Something about her felt different, but as he hardly knew her, it was possible that he was mistaken.

He again turned to his studies, gathering all the information he could on binding and sealing rituals—whether they came from Satanists or ancient witches was irrelevant. He searched them all for common motives, attempting to reveal their roots so that he knew where to look for the true and original form of the incantation. The internet made it possible for him to scour global resources and get into contact with societies and specialists that worked in his field. Many of these people had started speculating that the recent pandemic was a sign of the end times. It was less grand than the Armageddon we had expected, but it seemed fitting, given that humans were poisoning the planet.

When he found what he was looking for—in the forms of the ruins used by the Norse Gods to imprison the kaiju Fenrir, no less—he started familiarising himself with the area that had changed so much since he'd left for Egypt. Centurion was now a vast, sprawling suburb that had expanded beyond his wildest imaginings. The borders between Pretoria, Johannesburg, and the old Verwoerdburg used to be much easier to discern, as there were large patches of wild between them, but now it felt like one large city.

He returned to his childhood home in Irene, surprised that it was still standing with all that had changed. After revelling in the nostalgic value of its presence, he turned around to see the area where the fields used be.

A large estate containing many smaller, but still sizable, estates had been built on those lands, the estate management using their influence to keep certain areas green as a sort of owl sanctuary to preserve endangered life. It was a luxurious estate inhabited by upper-class earners and their families. It sported several schools, filling stations, and a shopping centre; but its best feature would also turn out to be his biggest bane: zero-tolerance security.

"I tried numerous times to get inside so that I could look around. I knew once I saw it, it would call to me somehow, but I needed the opportunity to search for that to happen. I ended up using a local social hot-spot to befriend folks, biding my time until they invited me over for a braai. Only then did I pretend to need fresh air, and ventured out into the streets. Once I saw your yard, I was certain," he confessed, gazing upon the motionless body of Miss Madison, waiting for a response.

Another lightning strike reminded him of the raging weather outside. He resolved to keep his back turned to the windows, ensuring that he didn't see whatever might be glaring at him. He admitted that he was not yet certain how, but through means related to the supernatural he would most likely find something to halt the spread of the virus, maybe render it harmless. Before he could do so, he needed to seal away his own shadow as it seemed to be interfering in his every attempt so far. He felt it was getting too close for his liking, appearing more and more frequently. That meant coming back to where he called it, where he would hopefully, finally, be rid of it.

Again, the lady across from him didn't respond.

He rose from his seat and approached her with caution, her face still concealed in shadow. As his hand extended toward her, she suddenly jerked forward, revealing her blackened eyes and emotionless stare, causing him to jump back in surprise.

The lights flickered and strobed, and then turned off all together, plunging the room into darkness.

Laughter that defied all description telepathically invaded his mind—menacing, loud, and victorious. His eyes searched the dark for answers, only finding the large shadow of claws as lightning briefly lit up the room, swivelling him toward the window he'd tried his best to avoid.

As he stared into the eyes of evil, the same voice addressed him. "Your time is up, madman. You were worthy prey." The laughter consumed his senses once more.

As he dropped to his knees in defeat, he slowly felt his psyche lose its tether to reality, its struggle to distinguish between what was real and what was not. From the clump of helplessness on the floor, laughter erupted, joining in with the disembodied voice, uncontrollably insane.

KAIJU

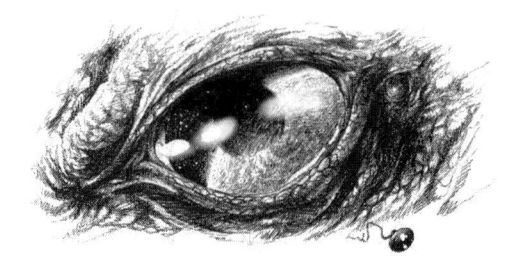

Starchild

A Kaiju Story

Erik Morten & Samantha Bateson

A lonely glass eye glistens in the dark, hanging by a thread off a plush toy rabbit, floating through space. As momentum carries it out from amongst the rubble it was hiding in, blinding sunlight shimmers against its frozen fur. A frozen hand, forever reaching for it. A large shadow is approaching, taking the sunlight away from them. Again, they are submerged in the deep and endless. Comforting calmness before two large masses collide, grinding both of them into icy fragments and dust.

***

"I think we're already on that course, sir." Hafsat Calgari was still stunned, trying to wrap his head around the situation. As he was re-checking the readouts the machines were giving him, he was sure that there must have been some sort of mistake. He wasn't being paranoid, either.

In interstellar travel, distances were so astronomically extreme that the slightest error could drag them off course by a million miles, if not more. Plus, you had to make sure you didn't crash into anything along the way, or got too close to objects with a strong gravitational pull.

Hafsat was new to this job, but there hadn't been a single time where he didn't have to re-adjust the course they were on at least a couple of times. The calculations to lay down a route would usually take several minutes, as well. Self-doubt at a time like this seemed pretty reasonable, he thought.

"Bas! Snap out of it!" That was the captain speaking, addressing him by his nickname. Hafsat had been staring into nothingness for several minutes now.

"Yes, sir!"

"Okay, Cadet Calgari, for the fifth time, just make sure we're heading to the coordinates on channel one. And no more distractions! Emeran, any new information?"

"They've gone silent again, captain, I will try to reestablish contact." That was Guiselle speaking in her role as communications technician on the bridge. She was probably the oldest person aboard the *Yaron* at this point. Having been amongst the first people to claim the kaiju over 90 years ago, she looked young for her age, even when she had her dark grey hair tied up in a bun, like she had today. Hafsat had known her for half his life now. Guiselle was the one who had taken care of him and his sister when things went bad, and he loved her like a mother.

Hafsat tried his best to focus again. He had been forced into active duty four days ago, after an accident had taken out two of the navigators, which had led to procedure being rushed in his case.

Being linked into the neural net still was a very new experience for him. Everyone was used to information just streaming in and out of their heads at this point, but it was something different when it was an entire kaiju's data grid being linked up to your brain. It felt overwhelming. Endless in a way, slow and heavy. Dragging. Like using all your strength to move through a stream you're fully submerged in, against the current.

He was not being inactive while trying to adjust, though, but constantly rechecking the data he was receiving, re-rendering the course, and re-running the calculations. His ability to multi-task was the reason he had been chosen for this position. "We're definitely on course, captain!"

All he got in response was a slightly exasperated sigh.

Their already being on course was most definitely a lucky coincidence, given that turning a kaiju around could sometimes take up to a couple hours.

The *Yaron Tautari* was their home. Installation crews had settled on her with the most modern technology available at the time. There had been no need to operate on the kaiju. Domes had just been clamped onto the *Yaron*'s spine plates. Afterwards, they had only needed to set up some electrodes to 'tickle' her a bit when they wanted to change course or speed. At least, that is how Hafsat understood it.

And now they were rushing towards the rendezvous coordinates at an estimated 74,000 miles per hour. Nobody knew exactly how kaiju could reach such speeds, or how they moved about in the first place. It was possible that it had something to do with their wings. Some speculated that they worked as solar sails, or something of the like. Then again, solar sails were absolutely not able to generate acceleration like this— at least, no man-made solar sails. Until anyone found a proper explanation however, solar-sailing kaiju had become the accepted scientific standard.

The *Yaron*'s wingspan was about 90 miles in length, with the human habitat-modules sitting on its spine, a little chain of domes, each about a mile in diameter and each hooked onto a single spine plate. After they had set up some supporting structures around them, the process had been completed.

Earlier kaiju settlements had been more complicated. The earliest ones, more than 3,000 years ago, had needed to drill themselves into the extremely thick tissue of the kaiju's outer layer of skin. They had needed to keep the kaiju tied to immense reverse thrusters to slow it down enough to keep apace with it, a whole little fleet of ships, working round the clock for weeks on end to install all the equipment and supporting machinery necessary to take control of a giant organism like this— even though control might be too strong of a word.

As far as humanity was aware, kaiju had been following certain migration routes for aeons untold. These pathways took them right past a surprisingly high number of inhabitable planets, seemingly effortlessly holding up speeds that were at the absolute upper limit of what human technology was able to achieve at the time. Even now, there were but a few, small—usually consultary—vessels that were able to outpace a kaiju going about its usual migration speed.

Plus, there was the gravity. Kaiju were so massive and incredibly dense, that they naturally projected a gravitational field akin to the ones of smaller planetoids.

KAIJU

The biggest kaiju on record almost achieved earth-like gravity.

The one they were heading towards at the moment was one such massive beast. The *Æterna Serenita* had been one of the first kaiju ever claimed—and certainly the first one of its size.

On this day, the people of the *Yaron Tautari* had received a distress call. This was why everyone on the bridge was on edge, jumpy. Especially Captain Rhaleffi, who seemed like he'd seen better days. Most of them were, after all, better days. The distress call had been strange. Hafsat decided to listen to it again.

"Mayday, mayday, this is Clive Byron of the *Æterna Serenita* calling out to all vessels receiving! We have lost all navigational control and are currently adrift with multiple celestial objects closing in! Our position is 14h 39m 36.49400s to 60° 50′ 02.3737″ to 284.578.5872AU Sol. We need assistance for the evacuation of 153,110 personnel. Repeat, mayday, mayday [...]"

How would they have 'multiple celestial objects' on approach? And how would they lose control like that? Hafsat decided he needed to read up on the *Serenita*. "Contact in T-3500."

The *Yaron Tautari* was rushing to the rescue. Flying through space at enormous speeds on seemingly endless wings, thousands of shimmering lights moving along the tissue, melting into the glittering vastness of the cosmos around it. Tails and tail-wings spreading out behind her for miles and miles. At its capitum, sensory feelers slowly weaving into oncoming reality.

***

The show host straightened his bow tie and smiled into the camera. "Professor Katherine Hauser was born on this very kaiju, and has dedicated her whole life to the research of alien life. I am Matthias Lorem, your host. Mrs Hauser—Katherine, if I may—what brings you back home, after all these years?"

"Good evening, Matthias. Well, *Serenita* has had some curious fluctuations in her behaviour over these last couple of months, and she is not alone in that. As you may know, some of the other early settlements have reported misbehavings of a similar fashion, so here I am, making my rounds, trying to figure out what is happening."

"When you speak of 'misbehavings', Katherine, what do you mean by that?"

"Unresponsiveness, most of all. The Exobiologist Society is aware of at least one instance where an unresponsive kaiju almost caused a collision. Our first and main priority is securing human life above all, of course. As you will understand, this matter is of a sensitive nature. I won't be able to disclose most of the details at hand, but I'll try and answer your questions as best I can."

"Katherine, in your professional opinion, and as a former citizen of this kaiju, would you say that there is cause for concern amongst the people living on board the *Serenita*?"

"Of course not, Matthias. Taking care of this issue is exactly why I am here. *Serenita* is probably the biggest settled kaiju at this point, and in this case, mass equals safety.

Sure, scanning through the kaiju's tough epidermis—that's the skin—is not easy, but we do have a lot of experience in these matters, and I can assure you, aside from some turbulence over these next few days, nothing noticeable will come of this."

"Alright, then! You've heard it from the expert herself. There is nothing to worry about! Thank you for being here today Katherine. This concludes our daily Info-Talk here on *Æterna Serenita*. Professor Katherine Hauser, ladies and gentlemen! Goodnight!"

Alysia Marx turned off the media feed.

"This is so typical. Always something to panic about. Such a convenient way of distracting the masses. What do you think? Jiro?" she said, turning to her boyfriend, who was sprawled out on the sofa.

Jiro barely even looked up from his game board. "Sure, lemoncakes, you know how it is. I've been saying it for years, haven't I?" Then, poking at the board. "This can't be right, is the connection still on?"

In that very moment, the entire room shook, roughly setting Alysia down on the floor. "What in all…" she gasped as she was lifted into the air, hanging there for a split second before the wall behind her caved in.

***

The *Yaron Tautari* was making her way through a nebular with a lustrous, warm orange hue, set aglow like golden flames by the light of the system's twin suns. One a red dwarf, the other bigger and almost white-gold in colour, they were seemingly forever bound in a dance of gravity and molten flame.

The shape of the *Yaron* cut through the nebula, leaving whirlpools of disturbed matter in her wake. Little breaths of saturated particles were pulled behind her, a trail of stardust. The light of the dual suns reflected on the starboard side of the little human domes, only for a moment making them visible to the Watchers' eyes, even through the clouds and whirls and confusion swirling around.

On the port side of the *Yaron*, the nebula was suddenly inked in blackness. The lights under her skin kissing the swathes around in a new flavour of light. The other particles resting in shadow for the first time in aeons.

Just a second. The *Yaron* rushes on.

"Okay but how are we actually planning to take them all in? I mean, space and supplies should be fine for a few days at the least. How about medical?"

"We're good." Tom leaned back in his seat, stroking his beard. "All stocked up at this point, but we should still activate the reserve medical personal per Catastrophe-Charta, just to be on the safe side."

"Understood. Reserve medical personnel should be activated. All in favour?" Nine raised hands confirmed unanimity on the subject. "That would be space, supplies, and medical taken care of. Now, back to the question at hand: how do we physically move more than 150,000 people off their kaiju and cram them into here?"

Captain Mars Rhaleffi cleared his throat. "Is it still completely out of the question to just let someone else handle it?"

Groaning around the table was the general answer to this. They had already spent over two hours weighing pros and cons, and eventually they had come to the conclusion that, even if another kaiju were to arrive on scene first and be better equipped to help in a situation like this, *Yaron* would be able to provide support enough to save countless lives. It didn't matter. As of this moment, they would be arriving on scene six to ten hours ahead of anybody else.

"In that case." Rhaleffi sat up straight, wearing a mischievous smile. "We should probably evacuate Dome Seven—and I mean completely." He held up a hand to halt the rising protest. "That is the only way. Yes, we could use our shuttles, conveyors, and probably even conscript some private vessels," he was listing the options, raising the digits of one hand, gesticulating with the other. "But even at full capacity, we could not hope to evacuate that many people in anything under two days."

Tapping on his data pad, he brought up several images and vector graphics onto the room's central presentation hologram.

"With the data provided by the *Serenita* and cloud-sourced satellite information, we have been able to outline at least three planet-sized objects on a direct collision course with the *Serenita*'s current trajectory." He used his hands to draw helpful lines across the display that appeared as glowing white strings with a minuscule delay, rearranging pictures and graphics.

"Moreover, these objects actually appeared to alter their course in line with *Serenita*'s slowing to a standstill two hours ago, while still remaining on target. We do not know what these objects are, but they will probably arrive no later than four or five hours after we get there."

He used gestures to zoom in on one of the unknown objects before continuing. "Data seems to suggest regular planetoids of varying mass, but that does seem unlikely, given what I just told you. Regardless, it is my foremost duty as captain of this vessel to ensure that none of our crew are being subjected to any unnecessary dangers. As such, coupling off the smallest, least integrated dome available and using it as a lifeboat is the most reasonable course of action. Wouldn't you agree, Seraphine?"

Seraphine had been silent for a while now, her forehead resting on folded fingers, silver hair streaming down to her elbows, which appeared to be almost penetrating through the table's anthracite-grey leather surface. The commander-in-chief of the *Yaron* was the daughter of their original founder, Argus Lorem, and had since set a strong standard for a very uncompromising brand of leadership. Everyone present knew she had a relative on the *Serenita*. Her nephew was the only family she had left. He was a talk-show host, cheerful type, lovable.

"It is the most reasonable course of action, you are right, Mars. Our neighbours in Dome Seven will have to suck it up."

"But, Miss Lorem, would it not be more practical to use Dome Four instead? The financial disposition alone—"

"Are you seriously this dense, Marcus? Dome Four has about eight times the population of Dome Seven, not to mention how this would disrupt the infrastructure between the Three and Five. And don't even get me started on structural integrity!"

Marcus Royl seemed to shrink and fade away in front of their eyes. Dome Seven was the 'luxury' habitat section, reserved for high-responsibility personnel and the occasional VIP, located at the very end of their chain of habitat-domes.

"Dome Seven will be readied for departure, 80 percent of available propellant redirected to Seven's capacitors, all but the skeleton personnel evacuated;

they can take up residence in Six and Five for now. Mister Royl will make sure everybody complies in a timely manner—and given this officially is a Catastrophe-Charta-situation, as per decision made at 1623 hours today, there will be no compensation of any kind. Anyone against?"

If there had been a way for the look she gave Marcus at this moment to be any more piercing, he would have required some serious medical attention.

No hands raised.

"Then it is decided. Get to work, people!"

***

Lloyd Marx was perplexed. This data could not be correct. The sensors that had been mounted to some of the lesser feelers on the *Serenita*'s 'head' were showing heat signatures and tissue reflexes that corresponded with those of kaiju biology. Where could another kaiju have come from so suddenly? He was certain he would have learned of such an occurrence, given that events like these were usually heavily celebrated. These serene giants weren't the most sociable of creatures, which might be easily explained given the gravitational pull of each body and the force it would unquestionably take for them to not crash into each other. As far as he was aware, such a collision had never happened before.

He was trying the comms-channel for the sixth time, but still couldn't get through to anyone in navigation. He had also tried to contact Tech several times, but those guys had made a habit of not answering him in the past, so he didn't really expect anyone to get back to him on that channel anyway.

He got up, determined to make his way to the observation deck and check out the situation by himself. Surely, no one could blame him, receiving nonsensical data like this.

A great tremor brought him back down onto his stool. A moment later, he opened his eyes again. He was down on the floor, his temple against the ground. There must have been a second tremor, more vicious than the first one, he thought to himself, head still dizzy from the impact.

There had been a couple of quakes like these ones over the last couple of days, but none had been nearly as extreme. Maybe this had something to do with those weird readouts? He really needed to make some sense of this. Lloyd got back up.

The door would not open. He tried to put his key code in. Maybe he had locked it by accident? The key code was accepted. The door remained firmly shut.

Oh, he'd had it with these tech guys now, pulling a prank on him, huh? Well, he was going to show them! He took one of the magnoclamps and proceeded to mount it onto the door when he noticed the door being quite a bit colder than he would have expected.

He stopped with what he was doing and put his hand flat against the door. It was definitely colder than it should be. *How in the world...*

He set his cheek against the door, trying to listen, and hastily ripped himself off the door with a yelp when he noticed his skin freezing onto the metal.

***

"I told you, Bas, I'm still trying to get a lock on their signals. We should be in range at this point. We really should be. But all I'm getting at this end is static and silence." Hadiza was getting annoyed. Both with the uncooperative machines and her little brother. She was ruffling up her short, neon-green hair as Hafsat started another attempt at helping with the problem.

"Have you tried compensating for stellar interference? Maybe there's a pulsar too close by?"

She sighed. "I appreciate you trying to help, Bas, I really do. But I have been doing this for a good long while now, as you know. Yes, I have checked all the star charts, I have been in contact with the Watchers, and there are no rogue planets or hidden anomalies in any discernible radius, either. So, unless there's something seriously wrong with our communications array, the problem is most likely on their side. Sorry, I will cut the feed for now. I need to think."

His troubled face nodded understanding and the screen switched back to the scouting drones' sensory output data.

"Damn these machines," she said to herself, cracking her neck and reaching for the other desk, but her arm was just a little too short, as per usual. "Too quiet in here for anyone to think properly!" she shouted into the otherwise eerily silent work space. She pushed herself towards the other desk. The wheels of her chair caught on a cable, halting her after she had moved only a few inches and almost throwing her to the floor.

She grunted in annoyance before finally grabbing a hold of the media pad and putting on some very noisy and distorted music. The speaker system of her workstation had absolutely not been made for entertainment purposes, and kept buzzing with every other high note, but it was still totally worth it. She got to her feet and fell into the sort of dance done at home when one was absolutely sure no one was watching.

She should not have cut him off like that, she thought, but handling frustration had never been something she was particularly good at—especially not while others watched.

Still dancing, she made a wrong move with her head and a painful pinching sensation started radiating from her neck. She slowed her dance, turning down the music, and reached up with her left hand to massage the painful spot. "I'm getting too old for this," Hadiza said to herself as she found her gaze being caught by the drone data monitor. The drones of the *Yaron* also were probably too old for this. They'd been brought in for some weird kid's school project from one of the older kaiju.

Drones were hardly used these days at all. There had been too many instances where machines like that just failed at all the wrong moments. They reached their intake of cosmic radiation and bugged out. When too many variables were involved, they made logical errors, like prioritising delivery routes over human transport and thereby causing crashes—things like that.

It hadn't been really bad. Very few people had actually been injured or killed, especially considering the extreme number of drones that had been active. Still, most captains nowadays tried their best to get around using them.

And there were always people eager to get off ship for a quick EVA, or just bored enough to take up the extra work, especially on the smaller kaiju like the *Yaron*, so getting human hands on drone-worthy tasks was anything but difficult. Older and bigger kaiju however…

She got back to her desk and linked the drone controls to the main comms-channel.

"Okay, searching for basically any drone-like signals on target coordinates... No, wait, they won't have the signal strength." She stopped typing and paused a moment "Ah, well then, reaching out to community satellites here, there and... Yeah, that one should work." She used her administrative rights to commandeer the main signal line of a few satellites between the *Yaron* and where the *Serenita* should be. She set a command signal on a repeating loop, leaned back, and waited.

The command was set for a simple response, but to actually send it, the drones would have to follow a couple of more complicated instructions. Each drone would have to link up with a least four or five other ones in its vicinity to send a unified response signal to whichever community satellite would be closest. They would also have to include a redirection command so the transmission would bounce forward to Hadiza's work station.

"Come on, you stupid robots, I know you can hear me." It had been almost three minutes now. Waiting and being patient also weren't exactly virtues of hers. "One of those days, is it?"

Suddenly, the inbox feed lit up like a Christmas tree. Over a hundred drone feed signals and counting, but even while she was linking them up for a permanent connection, some of them cut out again. "Just how old is that hardware?"

Hadiza gave the drones a new main command: Transmission of all sensory data collected within the last 72 hours, streaming backwards from this moment, as well as current sensory input. She then continued by setting up a sorting protocol and activating a couple of AIs to run an interpretation routine before she re-opened the comm-link to Hafsat. "Good news, we got eyes on target. A lot of them."

The hologram streaming onto the *Yaron*'s command deck was a three-dimensional vision of the *Æterna Serenita*. It had been put together by combining all the drone data Hazida had gathered and then implementing all that information into a working simulation. Different occurrences in time were being shown at the same time, colour-coded, one blending slowly into the other, showing four dimensions all at once.

The bridge crew was watching in stunned silence as they witnessed what had happened, and was still happening, at their destination.

Lieutenant Jasatuta spoke up. "It must be some sort of weapons system, some test gone wrong."

"And what kind of weapons system would be able to do something like this? Why would you want to do something like this in the first place?"

"Have you met the military?"

"Last I checked, you could be considered military yourself."

"Enough, the both of you." Guiselle appeared composed, but Hafsat saw her shaking ever so slightly, her jaw was more set than usual, and her hands uncharacteristically entwined.

"The captain will be here within the minute. Rather than speculating, we should be figuring out how to work around the problem." She cleared her throat and spoke with more determination. "All of you, how much do we know, and how do we handle whatever this is?"

Hafsat had been studying the drones' non-visual data while he kept looking at the hologram. Raising his hand, he said, "The gravitational disruption seems to be the most pressing concern."

Jasatuta locked eyes with him. "What do you mean, 'gravitational disruption'?"

"It's what's pulling all the drones in, making them crash. They're all trying to pull away from the *Serenita*, but can't get out of the gravity well. Look at sensor-sections Aleph and Rharta, it's all there."

"Bas is right, but that means we will get pulled in as well if we get too close! How are we supposed to help them evacuate like that?"

The bridge doors hissed open.

"Captain on the bridge!"

Rhaleffi strode in and started to speak, only to stop himself abruptly. He walked up close to the hologram, studying it. "What am I looking at?

The *Æterna Serenita* was bending in backwards on itself. Her multitude of tail-wings and fins were reaching way past her capitum, and had almost caught up with their own roots at this point, engulfing the kaiju. Every other minute now, she was being violently shaken by what looked like slow-moving cramps under her skin. Her main two pairs of wings kept moving erratically from side to side, seemingly in opposite relation to her twisting and turning around.

Only a very distinct few drones were still able to hold their distance, engines running almost beyond maximum capacity. Even so, their orbits were constantly descending.

The last human-operated vessel had gone down about four hours ago. Lucky enough not to be swatted away by any of the *Serenita*'s wings, it still had been hopelessly caught in the gravity well and had eventually crashed into its docking port, desperately attempting an emergency landing. Now a drone was remotely reading out data from the crashed ship's final log entries.

"Sir, you might want to have a look at this! We just received additional log data from a small transport vessel called *Vera* that had been trying to flee the immediate danger zone around the *Serenita*. They recorded extreme fluctuations within their engines."

"Okay, Bas, put them in with the rest of the data and hue them red for me."

As the erratic flight path of the *Vera* made its burning-red way through the holographic timeline, Guiselle spoke up first. "I have never seen flight patterns like that before. Is the information corrupted?"

The captain answered slowly, absorbed in studying the flight data. "No, the data is solid, there are no fragmentations…"

"I think I've seen similar behaviour with atmospheric flights, when there were air pockets or sudden drops in pressure." Jasatuta was thinking out loud.

"How would there be drops in pressure in space? It's not like we're going to get a lot less pressure than zero," Hafsat interjected.

The captain spoke up again. "No, Jasa is right, this does look similar to some kinds of atmospheric turbulences. It can't be changes in pressure, but the drones did already record other gravitational anomalies, so let's assume these are very compressed gravity waves. Look how they are preceding every move of the *Serenita*'s wings, right here. First, the *Vera* is hurled to the left and then, here, this wing right here moves in the exact same direction, could even be the same speed. All credit to the *Vera*'s pilot aside, I don't think the wings would ever have hit them like this."

Rhaleffi was massaging his temples with both hands, clearly thinking about how to work with the situation. "Let's summarise. We know that there is a gravitational anomaly, most likely centred on the exact location of the *Serenita*. The anomaly probably is what got them stuck there in the first place. Whatever the anomaly is, it would also be causing these gravity waves, which do seem to be at least somewhat predictable. Getting back to the task at hand, we need to get Seven close enough to use the docking system, so we can get everyone who is still alive on the *Serenita* out. Maybe we can try and ride these gravity waves, both conserving fuel and evading the wings at the same time."

"I hope I am not being too forward, Mars, but…" Guiselle had stood up and lain a hand on the captain's forearm, a doubtful, concerned look on her face. "I know you are a brilliant pilot—we all do—but we still have very limited information as to what is actually happening, and steering a huge structure like the Seven through an unpredictable situation like that…"

Rhaleffi started to respond. When she spoke up again, her voice hardened. "Attempting something like this would be reckless and irresponsible at best. We need to find another way."

Rhaleffi took Guiselle's hand off his forearm and placed it in between both of his hands, softly. When he spoke, his voice sounded younger than Hafsat had ever heard before.

"I know, Guiselle. And I thank you for your honest opinion, as always." He turned to the rest of the bridge crew. "We will take precautions. Hafsat, tell your sister to ready the drones she has on hand. We will need them to scout ahead and around Seven during approach. Jasa, have the technicians rig up the controls of Seven to a stable, light freighter. I want it docked and secured tightly in Seven's hindmost hangar, prepared for emergency release.

"Guiselle, I appreciate your concern and I hope these precautions are acceptable, because they are all we can do for now. I would go with another plan, but if we want any chance at saving these people, we need to use Dome Seven, because there is no time now to make anything else work.

"Any further objections? Good. Get to it, people."

***

Lloyd was making his way through the collapsed bulk of the third midsection.

He needed to find his daughter. He needed to find Alysia. He'd found about a dozen other survivors in an escape pod still sitting in its ejection module. The pod wouldn't budge, and they were now waiting for an emergency crew to help them out.

They'd be waiting a while. Lloyd hadn't come across any personnel fit to help anyone right now.

Lloyd was moving around in an EVA suit he had modified to the best of his abilities. The additional generator he had fused to the back section was heavy and made him sluggish and tired, but he needed it for the hydraulics and magnetic clamps he had mounted to the rest of the suit. He had placed the hydraulics in a way that would help increase his mobility during the stretches of heightened gravity that seemed to get more regular by the minute.

He had spent a total of two hours nailed to his workstation's floor because of those intense gravity stretches—and they were most definitely getting more and more intense. Even in his modified suit, he had been forced to use all his enhanced strength just to stay on his feet. It wasn't pretty, but it was getting the job done—the job, in this case, was being able to move around in a completely wrecked, over 3,000-year-old ship that was being bombarded by drones and debris and who knew what else.

He'd been stuck in that work station for hours on end. After he had taken care of his wounds, he had spent his time gobbling up emergency rations, smoking, and coming up with a lot of plans on how to get out—and survive once he did. Until he heard bits and pieces of a voice that sounded a lot like Jiro's amongst the radio static.

He had immediately sprung into action and done what he had been considering for all this time. Staying put had been the easy option, just thinking about his fate, pondering what could be done, without the risk of actually doing it. Even then, he dared not think of the impending doom that was possibly descending down on him while he was staying still and procrastinating. Hearing Jiro's voice, however, and consequently being reminded of the immediate danger Alysia was in, had changed things. His daughter being in mortal danger had triumphed over any and all other concerns.

Now he was rushing to the rescue without any doubts. There would be no distractions. No excuses. He would find her, he would make sure she was saved, even if it was the last thing he did.

***

Hafsat and the rest of the crew on the bridge sat still, stunned into shocked silence. After the captain had left for Dome Seven, they had broken through another small nebula and had come into visual contact with their target.

Hadiza was trying to contact him over the comms-channel, but he could not muster the will to take the call.

Suddenly, her voice came over the bridge PA system, breaking the crew out of their paralysis. "Repeat, this is Hadiza Calgari in engineering. Have you all gone deaf or something? What is going on up there?"

He unfroze from his daze, quickly opening the channel. "I'm sorry, sis, give me a second and I will link you up to the video feed. You need to see this for yourself."

The *Yaron* was slowly decelerating as she approached her destination. The Watchers behind her had just broken through the nebula as well and were now witnessing what the bridge crew had seen. A giant kaiju, many times bigger than the *Yaron*, dead ahead.

The *Æterna Serenita* had curled into itself at the epicentre of a titanic spiral of rock, dust, ice, and light. The spiral seemed to stretch on forever, made up from twisting shapes of grey, brown, yellow, and white.

Amongst the rubble were not only asteroids several miles in length, but also much larger objects. Slowly approaching from all sides and almost hidden in the chaos were what appeared to be objects the size of moons, bent into oval shapes, warped by incredible forces.

KAIJU

As he kept observing, the Watcher suddenly became aware of four distinct shapes he must have been ignoring for his sanity's sake. Planets, earth-sized. Four, at least. Their atmospheres were aflame, creeping towards the epicentre like the apostles of Armageddon.

"Hafsat, talk to me!" Jasatuta was shouting through the alarms. "I cannot get any response from the controls! Are we already stuck inside that gravity well?"

Hazida yelled over the radio. "Negative, the drones do not register any pull yet. We should still be good for another 6,000 miles!"

"Maybe the *Yaron* is overwhelmed by the sight as well?" Guiselle was close to tears, visibly shaking.

"I don't mean to blame her, but we need to get her under control. Setting impulses to 300 percent. Bas, get on it!"

"Roger, lieutenant!" But even with him trying his best, he could not seem to get any response from the *Yaron*. He kept trying, until suddenly—

It felt like being forced, stomach first, through hardened concrete. Hafsat was trying his best not to throw up. He attempted to scream, but the sound did not seem to leave him.

He looked around and saw Jasatuta falling to her knees, holding her head. Guiselle had collapsed on her stool.

Hafsat tried to get up, but his body would not obey him.

As the wave lessened for the first time, he realised he had not been able to breathe since it had begun.

As the wave lessened for the second time, he managed to get up, only to crash down to the floor again as it came back with even more force than before.

As the wave lessened for the third time, he realized what was happening: the *Yaron Tautari* was screaming.

***

Lloyd was staying awake—alive. He had spent the last ten minutes pressed flat against a collapsed support structure. At least two of his ribs were broken and the generator was running on fumes, but he had made it to Hub Twelve. She would be here somewhere, he knew it.

He slowly made his way through the collapsing hallways, the ceiling steadily sinking, ceramics, and composite metal structures being compressed. His feet were only able to move due to the motors on his suit working at maximum capacity.

He tried calling her on a broadband frequency again. "Alysia!" He used the speakers integrated into his helmet again. "Alysia, I am here, I am coming for you! Be brave! We will survive this!"

Lloyd broke through the apartment door and fell to his knees. The main room had been ripped in two, the two halves hanging more than fifty feet apart. Overhead, the gaping maw of vast space finally revealed the total horror of the situation to him.

He sat on his feet, stunned and unable to think, taking in the spectacle of burning planets and billions of tons of debris falling at him.

"Dad?"

Alysia was laying on the other side of the chasm in an emergency EVA suit. She was being pressed against the floor by the gravitation, clutching a human figure.

"Alysia! I am here, I am coming! Hold on!"

KAIJU

Lloyd could not hear anything but sobbing through the comms-channel, but at least she was still alive. Forcing himself back up, mustering the last of his strength, he slowly made his way down his side of the gap using whatever wiring or ledge was at hand.

He logged into her suit and checked her vitals. The emergency system had treated symptoms of acute exposure to zero space. Someone must have put the suit on her after it happened.

Still climbing, he logged into the apartment's surveillance system. He needed to know what had happened.

A playback of the last six hours started playing. Jiro, laying on the couch, Alysia walking around, motioning to the media feed, then, just a moment later, the feed cut off completely. He reached the bottom of the gap and started climbing up the other side as a rock the size of an elephant came crushing down, no less than twenty feet to his left. He tried the data logs. Just seconds after the cameras cut out, Jiro had activated the emergency drones using his up-link implant. One of the drones had been destroyed by the crash, however. Without a moment's hesitation, he had assigned the remaining drone to take care of Alysia. His vital signs had faded out 32 seconds later.

Lloyd continued climbing, tears running down his cheeks.

***

Several main structures had been disintegrated by the shock waves. Bulkheads were collapsing. The people of the *Yaron Tautari* were using the short intervals between the *Yaron*'s screams to breathe, recover, and to run—even if it was only a few steps at a time before the next wave hit them.

Captain Mars Rhaleffi was desperately trying to stay conscious as he readied the Seven for departure. Hafsat had somehow managed to send a message to him via the ship's neural net. Bless that boy. Once he had learnt what was happening, he had given the evacuation order for the entire crew. Everyone would have to try and make their way to Dome Seven. At this point, he was but hoping it would actually still be intact for long enough to achieve lift-off.

He checked the distance to the event horizon and felt a cold sweat break out on his back. They had already crossed the threshold. Rhaleffi did not understand; they should have had at least another two thousand miles at this point!

Then he saw the baseline moving. The gravity well was increasing. He had been right; there still were about three minutes left until they would pass the initially marked distance.

On the screen, the central hub was informing him of several transport crafts and private vessels that were starting to leave their docking bays. Only moments later, most of them had already left their designated flight routes, being drawn in by incredibly powerful tidal forces.

His only priority now was saving as many of his people as possible. Rhaleffi redirected all available processing power to a calculating-routine. He needed to know how long he would be able to wait before lift-off, factoring in both the steadily increasing pull of the gravity well and the continuously failing integrity of Dome Seven.

KAIJU

At this point, no more than 14 percent of the *Yaron*'s population had made it into his ship. Hafsat and his sister were still nowhere to be found, Jasatuta would not leave her post, and Guiselle was gone.

In that moment, the *Yaron* began to accelerate.

***

Lloyd had reached the level Alysia was on, but as he was starting to make his way forward to her, the generator burned out. He fell to the floor, unable to move. He had heard more of his bones breaking as he hit the floor. As all the air was being pressed out of him, his vision grew darker and darker.

Suddenly, gravity seemed to lessen. Lloyd coughed and started to breathe again. Using all the strength he had left, he started to crawl towards her, moving inch by inch.

All that mattered was saving her—against all logic, saving her. It did not matter how, nor did anything else. Screaming and kicking, making your way forward. Even if everything else failed, nobody should be alone like this. Nobody should die like this.

***

Planets were falling.

The *Æterna Serenita* was being buried. She was laying like an embryo in an eggshell still being assembled.

Dome Seven had managed to pull free of the *Yaron Tautari*, still rushing towards the other kaiju. The human craft was still desperately trying to achieve enough velocity to escape the pull of the abyss. They had burned through almost all of their fuel reserves, but there was still hope.

Hafsat was at peace. It had sounded like Hadiza would make it, just before the radio feed cut out. He was holding on to that.

He had needed to let the captain know, but nothing would work. Everything was falling apart and there was no time, so he had turned off all safeguards and fully integrated his thoughts into the *Yaron*'s neural net.

He had not known how to get back out, and he wasn't sure it mattered anymore. It had been too late, anyway. He felt a touch of eternity on his mind, senses that were used to tasting starlight, and wings that were forever weaving through the void.

He is listening now, and watching.

A lonely glass eye glistens in the dark, hanging by a thread off a plush toy rabbit, floating through space. As momentum carries it out from amongst the rubble it was hiding in, blinding sunlight shimmers against its frozen fur. A frozen hand, forever reaching for it. A large shadow is approaching, taking the sunlight away from them. Again, they are submerged in the deep and endless. Comforting calmness before two large masses collide, grinding both of them into icy fragments and dust.

KAIJU

Dominion
Tyron Dawson

Part One

Ireland, 1910.

The pristine streets of upper Dublin may have been enveloped by the bustle of commerce and joyous life, but the shadow of blight still hung over the city. The residents of the more affluent areas—those whose Balmorals were seldom spoiled by the soot and dredges of hard-living—knew nothing of the trials of those whose existences were confined within the walls of poverty. The wealthy had lorded over the less fortunate for decades, and had become accustomed to their lavish lifestyles, as well as the status they held.

The odours and grime that permeated through Oskar's forge on the outskirts of the city were a far cry from the swept boulevard and perfumed stores of the high street of Dublin. A dense fog of cool winter's air folded in through the open window and spread across the clay floor. Dew formed on the rusted bulks of metal scattered across the empty forge. Shimmering points of refracted light were strewn across the silent room. The clang of a hammer striking iron had been absent from this place for years.

WRITE LIKE HELL

Four years had slipped by since Oskar's father had been claimed by tuberculosis, but his bellowing voice was still fresh in his mind. It reverberated through his skull. It demanded more water to temper the steel, more coal, and more force behind each ringing strike. This six-foot-seven behemoth of a man had drawn a stark contrast to the slight frame of his only son. The old man had never held back in expressing his disappointment in him, whether it be his lack of physical prowess or his subservient personality. Oskar had tried in vain for years to earn his father's approval. The man's passing could have been likened to the double-edged swords commissioned by the resident militia some years prior: there were times when it was favourable, as well as instances when it posed a threat to the wielder. Beyond this, the fact remained that it could always be used to inflict harm.

Oskar Moore had tried his utmost to maintain the upkeep of his late father's forge since his death. Despite his efforts, he had lost the business of once loyal patrons, which led to the forge quickly falling into disrepair. Steam once sought out every crevice of the enclosed work area as orange-glowing metal was cooled in clay basins. Now the forge remained bone-dry for weeks at a time. Cracks spread through the dry wooden support beams like festering decay.

The forge was attached to the family's three-roomed home, and had once served as both workplace and source of warmth during the winter months. The only purpose the massive furnaces still served was radiating heat across the residential portion of the structure. It brought the family comfort and peace of mind when steam and smoke from the forge passed throughout the house. To the children, this had once been a sign that their father would be paid soon. It was a sign that they would eat. The memory remained, and could still convey a sense of comfort, even if the underlying reason had been extinguished. The forge was the heart of their dwelling, pumping life through their home.

The family lived as tenants-at-will, subject to the whims of their landlord, Mr Doyle. The threat of eviction hung over their heads, positioned to plummet at the first sight of disobedience or scarcity of coin on Oskar's part. The Doyle clan had originally made their fortune as farmers before subdividing and renting the land they had appropriated over the generations. The Purchase of Land Act that had passed twenty-five years ago had little effect on those who could barely afford the costs of daily life. Those in positions of power, who benefited from subjugation, always found a way.

Life under the glaring eye of Mr Doyle was difficult. He had used his affluence to hold Oskar's father under his thumb. Mr Moore, a man who had towered over his squat landlord, had portrayed the role of submissive underling when in his presence. As cowardly as it may at first seem, he knew that challenging Mr Doyle would not serve his family well.

***

Oskar woke to a loud knocking on his door. The sound cut through the early morning silence, waking Eliza and their children. He leapt from their bed and dashed to the door to find Mr Doyle waiting on the other side.

"I require the use of this property by the end of the month," he huffed as he stood on the cracked paving which led to the door. "My sister has obtained a position as a teacher at the preparatory school and will take up residence here four months from now. Time must be set aside for the necessary renovations. I am certain that there will be adequate time for you to make arrangements for yourself and your family."

The statement left Oskar astounded. Mr Doyle stared impatiently as Oskar gathered the thoughts swirling in his mind. He blurted his response in a panicked tone. "But Sir, we have nowhere else to go! My work is here. How will I provide for my family?"

"That is none of my concern." The condescension in his tone hung in the air. "Now, if you would excuse me, I have other matters to which I must attend." With this final nail driven into the coffin, Mr Doyle withdrew, mounted his horse, and began his canter back to his opulent family manor.

The Moore family were left in defeated silence. Never before had their future been so clouded.

Thirty miles away, a low rumbling reverberated through the hillside. Dublin had been built on the backs of the mines that surrounded it. The walls of the abandoned iron mine began to crumble and collapse. A gust of rancid air spewed out of a newly formed crack. An exhale thousands of years in the making had finally been released.

KAIJU

Part Two

A bone-white claw as large as a horse protruded through the entrance of the mine. The surrounding hillside began to crumble under the immense pressure of the creature's emerging frame. Stones and dirt fell away as it pulled each of its six limbs free and stretched for the first time in millenia. A shiver ran through the length of its gargantuan, pale body as it lifted a broad head in the cool air and inhaled deeply. It struggled at first to move, having been without nourishment for so long. It needed to feed.

The breeze carried a scent no human would have detected. It was the scent of joy and contentment. The creature began to move in the direction of the tantalising smell. Its lanky body cast a shadow over the shrubberies as it passed, while its bloated gut brushed the treetops. A thick, noxious mist began to issue out from a number of orifices along the creature's body. If any unfortunate soul had been present to witness its fledgling steps, they would have strained to see through the dark fog exuding from the behemoth. The white, ashen tone of its taut skin was the only thing visible as it drew closer to Dublin.

Oskar gathered his family inside their home. Cracks ran across the walls like a spider's web, and it seemed as if every drop was felt during rainstorms—but it had been their home. It was where Annabel, his eldest, had been born fourteen years ago. It was where Eliza had taught Grantham to read. Would these memories not disperse like vapour without the confines of these walls to hold them in place?

Eliza calmed the children in the bedroom before returning to Oskar. She had always been his voice of reason and calm, but now there was blind panic in her eyes.

"He can't do this! Where will we go? How can I care for our children if we are stripped of all sense of safety?"

The silence that followed seemed to hang in the air, slowly resting upon them as they contemplated their fates. Oskar knew what was required of him, but was filled with too much self-doubt to utter any words. He had lived under the pressure of his circumstances for too long. If his family were to survive, he would have to lay a new path for them.

"We will travel to the city in the morning. Eliza, there is nothing left here for us. I will find work in Dublin, as well as residence for us. We have no choice. I'll make the wagon ready for tomorrow."

Fear plunged deep through Oskar with every sentence uttered, but he tried to hide it from his wife. He tried, but knew it was a futile act; she could always tell how he truly felt. He drew her closer and said, "We will survive this."

The family left their home for the final time the following morning. Grantham, having been too young to truly grasp the gravity of the situation, was excitable and boisterous. He saw the journey as an adventure. Annabel remained silent. Her eyes were hollow, and her sombre expression set in stone. The precarious state of her family's well-being was all too comprehensible for her.

The wagon arrived in Dublin late that afternoon. Finding affordable shelter was the most pressing issue at that point. The Moore family were struck by fortune in the form of Mr O'Sullivan, an elderly innkeeper with a penchant for smithing. The Paiste Inn was located in an old, two-storey building with narrow passageways,

KAIJU

and even narrower rooms. He offered them accommodation in exchange for a few coin and willing ears. That night, he recounted how, on the brink of entering his years of youthful independence, he had faced the onset of The Great Famine that had plagued Ireland for seven years.

"Blight swept through the fields, spreading rot aimlessly. The white mould was the sign. It covered the leaves of every stem, marking them as corrupted. Every household in Ireland felt the wrath of that monstrosity. When the undertakers could no longer take in any more, bodies were laid out on the roadside, covered in shroud after shroud, hiding the visage of those who had passed," Mr O'Sullivan said, before lowering his gaze and concluding with a sombre point. "Some no more than thirty inches long."

Eliza focused her gaze on her husband as the innkeeper offered more tales from his youth. She knew Oskar's mind better than he knew it himself, and could sense his anxieties crashing at the doors, attempting to escape. He needed time to recover.

"Excuse us Mr O'Sullivan, but it is rather late and it has been a trying day. Would you mind if we turn in for the night? The worry and travel today have left me rather worn."

"Of course. I wouldn't want to keep you. You all can sleep in the empty room at the end of the hall."

The old man's words cascaded through her mind as she and Oskar returned to their children. It had been such a detached way of conveying something so horrible. *"...thirty inches long."* She inhaled deeply, refusing to let those words upset her. She had to remain strong for her children. She needed to provide the support she knew her husband required. She loved him, but knew that he would need her unwavering support during this time.

***

A mile or so beyond the edge of the city, the creature lifted its head in the brisk night air. The flesh along its neck quivered as it drew in a deep breath. The nourishment it required was near and in abundance, but the long years of its dormancy had left it too weak to go any further. It settled its skeletal body on the soft brush and shut its turquoise eyes.

KAIJU

Part Three

A new day offered new opportunities for the Moore family. The soft light of the morning illuminated the stone-faced buildings as they passed by. Mr O'Sullivan had pulled Oskar aside while Eliza and the children ate a surprisingly plentiful breakfast provided by his wife.

"If you're looking for work, notices are posted regularly at the library on Pearse Street. There might not be an abundance to choose from, but you have to take whatever you can get. You have a family that depends on you. This is not the time to turn your nose up at menial work. If the only position available is that of messenger, you take it!

A few hours later, buoyed on by a few witty words of encouragement provided by Mrs O'Sullivan, the Moore clan set off for the Dublin City Library. The face of the structure presented rows of tall windows along both floors that welcomed in an abundance of light. Oskar knew he shouldn't put all his hopes on their very first endeavour, but he couldn't help imagining all the opportunities this building could hold.

They entered the library via the large Scots pine doors, which led into a small foyer containing a clerk's desk. The young woman stationed at the desk lifted her head as Oskar drew the doors shut behind him.

"Good morning, Miss," Oskar replied, "I believe the library has the work listings from entrepreneurs in the city. Is it possible I could take a look at them for a while? I would be incredibly grateful."

The clerk's face softened as her gaze moved over to the children. "Certainly, I would be happy to assist you. My name is Miss Reilly." Her gentle expression conveyed genuine care and concern, far from the false mask of platitudes behind which most in the service of the public hid. She entered the main hall, followed by a bewildered Oskar. He had never before seen such a massive assortment of books. When Oskar was a child, his father had ensured that his son was taught to read. He wanted his son to have options beyond metalwork. The library contained a plethora of knowledge readily available to all those who were fortunate enough to have both access to the tomes and the words they contained.

***

Oskar wandered the stacks that stretched out before him. He reflected on how they were more than mere sources of knowledge. He saw them for what they truly were: a possible means of obtaining a better life. It was only when Oskar followed Miss Reilly further into the hall that he noticed the silence that hung about the place. Deeper than any he'd experienced before, it had an almost tangible quality to it, and rested upon everything in the library. Miss Reilly seemed to hesitate, pausing in her steps as she peered into the gloomy corners of the hall.

The large hall was immersed in almost complete silence. A few moments later, a number of bibliophiles began to notice a thick mist which had begun to seep in through various crevices along the south wall. The few whom the quickly dispersing smog had already reached fell to their knees in an eerie silence. A woman who, moments before, had been captivated by the thick novel before her, suddenly fell to the floor. A blood-curdling scream rang through the hall, shrill at first but quickly descending into a guttural stutter.

The floral-scented fog spread throughout the stacks like clawing fingers groping for their prey. Almost every soul in the library was suddenly overwhelmed by dread. It was peculiar how an odour so pleasant could evoke such desolate responses. Anxiety thrust its way through the hall. This fear of the unknown quickly devolved into a crippling state of submissive hopelessness. The opaque mist penetrated deep through the bronchial passageways of almost everyone present and suffocated all sense of hope.

A broad segment of roofing collapsed, revealing the pale creature to the despondent patrons. Joy was drawn out, and siphoned up to it, via narrow streams of mist. The hopes and elations of its helpless prey strengthened it and gave it dominion over their crippled forms.

Oskar watched from a distance, petrified, as one man crumpled under the influence of the creature and lay with his knees tucked under his chin. The subjected man lay there motionless, not trying to escape, whimpering softly. After a few minutes, everyone had succumbed to the pale creature's influence, except Oskar, his family, and Miss Reilly. The swirling tendrils of mist had not yet reached them. He gestured to the others and quietly led them towards the entrance. Oskar draped his arms over Grantham and Annabel's shoulders in a desperate attempt to comfort them while still remaining silent.

The pale creature demolished a row of bookcases as it lumbered across the library floor. The novels that now lay ruined amongst the rubble held no value to the creature. A rattling, booming sigh spread through the library as the group reached the front doorway. It didn't convey emotion of any kind, but rather a more primal sense that needs had been met; its appetite had been satisfied. Thoughts charged through Oskar's mind. Notions of how hopeless this all seemed. How he had failed at various junctures in his life. How Eliza was far more capable of navigating life than he was. Did his family really need him? Would they not have a better chance of survival without him? Perhaps the noblest act he could perform would be to distract the pale creature while his family escaped? He was brought back to reality by his wife's panicked voice before his mind could disappear completely into the void.

"We have to escape! There's nowhere to hide. Oskar, help!"

The signature fog began to fill the room, making it difficult to discern who was who. The walls separating the cramped entrance hall from the main library began to shudder, and then collapsed, not unlike Oskar's last reason for self-preservation. If his family perished, there would be no point in continuing to live. He loved them with all his heart, and the only world he could imagine without them would be one consumed by darkness and sorrow. A world of pure torture to which he, the lone survivor, would wake each morning.

He turned to his wife, grasped both her hands, and said, "Run, take the children and run as far as you can. Don't look back. The only thing that will give me peace is knowing that my family is safe. Take the children and run." He pressed his thumb to Eliza's lips one final time. An act that held more significance for the pair than any kiss could have meant. He knew this act would give him the will to face his demon and save his family.

The fog was now too thick for Oskar to see his wife's face. He felt her grip loosen and her hands slowly draw away. He was alone with the pale creature. Sorrow shrouded him as he turned to face it in its entirety for the first time. The creature hunkered down until its broad, curved head was level with Oskar's gaze. A voice whispered in the recesses of his mind and echoed throughout his subconscious.

"There is no point in resisting. I am inevitable, give in. Why would you force your family to endure any more of this? Allow me to take you and I will let them go. Your life is worthless. Surrender it to me so that your family may survive."

The voice resonated in Oskar's mind. He had recognised it as soon as he heard it. It was the voice of his most outspoken critic. It was the voice that degraded him at every opportunity. That sickening tone, he thought, it's the voice of my father.

He slowly took the first step toward the conclusion he believed his life deserved. The innocent should not be forced to suffer due to the cowardice of the weak, he reasoned. The fog surged through his body. Its influence on his mind was immediate. He feared what might come next—the finality of it all. The immense, turquoise eyes of the pale creature loomed ahead of him, robbing him of the last of his ambitions and confidence. The whisper invaded his mind once more.

"Why continue to suffer when relief may be found in one simple act? I will take everything from you. I can see the path on which you are set. It is nothing but a downward spiral into a bottomless chasm. End it now."

The voice tore through Oskar's mind. It felt as if an ice-cold axe had been thrust into his skull. He collapsed to the floor and shut his eyes, wishing it would come to an end. He reached out, searching for something heavy enough to do what needed to be done. A moment later, his fingertips brushed against something coarse. A muffled but familiar sound reached his ears as he lifted the brick above his own head. The sound shook him to his core and gave him pause. He strained to identify what he was hearing. A voice, a stern but loving voice said, "Oskar, don't do it. We love you. Our lives would not be the same without you."

KAIJU

Part Four

Oskar felt a hand grasp his shoulder. The familiar grip instilled him with the bravery to open his eyes. The first things to come into focus were a pair of green eyes. These were the eyes that had watched him work over the years. These were the eyes that had seen him achieve small triumphs that had meant the world to him, but had also witnessed his most devastating failures. Those brilliant green points had witnessed his soul being dismantled, but had remained to help build him back up. He lay the brick down on the ground. Slowly, he sat up and stared into the eyes of his saviour. Despite all the destruction surrounding them, his wife had never looked more beautiful to him.

They rose to their feet without breaking eye contact. Oskar wrapped his arms around Eliza's waist, embracing her as tightly as he could. "I'm so sorry," he said. "At first I thought I was acting in the best interests of you and the children. I thought I could spare you any more pain by offering my own life to this creature. Your words pulled me out of the void."

The Moore family, together with Miss Reilly, ran out of the ravaged structure into the vacant street out front. They were met by a scene so bleak that it would stay imprinted on their souls until their final breaths escaped each of their chests. Businessmen, matriarchs, children, vagrants, and people of all other walks of life, were motionless in the streets. Some were cowering on their knees, others were silent and breathing heavily, and a few were suspiciously still. The absolute hold the pale creature had on each of their minds had brought them to their own personal points of unrelenting despair.

In the end, it had been too much for some of them to bear. This was the outcome of an absence of all hope.

The group fled. Without sparing a moment to consider what had happened, they collectively decided to run from the crushing presence of the pale creature. They did not need to consider their options. There was no need to address the possibility that the creature may still have a hold on their minds. Amorphous taunts still echoed through each of their thoughts. The only thing that mattered was that they attempted to get as far away from the source of their suffering as quickly as possible.

The city lay in ruin. Shops and homes had been reduced to rubble, strewn across the ravaged roads. The rancid odour of death hung in the streets like a curtain. The façade of every building along Main Street was obscured by fog.

Eventually, they came to a halt outside a small house at the end of a street. A stuffed bear lay near a hedge of bushes. Something was protruding from the bushes—small, pudgy, and motionless. It was the leg of a young boy who had tried to escape the horrors that had surrounded him upon the pale creature's arrival. He had fallen short.

"We can't run from it any longer," Eliza cried out. "We have to turn and face it. There is no escaping it by running blindly, without any support. Whatever the outcome, turning our backs on this beast will not lead to our salvation. She turned to her children, her eyes filled with love and devotion. "It will be frightening, but it will all be over soon." The children did not detect the ambiguity present in the statement.

Oskar's eyes widened as he realised the gravity of his wife's words. His mind cycled through every instance where he considered himself a failure as a father. This was his final chance to redeem himself. He would face the creature.

He turned to Miss Reilly and, in a low voice, said, "We have to turn back. If we run, it will continue to seek us out, hanging over us forevermore. This is the only choice we have." Miss Reilly nodded solemnly. They turned together to face the pale creature.

The journey back into the shadow of the looming beast was laden with anxiety for Oskar. He had found the mettle displayed by Miss Reilly during their trek quite surprising. She walked in silence with a look of steely determination in her eyes. This was the end, he thought, as they reached the shadow of the creature. No matter what the outcome, he had tried his utmost to protect his family. The creature turned slowly to face them. Its bright turquoise eyes shone brilliantly.

Oskar stepped forward through the thick fog. He began to mutter as he walked, more to himself than any attempt to address the pale creature before him. He said, "It may not be easy to rise and face the light of each new dawn, but if I do, I will have overcome the first oppressor of the day. To know that many obstacles lie in wait of me, but to continue in spite of this requires true courage. My greatest persecutor isn't this creature grasping for control of every thought which passes through my mind. I am my own greatest foe. The ones I love will continue to suffer as long as I turn a blind eye to the consequences of my actions." He turned his gaze to the source of his anguish and shouted, "I do not fear you! As long as I have the love of my family, I will survive. I still have a purpose, a reason to live!" At the moment his final words left his mouth, a ripple shot through the fog in the direction of the pale creature. It emitted a strange, high sound, barely within the range of human hearing. For lack of a better word, it could be described as a soft whimper.

The wave of pressurised air was followed by a dense silence. The silence bore down heavily on them, and led each of them toward their own personalised line of tragic thoughts. Miss Reilly was the first to break the silence.

"Do you realise what just happened? It uses the fog to feed on us."

Oskar, confused by this sudden statement, turned to her and asked, "What do you mean? How can fog eat?"

A stream of fog suddenly surrounded Miss Reilly. She could feel it trying to take control of her subconscious. Her mother's shrill voice pierced her mind.

"You will die a spinster, unworthy of love. No one would ever want to marry you."

Miss Reilly turned to the creature with an expression of resilience on her face. She was scared, but she knew that she had to attempt to summon enough courage to face her fears. She began to speak, softly at first, "I may not have anyone with whom to share my life with today, but that has no hold over me. I do not seek fulfilment by attaching myself to the life of another; I can find contentment in myself and my own accomplishments. Today may be bleak, but I have the rest of my life to live. The possibilities for what the future may hold are endless."

The fog that surrounded Miss Reilly dissipated as quickly as it had appeared. An aura of clear air surrounded her. The creature could no longer reach her through the fog. Oskar felt a glimmer of hope in the recesses of his soul. He turned to face the pale creature and said, "You tried to take everything from me. You would have me devoid of any desire to live." He turned to face his wife and children before completing, "I will always have a reason to live, as long as I have my family."

The fog began to recede from every corner of the city. It was wrenched out of every citizen's body and drew back across the streets. The pale creature's broad jaws hung open as multiple streams of surging fog entered through its mouth and eyes. It shrieked as fog penetrated the multiple, small orifices along its body. The distressed beast stumbled as its pallid skin began to harden and turn black. It eventually collapsed to the ground and shattered into thousands of tiny shards. The pale creature's oppressive control over the city had come to an end.

The silence that remained in the wake of the beast was palpable. Oskar remained motionless for a moment, fearing that any action on his part would somehow restore the fragmented creature. His mind went to his family once he was certain that it was finally over. Eliza stood a few feet behind him, near the half-demolished wall of a small cottage. Her arms were wrapped around Grantham as she tried to comfort him. Where was Annabel?

The world, and all the sights and sounds it contained, began to flood into Oskar's head as he veered in every direction, searching for his daughter. He did not have to search for long. Her slight figure lay lifeless behind a bed of blackthorn. She had wanted to support her father in his time of need, but had succumbed to the overpowering onslaught. Oskar fell to his knees and cradled her as he wailed.

An eternity passed before Oskar could lift his head once again. The widespread devastation the creature had left behind ran through every facet of his life. It had torn him open and left a wound that would never close. Nothing could change what had happened. The remnants of the Moore family would have to live with the consequences or risk summoning a new creature to wreak havoc over their lives.

KAIJU

Kaiju Noir

Matthew Fairweather

It's an hour before the sun will creep its way over the city walls, high as they are, but the dust rolls in, steady as always. I sit at my desk and try to kill yesterday's hangover by getting an early start on tomorrow's. A tremor rattles my office as giant monsters that people haven't seen in generations tussle on the other side of the mountains that stand watch over the city. Fate ruffles her cards and starts dealing me my hand for the day, starting with a queen that knocks thrice on my door and lets herself in.

"Detective Murphy?"

Even after having tipped a few, I could tell from across the room this dame had eyes like the moon's reflection in the reservoir, and god damn if I didn't feel like wading out and drowning.

"Who's asking?"

"My name's Penelope, Penelope Jochovic. Mr Murphy, I have a case for you." She strides up to my desk and makes motions towards the chair opposite. I nod, and she sits down.

"Call me Mick."

"As in Micheal?"

"As in Donald. Every Murphy man since time immemorial has been lumbered with the handle Mick, same with the O'Brien men until the last of them cashed their chips. No one remembers why, but here I stand, Mick."

Penelope looks around my office and shifts in her chair. I'm guessing the slightly ramshackle nature of both the office and myself was not what she was expecting. She ain't no damsel, though; I can tell by the set of her jaw. It takes grit to come to this end of town alone, and she is chock-full of it.

"Mr Murphy, my father's gone missing. I believe he may be in trouble."

I unclip my pen and pad from the desk and start taking notes. I also loose a cigarette from a deck in my pocket. I offer one to Penelope that is flatly refused. "So, when was the last time you saw your father?" I ask, lighting my smoke.

"Yesterday. We had lunch together at a bistro on the square."

"You mean to tell me it hasn't even been 24 hours? Listen, dollface…" Like a flash, I take a mitt to the kisser that loosens my molars and sends my smoke flying to land neatly in my drink. I sit a moment, stunned, as Penelope looms over my desk.

"I will not have some booze-hound gumshoe talk to me that way, Mr Murphy."

"Listen, you lousy skirt, if this is how you ask for help, I dread to see how you pay. I'm sorry your old man *might* be in a jam, but I think it's time you leave."

"Mr Murphy, people have seldom good to say about you, and in person you're worse. But the word is that, despite your flaws, you can be trusted to get things done. The word is that, when it comes to finding people, there are none better." She takes a beat and sizes me up before she continues. "As for how I pay, the answer is well. Providing you can keep a civil tongue from this point forward, how does a $100 a day strike you?"

"It strikes me like your left cross, Ms Jochovic," I say, cradling my jaw. "So, fill me in on the particulars. What makes you think your father is in trouble? What was his daily routine? Who was the last to see him? Does he have any enemies?"

"I worry for my father's safety, Mr Murphy, because of his line of work."

"Oh, yeah? What line of work is that? He a boxer? He teach you how to throw like that?" As allergic to sincerity as I am, I try to resist a smirk. A hundred clams a day will keep my whistle wet till Christmas.

"Where do people like you come from, Mr Murphy? I just can't picture it."

"According to my grandma, my family came here on a boat."

Penelope cocks her head to one side. "A boat? What's that?"

"Water vehicle of some kind or other." I light a new smoke, and as a precaution, lean back as far as I can in my chair.

"Oh yeah, did she take it for a spin across the reservoir?"

"Water used to come bigger than the reservoir, they say."

"Sure, Mr Murphy. Wetter, too, I bet."

I pick my pad and pen back up and ask again what her father's line of work is.

"He's a scientist Mr Murphy, a Kaiju Scientist."

***

I hop a streetcar a few hours after Penelope leaves my office. Ain't no good putting the squeeze on folks still napping. I'm heading uptown, not so far uptown that a couple of the parlours don't have brunos on the door, but close enough that you can see the odd senior with their glad rags on, heading out for some sautéed protein. I've left my goggles and mask on, even out of the dust. Screw etiquette, I don't need to know these people, and they sure as hell don't need to know me. The ground shakes, rocking the car on whatever suspension keeps it on the track. I look out the window into the blanket of dust. I swear, living in a world that seems to want to shake you off it, without a drink, I might just let it.

"Maybe it's mating season," says some rube to my left.

"Sure," I say. "We're all nothing if not screwed."

I jump outside Johnny Wilson's Place, a known watering hole for those behind the eight ball and the hatchet men who've made them their marks. It was the last place anyone had seen Dr Jochovic, and to my surprise, apparently he was a regular. I walk through the doors into the lobby, dust myself off, and enter the bar proper. I walk through the crowd of early drinkers dipping their bills to drop my gear on the bar. The oldest canary I ever laid eyes on has just taken the stage and is already visibly losing the will to live.

"Mick the Dick!"

Behind the bar is Ron Jackson. We walked a beat together before the beat became too literal and the number of cops shakin' down stores outnumbered those that didn't. He'd stuck it out longer than I did, even with the hard time he got 'cause of his pigment.

KAIJU

"Big Ron, how's the kids?"

"Ain't customers here yet, so I must be doing something right."

"Good to hear! Look, Ron, I'm looking for someone. Older, bookish-looking guy who must stick out in here like a sore thumb. Can you help me out, for old times' sake?"

"Look, man, you want a tip? Try the protein here—best in town. Part from that, loose lips in this joint gets you a pine overcoat, feel me?"

I pull my ration card out of my pocket, two stamps for protein this week and we just hit Sunday service.

"This all you eating? You must be working your green house to dust." Ron says, taking my card and stamping it.

I tap the flask in my breast pocket. "Liquid lunches."

Ron leans heavy on the bar and looks me in the eye. Then he asks the question no man should ask another. "How you doing, Mick? Really."

"I'm all peaches and cream, Ron. Fine and gosh-darn dandy. Now, come on, you gotta know something." I pull a couple sawbucks from my pocket and slide them across the bar.

Ron snatches it off the table and stuffs it in his apron. "You don't want nobody in here seeing you do that. You need to cool your jets, take a load off, and like I been tryin' to tell you, try the freakin' protein."

Something twigs, I take a step back and see where my man's coming from. "Sure, hook me up."

Muscles that had been rising in bunches over Ron's shoulders relax, and he walks off into the kitchen. I wonder if he's going to slip me a note in the brick, or write a code in the sauce. I'm intrigued by all the cloak and danger for one old man. Maybe this case ain't as cut and dry as I thought.

A tremor sets all the bottles dancing in their spring-bottom holders and rattles any cups not clipped down to the lips of the tables. It also covers the advance of two goons creeping up on me. One lays a massive paw on my shoulder that has me reach for my piece.

"Not so fast," I hear as a barrel is pressed into my back. "Heard you askin' questions. Boss is gonna want a word."

The canary has stopped singing.

***

I've seen the backroom of a few dives in my time, and they often reflect the personality of the owner. Johnny Wilson's back room had delusions of grandeur painted all over it. The chair Johnny was sitting on couldn't have been more of a throne if it flushed. That being said, Johnny had become a known name over the last couple months. He'd picked up a bit of sway with the egg and butter men of this city, even slipped the bracelets by calling in favours. He wasn't in charge in any way that counts, but he knew people who were.

"Donald Murphy."

"You know, I'm having a day where everyone's saying my name and not a soul has said it how I like yet."

"What are you doing in my bar, Donald?"

"Lost dog case. You seen him? 'bout yea big, answers to Fido?"

Johnny's fuse burns out like I ain't seen before and he blows his stack. He jumps to his feet and slams a fist down on the table, which has the effect of making all his hired muscle take a step towards me. "Listen, you miserable flatfoot, don't play games with me!" he says, standing up at his full height of five-foot nothing.

Now, if you're a good detective, information is only meant to flow one way, but I can see if I don't give him something, I'm in for the big sleep. It's a shame, really, an older class of criminal would've known how to play.

"Some dame's father's been gone a day or so. Figured he was just making use of your fine establishment is all, nothing sinister," I say, fully aware I'm relieving myself in a psychopath's pocket and calling it rain.

Johnny sits back down and grabs the fattest cigar I've ever seen from a box on his desk. In deference to my host's apparent unstable tendencies, I ask permission to light a cigarette of my own.

"You go right ahead. Now, as for Dr Jochovic, he's no longer any of your concern."

"Believe you me, if I had known my client was sending me to snoop in your business, I would have told them to ride their thumb—if you'll excuse the colourful turn of phrase."

The little volcano in a pinstripe suit puts his feet up on the desk and stares at me from behind a thick cloud of smoke. I can tell he's considering whether I get to see tomorrow, or if I leave his office and go straight for a dirt nap.

"Here's how it's going to go. I catch you anywhere near my business again and I'll cut your fingers off, I'll cut your toes off, and then I'll start working on you. Am I clear?"

"As a day without dust Johnny," I say, before I feel hands move towards steel. "*Mr Wilson*," I correct.

"Very good. Now, there's only one thing left." Johnny clicks his fingers and everyone starts getting real helpful. My cigarette is taken from my mouth and stubbed out for me. I'm also helped to my feet in a manner I don't really appreciate. Once all the formalities are taken care of, I'm marched out a side door and held in place while everyone gets their goggles and masks on. Looks like we're going for a walk. I spot a big palooka in the back with my gear, all balled up under his arm.

We get to the alley that runs behind the bar. The dust stings my eyes and makes it hard to breathe, even before any of the gorillas start playing chin music. One guy gets behind me and holds my arms back. Through the dust I can see two figures donning brass knuckles and grinning to themselves. "Ever have a day where fate just deals you crap? Between the joker in there and you pair of deuces, how is a guy meant to get ahead?"

They work me over good. One of them, wide-set, hits like a train. Lots of power but slow, and always to the gut. The other's a whippet of a man, and he's worse—lots of short, sharp jabs. He likes to work the puss. I hear two crunches—my nose and my rib—before they run outta steam, though I can also feel warm streams of blood coming from a cut above my eye and a busted lip. When the guy behind me lets go, I drop like a sack of spuds. I can't breathe and I sure as shoot can't see. The last man, the big one holding my gear, steps forward and drops my goggles in front of me. I reach out for them, and just as I'm about to thank the patron saint of kind-hearted goons, he steps on my hand.

"Remember, Donald," he says, "fingers and toes." Leaving my goggles on the floor, he throws everything else in a skip, and all four head back inside, laughing.

KAIJU

I put on the goggles, blink as much dust out of my eyes as I can and try to crawl. Each inch I make hurts, and I cough great, wet hacking coughs. I make it to the skip, but there's no way I'm pulling myself up. Round the corner of the building I make out what I hope is a pay phone. What can't have been more than eight metres feels like a mile. When I get inside, I reach up and knock the receiver off its cradle with my fingertips and hit the vac-o-matic, which sucks all the dust out of the booth. Looking down, I see my blood flecking the floor. I feel my breast pocket, only to find my flask missing. I turn what little focus I have left to the keypad and think of all the phone numbers I know and the short list of people who would pick up for me. In the end, I dial Penelope and get her machine. "Hey, Pen, so I'm off the case. Your father was mixed up with a real bad crowd, and it ain't worth even what you're payin'. If I manage to get outta this phone booth, I'm gonna go pick my clothes out of a dumpster and lay low for a while. So, that's how my day is going. Hope the world's treating you better, doll…"

The world trembles, and that's all she wrote.

***

I wake up and the world's in black and white. Hazy shapes move in the distance and it feels like someone is tap-dancing on my skull. I go to sit up, but a shooting pain in my side tells me in no uncertain terms to lie back down.

"You're awake."

The voice is soft, and when I see her looking down at me, there's colour in the room again, colour in the form of a full pair of ruby-red lips.

"Ms Jochovic," I say, mummified in bandages. "Where am I?"

"My place. I got your message and went looking for you."

She's mopping my brow with a damp cloth. Her perfume fills my nostrils, and the ground shakes. I shift my weight best I can and start trying to get my bearings, taking what weak grasp I can of the world and pulling it back into focus. Penelope's apartment is as classy as her, and it's the tastefulness of the décor, and its stark contrast to my garbage pile of belongings, that helps me spot them on the chez longue. "You went dumpster diving for me?"

"Seemed the least I could do, given what happened to you on my behalf," she says, unable to make eye contact for a moment before regaining composure. "Can I get you anything?"

"Pass me my coat."

She leans across and grabs my bundled-up coat. As she does, my hat, mask, gun, and a brown paper bag fall to the floor. I rifle through my pockets and breathe a deep sigh of relief when I come across my flask. "There you are, baby. Thought I'd lost you."

"You've been beaten up that badly and you still think it's a good idea to have a drink?" Penelope says, picking my stuff up off the floor.

"I've been beaten up this badly and you think it's a bad idea that I have a drink?" I say after a hefty pull. "Hey, what's in the bag?"

"I don't know," she says, handing it over to me. "It was with your other things—at least, I thought it was when I scooped them out of the trash."

Opening the bag, I find an A-grade slab of protein. None of that rat-and-sawdust stuff the government hands out. I hadn't seen meat this fresh since my last case took me down the morgue.

"Wow, this looks good enough to eat," I say, showing Penelope the brick.

"I wouldn't."

"Why, because it was in the trash? Half the city is eating out the trash. Food this good is hard to come by," I say taking a bite.

"I wouldn't, because that bag was sitting on a corpse when I found it."

I spit the protein back into the bag, then hawk up a couple fresh ones for good measure before chasing it with a hit from my flask. "Who was the lucky contestant in trash can number one?" I ask, before realising if Johnny is icing people, it don't bode well for Dr Jochovic.

"A big guy, dark, looked like a barman from his apron."

A chill hit the air. They couldn't have—there wasn't time while I was in the back room. What am I talking about? Of course there was, the way a hothead like Johnny would have it done. They would have walked him out back and capped him with no ceremony whatsoever. I grit my teeth and ball my fists as what happened unfurls in my head. They didn't even let him take off his apron… or put down the protein. The protein… *my* protein. I pause a beat, then slowly turn the paper bag upside down. The protein, my chewed lump and some spit hit Penelope's rug. I toss it all over, looking for the note or clue Ron was going to give me. The pain in my side lights up like a match hitting gas, but I dig all the same.

"What on earth are you doing?!" Penelope yells, diving down towards the mess.

"My friend Ron, the body you found, was going to give me a clue—least I thought he was. Come on, Ron, where is it?" My digging becomes more frantic as I tear the protein into little pieces.

Penelope takes hold of my hands and I stop. I look into her eyes and see fat tears swell at their corners.

"I'm sorry about your friend," she says, doing everything she can to keep her voice steady.

"Sorry about your father."

***

I spend the night laid-up on Penelope's sofa. By morning I'm mobile enough to shamble into the kitchenette and put on a pot of java. I pull a couple of eggs from a coup on the balcony and crack them into a pan. While looking through the cupboards for some bread, Penelope gets the drop on me.

"Making yourself at home, I see."

"One of those eggs is for you."

She smiles at me and tucks her hair behind her ear in a way that makes my knees weak.

"I was thinking of heading over to father's office, maybe find out for myself what happened. Back in the family home, he had a false bottom installed in his drawers so that he could hide sweets from my sister and I. I feel it would be worth taking a look."

"Forget it. Too risky. Clients that come down with lead poisoning seldom pay their bills. I'll go after breakfast."

Penelope's ears prick up and she looks at me with a half-smile. "So, am I still your client?"

As I look at her, I want to tell her that she's more than a client—that I'm starting to have feelings for her that I haven't felt before. The eggs hiss in the pan and I tend to them, pulling my eyes off hers.

"A good man don't stay down for long, neither do us 'booze-hound gumshoes', for that matter."

"I think you're a good man, Mick, a very good man."

I tell her that I'm staying on the case, as it's the best way to pin something on Johnny for killing Ron; that the money's good, and that I think I can carry on from here giving the mob a wide berth. When I get back to my place, while I change my shirt and pick up my motor, I think about the things I didn't tell her. Firstly, that someone who studied kaiju, like her father, would have had access out of the city to the observatory in the mountains. That'd make him a handy smuggler if he could be threatened or bribed. And secondly, that being a scientist probably meant he had the kit to test Johnny's black-market protein and see whether or not it was human.

It was a horrible suspicion to hold, but it was the only way I could see someone low-rent as Johnny Wilson pulling together that much protein. The mountains keep us safe from the kaiju, but it leaves our whole world only about twenty-miles wide, and with almost a hundred thousand mouths to feed, livestock is worth more than people to those at the top. Johnny wasn't getting his hands on anything larger than a goat, even with all the grifters and swindlers in his employ, but making people disappear, that was something he could do. The worst thought was, that would explain the sway he had with the politicians. Someone who could feed the rough side of town, and curb its population at the same time, would be worth his weight in gold.

WRITE LIKE HELL

***

Driving in the dust is slow-going, but gives someone like me more options when it's time to vamoose, should things get hairy. It also gives me time to put my head on straight and push ugly thoughts to the back.

When I get to Dr Jochovic's office, I tip my lid to the receptionist and do my best to smooth-talk my way through. The Doc shares the building with a shrink and a couple mouthpieces. With my bandages I probably look both criminal and crazy, so I pick a random name from the plaques on the wall and make my way through. Looking at the building plan I see I'm in for a climb, as I'm heading to the fifth floor in a building without an elevator. In the stairwell on the third floor, I pass a guy with his beak firmly in a newspaper, and without looking back, I feel him shadow me all the way up. By the size of him I guess he ain't no scientist—potentially a specimen. A tremor knocks the wind outta me on the last couple stairs and the guy behind me gets a little closer than he means to.

When I get through the door to Dr Jochovics office, I spin on my heel, reaching for the revolver in my shoulder holster. I realise too late that I don't have enough movement in my upper body to reach it at speed. Instead, I spasm in pain and drop to my knees. When the mug who's been following me tries to burst in through the door, it hits my shoulder and I slam it back on him. He fires six slugs through the door. Luckily, he's not expecting me to be down so low and they fly above my head. Bent over, my fingers finally make it round my pistol, and I return fire upwards. I hear a body drop and a gargling plea for help, before whoever's on the other side of the door kicks.

KAIJU

Patience may be a virtue. Had the big guy waited for me to get further ahead before making his play, I may not have noticed him and he'd have had me dead to rights. That being said, I don't fancy coming face to face with uniforms who would undoubtedly be bought and paid for by Johnny or his high-flying friends, so I have to make it quick. The room's already been turned over. At first glance, it seems anything of import has been shredded or is long gone. I go to the desk, rip the empty drawers out and flip them over. Going for power over finesse, I step on them. The first collapses like you'd expect, but the second collapses once and then a second time as the secret compartment gives. I toss the planks aside and spread the contents out over the desk. It's a map showing a location marked with an 'x', about a mile away from the observatory, in the mountains, as well as a list of names. I go through any other scraps I can find in the office and piece together enough papers that, with a little luck and a whole lot of manure, might get me past the checkpoint at the wall. The last thing I do before heading to my car is call Penelope and tell her to lay low for a bit. I'd been stupid enough to finger her as my client, and I feared for her safety. I open the door to see the guy on the other side is Johnny's man that was holding my arms behind my back. He didn't look so tough with a hole in his neck. Rather than holstering my gun, I stow it in my coat pocket where I can reach it, fully loaded with the safety off.

***

The checkpoint out of the city is a little too easy to get through, but I figure it's because no one would be stupid enough to want to tango with the kaiju. The dust is thicker this side of the wall, and as the sun goes down, the lack of visibility slows my drive down to a crawl. A quarter mile away from my destination, I stash the car on a side road and make my way on foot towards a faint glow in the distance. I very much doubt I want to be announcing my arrival to whoever is on the other end of this thing.

At the end of the road I see a forest of spotlights. The beams don't reach far in the dust, but manage to pick out the edges of a large, barn-like structure nestled at the foot of the mountain. I climb to higher ground and circle to what I hope is the rear of the compound. When I get closer, I see the barn itself is a hive of activity. I hear men—drunk, yelling, and fighting. What I don't hear is any livestock. A light goes off in a small side-building as what I hope is the last man leaves to join the ruckus, and I see an opportunity to investigate.

When I get inside, I pull my goggles down and use a lighter from my pocket and give myself just enough light with which to see. At first glance, it's a locker room, overalls hung up on one side and storage on the other. As I inspect one of the overalls, I can't help but notice the taste of copper on the air—the smell of blood. The overalls are rubberised and droplets of water cling to their exterior. I recognise the name written on a helmet on the shelf above, as well as the name on the one beside it. They were from the Doc's list. I had assumed the names belonged to the unlucky victims of the black-market protein operation, but it looks like they work here.

Going deeper into the room, I see shower heads affixed to the ceiling and feel a slant to the floor that leads to a drain. Kneeling down, I can see a tinge of reddish brown around its rim. At least now I know where the smell is coming from.

I have 'em. All I have to do is make it back into town, grab a handful of newsies and any honest cop I can find, bring them up here and blow the whole thing wide open. My city can turn a blind eye to a lot, but this... Nobody could ignore this.

I get low and creep out of the wet room, spinning back to make sure the door closes slow and soft behind me. Before I can turn around, someone throws the switch on a pair of headlights directed straight at me.

"Hands in the air! Be a good boy, now," says a voice through a mask. It's slightly muffled, but I recognise it.

The voice belongs to Johnny's goon that hits like a train. I put my hands up and turn around to see him and two silhouettes. I presume one to be the whippet, and that would make the other the patron saint of goons, who act exactly like you'd expect. The first two have pieces drawn on me. The last is leaning on the car, using a knife to pick grit from under his nails.

"Fingers and toes, Micky!" says the big silhouette at the back.

"I'm unarmed," I say, gingerly reaching to my lapels and opening my coat to reveal an empty holster.

"Wouldn't matter if you were," says the whippet, chuckling from under the rag wrapped around his face. "We found your car. You're not going anywhere, even if you could bust outta here."

I should've known it was too easy to get here. The checkpoint must've tipped them off as soon as I was outta sight. I shrug and lower my hands, slipping them into my pockets. "Well, then, what's a fella to do?"

Whippet looks giddy at the opportunity to get his hands on me and advances, lowering his weapon. The train, not so foolhardy, still has a bead on me, luckily, he's standing right at my twelve-o-clock. I grab my pistol and blow a hole through my coat pocket, and his ribcage. After that, I spray wildly while trying to get around the corner of the building at my back. I hear one wet thud that I hope is a bullet connecting with the whippet, and another that must've been the radiator of the motor, as it was followed by a long, loud hiss. That'll teach you for messing with another man's automobile.

I turn to run, but can't breathe. The recoil from the pistol has aggravated my injury and my chest is on fire. I give myself to the count of three to get it together and start putting one foot in front of the other. I don't need to make much distance before I'm hidden by the dust, and it won't be long before a tremor covers my tracks. I can't raise my gun arm, and drop my spent pistol. Looking up, I see the mountain loom over me. At that moment, I know three things: if I don't take the road, I have a better chance of not being followed; I know that trying to grab a car from the slaughterhouse is suicide; and finally, I know where to go for my best chance of survival.

It takes me all night to climb the mountain. The path is relatively forgiving, not too steep over mossy stone, but my condition continues to worsen as I press on. By the time I reach the observatory, I'm half-dead—and worse, my flask has run dry.

There are two vehicles outside the observatory, one civilian, and the other sporting government plates. Maybe they're just checking in for a report on the latest kaiju research, or maybe they know every blood-soaked detail of Johnny's operation and this is as close as they're willing to get. Either way, I doubt the people inside are friendly. Seems no one is these days. I don't have steel to jimmy the lock on the civilian car, so I smash the window with a rock. The effort saps what little strength I have left, and as I work on hot-wiring the vehicle my vision splits and I'm seeing more wires than is useful. I lay my head on the seat for a moment, but instead of resting my eyes, I slip into the black. Second time out cold in as many days—this is getting embarrassing.

***

When I come to, I'm sat upright in a chair with my arms bound to my side. Light, unfettered by the presence of dust, streams through the window. I must be getting used to this falling unconscious business, though, as my eyesight returns to normal quicker than before. Within a minute I can see clearly again, but, if I'm honest, I wish I can't. I let out a short barrage of obscenities, and a cold sweat instantly soaks my bandages as I see, sitting across from me, the patron saint of goons.

His eyes look dull as he stares at me, none of the psychotic intensity of the last time he had me cornered. It's then I realise the small wet clump of hair on one side of his head, the larger clump on the other side and the brain matter on the wall next to him.

"Detective Murphy, good of you to join us," a voice says from behind me.

"Pleased to make your acquaintance. Big fella, good to see you again, too," I say to the stiff winning a staring contest with me. "I'm afraid you have me at a disadvantage—several, actually."

"Call me Jack, Detective Murphy. As for our mutual friend here, he was just telling me that you've been asking about our Dr Jochovic, and that, rather than buy you off or kill you, all he accomplished was piquing your curiosity enough to lead you up here."

"Talking to you seems to have done him a world of good, Jack. Hey, not to look a gift horse in the mouth here, but can we cut to the chase? Why did you use him to redecorate the walls, but I get to sit here and jabberjaw?"

"Oh, I do like you, Detective! Yes, well, there's something you can do for us. Something we would appreciate very much."

"Plait your hair? Bake you a cake?" I retort, feeling close enough to death's door that I don't want this guy to start singing carols before I get to go through.

"Kill Johnny Wilson."

"Oh, I see, you want to take over this sick little operation. I figured the only reason Johnny was involved was because this was beneath you."

Up until now, Jack's been wandering behind me; this is the first time I can feel him standing still. Without being able to see his face, I can't tell what I'd said to provoke a reaction. Indeed, I wasn't altogether sure what the reaction meant.

"You think this is Mr Wilson's operation? Oh, no. When he found out about the kaiju, he pushed his way in. He had just enough muscle to keep us from taking care of him, and a wide enough network that if he wanted to put the word out, he would have done some considerable damage. It's always been *our* operation. Mr Wilson has just gotten a bit greedy of late, trying to claim the good doctor and his research for himself."

I struggle to wrap my head around what Jack is saying. "What do you mean when Johnny found out about the kaiju? What would that nickel-and-dime mob boss even do with kaiju research? Unless it tells him how to use them for muscle, or to teach them to turn tricks, I just can't see it."

Jack laughs, clearly relishing my confusion. "I was under the impression you had been to the mine... Seen for yourself."

"*Mine*? You mean the slaughterhouse, you cannibal psycho?"

"Cannibal? Oh, this is great, you think our protein is people. You really haven't figured it out, have you? You have no idea!" Jack grabs the back of my chair, tilts me backwards, and drags me through a pair of double doors. "Let me ask you this, why do you think the city is built in the mountains?"

"Kaiju are huge and flat-footed, they don't travel well over terrain that's not level. They can't get past the mountains."

"Sure enough, that's what people say. So, have you ever wondered why we need a wall? If the mountains keep the kaiju out, then the wall..."

"Keeps the people in?" I say, starting to wonder how far off I was in my estimations.

"Bingo, that's the important one. Now, are you ready for the kicker?" Jack rotates my chair, and I find myself looking at the end of the observatory telescope and a scientist scribbling on some papers. "Detective Murphy, Dr Jochovic. Dr Jochovic, Detective Murphy."

"Doctor, you're still alive?"

The doctor looks blankly at me, and then behind me, at Jack. He shrugs, nods quietly, and goes back to his papers.

"That's not the kicker, detective. You need to get quicker. You're starting to bore me. The good doctor has merely been kept here as a precaution, for his own safety. Now, if you'd be so kind, please, look through the telescope."

I lean forward best I can to look through the eyepiece and search for anything that would have all of this make sense. At first, I'm surprised by the lack of roving monsters—in fact, the lack of anything at all. The only thing I can make out is the sea of dust and the mountains that break its surface. The mountains form a narrow range that stretches out, connecting those that surround the city to a huge land mass in the distance. I wouldn't have been able to tell were it not for the markings on the lens, but what is strange is that the landmass in the distance seems to be moving. I adjust some settings on the knobs and dials at the base of the telescope, and through trial and error, I find a way of zooming in. That's when I see it: the land mass is definitely moving, and it has an eye.

***

I'm loaned Dr Jochovic's car, the car I had previously attempted to steal. As such, dust blows in through the broken window, forcing me to wear my mask and goggles on the way back to the bar. I've left the observatory having been furnished with a new gun in the glovebox and a stiff in my trunk. I'd been told straight: I go kill Johnny, and when I do, not only is my slate wiped clean, but there's a bonus in it for my silence. As simple as the terms are, it takes a while for them to sink in. My world has been turned upside down or, more accurately, put on the back of a giant reptilian beast. I feel smaller than ever and dirtied by the task at hand. I think about my reputation as a man that will do anything for a quick buck and cares for nobody but himself. Looking at myself in the rear-view, I wonder if I am that same man.

As I drive through town, I look at the hungry faces of a population that doesn't know it's riding on the back of a continent of steak—a continent that the rich had claimed for their own. Every one of them collecting stamps for scraps and being grateful to their benevolent captors; kept in constant fear that, if they leave, they'll be stomped to death by the giant monster that's, in truth, keeping them alive. The whole thing makes me sick to my stomach.

When I get to Johnny's place, I set about what has to be done with cold efficiency. I walk up to the back room, and before the guy on the door has a chance to even think about frisking me, I stick my gun in his ribs. He opens the door and I use his massive frame to conceal myself from view as I walk in and count how much muscle Johnny has left. Besides the bruiser I've brought in myself, there's only Johnny and one other person in the room. My man-with-nothing-to-lose gambit goes to pot when I see Penelope being held at the business end of a letter opener.

As Johnny pulls Penelope in to use as a human shield, I see a red mark under his eye that's already started swelling, and I realise the scene I just walked in on.

"Got a hell of a cross, don't she?" I say, pushing the doorman towards his boss and raising my gun to avoid any misunderstandings.

"You're a piece of work, you know that?" spits Johnny. "I let you live, and this is how you repay me."

The goon must have panicked, because as tensions flair, he reaches for his gun. I burn powder and cap him twice in the chest. Johnny drops the letter opener to go for a gun on his desk, but as soon as he loosens his grip on Penelope, she elbows him in the nose and makes a break for it. She's not quite clear enough for me to take a shot before Johnny regains a hold of her and pulls her back in.

"I am repaying you, Johnny. They sent me here to kill you, but I'm planning on letting you live."

"Now, why would you do that?" Johnny says, eyeing up the gun on his desk.

"Our friend, Jack, says you have a big enough network to get the word out about the kaiju."

"Get the word out?" Johnny scoffs. "I only said that to keep the guys upstairs at bay. We all know what would happen if the rubes knew the truth. They'd go into their basements and dig straight down. Our innocuous little infestation would be a bleeding wound within a week."

"We could organise, open new mines controlled by the people!" I plead as Johnny is trying to drag a struggling Penelope to the back door.

"Not gonna happen. The mines need to be under someone's control—my control. Anyone else might hit a nerve or make the kaiju itch. All it needs to do is roll over and it will wipe our species out of existence."

"Our species?"

"Do you know why there's so much dust? You never even wondered did you. The whole world is dead, you moron!"

There's no way I'm going to win this thing with reason. My focus quickly switches to stopping him making it out the door with Penelope. He's small but powerful, which means he's doing a good job of keeping her between himself and my gun. Then an idea hits me like a streetcar in the dust.

"Penelope, did you know I originally thought this jerk-off's protein was people? Not an uneducated guess, given his habit for making people disappear and his limited means." I see Johnny's temper starts to flair up, and he stops trying to drag Penelope towards the door. "It made sense. That's why you were slinging it in this dive, because they wouldn't touch it uptown. But uptown has its own supply, and you were just doing what you could to control those that had nothing." At this point there's an audible snarl emanating from the hot-tempered little crook. "You know what Johnny? I had more respect for you when I thought you were a cannibal."

Like a flash, Johnny loses his cool. He throws Penelope to the ground and makes a dive for his gun. I plug him once in the shoulder and then perforate his pump. He collides with his desk and scatters a box of cigars across the room, one of which lands at my feet.

"Don't mind if I do," I say, picking it up and putting it in my pocket. Then the room is still, Penelope's eyes meet mine and I see the rest of my life laid out in front of me.

With Johnny dead, I'd held up my end of the deal with Jack, but still, I wouldn't be holding my breath to see the pay day. Every dirty cop in town is probably staking out my place, if they aren't already on their way here. I know the truth. The world as we know it starts at the snout and ends at the tail of a giant kaiju. A story so absurd, people wouldn't believe it even if I didn't have a government trying to actively discredit me. No, my time in this city is done. I've solved the case I was paid to solve, and, in my book, that earns me a vacation. I may be beaten all to hell, but I have a car outside, a lot of road ahead of me and someone special to take the journey with.

Penelope runs over into my arms. She's warm, and her scent fills my nostrils. I look into her eyes and tell her we're heading out of town to the observatory, that I'm going to show her the world and something else, a surprise just for her.

She calls me Don, and I smile. We kiss, and the world shakes.

Cthulhu vs. Kaiju

Mitchell Lüthi

EMERGENCE

The elevator doors opened with a jolt, and a silky female voice announced our arrival. "Platform 53D," she stated in a southern drawl. They changed the automated voice every day. Yesterday, she'd been from Eastern Europe. Today, she was a southern belle.

I nodded to my ward, and stepped out of the elevator, not waiting to see if she'd follow.

Aside from a few figures hunched over their computers, the floor was empty. The service staff were not due for another hour at least. Most of them would still be sleeping off their last shift, or grabbing a quick bite at the local, enjoying what little time they had off before the next one began. When they did arrive, the level would be a hub of activity. Scientists, research teams, statisticians, a whole ensemble of the intellectual elite, gathered from around the world, all in one building. Languages and ideologies would collide, conflicting theories, beliefs, and assumptions would be thrown from one end of the hall to the other—but that would only come later.

For now, the level was quiet, and I walked across the floor unimpeded by the usual scurry of bodies. From the scuff of her cheap sneakers against the tiles, I knew that my guest was right behind me.

We reached the end of the room, and I flashed my security pass at Edgar, only to roll my eyes when he stopped us to examine it properly. He'd seen my face day in and day out for the last five years, with the one notable exception of a sick day sometime in May of 2026.

"You know the rules, Captain. I have to swipe you in." He took my pass, pressing it against the red eye of the scanner embedded in his desk. "Haven't seen you around before," he said, accepting the ID of the woman who'd trailed me around most of the morning.

"She's just an observer," I said before she could reply.

Edgar handed back our cards and smiled at my guest. "Well, enjoy your stay, Miss Fern."

"*Doctor*," she replied, looking up from her clipboard. "Thank you."

We passed through the checkpoint, and took another elevator up to our last stop for the morning.

"Observation Deck 1A," the belle informed us as we stepped out. A far cry from the open space of the research centre below, the passage to Observation Deck 1A was narrow and claustrophobic. An orange light blinked overhead, and about a dozen unseen lenses zoomed in on our persons. A whole security team would be sliding through our biometric scans, t-rays, viral diagnostics, heat signature trackers. Edgar's little security booth really was a waste of everyone's time. We were currently undergoing one of the most intense security checks in the world, and I doubted the young doctor even realised it.

"What did you say you do again?" I glanced over my shoulder, catching her eye as she scribbled something down. She was pretty, in a matter-of-fact sort of way. Mousy blonde hair hung down to her shoulders, and she wore glasses a size too big for her face. Her lips were thin, which made her seem colder than she probably was.

"I teach ancient languages at Princeton."

I snorted. "What's a professor of ancient languages doing in a UNGDM facility?"

She smiled. "Sating my curiosity."

Hardly a reason to be granted access to one of the most secure compounds in the world, but I didn't really care. I'd been told to show her around, and that's what I'd do.

The passage ended before a steel door, and I underwent one final retinal scan before gesturing at her to do the same. I knew that if either of us failed, or if any of the scans prior to this one had triggered an alert, the air around us would have been sucked out within seconds, leaving us floundering while security teams moved in.

We waited a tense moment, before the light flashed green above the door and it slid open.

I took a breath, feeling that oozy feeling I always did when entering the negative pressure room. There were two yellow hazmat suits waiting for us on the walls, and I took the one laid out for me, gauging by its size that someone under six foot would be swallowed up by it.

The doctor followed my lead, pulling her own suit over the lab coat and jeans she'd chosen to wear for her visit.

"Have you had contact with anyone suffering from radiation poisoning, swine flu, influenza, or ebola in the last two months?" I pulled on my gloves and stared at her pointedly. The scans would have picked up anything out of the ordinary, but it didn't do any harm to double-check.

"Negative."

"Any known terrorist cells, revolutionary bodies, or persons listed as dissidents by the United Nations, NATO, or the Pacific Defence League?"

She snorted, pulling on her own gloves. "I'm sure I'd tell you. Anything else?" She picked up the mask and visor, dropping the helmet over her head, then fastening the clasps with a practised hand.

I shook my head and latched the seals to my suit, repeating the process with hers. Once we were entirely concealed by the clumsy, yellow body-bags, I gave the thumbs up to the closest camera and braced myself.

A high-pressure pump pounded us with anti-bacterial agents from all corners of the room, forcing me to arch my back against the force. The first time I'd gone through the chamber, I'd nearly been blown off my feet by the shock. The doctor seemed to be managing okay, though. Still, I smiled behind my mask, seeing that the sheet she'd been filling out so tirelessly was soaked through, and black ink had bled out all over the page.

"I hope that wasn't anything important," I said with a nod to her clipboard, once the pressure had worn off. She pursed her lips behind her visor, and gifted me with a raised brow, but didn't reply.

"I doubt they'd let you keep your notes, anyway." I walked to the other end of the chamber and pressed my hand against the red seal-lock. The oozy feeling returned for a second, before the door swung open and we were granted our freedom.

We waddled down a series of steps, hands held to the railing to keep ourselves from slipping. Industrial-grade fans whirred beside us, drying out our suits as we crossed the final passage before Observation Deck 1A.

"Ever seen one of them up close?"

The doctor was quiet while we walked, and I didn't think she'd reply, but then she let out a sigh and nodded. "I was in Kyoto when the first of the Lake Biwa brood emerged, but I didn't see much before the embassy airlifted us out. Then again in Porto Alegre... I just made it out that time."

Lake Biwa. I remembered the reports. The city had been ravaged by what appeared to be at least three class-four kaiju. The Pacific Defence League had hardly been ratified when their first challenge had arisen. The engagement had not gone well, and the city had been left as little more than a ruin.

"Ancient languages sure take you places," I said, gripping the handle of the door to the observation post.

She laughed. "You have no idea."

***

Observation Deck 1A always reminded me of an air traffic control tower. Hundreds of screens covered every inch of space, and reams of data flowed in a never-ending stream upon them. Aside from the off-white glow from the screens, the light in the room was carefully maintained, and I had to squint while my eyes adjusted to the gloom.

Unlike the platform below, the observation deck was always busy. Research teams migrated from one desk to another, squeezing their way past security personnel and intelligence agents, then flocking to the next computer screen in an endless loop. At any given moment, there were perhaps fifty people crammed onto the platform, like sardines—a description I found more apt given what lay beyond the viewing ports up front.

I nodded to a few familiar faces and waved the doctor ahead of me. "Seeing them up close tends to knock people," I said as we walked between the blinking screens. "It's a power thing. Knowing you're no longer the apex predator on this planet is one thing, but being confronted by that reality in the flesh is altogether more meaningful, more real."

"How philosophical."

I snorted. "See for yourself."

The last row of desks came to an end in front of a short flight of steps, which I took two at a time, emerging at the top before the doctor.

The viewing ports were massive, translucent panes, spread out across the surface of the wall. I briefly remembered the first time I'd stood on the platform, staring out the bullet-proof glass, knowing that if the things outside willed it, they'd tear the platform apart like it was cardboard.

Through the glass I could see the heart of the facility laid out before us. About as tall as a football stadium, and twice as wide, the area was ringed by other observation posts like the one we were in. Beneath each of the platforms hundreds of steel pylons had been erected. About a million miles' worth of cable ran between them and the viewing decks above.

But the reason for all of this—for the pylons and observation posts, for the thousands of staff and security protocols, for the facility's existence—stood on the other side of the window.

I smiled, feeling that thrill I always felt when being there, and turned to the doctor. "See what I mean?"

She'd somehow managed to find a dry page, and was jotting down notes on her clipboard. I couldn't make out her expression behind the mask, but she seemed relatively unperturbed.

If a 100-foot-tall killing machine didn't impress her, I didn't want to know what would. I rolled my eyes and stared out of the window.

King was a killing machine—that was beyond question. Standing just over 100 feet tall, he could switch between bipedal and quadrupedal in a heartbeat. His thick, leathery skin was near impenetrable by conventional means, and the spike-like protrusions on each shoulder doubled as a battering ram. I'd seen his triple-barbed tail rip through steel and flesh with ease on a number of occasions. Like the other two kaiju in the facility, King's arms were fused, and ended in four-digit claws. His reptilian face was angular, not unlike that of a tyrannosaur, but that was where the comparison ended. Two red eyes stared down at us from each side of his head. A pair of curved tusks hung from his jaw, and he emitted a constant green, bioluminous glow from his mouth. A single drop of the venom in his saliva would pollute a city's water supply for a month, if not longer.

Behind him, kept in stasis before their own observation posts, were Riptide and Bonehead. Though they shared some physiological traits—the fused arms and barbed tails—they were otherwise quite different. Riptide was lighter than King, more nimble on her feet. Her features were altogether more serpentine, and where King's shoulders were covered in bulbous protrusions, hers were slender and narrow. The gap between her arms were webbed, and gills ran along both sides of her body. As a bio-weapon, Riptide was more advanced, and she had a number of Destroyer capabilities. High-yield plasma bursts could be generated in an instant, and deployed from the two bio-organic tubes on her chest. I'd seen the devastation they could inflict, and knew that, despite her slender size, she'd pose a challenge even to King.

Bonehead, on the other hand, was squat and muscular. Standing at around 80 feet tall he was the shortest of the three, but what he lacked in size he made up for in sheer strength. His face was more spherical than the others and covered by a hard exoskeleton that put King's own leathery shell to shame.

The doctor moved up beside me and tapped the glass with her pen. "And who is this little guy?" There wasn't a hint of insincerity in her voice.

I frowned and turned to her. That *little guy* was a 2,000-ton class-two kaiju. "This is King. He took out both Han'nin and Tappaja before they could even make it ashore." I could feel the irritation in my voice, and I ground my jaw before continuing. "He's been deployed in over twenty operations, and succeeded against every Emergence he's been pitted against."

She nodded, and jotted something down on her clipboard, before stepping closer to the window. She stared at King for a moment, then glanced at the other kaiju and nodded.

"They'll do."

KAIJU

THE DREAMS OF TIME

I was just twenty-two when the first sighting was recorded. Drunk on my arse, on the other side of the world, and busy with a gap year in Asia after graduation. When the news came in, I hardly believed it. I'd thought I was still working off the shrooms from the night before. But no, Venice was gone. Not destroyed, not turned to rubble and ruin—simply gone. A black scar marked the place where the city had once stood. 300,000 people wiped out in the blink of an eye.

Then the footage started rolling in. Like some great horror out of myth, the first kaiju had risen from the Adriatic and put the city to the torch. It's not clear what triggered the Emergence, or why he picked Venice, but on the 15th of April 2023, death came to the city.

The media dubbed him "Emperor," and the name stuck. We couldn't kill him—God knows we tried. Tactical nukes, hydrogen bombs, fully mechanised units... Nothing worked. Emperor was a class-five kaiju at the very least. Easily surpassing 300 feet, it was estimated he weighed over 7000 tons, with multiple Destroyer abilities. He was the first and he was the largest.

But once he wrecked Venice, he disappeared. Nobody knows why, and we weren't given much time to think on it. After Emperor, Emergences began all across the world.

Turns out the kaiju had been resting beneath the ocean for millennia, and now they were waking up. Why? Nobody has quite figured that out, but teams like mine are working constantly on it. As to how we got our hands on three kaiju of our own? Well, it wasn't long before some smart-arse in a lab realised that some of these things *could* be controlled. Not the largest—not the dominant category fours and above—but the others. It had something to do with how their minds are programmed to think. The term "hive mind" had been thrown about, and "neural linking." It means they can be trained and used as tools. It also means that, in all likelihood, some other vast consciousness is controlling the actions of the kaiju. I'll likely never understand quite how they operate, but that's not my job. What I am paid to do is pilot King, and I do that better than anybody.

***

The morning after I'd showed Doctor Claire Fern around the compound, I got the news that our unit was being relocated, and command seconded to Admiral Armitage of the South Pacific fleet. The news took us all by surprise; we hadn't moved facilities since operations began on the Faroe Islands almost five years ago.

"Any idea what's going on?" Kiyo was my second, and Riptide's pilot. She took the seat opposite mine and took a bite from her egg roll.

"No clue." I sipped from my coffee and watched as Maks pushed his way through the canteen line. The fat Russian had a way with words, and even the larger security personnel shifted out of his way. "Ever heard of this Admiral Armitage?" I asked, placing my empty cup on the table and turning to Kiyo.

She shrugged, then took the salt shaker from the table and applied it liberally to her breakfast. "I don't keep track of the comings and goings of the South Pacific fleet," she said, licking sauce from her fingers. "I just go where Riptide goes."

KAIJU

"Aye, and I go where Bonehead goes." Maks dropped a tray piled high with food on the table and pulled up a chair. "I kept telling you that they were going to send us after that big bastard, and here we are!" He shoved a pork rasher into his mouth and waved a finger. "They've had it out for us since we rolled over Antwerp, fighting those nasty spike-back twins. Not my fault if the city can't take Bonehead's weight, not my fault, I say."

I stole a chip from Maks' plate and winked at Kiyo. "You did send Bonehead through the Old District when he could have stayed in the river, though. Buildings as old as the city itself turned to dust under that fat monster."

Maks slammed a palm against the table and glared at me. "Not my fault, I say."

"Alright, alright." I caught Kiyo's smile, and patted Maks on the shoulder. "But I don't think they're going to send us after Emperor just for that."

"We see," said Maks, his mouth still full of pork. "But don't say I didn't warn you."

I left my hand resting on the Russian's broad shoulder and reclined into my chair. Through the windows of the canteen I could just make out one of the leviathan haulers, hovering above the compound. It'd take a dozen of them to move just one of our kaiju. Luckily, we had a whole fleet of them dedicated to our unit.

They'd leave today, while we'd get a few days off, before being jetted over to our new base of operations on the furthermost tip of South America, in Chile.

"I hope one of you picked up Spanish in college. I think it's going to be a while before we see this place again."

337

***

I slept on the flight; I always did. I wasn't in the mood for Maks' stories, and Kiyo was an anxious flier, which made me nervous.

We landed on a private strip, just south of Punta Arenas, and took a chopper to our new compound. The weather wasn't bad, but after years of acclimatising to Scandinavian temperatures, my shirt was already drenched.

The facility was smaller than our previous one, but not by much. I could see it'd been built with some haste, and construction vehicles were still parked all across the premises.

"They're not mucking about," said Kiyo, pointing out the window of the helicopter.

I scrunched up my eyes against the sun and stared down at a coned building beside the compound. I'd seen one of them before, in a brief foray into Russia some years back.

"A Bumblebee," Maks chortled. "We must be facing the devil himself."

I frowned at Kiyo, and then stared back down at the launch site. The "Bumblebee," as Maks referred to it, was a second-generation thermobaric missile. Capable of levelling a city in seconds, they had a tendency to make entire regions uninhabitable. As such, their use had been prohibited by the UNGDM. The Russians had still used one in Ukraine about three years ago. Supposedly to take out a class three, but the reports had been conflicting, and it was better not to bring it up with Maks.

The helicopter dropped us off on the rooftop pad of the compound, where we were escorted in by a team of all-business marines. I couldn't tell by their badges where they were from, but most of these operations had dedicated special forces attached to them, so I wasn't surprised. They led us to our rooms, where we left what gear we'd brought with us, before being marched to a conference room on the upper floor for a briefing. There were no elevators, so we were forced to walk the fifty odd flight of stairs by foot, a task Maks would not shut up about.

When we finally made it to the right floor, the marines left us at the door. We waited hesitantly for a moment, before Maks took the initiative and barged in.

"Bloody hell, Maks," I said, following him. "Who needs an invitation when—" Whatever I was going to say next stuck in my throat, and was replaced by a wry laugh. "Fancy that. Ancient languages really do take you places."

Claire Fern looked up from the head of a long table that occupied most of the room and smiled. "Nice to see you, too, Captain Reynolds."

"I take it you're responsible for our relocation?" I sat down on the edge of the table and cocked my head. "What's a civilian doing in a top-secret military facility at the bum-end of South America?"

Kiyo and Maks exchanged bemused looks and pulled up seats beside me.

"All will be explained, captain. Now, please, if you'd take a seat, I can begin the briefing."

"You're leading the briefing?" I said, slipping down into the chair between my squadmates. I glanced at Kiyo and shrugged. This wasn't what I had expected, and from the look she gave me, she hadn't either. Maks seemed quite content, though, and was in the middle of mining one of his nostrils.

WRITE LIKE HELL

The doctor clicked a remote and a screen blinked into life behind her. I thought I was staring at an empty set before I realised it was a satellite shot of the sea. Grid-lock coordinates appeared on the bottom left of the image, and the lens zoomed out further.

"Point Nemo," Claire said, leaning back in her chair to look at the screen. "The furthest point from land in the entire ocean. These are from last week." She clicked the remote again. "And this is from two days ago."

At first, I thought it was the same image, but I quickly realised my mistake. A shadow had formed beneath the sea, spreading out across the entirety of the shot. I had no way of telling how big it was—not without another point of reference—but I guessed we wouldn't be there if it was a simple blip beneath the water.

"A passing cloud?" Maks said. He crossed his arms and leaned forward against the table. "Or perhaps it is a big fish, yes? One that you want us to kill, perhaps?"

The doctor rolled a finger over the remote, pulling the image back until most of the South Pacific was in the shot. The black spot was still visible, a massive inky stain beneath the sea.

"What is it?" Kiyo asked. "An Emergence?"

I hoped not. God, whatever it was looked to be bigger than the entire state of New York.

"Land," said Claire without pause. "A new landmass is emerging in the middle of the South Pacific. We've seen this sort of thing before, but nothing close to this size. It is unprecedented."

"Interesting," I replied, "but what's that got to do with us? Exploring the lost city of Atlantis isn't exactly in our job description."

Claire put down the remote and turned in her seat to look at us. In the few days since I'd met her, dark circles had formed beneath her eyes, and I noticed a couple of new stress lines on her forehead. Whatever this was had taken its toll on her.

"I'm well aware of your areas of expertise, captain. However, Kiyo is right. We're dealing with an Emergence... of a sort."

"I knew it," Maks chortled. "It's that big bastard, isn't it? You want to send us after the devil. Me and Bonehead will do it, we don't even need these other two. I always knew it." The Russian clapped his hands together and looked at Claire expectantly.

"I don't know anything about Emperor," she said, to Maks' disappointment. "In fact, we're not dealing with a kaiju at all. This is something entirely different."

I felt my brow furrow as the doctor got up from her chair. If exploring lost cities wasn't my forte, neither was solving riddles. Claire picked up a small stack of files and slid them across the table towards us, then opened up her own file and waited for us to do the same.

I glanced down at the cover and blinked. "Project Dreamer?" I flipped through the pages, browsing through datasheets, map coordinates, and what appeared to be old journal entries. Most of them were written in English—or in what I took to be Arabic—but there were others, in a language I wasn't familiar with. I scanned through them before settling on a photo of a white landscape beneath towering glaciers and mountainous peaks. In the centre of the image stood a group of explorers, huddled together for warmth, but grinning like madmen all the same. A burley, bearded fellow in the middle of the group held up a sign with the words *Starkweather-Moore Expedition - 1933.*

"What is this shit?" said Maks, waving his folder at the doctor. He had a habit of being direct, but I still winced at his bluntness.

"This is all we have." Claire took off her glasses and pinched the bridge of her nose. "The culmination of years of work, sacrifice, and the lives of *great* men and women, some of whom were my friends. This *shit* is the reason you are all here."

Maks sunk into his chair a little, and stared fixedly at his file. "Apology," he said, keeping his eyes lowered. "I mean no offence."

The doctor ignored him, and turned back to the screen. "When the kaiju first appeared, I thought it had something to do with this, something to do with *Him*. But I was wrong." She pressed a button and Point Nemo disappeared. Another image took its place, this time of the stars. "You see, while your kaiju rampaged across the globe, another threat was preparing to unleash itself. It has been waiting for a long time, but I believe that wait is coming to an end."

I squinted at the screen and felt my jaw clench. There was something *wrong* with the stars. Scattered about the black sky, they shone with dizzying intensity, but in a manner I found entirely unfamiliar. It was only later that I realised why—the constellations had started to shift, turning into some corruption of their former selves. More than that I couldn't put into words, but a sense of foreboding washed over me like a warm tide.

"So, the stars are sick," said Maks. "What's that to us?"

Claire swiped to the next image. It was of a rock face, or wall—it was taken too close for me to tell. Drops of water covered its surface, and slime hung to it in great clumps. But what caught my eye were the inscriptions carved upon it. Various shapes and symbols had been etched into the stone, their individual meaning completely unknown to me. Yet, somehow, I felt I understood the message they were trying to get across.

"In his house at R'lyeh, dead Cthulhu waits dreaming." Claire gave voice to the words I felt were already bouncing around inside my head, and I shivered.

Beneath the sprawling text, a hunched figure had been carved into the wall. The style was primitive, and the artist had lacked the skill necessary for the task— and yet, it triggered some primordial fear in me that I had not felt in years, not even in the face of kaiju. Thick, tentacle-like tendrils hung from the thing's pulpy face, while its grotesque body was simultaneously humanoid yet impossibly alien. The cephalopod head was bent forward, allowing the ends of the tendrils on its face to brush the back of the huge forepaws that clutched the thing's elevated knees. I blinked away from the screen and looked at the doctor instead, only to find her eyes fixed on me, as if I were some patient ready for examination.

"This is real, captain. A being so vast and unknowable has chosen our little world to be the subject of its administrations. Even as he rests, his minions conspire to bring about his eventual awakening. If this were to ever happen, it would doom us all."

She tapped the remote again and nodded towards the screen. A new image had appeared, this time of a barnyard. Livestock walked freely around the driveway, and an old pickup with a flat tire sat parked outside. I felt Claire's eyes on me again as I studied the image. A pair of pigs were rifling through a garbage can next to the barn, but their limbs were bulbous and deformed. Pustules and warts grew out from their distended bellies, and horrific growths hung from their necks. The other animals seemed similarly afflicted, and I struggled to maintain my focus on the image.

"This was taken two weeks ago in Arkham, Massachusetts."

The next photo was of the sky above the barn house, taken during the night. Instead of the stars, a shifting blur of colours covered the heavens. It reminded me of the aurora borealis we sometimes saw when we were still stationed on the Faroe Islands. I frowned as I tried to make sense of the colours.

"What you're looking at does not fall inside anything known in the visible spectrum. The electromagnetic—"

Someone was screaming.

I tried to look away from the colours, but I couldn't move my head.

I felt my lips go dry, and I struggled to even blink. That voice. I tried to focus on it, to pinpoint where it was coming from.

It sounded like an echo from the bottom of the well, but I recognised it.

A chill ran down my spine, and I felt goosebumps cover my neck and arms. My breaths started to come in short, tight rasps, and all the while the screaming continued.

I knew that voice.

It was my own.

I managed to tear my gaze from the photograph, nearly pulling myself out of my seat in the process. I was breathing heavily, and I could feel my heart pounding against my chest.

"Everything alright, captain?" Claire was staring at me, a look of genuine concern on her face. I glanced about the room and saw that Maks had started praying to himself, something I hadn't seen since Brussels. Kiyo looked like she'd just seen a ghost, but she managed a smile when she saw me looking.

"Captain?" Claire switched off the screen and took a breath.

"I'm fine," I said, gathering up the strength needed for a smile. "I don't know what came over me."

She nodded and sat back down in her seat. "You understand a little bit more now, I think. All of these events tie in with a mythos I have been studying for years. But I am not the only one who has been watching, and not all who have been watching have good intentions. There are those who seek to bring about the end of the world, to raise the Dread Lord from his slumber. I believe they are on the cusp of succeeding."

"Who would want to do such a thing?" Kiyo seemed to have recovered, and was staring down at her file.

"Madmen, lunatics, and those who desire power," said Claire. "I have only met one such man before, and he fell quite comfortably into the first category."

"Can we stop them?"

"Perhaps. I have teams moving in on known cultists as we speak, but it may not be enough. In all likelihood, it won't be." She pressed her glasses against her brow and stared at us. "We are about to witness a paradigm shift, a significant change in the global hierarchy. Earth will become the playground of beings beyond our understanding, and we their playthings… Unless we succeed, unless we stop Him on R'lyeh."

WRITE LIKE HELL

EX OBLIVIONE

We were eating a late dinner in our new canteen when the leviathan haulers finally arrived. They'd flown over ten thousand miles without stopping, slowing only for in-air refuelling and safety checks. Their cargo, over 6,000 tons of kaiju, hung in harnesses beneath the squadrons of helicopters, and were secured by reinforced plasma rope. They'd been kept in stasis the entire journey, and would be grumpy when they woke up.

"You think she's right?" Kiyo stood beside me, munching on a granola bar as we watched the leviathans deliver their cargo.

"I think enough important people do, enough to justify our being here, anyway."

"That's not what I asked, Daniel."

"I know, but I'm still trying to wrap my head around this *end of the world thing*. I definitely felt something looking at those pictures, and you can't tell me the stars haven't started looking a little weird right now."

Kiyo leaned against my arm and stared up at the sky with me.

"They look like tiny lanterns against a stormy sea."

"Poetic," I said with a smile. I turned to get another hot dog when Maks rushed into the canteen, waving his arms at us.

"Turn on television," he said, still chewing on his dinner. "Quick!"

"What's up?" I looked around the table for the remote, before Maks turned on the television manually.

"It's bad." He swallowed his food and flipped through the channels, muttering beneath his breath. "Real bad, cap, real bad."

KAIJU

He settled on a channel and turned up the volume before coming over to join us. A curly haired blonde reporter was staring into the camera, reading out a breaking news story while images played out beside her. The footage looked like it was out of a dystopian horror. Tanks were rolling through Washington DC. Military personnel were setting up roadblocks all across the city. More footage showed a firefight between the military and private citizens. It was over in seconds.

And in China, calamity has struck after nuclear warheads were deployed in the cities of Shenzhen, Guangzhou, and Nanjing. Casualties are estimated to be in the hundreds of thousands, with unconfirmed reports listing President Xi Jinping among those who have died.

"What the hell is going on." I watched in horror as scenes from all over the world played out on the news. A military coup in the United States, assassinations across all levels of government, riots in India, Europe, and Russia. The complete breakdown of order.

The television went off, and I turned around to find Doctor Fern standing with the remote pointed at the screen.

"It's happening sooner than I expected." She dropped the remote on the table and waited for the questions she knew would follow.

Maks was furious. "You knew this would happen? How? Why?"

She raised a placatory hand and waited for the redness to leave his face. "I had an idea," she said once he'd calmed. "You must understand, His worshippers have been preparing for this for centuries—infiltrating governments, military, media, everything they can get their fingers into. Now, they are making ready for His arrival." Her voice quivered for a moment, before she composed herself. "My teams have failed to uproot the cults. We'll only have one more chance to stop Him before it's too late."

I flinched as the first siren in the compound started to wail. It was joined by another, and then another, until the whole facility was one blaring alarm.

Claire nodded sadly and stared up into the night sky. "He is awakening."

***

I was strapped into the chest of a refitted CH-53K King Stallion helicopter, along with the rest of my team. The hold had long since been cleared out of anything deemed unnecessary, and a unit of tech wizards sat scrolling through reams of data. Three of the screens were dedicated solely to King's vitals. I could see his dual hearts beating a steady pace as the pressure from stasis was slowly lifted. He'd be fully awake by the time we committed to neural linking, and then my work would begin.

Doctor Fern sat beside Kiyo to my left, while Maks had taken to standing beside the port-side gunner, putting everyone in the hold on edge.

"Stars aren't right," he said into his headset, glancing back at us.

I looked out of the closest window and took a deep breath. I'd seen photos of Westerhout 5 and the Taurus Cloud Complex—beautiful, celestial clusters of red and blue that shone like fire from space—but even they paled in comparison to the sky above our heads.

A dense mass of swirling light and colour blanketed the heavens. Star formations I'd never seen before hovered between great clouds of molecular gas. Wisps of colour rippled between the clusters, and I felt my head start to spin. Everything appeared closer than it should, like someone had magnified the sky and brought it closer to us.

"We're nearly there." Claire had unstrapped from her harness and was standing next to me, staring out the window. "It won't be long now before He awakens. It's best you ready yourself for deployment."

I nodded, and then signalled to Kiyo and Maks as I undid my harness. My squadmates moved in beside me as I walked across the hold, a hand gripped tight to the railing for balance. One of our support staff helped strap us into the seats of the cockpit, before he plugged us into the interface. A screen was shoved in front of my face and cables plugged into pads on the side of my head. Finally, I felt the cold steel tip of a needle pierce my arm as relaxant was pumped into my veins. The whole process took less than a minute, and I settled into my seat, waiting for the neural link to activate.

The first time I'd linked to King had nearly been the last. His vast consciousness had threatened to swallow my own, and it was only through the quick thinking of my team that I'd managed to get out at all. The second time had been better, and by the third time the operation was deemed a success. Still, there was always the threat that, one day, I'd slip and disappear forever. Pilots don't like to dwell on that fact, and most of us acted like it couldn't happen at all. But I knew... I'd been close enough to almost touch it.

People think neural linking gives us control of the kaiju we pilot. Even the term 'pilot' seems to indicate as much. In reality, we're more like handlers than anything else. We don't gain direct control of our ward, but we can make suggestions and try to influence the way the kaiju think. We just stopped them from going on a rampage, mostly. Maks had once said we were "passengers in the back seat, trying to tell the driver where to go." I liked that.

Claire walked across the hold towards us, her hair flowing out behind her in the wind. She stopped beside my seat and stared at the visual on the screen before me. Our chopper was trailing just behind the leviathan haulers, and King, Riptide, and Bonehead still hung from their harnesses. From King's twitching tails, I could see he was close to waking up.

Beneath the squadron of haulers, the sea was a heaving mass of thundering waves and murky black water.

"There's nowhere to deploy," I said, still watching the screen. My words were slightly slurred as the relaxant started to make its presence felt. "Unless you want to drop us right into the sea?"

"Give it a second."

We waited for a minute, and then another, before Kiyo nudged me with her arm from the seat beside me. "Look," she said, pointing a finger at a dark smudge on her screen.

I stared hard at the smudge, before I realised what it was I was seeing, and then gasped despite myself. Land was emerging from the ocean, even as we watched.

A coastline of mud and ooze rose steadily before us, buffeted by the waves that hammered against it. Strange buildings grew from out of the sea, monolithic edifices formed from colossal, greenish stone blocks. Cyclopean statues the size of skyscrapers pierced the night sky triumphantly, their blasphemous visages leering loathsomely across the mud banks.

Behind them, a great acropolis broke out from beneath the waves, and streams of water ran off the structures like steaming rivers. There was something strange about the architecture of the buildings, something that made my stomach flip. The shapes and angles had no logic to them, no bearing on our reality. They *should not* have worked, adopting some contorted form of spherical geometry that had no place in our universe. And yet, there it stood, rising from the sea like some dread citadel.

"R'yleh," Claire whispered.

I pulled my eyes away from the screen and turned to the doctor. She was breathing heavily, and sweat covered her upper lip and brow. There was fear in her eyes, but something else, too.

"You're excited," I said, recognising that look. It was the same look I got just before linking with King.

"Of course I am." She brushed aside her hair and met my stare. "For years I've studied every scrap, every word I could find on this city… on Him. People told me I was as mad as the cults I studied, that this was all nonsense. To see my theories confirmed, to know that my colleagues did not die in vain… Of course I'm excited. I've just seen my life's work validated."

Maks chuckled on the other side of the hold. "Let's just hope you live long enough to enjoy it." He tapped a chubby finger against his screen and nodded towards it. "You see."

In the centre of the acropolis, beneath jagged spires that made my eyes hurt to look at, were the doors to a titanic vault. Covered in weeds and slime, innumerable markings had been etched onto the surface. The doors of the crypt seemed to distort as I stared at them, shifting from impossible shape to impossible shape. I knew then, without a shadow of a doubt, that no mortal hand had been responsible for their creation.

"It's now or never, captain." I felt the doctor grip my shoulder, and knew that she was right. If whatever was in there was allowed to get out, it'd be tickets for the lot of us.

"Maks, Kiyo, engage neural links on my say so." I glanced at the screen one last time and thought I saw a flicker of eldritch light emanating from within the crypt, but it was gone before I could focus in on it.

***

Bonehead landed with a thunderous crunch upon the still-forming land mass. His thick pads cracked the tiles beneath him, and gouts of water sprayed from a crevice his one foot had caught in. He pulled it out with a satisfying pop and rose onto his hind legs to take in his surrounds.

For the first time—perhaps in Bonehead's life—he found himself in a city built for a being of his size. He turned his head from side to side and sniffed the air. I knew that Maks would be working on gaining a foothold on Bonehead's consciousness. It usually took a couple of seconds for the pilot to adjust, then it was game time.

"Ready to deploy, captain." Kiyo's voice sounded in my helmet, and I confirmed with a quick glance towards the digital relay in my visor.

"Activate Riptide," I breathed into my mic. The leviathan haulers responded in an instant, releasing the fastenings that kept Kiyo's kaiju airborne.

Riptide's landing was more graceful than Bonehead's, and she was already moving forward when the last of the plasma ropes fell from her side.

KAIJU

I monitored her progress for a second, noting how quickly Kiyo had her under control. She was getting faster than me. Then again, Riptide was far more docile than King, even if I'd never say as much to Kiyo.

"Ready to deploy," came a voice through my helmet. One of the leviathan carrier pilots.

"Just a second," I said as Riptide and Bonehead approached the monstrous portal, the supposed lair of the Enemy. It towered over even them, and seemed to shift and move, disrupting all known laws of matter, warping my perspective.

As Riptide got closer, I noticed that flicker of luminosity once again. It came from inside the vault, despite it still appearing to be sealed tight. I frowned and ran a heat scan of the crypt, but what came back was a garbled mess.

"Captain." Claire crouched down beside my seat and nodded to the screen. "You must deploy now, there's not much time."

Even as she said the words, a bright beam of light of blinding intensity shot out from the crypt—or was it from the stars to the vault? I couldn't tell. When I opened my eyes again, the light was gone, but a gaping black abyss stood where the sealed doors had once been. The darkness was so thick, so all-consuming, it almost had a material quality to it.

"There's no time!" I felt Claire's nails dig into my arm, and I smashed my hand on the activation seal without a second thought.

***

I fell to the ground with King. We landed on all fours, even as our consciousnesses danced around one another. He was always hesitant to accept me, to lose full autonomy. I didn't blame him. Before we'd figured out how to break the synaptic control of whatever hive mind governed the kaiju, he'd been little more than a drone, carrying out the vicious desires of some other sentient body.

After a moment, King stopped pushing back, and I settled into the narrow mental corridor he'd provided for me. I could still see everything from my seat in the helicopter above, but another POV had been superimposed over my normal vision—the result of a superchip embedded in King's skull that activated once I'd committed to neural linking.

King quickly moved through the strange city, unconcerned by the warped architecture and hexagonal structures that surrounded us. His clawed pads cut deep grooves into the green stone beneath us, and I could feel his triple tails flicking out behind us. This sunken city meant nothing to him, and I felt myself relax a little. Doctor Fern had spooked me—that much was true—but whatever lurked within the depths of R'lyeh had never fought kaiju before. Not like ours, anyway.

Riptide and Bonehead were still standing before the black portal, and they both turned at our arrival.

"It's like nothing I've ever seen before," I heard Kiyo's voice in my ear.

"Smells like shit, too," said Maks.

I let King's senses roam, exerting my will only lightly as I stared into the cavity. Maks was right. The smell emanating from the gaping hole was intolerable, and I would have gagged had I not been hundreds of feet above, in the helicopter.

I felt King flinch as he picked up on a disturbance in that great cavernous pit. The kaiju tilted his saurian head and took a cautious step forward. I could hear it, too. A wet, sloshing sound coming from deep within the doorway. Bonehead and Riptide moved forward beside us, listening intently to the jarring slopping noise.

"It's too late," said Claire, her voice on the edge of panic. "We've left it too late. The seal is opened."

"Look at the stars," said Kiyo breathlessly.

I exerted my will over King, and he tilted his head towards the heavens. The sky had taken on a velvety red tinge, and I watched as a ripple of energy coursed from the furthermost constellations to those directly above us. It wavered for a moment, hovering just above our heads, and then shot straight down toward the open tomb, a coursing current pumping directly into that gaping maw.

The slopping noise came to an immediate halt, and was replaced by the sound of a thousand horns, blaring their distorted notes until I felt my eyes start to water and my ears bleed. The fanfare ended as abruptly as it had begun, and finally, the being it heralded began to emerge.

I felt an alien consciousness brush against my own, something so vast and loathsome that I nearly decoupled from King. As it was, King's own immense consciousness acted as a buffer, and saved me from what could only be madness.

Maks and Kiyo were in similar positions, and I heard Kiyo cry out as the Dread Lord finally emerged from his vault.

A flabby claw gripped the edge of the crypt, and the masonry cracked beneath it. Another claw appeared, dragging itself across the chipped stone as the immensity within pulled itself from the tomb. A sickly green form, an accursed shape, squeezed itself out from the black doorway and onto the slimy flagstones of R'lyeh.

Though vaguely anthropoidal in shape, the being's massive head was not unlike that of a cephalopod, with rubbery feelers and scaly, amphibian skin. The outline of the thing seemed to flicker as I stared at it, shifting between our reality and another, imposing itself on our cosmos. I was immediately reminded of the carving Claire had shown us during her briefing, and realised the being depicted was the very same.

The creature lumbered forward, and I saw that two bony wings jutted out from behind its back. It towered over us, standing at nearly double Bonehead's height, and was at least a third taller than King. There was something about the way it moved that hinted at a great density, like that of a star compressed into a living form.

"No bigger than a class 3," I said into my headset, trying my best to hold my nerve. "We've dealt with worse." Even as I spoke the words, I knew them to be false. I could feel my mind starting to fray, and chattering, gibbering voices tugged at the tattered ends of my consciousness. I tried to drown them out, focusing instead on reining King in. The presence of that thing had stirred something within the kaiju, and he was champing at the bit. "Kiyo, give him a barrage, will you? Let's see what this thing is made of."

A green light flashed in the top-left corner of my visor as Kiyo confirmed, and a moment later Riptide was on the move. Her pilot led her past the crumbled remains of a spire until she stood directly in front of the thing from the star-vault.

It was only then that Cthulhu appeared to notice our presence at all. Two black eyes, as deep and old as the universe itself, stared down at Riptide. I saw a spike in

KAIJU

Kiyo's vitals—her heart rate was peaking. "Kiyo." I turned in my seat and placed a gentle hand on her shoulder. She was sweating profusely, her eyes fixed before her. She was staring right into its gaze.

Somehow she managed to jerk out of whatever trance held her, and she nodded towards me curtly, before dedicating herself to controlling Riptide. "Volley fire," she confirmed.

Two cylindrical organic pipes emerged from Riptide's chest, already glowing red from the heat the kaiju was generating. The air around them crackled and started to blur as energy was channelled towards the bio-weapons.

"That'll pump him," Maks chortled. Bonehead was already moving in, ready to follow up on the vicious volley Riptide was about to deliver. We'd repeated this manoeuvre countless times, to devastating effect. Riptide would open up on any Emergence with a salvo, while Bonehead and King moved in to finish off anything that managed to survive.

Riptide dug her heels into the concrete beneath her and opened up her chest just as Cthulhu started to move towards her. Two gouts of burning-hot plasma shot out at the Dread Lord, melting stone and sand as it raced towards their target. A blinding flash followed, and I turned away from the screen, blinking rapidly.

"Again," I said, trying to catch a glimpse of what remained beneath the smoke. Bonehead was pounding forward, cutting great grooves into the green stones as he moved in.

Riptide started drawing in the energy needed for another shot, allowing the already superheated cylinders no time to cool.

"Quickly." I squinted into the cloud of dust and ash particles. There was a flicker of movement, and then a shadow shifted. A great, oozing green appendage emerged from the billowing cloud, and then the Dread Lord stepped forward. Though the plasma had hit him head on, he appeared unscathed by the barrage. I'd seen similar volleys tear open class 3s and cripple at least a few class 4s, but they'd done nothing to him.

The looming figure ignored Riptide and turned to face the charging Bonehead, lifting its gigantic limbs to tackle the kaiju head-on. I heard Maks' roar through my headset, and watched as Bonehead switched to all fours.

The kaiju slammed into Cthulhu with a crunch, nearly lifting him from his feet, pushing him across the flagstones. But the thing from the vault was not to be undone so easily, and it quickly found its balance. It shifted against Bonehead's weight, grappling with him for control, until he managed to get an arm around Bonehead's fortified skull. The crypt creature dragged a malefic talon across the kaiju's back, tearing through flesh and bone like it was nothing, and I watched as Maks' ward struggled to get out of the thing's grip.

"Again!" I shouted, turning to Kiyo.

"But, Bonehead...He's in the way."

"Get him out of there, Maks. Kiyo, take the shot!"

I prompted King forward, releasing the brakes and letting his instincts take over. Bonehead managed to get out of the headlock just as Riptide launched another volley. The barrel-chested kaiju rolled out of the way, narrowly avoiding the scolding-hot torrents of supercharged energy. Another cloud of ash and magnetic energy formed, but this time Cthulhu did not wait for it to clear before making his move.

KAIJU

The Dread Lord seemed to materialise out of nothingness behind Bonehead. The cephalopod limbs on its face whipped out like tentacles, attaching themselves to the kaiju's neck and wrapping around his face before he could get out of the way. I heard Maks grunt as the creature began to exert pressure on Bonehead's skull, clenching tighter and tighter.

King broke out into a run, sensing the danger, but it was too late. With a sickening crunch, Cthulhu crushed Bonehead's skull and let his lifeless body fall to the floor.

Maks' anguished screams pierced through the neural link, an explosion of hurt and anger that threatened to knock the connection between me and King. I could feel him bucking in his seat beside Kiyo, and it was only when one of our support staff tranquilised him that the screams subsided.

King drew up alongside Riptide and watched as the Dread Lord moved away from Bonehead's carcass, trudging slowly through the towering buildings. It seemed unconcerned by the presence of the other two kaiju. Why shouldn't it be? It'd just crushed the skull of the most resilient of the trio like it was made from paper.

King bristled at the lack of respect, and I felt my control on him lessen as anger pulsed through his veins. Riptide was already lining up for another shot, and I heard Kiyo urging her on to greater strengths.

I felt the same confusion King felt as the great being turned away from us, instead making its way toward the sea.

"You cannot let Him get away." I heard Claire's voice shrill in my ear, and I nodded. Whatever happened, we couldn't let this thing get off the island. It would sweep across the world like a rotten tide, leaving nothing but chaos in its wake.

"That Bumblebee operational?" I turned in my seat to stare at the doctor. Her thin brows knitted together, and she nodded.

"Good," I said, flicking back to King's POV. We'll keep him on the island as long as we can. Blast this place to hell."

It'd take a few minutes for Claire to get authorisation, and then another minute or so for the thermobaric missile to be launched. But once it was, it'd arrive in seconds.

"We've got to hold him," I said, signalling to Kiyo through my visor. "For at least a few minutes, but as long as we can." We'd come to kill him, and it had taken hardly a few minutes for us to realise we never stood a chance.

King started moving through the buildings, barrelling through the grotesque stone structures as he built up momentum. The being from the vault was a couple hundred metres away, already on the outskirts of the sunken city. It wouldn't be long before he reached the muddy shoreline and disappeared forever.

"Light him up." I blinked a confirmation into my visor, and watched from above as Riptide commenced one final barrage. Her aim was true, and dual beams of plasma scorched a path across the ruins, smashing into Cthulhu's exposed back. The Dread Lord stumbled forward, extending a claw to try and maintain its balance, but then King was on him.

The kaiju bellowed out in rage as it connected with its target, slamming the bulbous growths on its shoulders into the thing's side. Cthulhu staggered, still recovering from the force of Riptide's plasma volley.

KAIJU

Still maintaining his grip on Cthulhu's midriff, King dropped a fused arm, clamped down on the Dread Lord's exposed leg, and heaved. There was a moment where nothing happened, and it looked like the thing would recover its balance entirely. Then, with a colossal groan, the Dread Lord fell.

King stayed on him, even as they tumbled, pressing home the advantage. He slammed a clawed fist into Cthulhu's side and swiped away the tentacles that tried to grip onto his face. The two titans collapsed against a sprawling temple, no doubt the home of some fell pantheon, leaving ruin and rubble in their wake.

When the dust settled, King was sat upon the Dread Lord, digging his massive claws into the creature's neck and chest. Ichor spurted from the wounds, drenching the kaiju in a sickly lather. Cthulhu bucked beneath him, but still he clung on.

"So, it can be hurt." I tagged Kiyo with my visor relay. "See if you can't help King keep that thing down, maybe drop some plasma down its throat."

Riptide responded instantly, loping through the wreckage of the dread city as she made her way to the battle. If they could just hold him in place for another minute or two…

A spike on King's monitor drew my eyes back to the fight, and I found myself smiling. The kaiju had managed to get both its legs over Cthulhu's midriff, and was holding down his head with a fused limb. Despite the crypt thing's size advantage, he didn't seem able to get out from the hold.

King brought his head closer to the Dread Lord's, snapping at any of the appendages that tried to attach themselves to him. A sickly, bioluminescent glow shone from out of his mouth, and venom dripped onto the cephalopod face beneath him. I thought I heard a hiss of pain coming from the thing's mouth, but I couldn't be sure.

The glow grew, until a yellow orb of putrescent light oozed out from between King's teeth, bathing the area around them in an eerie tinge. Cthulhu lashed out beneath him, intensifying his efforts to break out of the kaiju's hold, but it was in vain. King's grip would not be broken.

With a bestial roar, King unleashed a torrent of bio-toxins directly into the Dread Lord's face. Hundreds of gallons of poisonous, gelatinous liquid washed over him, covering his eyes and mouth, entering every crevice and hole it could find. Steam rose from Cthulhu's rubbery flesh, and I saw his tentacles try to retreat from the poison, before his entire face was hidden beneath King's toxic spew.

The kaiju vomited out a final spray of bio-toxin and stared down into the bubbling swamp that now covered the Dread Lord's face. Nothing could survive that, I was certain. It didn't matter what dimension you came from, or how many worshippers you had, taking King's 'kiss' directly in the face was a death sentence, even for a 'god'. But I was wrong.

The air around Cthulhu shimmered and distorted, even as the venomous spray evaporated or seeped into the ground beneath him. King tilted his head, and I felt his uncertainty across the neural link.

Before King could make another move, the Dread Lord's massive paw shot out from the ground and wrapped itself around his neck. The kaiju tried to claw it away, angling his razor-sharp mandible horns downward to cut at the flesh. His triple tails flashed behind him, slicing through the air to pierce Cthulhu's arms and face.

The Dread Lord shifted beneath King, leaning his body against his other arm as he lifted himself from the ground. His modest wings angled out behind him, fluttering as they added power to his movements. I managed to catch a glimpse of his face as he rose. King's attack had left it a smoldering wreck of boiling blisters and scarred flesh. Many of the tentacle-like tendrils had been fused together or burnt away entirely, leaving black-stained flesh in their place.

King sliced down with one of his tails, cutting into Cthulhu's ruined face, but the Dread Lord was ready for it, and a clawed hand caught the tail before King could recover.

"Get in there!" I shouted into my headset with a glance at Kiyo."

Cthulhu now had King by the neck and tail, and was starting to pull. I had no idea if he had the strength to tear the kaiju apart, but after seeing what he'd done to Bonehead, I didn't want to wait to find out.

Super-heated plasma heralded Riptide's arrival, slamming against the arm that held King's tail. Cthulhu's grip slackened long enough for King to pull his tail away, and the kaiju put all his strength behind getting out of the Dread Lord's vice-like grip.

Riptide swung around from the other side and held onto the thing's other arm, preventing it from doubling down on its hold on King. With the strength of two kaijus on him, Cthulhu finally relinquished his grasp, letting King slip out from between his claws.

The kaiju rolled back on his heels, pushing himself away from the Dread Lord, while Riptide did the same from the other side.

"It's face," said Kiyo, almost too soft for me to hear. "It's healing."

I stared hard at the screen, and then waited for King to get a better look. Kiyo was right. The charred mess of flesh that made up Cthulhu's face was repairing itself, knitting back together the scarred flesh, even as we watched. The cuts on its chest had already disappeared, and any sign that it had ever been hurt was gone.

"We can't win this." I shook my head and took a deep breath. I didn't even know if the Bumblebee would make a difference—if there was even a point delaying the inevitable.

"It's not coming." I felt Claire's hand on my shoulder. "They won't authorise the strike. Something has gone wrong."

"What do you mean?" I nearly pulled my helmet off, and felt a bit of King's anger course through my veins. "Tell them to fire the damn missile. We need to kill this thing here and now."

Claire shook her head, a tired look in her eyes. They spoke of resignation, of failure. "It's the cult. I think they've somehow managed to infiltrate the facility. We're on our own."

I swore. "Then we're done for."

Below us, the Dread Lord waded forward, seeming to grow in size and stature as our last hope was dashed. I could feel that gibbering madness again—just on the edge of hearing—and I recoiled as the lumbering behemoth turned its gaze towards our helicopter.

I knew then and there that there was no God. That this titan from the stars, and the gibbering voices, were more real than any belief I'd ever held. I wanted to laugh and scream at the realisation, but something anchored me to my sanity.

KAIJU

I looked down and saw that King was still circling the Dread Lord—was still willing to engage, despite the impossibility of the task. Riptide, too. Perhaps they sensed the apocalyptic nature of the being they faced. Perhaps they didn't want to lose the first home they'd found—not without a fight.

I wasn't going to get in their way.

"Decoupling from King." I moved my hand over the deactivation seal and nodded to Kiyo. "Let's see what they can do without a leash."

I pressed the button and felt the pressure lift immediately. King noticed it, too, and rolled his massive shoulders as he adjusted. Kiyo followed my lead, closing the neural link with Riptide. She exhaled heavily beside me and removed her helmet.

"Now what?"

I shrugged. "The law of the jungle prevails. They've got a better chance without us slowing them down, and it's not like we need to stop them from destroying this place. It can go to hell for all I care."

My second nodded and focused back on her screen. "The law of the jungle, then."

Down below, King bellowed out a challenge and slammed a meaty fist against the ground. He moved onto all fours, keeping his body close to the shattered tiles beneath him. Riptide was already generating the energy required for another shot. This time, however, she was moving in step with the other kaiju.

Cthulhu stretched out his wings and broke out into a loping run. With each stride he took, the wings flapped gracelessly behind him, but he picked up speed at a remarkable pace.

The colossal titans met with a scream of tearing flesh and broken bones. Riptide unleashed her load on the Dread Lord the moment before they collided, while King slammed upwards at the last second, trying to skewer Cthulhu with his horns.

The thing shrugged off the plasma and smashed a fist into King's face, halting the charge in its steps. Riptide crashed in a moment later, swinging her fused arms at the Dread Lord's face, forcing him off the other kaiju. She was lighter than King, but she was fast, and managed to pull back before Cthulhu could hook onto her with his feelers.

King shook off the blow and reared up onto his haunches. His barbed tails shot out with blinding speed, and I heard the Dread Lord groan as his stomach was punctured by the blades, his arms floundering as they tried to block the strikes.

Riptide swung in again, lashing out with her own tail as she tried to flank her prey, while King moved in the opposite direction. The two kaiju began to circle Cthulhu.

"Is it just me, or does he look a little slower?" Kiyo shifted on her seat and tilted her head as she watched the fight play out.

The Dread Lord trudged forward, clumsily blocking another attack from King, but opening up his side to Riptide, who didn't wait for a second invitation. She knocked aside his arm with her shoulder and sunk her teeth deep into his belly, tearing flesh from him. The kaiju spat it out on the ground as she retreated, before the Dread Lord could respond.

The thing let out an ear-splitting bellow and held a clawed paw to its side, turning its great head from kaiju to kaiju.

Kiyo was right. He was slower, more lethargic than he'd been when he first emerged.

KAIJU

"The stars," said Claire. She pulled herself towards the helicopter door and stared out into the inky black sky. "They're changing again."

I glanced out the nearest window and saw that she was right. The red tinge had disappeared, and the heavens no longer felt like they were about to fall on our heads. Though far from normal, they were starting to resemble something less foreboding.

King sprung forward again, sensing weakness, and slammed a shoulder into the side Cthulhu was favouring. The Dread Lord stumbled back, lashing out with a talon, landing a glancing blow on the kaiju's head, but the impetus was gone and King shrugged it off.

Riptide darted in, narrowly avoiding a swipe from Cthulhu, and sprayed a torrent of plasma at the Dread Lord's chest. The thing stumbled back, nearly collapsing against the side of a monolithic building, but somehow managed to retain its balance. The other kaiju bounded in, spewing his vile, luminous sludge across the Olde One's leg, before snapping at the hand that tried to push him away.

The Dread Lord howled as the bio-toxins burnt through his flesh, leaving tumorous welts in their wake. He took a step back, and then another as the kaiju circled him like sharks in open water.

"They're herding him back to the vault," said Claire, glancing at me from the helicopter door.

With each step, King and Riptide were forcing the Olde One back into the city. I don't know if they thought they could force the Dread Lord back into his tomb, or if it was just instinctual, but it was working.

The Olde One ducked beneath a flurry of King's strikes and kicked him back with a massive foot, before weaving out of the way of another plasma volley. He'd grown even slower, and the high-density plasma shot knocked him on the shoulder, flinging him back against another ruin.

Cthulhu howled his defiance and clambered back to his feet. His movements were unbalanced and tired, and he barely managed to pull himself upright.

Perhaps sensing the change, he stared up into the sky and watched as the stars that had brought him forth slunk back into the abyss of night. He let out a single, mournful bellow and then turned his back on the kaiju, before walking back of his own accord towards the vault.

"What is he doing?" Asked Kiyo.

I shrugged and turned to the doctor.

"The stars aren't right," she said, taking off her glasses and wiping away the sweat from her brow. "It is not His time."

I raised a brow, but nodded anyway. Whatever the reason, Cthulhu was making his way back through the city. He barely attempted to fend off King when next he struck, and the massive kaiju bit off great clumps of the Olde One's flesh.

Riptide slammed into his back, tearing into his exposed wings and flesh with tooth and claw. The Dread Lord ignored her and continued his march towards his crypt, picking up speed as he did so, despite her added weight.

When the vault finally appeared, Cthulhu's flesh was torn through in a dozen places, and great gashes had formed all along his head and sides. King and Riptide backed off, content to watch as the Dread Lord limped across the flagstones towards the gaping black hole. His body's regeneration had slowed, and the wounds that covered him festered and bled across the tiles beneath him.

When he reached the vault, the Dread Lord placed a hand on the slimy stone door and stared up at us. I felt the whispering voices, the soft hysteria of madness as it brushed against my mind. I heard the gibbered chants of beings I hoped never to encounter, and saw the Dread Citadel reflected in his eyes, a place of eldritch light and sickening despair. And then it was gone.

The Olde One squeezed his girth between the stone doors and pushed himself into the great chasm that lay at the centre of R'lyeh. The last thing I saw of him was the flick of his great tail, just before the doors to the vault closed shut behind him, sealing him in his tomb even as the sea began to reclaim the lost city once more.

Perhaps King and Riptide wore down that thing from the vault, beating it into submission until finally it was forced to concede defeat and return to the black hole from whence it came. Maybe, there in that dark crypt, the creature died from its wounds. That's what I like to think anyway—that our kaijus beat down on a cosmic being beyond our comprehension and punished it for its hubris. But maybe Claire's theory is correct and the stars weren't right. Perhaps, one day, the Dread Lord Cthulhu will rise again and bring forth an age of madness and unspeakable horror. Maybe, when the stars are right, He will come back to conquer our world, His emergence heralding a reign of darkness that will last for all eternity and scar the minds of all those who live to see it come to pass.

I plan on being long dead before that ever happens.

WRITE LIKE HELL

KAIJU

ABOUT THE AUTHORS

Adam Gray lives and works in Johannesburg, South Africa. After completing his studies in English, Psychology and law, Adam began a career in law. Adam is passionate about the written word, and seeks to put pen to paper whenever the opportunity arises.

Big Bloody Ben is his first foray into the world of horror.

Andrea Speed has been a fan of Mothra since the very beginning, and will fight you over it! Made ever loopier by the current social distancing, you can find her writing from her crawlspace, somewhere in Washington State.

Her previously published works include the multi-volume *Infected* series, originally under Dreamspinner Press, but now self-published. She also wrote the *Josh of the Damned* series for Riptide Publishing. Speed's works have also appeared in several Less Than Three Press anthologies.

André Uys has cultivated a love for literature and language from a young age. Having it in mind to become a writer or linguist, he studied Languages & Cultures at Stellenbosch University, but has since moved on to other ventures. The recent lockdown in South Africa provided him with the perfect opportunity to pen some fiction. This is his first published work.

Clint Lee Werner is the author of over thirty novels, and has written stories for the Black Library in both the Fantasy and Age of Sigmar settings—though he has dipped his toes into Warhammer 40,000 on occasion. He has also written stories for Iron Kingdoms, Wild West Exodus, Kings of War, Keyforge, Beyond the Gates of Antares, and City of the Gods. His original fiction has appeared in anthologies such as *Rage of the Behemoth*, *Kaiju Rising*, *Sharkpunk*, and a few issues of *Tales from the Magician's Skull*.

Erik Morten is a writer, composer, and audio producer from Eastern Germany. When he isn't practicing martial arts or reading up on religion and philosophy, you'll find him busying himself with Nerd culture. Erik is currently living in the heart of his home town of Hannover, Germany, with his wife Samantha Bateson.

Tyron Dawson lives and works in the Eastern Cape, South Africa. He currently works for a small Monumental Works business. This is Dawson's first published story.

Justin Fillmore lives with his wife and son in Fish Hoek, South Africa. He enjoys relaxing at the ocean's edge with them. He studied Theology and Counselling Psychology, and has worked in both fields. He now works from home and raises his son. He has been exploring the many worlds conjured by writers, actors, and musicians since childhood, and has now felt the call to contribute his own. His debut novel, *The Jethro Parables* is available now.

Leon Fourie has written reviews and opinion pieces on gaming culture for NAG Magazine and 925 Rebellion.

When not obsessing over comic books, anime, dark fantasy stories, and video games, you can find Leon riding motorcycles, drawing, or writing. This is Fourie's first work of published fiction.

Scott Miller is a dark fiction and psychological horror writer from Cape Town, South Africa. His keen interest in philosophy and the human condition informs his work, as does his passion for understanding what makes people tick. He is inspired by a broad range of authors and theorists including, but not limited to, Thomas Ligotti, David Benatar, Percy Shelley, and Neil Gaiman. While his academic qualifications include majors in both philosophy and English literature, he dabbles in a variety of extracurriculars, such as pessimistic philosophy, drumming, singing, voice acting, and animal ethics. Like most writers, he has a soft spot for cats and good coffee. You can read his previously published works in volumes 1 and 2 of *Write Like Hell*.

Samantha Bateson lives and works in Hannover, Germany. When she isn't sating her passion for the natural sciences or obsessing over seals, you'll find her spending much of her free time painting surrealist and abstract pop art. All the science 'stuff' in *Starchild* comes from somewhere a little closer than fiction – Bateson once worked a contract on a research vessel affiliated with NASA. This is her first published work of fiction.

WRITE LIKE HELL

Matthew Fairweather has been writing for the better part of a decade, but has only recently taken the plunge into publication. This is Fairweather's first published work.

Mitchell Lüthi is an epic fantasy author based in Cape Town, South Africa. After completing his studies in history and law, Mitchell turned to the fulfilment of more personal pursuits, including entrepreneurship and recreational writing. More recently, the latter has been undertaken in earnest, with the hope of releasing a great many literary works.

He is an avid board game and tabletop player, and, when not devouring the whole gamut of fictional works—from historical fiction to fantasy—spends much of his free time composing scores.

His debut novelette, *The Ritual*, was born from a fascination with the darker chapters of human history, as well as an abiding love for gripping, character-driven fantasy.

KAIJU

Looking for more from Sentinel Creatives? Join the Sentinel Creatives Book Club for more books, audiobooks and featured content!

Printed in Great Britain
by Amazon